# St. Jude's

## A Castlehead Novel

## Joshua Meeking

Grosvenor House
Publishing Limited

The right of Joshua Meeking to be identified as the author of this
work has been asserted in accordance with Section 78
of the Copyright, Designs and Patents Act 1988

This book is published by
Grosvenor House Publishing Ltd
Link House
140 The Broadway, Tolworth, Surrey, KT6 7HT.
www.grosvenorhousepublishing.co.uk

This book is a work of fiction. Any resemblance to
people or events, past or present, is purely coincidental.

A CIP record for this book
is available from the British Library

ISBN 978-1-80381-738-5

# AUTHOR'S NOTE

Before you continue, I would like to acknowledge that this book may not be suitable for readers under the age of sixteen. Expect references to death, grief, mental health, and forms of discrimination. I would also like to point out that the social and political views of some of the characters in this novel – and any other books of mine you might have come across – do NOT reflect that of my own. This is only a work of fiction, and, like all works of fiction, its purpose is to present a story to readers that they can enjoy.

With that said, *St. Jude's – A Castlehead Novel* is set during the events of the "THEN" timeline in *Isolation – The Story of Isabella Rose-Eccleby*, in 2009. Writing a story in which its events align with that of another allowed me to dive a little deeper into some of the questions that might have not been answered previously, *possibly* setting up key events and plot points for the Castlehead Novels still to come.

I hope you enjoy reading this book as much as I enjoyed the process of writing it. Please do leave a review wherever possible, it really does help, and I appreciate it more than anyone will ever know. If you'd like to see some of the things I get up to in my spare time, as well as see updates for any future projects, you can find me on Instagram (@joshuameeking) and on Facebook (Joshua Meeking – Author).

Thank you, and welcome back to Castlehead!

# ACKNOWLEDGMENTS

First of all, I can't thank Grosvenor House Publishing enough for putting up with me during the making of this book. They are a splendid team and always find a way to outdo themselves. I have worked with them on my first two books, *Isolation – The Story of Isabella Rose-Eccleby* (released in September, 2020) and *The Corrupt – A Castlehead Novel* (released in April, 2022), and I will continue to work with them on all future Castlehead Novel projects.

I highly recommend their services should anyone reading this have the desire to publish a book. When I had finished *Isolation* I initially thought to just send the manuscript into various publishers because, well, I had nothing to lose. Little did I realise back then that, because of this team, I would have a book out at eighteen. It just proves that hard work does pay off in the end.

Another special thanks goes out to my A-Level Drama class, and those who worked on the original devised piece that this book is based on. Although it was a weird time trying to get through sixth form during the pandemic, we managed it and if we hadn't created the pieces we presented for our exam, this book wouldn't have been possible.

And finally, thank you always to my family and friends who continue to come on this journey with me. They have done so much to support me and what I love to do, and I wouldn't be here without them cheering me on. I am forever grateful.

# BOOKS BY JOSHUA MEEKING

*The Castlehead Novels*
Isolation – The Story of Isabella Rose-Eccleby
The Corrupt
St. Jude's

*Still To Come…*
It's Good To Be Sixteen
The Way – A Castlehead Novel

This book is dedicated to my Dad, Nana, Grandad, my little brother Josiah, Lisa, and all my aunties, uncles, and cousins in the Meeking family. I love you all dearly, and I am so thankful to have you in my life.

# ABOUT THE AUTHOR

Joshua Meeking was born in October, 2001, in London, England. At the age of three he moved to Newcastle Upon Tyne with his mother, Gillian, and has lived there ever since. He has always been compelled by storytelling, whether it's through film, prose, theatre, or even through professional wrestling or video games like *Red Dead Redemption II*.

By eighteen he published his first book, *Isolation – The Story of Isabella Rose-Eccleby*, which was released in 2020. At first, it was a passion project based on his GCSE Drama devised piece of the same name, believing the story could be something more. It was then that he realised writing was what he wanted to do with his life, and in 2022 he released *The Corrupt – A Castlehead Novel*, the first official book of the Castlehead Novel series. A couple of inspirations include Stephen King and the stories told by Pixar Animation Studios.

While studying English Literature with Creative Writing at Newcastle University, Joshua never stopped writing in his spare time, completing two full manuscripts during the three-year course. As long as the ideas keep coming, he's never going to stop writing books. He doesn't want to be tied down to one genre, either, working on a plethora of stories appropriate for various ages and various tastes. He likes to test himself and experiment with new ideas that may or may not work, and he can't wait for what the future holds.

# PROLOGUE

## 2020

With the sky clearer than the Caribbean Sea and the sun beaming down like Earth's constant lamp, it appeared that everybody in town had the same idea; the traffic on the motorway to Jaxson Bay had become quite anger inducing. However, the cars coming to a halt once every few minutes wasn't necessarily a bad thing, for it gave many the opportunity to peer out of their respective car windows to examine the hills and countryside that surrounded – some might say trapped – the town of Castlehead.

The rusty, possibly second-hand minivan that Clarke Smith drove rumbled along. He had kindly agreed to chaperone the group, all of them friends of his recently deceased son, to the beach so they could take advantage of the very rare clement weather that had settled in the north-east of England. In the back seats were Jason, Brandon, and their new friend, Josh, and in the front passenger seat was Anna. Josh looked through the window on his left and his eyes immediately grew wide, intrigued by the winding sandy road that made its way up the hill like a ladder as it reached a great wall.

"What's that?" asked Josh, to Clarke's surprise (and secret distaste).

Clarke kept his eyes fixed on the road.

There used to be great metal gates attached to the intimidating fifteen-foot brick wall; the bricks were mouldy with age, with moss growing uncontrollably wherever it could.

It stood and sent shivers down people's spines; enclosed within those walls stood a building that had an equally uncontrollable amount of moss growing from the corners of its pointed roof, a roof that – even visible from the motorway – had gaping holes. The damp, wooden cross with Jesus Christ nailed to it above the entrance told everyone that it most probably had Catholic origins. The windows to the outside world had been heavily boarded up, and if you squinted just enough you could make out the padlocked chains over the entrance.

"They call it St. Jude's," answered Clarke, forcing himself to keep his eyes locked on the road still. He tightened his grip around the wheel as his hands began to sweat. A sudden tingle shot through his neck like a thousand ants crawling into his head. And after a long, well-needed deep breath, Clarke continued, "Back in the 80s and 90s, it was a mental asylum. Since the government didn't – and still don't – acknowledge the town, the mayor at the time was able to get away with its construction after the attempt to close asylums for good in the 60s."

All the kids were entranced by the information, as if they were at a museum. They were still struck by the building that drifted off into the distance behind them even as the traffic started to shift towards an upcoming junction.

"The building shut at the turn of the millennium, but it was *rumoured* to be refurbished back in 2009. There was a ceremony planned and everything. Think it was going to be a fancy hotel or something. I don't know. But what I do know is that when patients entered, they never left." Perhaps *escaped* was a more suited term, he surmised. "Rumours of people hearing blood-curdling screams and the sound of torture contraptions spread quicker than wildfire. But when the C.C.I.D went to investigate…" *Just before the planned ceremony*, he recalled, "…the noises at the end of '09, there was no sign of anyone. No doctors, no patients... Nothing."

He purposefully forgot to mention the one thing the Castlehead Criminal Investigation Department did in fact find: a blood-coated hospital bed.

You shouldn't always believe rumours.

## 1985

It was the place where freaks belonged, he thought as he came to a halt in his car in front of those great metal gates. He heard the child in the passenger seat gulp hard; he could sense the fear.

"Dad?" muttered the boy, double taking from the gates to his father. "I... I thought we were going to the beach?"

The sun beamed down, with not a single cloud in sight, upon the town of Castlehead that morning, and everybody had appeared to have taken advantage of this rare weather. The boy had finished school for the summer just two days before, and all he wanted to do now was meet up with friends and ignore the pressures that came with growing up – the pressures that came with secondary school. Teens weren't expected to wonder what they were doing parked in front of a place for freaks.

"I just have to run in and sort out a couple of things, son," the man said as he unbuckled his seatbelt and hopped out of the car. He stopped before shutting the door, bent down, holding the door open slightly, and looked into his son's eyes. "Don't move. If I find you've taken one step out of this car, then you can kiss goodbye to your trip to the beach. Got that?"

The boy nodded and said obediently, "Yes, sir."

He watched his father walk up to the gates and heave them open. The screeching could be heard from where he sat parked. His father vanished beyond those gates, entering the grounds of St. Jude's. The home for freaks. It was clear to the townsfolk what proceedings occurred within those neat walls, but the odd scream that was rumoured to be heard at night was pretty much all the townsfolk needed for them to stay away. Rumours had already spread around his school, Thomas Hill High, that the place was haunted. Like Michael Manor. Teachers, however, instantly targeted the students who said those ridiculous things, threatening that they'd get their own spot in the looney bin if they didn't behave.

As the boy sat making shapes with his fingers and thought back to those times, he knew in his heart that the rumours were stupid. In History, one time, the class reflected on the institute's opening just mere days after WWII. Even though historical facts weren't exactly the boy's strongpoint, even he had to admit learning just a smidge of the town's past was mildly interesting, that was all the hook his imagination needed.

So there the boy was, looking on from the car to the gate that kept the building away from the public. *Good idea to build it on a steep bank*, he thought. Thoughts like that told the boy boredom was steadily setting in. All he wanted to do was inhale that salty scent of the North Sea. But, like the boredom, it quickly became clear that the beach had to wait.

The inside was dimly lit; the wooden floorboards beneath his and the female doctor's feet croaked as they walked through the narrow hallway and entered a wide space. The space could've been a reception or waiting area, but instead it was just empty. The man looked around, noticing four reinforced steel doors in each of the walls around the two of them. A single wooden door stood by the end of the area, leading to what looked like nothing. He smartened up his jacket, then felt his back trouser pocket.

*Only use it if absolutely certain*, he thought. *Which is always the case.*

That morning, the mayor had told him in the meeting, "Just make sure they're recovering."

*Recovering?* He repeated the statement in his head. *They're in here for a reason.* Yes, that much was definitely true, but somehow in the mayor's and many others' eyes they were only there to receive help and care. *Yeah, whatever.*

Nothing happened and the prolonged silence made him feel like something was going to jump out. The flickering overhead chandelier made the man flinch; smirking at his timidity, the doctor led him forward a couple of steps and waited.

And waited…

And waited…

And waited…

Each door opened simultaneously, so he didn't know which one to focus on. Four pale doctors appeared in the doorways, each restraining a patient in matching hospital gowns by clutching their wrists behind their backs as if they were being cuffed. He noticed nobody came from the wooden door by the far end of the space. *They should have put fucking straight jackets on them*, the man thought as he watched the doctors struggle to push the patients towards him. After all, he did ask for an audience with these freaks.

All of the doctors held their respective patients by the collars of their gowns, planting them in front of the man. The doctor beside him noticed he scolded them, distorting his face at the sickly sight. But after a moment, he straightened up, smartened his jacket again, and cleared his throat to speak.

"So, nothing's working I'm guessing, Doctor?" he asked rhetorically.

"No, sir…" said the doctor next to him. "Oh, and please call me Carrie."

"Okay, Doctor." He felt it was unprofessional to reveal one's first name, especially in the line of work these doctors had found themselves. And what he himself did. He cocked his head towards Carrie, and asked in a whisper, "Would we be able to have a moment with these…" He had to use his words wisely, already feeling sick coming up his throat. "Can we have a moment with these patients alone? Just for a couple of minutes?"

Carrie looked at the four doctors that still held the patients in place like they were forcibly training dogs to sit. She jerked her head to the side as an order for them to leave the room. To the man's surprise, the patients kept themselves frozen in place; they all had that dead glare, and it was a type of look, he thought, that no human being should have.

The doctors left with no argument and made their way down the hall towards the entrance. Carrie didn't really understand why the man wanted them to be alone, but for the man this was a long overdue visit.

"As I said, sir," said Doctor Carrie, speaking as if the patients in front of them didn't even exist, "we've tried everything. Hypnosis to dive into their psyche, one-to-one therapy, etcetera. If you can think of it, we've done it."

The man huffed, his hands on his hips, and said, "What about the approach I suggested?"

"With all due respect, sir, we both know that that's not what Madam Mayor wanted. Ever since the assassination in '77, you can't deny that all she's ever tried to do is help those in need." She added hesitantly, "Also, with that fiasco a few years back—"

"What happened back then just shows, Doctor, that not everyone can be helped."

That day in 1980 still haunted the man, even with his deputy assuring him that the two escapees had been dealt with. Still, he felt like *he* needed to be the one to do it.

ST. JUDE'S — A CASTLEHEAD NOVEL

"So, what do you suppose we do with them, then?" asked Carrie.

The doctor acknowledged the patients for the first time in the conversation. The man followed her gaze, and he stepped forward, looking into the eyes of the first patient in line; he was bald, his skin like a Halloween night – dark and intimidating. Well, that's how the man saw him. He took a big step to his left and examined the second patient in line. Frail, her face was wrinkled and strands of hair drifted down to the ground every time she shook. Another step to his left brought him to the third patient, who kept their – he couldn't tell if he was looking at a male or a female, which was an immediate red flag – eyes on the floor. But he could see *it* was on the verge of tears. *I never knew these things were capable of emotions*, he thought as he took one final step to the fourth and final patient.

It was like a staring contest when he faced this one, neither of them budging. Sneakily, the man grabbed at his back pocket again. But before he knew it, the patient leapt forward, launching at him with all of his force. He had to admit, this patient's hands pressing down on his shoulders felt like a pair of cranes. Doctor Carrie froze; she didn't know what to do, whether to push the emergency alarm, call the other doctors back in, or...

"Don't do anything," the man said, strained.

He was almost brought to his knees by the patient, but he broke free with a kick to his kneecap. The second patient cheered as if she were watching Mr. T and Hulk Hogan defeating Roddy Piper and Mr. Wonderful, tugging at her hair in delight and jumping excitedly. The man swept the other knee from under the fourth patient with another kick. The patient cried out, unable to stand, forced to stoop like a follower bowing and acknowledging their leader.

One last grab of the back pocket… He revealed a pistol, aiming it at the patient's head without any sign of hesitation.

"Sir!" cried Carrie.

But all the sounds around him went fuzzy; after all, he was focused on accomplishing what he came here for. A pleasurable gunshot later, the patient collapsed at the man's feet with a bullet hole in between the eyes like the red recording light on a camera.

"As *I* said, Doctor," he said blankly, turning to Carrie and the three remaining patients, "some people… just can't be helped."

BANG! BANG! BANG!

Doctor Carrie hid her face with both hands, flinching at all three shots. She thought for a moment they might've been for her, but she didn't feel herself fall nor did she feel cold and lifeless. She peeked through her fingers and saw the other three patients lying there almost on top of each other with the same matching red dot in between their eyes.

As she watched the man check the gun over, Carrie straightened up and wanted to say the hundreds of things that came to mind in that quick moment. The man placed the gun back in his pocket and ignored the bodies as he stepped in front of the doctor.

Carrie couldn't stop glancing back and forth from the man to the bodies as she stammered, "W-W-Why…?" She cleared her throat. "What did that achieve?"

The man chuckled, aware of Carrie's distaste for the entire situation, and said, "It was the only way." His tone was low, but he exuded pride. "You might not understand now, but you will. I've done all of us a favour, and it's my job to help the people of Castlehead. If that means ridding this town of those who don't deserve a place here, then so be it."

Carrie couldn't believe what she had just heard. St. Jude's was built on a foundation of care, and it was an attempt to help those who needed it most, no matter what they had done. Madam Mayor was lucky enough to keep the institute open after the impetus to close all of these kinds of places in the '60s, and change was needed. But anyone with a conscience knew this wasn't the way.

"But…" she started.

"Now, if you don't mind, my son's waiting for me to take him to Jaxson Bay."

The man brushed her aside as he made his way back through the hall to the entrance, leaving Carrie with the mess he had created.

The doors to the outside world were wide open, and the other doctors stood there. Curiosity quickly filled them. They had all heard the same thing, but they couldn't speak up. The man passed them and gave them all a nod as a way to thank them for their service. Should they have attempted to bring up their worries, they would've been risking their jobs and their lives.

One by one, the doctors walked back through to where Carrie was; they all stood over the four patients, speechless. None of them could manage to say a word, but they were all thinking the same thing: *If killing four sick patients is what he thinks is best for this town, imagine what he would do to us if his actions were ever released to the public.*

"What do we do now?" said one of the doctors.

Carrie didn't care who it was; she was solely focused on the bodies.

"We clean this shit up," she said.

"Should we tell Madam…?"

"We can't," barked Carrie suddenly. A beat passed, she composed herself, and continued more formally, "There's no chance the mayor would believe us over him." All the doctors looked at her. She was right. "He's overseen this project for years now. He has the mayor in his pocket. I guess that's one of the main perks of being the chief of the C.C.I.D."

Howard Pattison, chief of the Castlehead Criminal Investigation Department (which he had been ever since he had taken over from his father in 1965) had big plans for his son to, like his father before him, be entrusted with the responsibility of making sure this town was cleansed and free from anyone who might be a threat to their cause. He was one of the very few who knew the truth: the only reason they had managed to keep St. Jude's open was because the government simply didn't care. The mayor said a deal was set, but he knew the truth.

Envisioning the town as a historical tourist attraction in the years to come was an obsession for Howard, and he knew the way to make that possible – the way to make the rest of the United Kingdom care – was to show that those who ran Castlehead cared for their community so much that they would do anything to keep it safe. It was obvious that it was going to be a slow step-by-step process. But that was why he had to teach his son the right way from a young age.

A proud smile spread across Howard's face as he noticed his son had obeyed his orders to remain seated. His son wasn't ready yet to experience what had just occurred back there.

He opened the door to the driver's seat and smiled at his son. His son mirrored the smile as they both clicked in their seatbelts.

"Jaxson Bay, here we come!" Howard cheered as he revved the engine.

But he was too in the moment to see that his son's smile had slowly faded.

"Dad? Is… everything okay?"

Keeping his eyes on the road, Howard put the car into reverse and said, "Absolutely."

"Okay," replied his son. "It's just that… Well, it's just that I heard lots of banging."

"Son," said Howard, "you'll understand one day when you become chief. Your dad does everything for a reason. For a good cause."

"To keep us safe?"

"Exactly. You'll do things in life that may not seem right at first, but it'll all be for the greater good."

*For the greater good.*

The boy that was destined to become the next Chief Pattison trusted his father every single time. Even if he felt like he shouldn't, and this was one of those times… *No! Trust him.*

They were finally back on the motorway on their way to Jaxson Bay.

Throughout the rest of that day, and until he had become chief of police a decade later, his father's words kept racing through the boy's mind: *You'll understand one day.*

*One day.*

# CHAPTER ONE

## Just Another Day

### 2009

The clanging of metal, the screeching of tires, and the explosion at the end of it all were the things that woke her up that morning. *Time is a construct*, they say; a day can pass quickly, whilst a week could crawl along like a snail. And this was the case for Mrs. Elena Sullivan. It had already – *already*, yeah, she couldn't believe it either – been a month since that night, and within that month… well, for now let's just say that *things* happened.

As much as she wanted to forget, she constantly remembered.

Elena found herself staring up at the ceiling, unaware of how long she had done so, but as she turned her head for what felt like the first time all night, she saw that her digital clock on her bedside cabinet read 6:00am. She sighed as she took one last look at the ceiling, knowing it was time to muster the strength to get out of bed. She had usually kept to her side of the bed for the better part of four decades, but lying in the middle for the past few nights suddenly reminded her of the main thing they had been promised when they had bought the bed in the first place: comfort, or at least some form.

She ignored the drawn curtains as she made her way around the bed and towards the door. A speck of light shone through the drapes, but even that didn't make her want to open them and say hello to the ocean view that was presented to them upon purchasing the property.

Unhooking the red-stained dressing gown – which needed a wash to regain that glowing, pure white colour – off the door, she brushed her glittering grey hair to the side and out of her face with her other hand. It was the typical wild morning hair that she supposed most long-haired women had to put up with first thing in the morning.

As she tightened the gown around her, she yawned her way across the narrow landing, passing an ajar door which she completely blanked and the staircase that led directly into the sparkling foyer. On the other end of the landing was a closed door, but it was the door she needed to open – the bathroom, a staple of everyone's morning routine, and for Elena it was the place to attempt to motivate herself to plaster on a believable smile.

But maybe this time it would be different…

Despite being the only one in the house, she still instinctively shut the bathroom door behind her in case of intruders. She undressed and entered the walk-in shower. The gushing water that sprayed over her, she dared to argue (to herself of course), was more relaxing than laying in that king-sized bed every night. She closed her eyes, bent her neck backwards, and allowed her skin to embrace the H20.

Then something flashed in her mind, and it felt like the screeching that followed echoed through the entire house. Friction… Tires burning on asphalt… Elena instantly opened her eyes, her heart in her throat.

"Pull yourself together," she whispered to herself in between calming breaths. "Just forget."

She reached for the knob and twisted it, stopping the water from gushing down and turning it into a light sprinkle.

But eventually, it stopped entirely. Finding the nearest towel on the radiator, she dried off and wrapped herself tightly in it as if it were a blanket. Waddling over to the sink, Elena firmly grasped the corners and looked up at the mirror hooked on the wall above it. Her reflection stared back at her blankly through the condensation, water droplets racing down her face.

And a smile was let out. Was it forced? The smile then widened into a laugh. She continued to laugh until she became breathless. The last time she recalled laughing this much was when... Actually, that was something she really couldn't remember.

Keeping her eyes on her reflection, making sure that the smile didn't fade in the slightest, a thought popped into her mind: *I'm so happy*.

She couldn't allow the smile to fade; she just couldn't. But a sudden twitch began to irritate her just above her eyes. *No*, she thought. *Don't lose it*. In the mirror, her eyebrows began to narrow and sharpen.

"No, Elena," she barked sternly. "You're happy." She smiled and forced out the same breathless laugh she had let out mere moments before. "You're so happy, aren't you, Elena?" The reflection was talking to her, and she was talking to it – demandingly. "You're so happy. You're happy as bloody Larry."

Changing her nightgown – or *nighty* as she called it – for a navy-blue blazer, a white polo, and pants, with heels to match, Elena was ready to head down into the foyer. Her hair now was sparkling and straight; proud of her efforts, she smiled one last time at her reflection in the mirror, then made her way back onto the landing before slowly walking down the stairs. She took one step at a time, clutching onto the banister as she went.

When she reached the last step, she looked around. Like any successful person, Elena just wanted to take in what she had made for herself; dead ahead was the front door; to her left was the glistening kitchen with its marble counters and island, which also acted as a dining table from time to time; a dozen steps to her right was a couch that faced the wall of books – with no television in sight – and beside the couch and coffee table, which was home to coasters and a laptop, was a grand, antique piano.

*Why did we even get that thing? We never used it... Well...* She tilted her head to one side to get another angle. *Actually, it still looks as good as the day you bought it for us.*

Getting on the property ladder in Valeland, England, was actually much easier than Elena had ever expected; even after she had constantly been told not to worry. The argument was simple: if you had money, you could get whatever you wanted. That was definitely the case if you were born into a wealthy family, which Mrs. Elena Sullivan proudly was. She remembered when they had first purchased the house, sometime back in the mid-80s (she couldn't remember specifically, and frankly she didn't want to), for a reasonable £30,000 – and that had been with all the trimmings, like a fine meal. They dreamt of privacy, so the house being detached and at the end of the close was a tick off the ol' checklist; with that, add a spacious flower garden out back and a front yard with a driveway, a garage, and an extra patch of grass on which to rest upon sun loungers, they had themselves their dream home.

Although she was born into money, her parents never allowed her to take anything for granted. Mrs. Sullivan rightfully earned what she got, and that was through hard work. That was why she was never ashamed of being the "stuck-up rich girl" in primary school. That doesn't hide the fact that the money her parents had was put to good use,

4

getting her into the best private school without any applications whatsoever: the Desmond School for Creative Arts. But even there, she earned her grades; and it was there where she met *him*. Of course, teamwork, resilience, and hard work got them both into Oxford and Cambridge respectively. Without question or debate, it was the best time of her life; they both successfully graduated with honours, and that was when the question quickly sunk in: what next?

"Let's go home," Emmett Sullivan suggested. By her smile that day, he knew she thought it was a good idea to return to Valeland. "But before we do... will... will you marry me?"

The immediate answer was, "Yes!"

And the rest was history.

She *had* to walk to work that day. The sun was trying to break through the clouds above, and that glimmer of light was like a beacon of hope – hope that she could start anew. *Walks help,* she thought as cars raced passed trying to beat the morning rush hour. *The easy option shouldn't always be the right one.* An image of a shredded car in the garage flashed in her mind. Up until that point, Mrs. Sullivan had only driven the temporary Volkswagen Polo once and, okay, it got her from A to B, but it wasn't exactly the pure white Rolls Royce they had received as a wedding gift from both Emmett's parents and her own. If anything, it would've just been idiotic even considering taking it away from the motorway heading into the Alfred Mountain Range...

*No! Don't think about how it is, just how it was.* Smooth, white, attractive, a perfect vehicle to make everyone on the path turn their heads with jealous lust. Today, though, she had to reassure herself that walking was the best option. She knew she wouldn't have been late per se, but she liked the old saying: *Better late than never.* Elena continued, clutching the strap of her small handbag around her shoulder until she reached a roundabout.

*When did I even pick my bag up?*

All she focused on was the exit dead ahead, that took her to where she needed to be. She crossed to the opposite side of the road, but only when the traffic lights were on red and when the green man appeared of course. Then she continued on up towards the exit she needed. Alongside each exit's respective traffic lights, a green sign was displayed to inform drivers and pedestrians where the roads would lead them. *You can't be careless with traffic, whether you're driving or walking,* she warned herself as she stepped onto the path across the road. *Carelessness leads to consequences.*

*Main Street.*

If she took the right – the third exit – she'd be heading towards the station. Valeland was her home, and this was where she needed to be. For herself and for her Emmett.

On the corner of Main Street and the third exit, she pressed her hand along the tall brick wall that stood alongside the pavement. As she walked, her hand brushed briskly along the wall; the grains of dirt, stone, cement and brick that dug into her palm didn't bug her one bit. That sparkling horizon before her drew her in, and the wall looked like it too went on for as long as the sky and sea met upon the horizon. *A tourist would think a prison was hidden behind it,* she thought, feeling a chuckle coming on, for she knew what stood inside the perimeter of that wall. It was not a prison, that was for sure, although it was still a place only a few could ever visit.

She reached the entrance, and the twenty-foot steel gates were closed.

*Normal.*

On the other side of the gate's steel bars, as if in a cell, stood a security guard.

*Normal.*

The guard's face was blanketed in the shade of his hat. Elena could tell by his hunched posture that he didn't notice her. Or that he was just bored out of his mind already.

"Eh-hem." Elena coughed. The man looked up, and the sun shone on his familiar face, prompting a smile on Elena's. However, this time he didn't respond with the same natural enthusiasm. To her, he looked surprised in spite of trying to hide it. She added, "For a man who works as a security guard, you're not very good at keeping a straight face."

The guard walked towards the gate, to a point that was close enough for them to both smell each other's breath, and he responded, "Oh... Elena? Good morning... I... We weren't... What're you doing here?"

*Oh?* she recited in her head, in that exact light tone. *What am I doing here? I'm working,* she answered – although it would again remain only in her thoughts. Things weren't adding up.

"What do you mean?" Elena chuckled nervously. "Why wouldn't I come to work?" She didn't let the guard answer, for she added with another – nuttier – chuckle, "Not just that; why wouldn't I come to work at the best school there is, the Desmond School for Creative Arts?"

She didn't notice him scooch back a touch.

But she did notice the shrug he gave when he finally replied: "Elena..." He sounded concerned, although she didn't feel a need for him to. "We've been thinking a lot about you, but we were thinking you wouldn't..."

"Awww, thank you. I appreciate the sentiment, but can you please just let me in? I want to get back into the swing of things, if you don't mind."

Although it was his job to oversee who did and didn't enter the premises and school facilities, he felt guilt surge through his body if he dared to argue with one of the most well-respected teachers at the Desmond School for Creative Arts. He didn't want to make it too obvious that he wasn't keen on allowing her in, but what more could he have done? With one last shrug, he stepped forward and pulled the heavy gates open with a toe-curling screech against the concrete floor.

He stood aside and said softly, "Welcome back, Mrs. Sullivan."

Before entering, letting the guard stand there for just one moment longer, Elena brushed her hair behind her ears and walked into the Desmond School premises. A warm smile suddenly spread across her face, and, as she headed across the main campus courtyard, that exact same smile greeted students and staff alike. She completely blocked out all the mumbling behind her.

The guard shut the gates and reached for his tight belt. Hooked on it was a keychain and a walkie-talkie. Lifting the com close to his mouth, he radioed in, "Main Entrance to Reception, do you read me? Over."

As per usual, the radio signal – and many guards would concur with this opinion – was crap. Holding the radio close to his ear, all the guard could hear was an irritating crackling and a faint mumbling. He turned around and looked ahead, taking a few steps toward the main courtyard.

The signal was improving.

He made out, *"Reception to Main Entrance, we read you. Does there seem to be a problem? Over."*

"A massive one," said the guard quietly. "Elena Sullivan has just walked onto the school grounds. Over."

*"What?! What shall we do? Over."*

"She'll most likely be heading to her classroom. Inform Desmond immediately."

*"Roger that. Reception over and out."*

The radio crackled again, and suddenly went silent. The guard hooked the walkie-talkie back onto his belt as he continued to watch Elena cross the courtyard.

She had walked across its grounds countless times over the years she and Emmett had worked there, but every new day, coming as it did with a fresh view of the commemorative statue of the town's founder, Lord Alfred Vale, was a breath of fresh air. Her co-workers knew she was especially fond of the main building behind the statue, which many said resembled St. Paul's Cathedral. The other two on each side of the courtyard looked more like town courthouses with their three stone pillars connecting the stairs and the roof together.

The admiration and emotion on Elena's face when she looked up at that stone Alfred Vale was something that people called a rarity; the black plaque with gold writing affixed to the pedestal on which Alfred stood heroically drew Elena in. Reading it for the millionth time in her life still felt like that first time; it was so intriguing, so inspiring, to know that this man had put everything on the line to make Valeland a functional town for its residents to thrive. He had made sure that there was never an issue in the town, and that's what made the Sullivans proud to be born and bred in this picture postcard town. If there was ever a problem, said problem would be sorted in a matter of moments.

Mrs. Sullivan pressed her chapped lips against the tips of her fingers then lightly tapped the plaque. *Always show respect to those who came before us*, she thought before walking around the statue and up the cobbled path to the domed building.

*Always show respect to those who came before us. Don't be ashamed of where you have come from. Love is a complicated thing. Death is imminent, but it's fate that decides when we go. Fates can be sealed through a single act… Fates can be sealed through a single act… Fates can be sealed through a single act…*

Fates. Can. Be. Sealed. Through. A. Single. Act.

"Yes… Yes, everything is fine here… No, unfortunately no new recruits yet, Chief. I understand that we agreed that this partnership and program was to help inspire people to do the right thing, but I… I don't know, Chief. I still have that feeling that it won't work." Desmond Edwards felt the telephone crack in the grip between his shoulder and ear; he was so used to landlines that these new iPhone thingies felt flimsy and useless. "I understand that it has to… Okay… Yep… I'll keep an eye out."

There was a knock at the door, and Desmond saw the knob turn as the door slowly opened. A young face peered in, her nose petit, and from the lack of hair around her face Desmond guessed she was formally wearing it in a ponytail. He waved her in. She was in a security guard uniform, and Desmond thought, *This can't be good.*

"Sir, I've—" started the guard.

Desmond raised his finger, silencing her.

"Yes, Chief… I will," he said, wanting this call to be over. The guard clasped her hands in front of her as she waited for Desmond to finish the call. There was lots of talk around the security offices that the headmaster had been on call with the chief of the Valeland Citizen Protection Agency a lot more than usual. It was no secret to many, especially those who studied at the school, that Desmond and the V.C.P.A maintained a partnership that helped both parties; when scouting out for possible applicants for the school, the team at the school would also take into consideration those possible applicants – if eligible, obviously – to join the V.C.P.A's new junior detective program. In the end, it was all for a good cause. "Bye bye, my friend."

Desmond reached forward, straining his back and stretching his suit, and placed the phone on the desk in front of him. His body looked too wide for the chair, and the guard supposed that there must've been a neck under those many chins, although that was only guess work. Nothing would ever be said about his size in front of him, otherwise they would've been fired quicker than contestants on *The Apprentice*.

"Sir," said the security guard seriously, "sorry to barge in like this…"

He waved his hand as a way to show that an apology wasn't needed, and roared, "What's the problem?"

Without hesitating, she answered, "Apparently Elena Sullivan has entered the grounds."

The chair croaked like a colony of frogs as Desmond leaned as far forward as he could without putting pressure on his stomach. He scratched the bushy beard he had been cultivating over the past few months. By his raised eyebrows and the biting of his lip, the guard gathered that he was considering only plausible solutions.

"Okay…" he breathed. The frog colony echoed again throughout the office as Desmond rose to his feet and walked around the desk. The guard felt the vibrations of every step he took towards her and the door that led back to the narrow hallway. He held the door open for the guard, and added with a groan, "She clearly doesn't know it's far too soon for her to be coming back to work."

Each door down every hallway on the entire campus had a sign telling students and the faculty what number room they were about to enter. Mrs. Sullivan kept her eyes directly on the final door at the end of the brightly lit hallway; the overhead lights were like a series of suns beaming down on her. It was discomforting in a way because it obstructed her vision just a touch. But she just couldn't wait for the wave of happiness that was about to pass over her as she walked through that door to her classroom.

"Happy as bloody Larry," she mumbled to herself as she wrapped her hand around the door handle.

The door clicked open, and she needn't need to use much strength to push it slowly open with one hand. She took a step forward into pure silence; she seized up in the doorway as every head in the room turned to her. The room resembled a lecture auditorium, with its elevated seats, a cinema-sized screen at the front, and a microphone connected to the desk so the students at the far back were able to hear the teacher.

A few scattered mumbles and whispers began to grow throughout the theatre; Elena couldn't explicitly hear what was being said but she believed there was a better than 90% chance they were talking about her.

"Um… Excuse me. Can I help you?"

Elena snapped her head towards the desk at the front of the class. There, where *she* was meant to be standing, was a slim, well-dressed blonde. While she was curious as to who this woman who had just disrupted her lesson was, Elena's eyebrows narrowed. She needed an answer right this second.

"I can ask you the same question." There was a sarcastic undertone in Elena's response. The chatter throughout the class grew. "This is my class."

"I'm sorry, but this has been my class for two weeks now," argued the woman, matching Elena's sarcastic undertone. "I think I know which class I'm supposed to be in."

"Elena!" called a voice down the hall. Now that was a voice she was happy to hear. Elena felt the vibrations of the headmaster's rushing footsteps as he, along with the security guard, entered the room. The class was fully invested, not a quiet soul in the room now. All the students rose at the sight of their headmaster, offering the usual sign of respect, and he nodded at them as an instruction to return to their seats. He put a gentle hand on Elena's shoulder, and added, "Are you okay, Mrs. Kay?"

So much for Desmond being a sight for sore eyes. Elena brushed her boss's hand off her shoulder and kept snapping her head back and forth from Desmond and this woman called Mrs. Kay.

"Yes, I'm fine, sir," Kay responded honestly.

"Okay," cried Elena, "what is going on here, Desmond!?"

"*Shh* Mrs. Sullivan," Desmond whispered, "I think you should come to my office. Please."

He didn't let her respond. Desmond wrapped his arm around Elena's shoulder and ushered her back into the hall, with the guard following. She shut the door behind her and the class resumed.

There were so many words and phrases Mrs. Sullivan wanted to use to describe how she was feeling. Not a single sentence, however, was exchanged until they made their way to his office and sat on opposite sides of the desk. For those first few moments there was a silence unlike any meeting they had had previously. She needed answers as to what was going on; she couldn't quite put her finger on why the Desmond School for Creative Arts was suddenly treating her like a trespasser, rather than one of the most respected teachers on campus.

Desmond clasped his hands together, planted them firmly on his chest as he took a deep breath, and said, "Mrs. Kay is your temporary substitute." Forget about the ice; nothing she could say would defrost this conversation. "We weren't expecting you back so soon, that's all."

His calm tone, as if he was all-knowing, irritated Elena. She scoffed and turned her head away from him; she looked at the bookshelves against each wall and noticed how there was no more space for any new additions.

Keeping her focus on the shelf to her right, but to Desmond's left, Elena said, "I'm fine. I came back because I'm ready to work again."

"You... y'see, that's the problem: We don't think you are." Elena opened her mouth, but Desmond quickly continued before she offered any of her own assumptions. "And that's not because you're a bad teacher. We love having you; in fact, between you and I, you're my favourite. We're just thinking of your wellbeing, Elena."

"I said I'm fine," she repeated.

Watching her employer lean forward and take another deep breath, Elena predicted rightly: *Come on, don't try to sound like you're making a valid point. It may have worked when I first started, but it sure as hell doesn't now.*

"Look, Elena, we're sorry for what happened. I know your husband..." He caught a glimpse of a triggered look in Mrs. Sullivan's eye. *Be careful with your words, Desmond,* he warned himself before adding, "I know he meant a lot to you, and what happened was a tragedy. Your emotions are still running extremely high, and that's common. They say that the first stage of grief is denial, and we don't want you feeling the way... you do around here. We would prefer you to come back in true good health, not two weeks after your husband's funeral." It was like solemnly telling a child why they couldn't get that special toy they wanted from the shop. "Elena," he continued softly, "the last thing we would want is to make a decision all of us involved would hate to make in the long run. So, please, we want you to take some time off. Just for a little while longer."

Elena wiped her face with her hands, tears forming. She slowly rose with the support of the arms of the chair and began to steadily manoeuvre herself towards the office door without looking back. Desmond sighed behind her, rubbing the back of his neck as he watched on. It wasn't like she was being fired; he was just thinking of what was in her best interest, that was all. He didn't see the harm in that.

As she placed her hand on the doorknob, she said simply, "Thanks."

And, as if she were actually being let go by the Desmond School for Creative Arts, her employer responded with two simple words: "I'm sorry."

*I'm happy as bloody Larry, right?* she thought as she walked out onto the main courtyard towards the gates. *Happy as FUCKING Larry.*

# CHAPTER TWO

## In Loving Memory

As Mrs. Sullivan walked with her head down along Main Street and back towards the roundabout, she felt a breeze growing; it wasn't as light as a wind caused by the tide, though. She looked up and saw a blanket of grey and black clouds cast over the entirety of Valeland.

*"Are you coming to see me?"*

It was Emmett; Elena knew that calm, well-spoken tone better than anyone.

"Oh, all right. I will," she said, her lips barely moving.

Just the sound of Emmett's voice was enough to persuade her. There was no need to ask where he may have been – he had been lying in the same place for a fortnight. She threaded along instinctively up past the roundabout, across, and continued to walk until she reached the rendezvous point: St. Patrick's Cemetery.

Again, she indulged herself in the walks she had. Even when they were to the outskirts of town.

It was no secret, like everything else in this world, that stories about St. Patrick's spread across town, commonly being passed on or made up by Valeland's youth. It wasn't helped by the fact that the cemetery and church grounds stood in the dead centre of Lily Park. Elena didn't understand why a community would decide to build a park around a spiritual place of life and death, but she assumed that it had something to do with giving the grounds just that – a pinch of life.

And death.

By day, a hotspot for children, dog walkers, and family outings; by night, however, a desolate land of folklore, the supernatural, conspiracies, and parlour trickery – a place for people to scare themselves into a fit. And as the common trope of horror stories insisted, the Valeland Citizen Protection Agency shrugged it off and brushed these rumours under the rug like the worthless remnants they were.

Elena reached the cemetery and the grey clouds above released a light drizzle. She listened out for the odd dog bark and scanned the distance for the specks that were the rare joggers. But when walking up that stone pathway, the thing that was in plain view was a towering, blossoming tree. *The* tree.

Under the weathered branches, the leaves, blossoms, and dangling vines – that all acted as a makeshift shelter from the rain – was the headstone of Emmett Sullivan, down by the base of the tree. With the season already at the tail end of winter, slowly sliding into spring like an inevitable realisation, Elena felt the sprinkle of rain as she stood under the tree. She felt like it was only right to make sure she stood at the foot of the grave, chuckling at what she knew her husband would say if she did anything different.

*"You would do that to your own husband? Trample over him like he's nothing,"* she heard, that overly dramatic tone she imagined Emmett talking in making her laugh even more. If he were there, lying in their bed and cuddling their way into a good book, she might just have done it to continue the joke. Knowing the reality, she thought to let him rest peacefully. *So, just stay six feet away from the headstone*, she thought. *"Do you miss me?"*

"With every passing minute," she said. The stones crackled behind her. She turned her head and two men, side-by-side, walked past, their eyes on her. "All right, boys?" she said to them.

They didn't respond, both of them making faces at her. *They must've heard me*, she told herself. *They must think I'm mad.*

But they looked past her and towards the tree; she caught the glance they made at one another, and then back at her. Their looks took on a realisation because they saw it:

## IN LOVING MEMORY
## OF
## EMMETT SULLIVAN

Neither of them saw the epitaph below the name they assumed had belong to this woman's husband.

"We're sorry," one of them said softly.

Then they continued down the path, leaving Elena in the shadows of the tree. She turned back around to the grave, her lips curving into a smile like Emmett was standing right there with her. She managed to glance towards the headstone, but her eyes darted back to the level of the tree trunk; there was no way she could bring herself to look at that epitaph again. No way. Elena couldn't recall a time before the headstone being planted at the base of the tree, but if Emmett were in fact standing there in that moment, then all would be right in her world. Wanting him to stand there under the blossom tree with her, like they did many times prior, was – to her – better than not imagining him at all.

*"How have you been?"*

"You know what?" she said quietly. "Absolutely fine." Elena turned her head and another couple walked past, like she was a ghost herself. *They didn't hear me.* Turning back to her husband, she added, "Work fired me, to tell you the truth…"

18

*"Fired?"*

"Well... Not exactly." She was forced to think. "Yeah. They fired me. They think I should be taking time to cope with what happened. To you." A distorted, almost disgusted expression appeared on her face. "I don't think they grasp that people grieve differently; everyone... everyone just expects you to constantly get upset about it. Maybe they think I'm still having difficulties... *difficulties* processing it, but you know that's not true, don't you? I'm doing what you told me—"

*"Please don't be sad or angry."*

*"Please don't be sad or angry,* so I'm not. I'm fine. Some just handle death better than others. And that will never be understood."

*"Elena, my love, I understand. But that's not—"*

"I knew you would. You always do, my love. Look, I'm going to go home. I'll come back sometime through the week with a little surprise." That smile came back. "I love you."

*"I love you, too."*

## TWO WEEKS EARLIER – THE FUNERAL

It had been requested that the casket would be closed for the service. Mrs. Sullivan wouldn't have been able to cope if she had to catch sight of her late husband's disfig... dead body. There was nothing wrong with that decision, and people – the few she told, that was – respected that choice. They understood the situation; losing a husband must've been bad enough, without even thinking about *how* it had occurred. *No! Don't remind yourself of that,* Mrs. Sullivan thought.

"Ladies and gentlemen, we are gathered... I didn't know Emmett well, but his wife... Let's all bow our heads in silence."

Mrs. Sullivan faded in and out, dreaming of being anywhere else other than in the front row of the church about to say goodbye to her one true love. *True love?* She considered the term, staring vacantly up at the coffin and the velvet-covered platform it lay over. *Emmett, you're my true love...*

*Am I yours?*

Of course she was; there was no doubt. She tried to curve her lips into a half smile, but her body didn't react in the way she had hoped. The priest continued to talk, and Mrs. Sullivan blocked everything out.

Anywhere else, that's where she would've preferred to have been. Anywhere else. *Anywhere else;* how about in the park, sitting under a lonely oak tree, hand-in-hand as they read their books? Holding hands was just instinct; it never felt forced. Or, actually, how about cosying up in the corner of the couch with a different book in one hand and a nice – but not too large – glass of red wine? *Perfect. Anywhere else...* Or perhaps she could be as far away from this service as possible? London? Afghanistan? Japan? Hell, how about the bloody moon? *Yes!* The moon! Alone with her thoughts, where nobody else could feel sorry for her... She would find a good spot... She would sit down in the spacesuit... *How good would it feel to just be alone with my thoughts?* she thought. *I bet the moon is so peaceful; in fact, it sounds delightful.*

"Take it off..." a voice would say. *"Take it off and see what happens..."* Elena would look around and see nobody there but herself. Alone with her thoughts. *"You want peace? Then take it off."* She would look around again, considering the option. *"You want to feel free from this pain? THEN TAKE THE FUCKING HELMET OFF!"* She would feel for the clips of the space helmet, fingers gingerly sliding up her neck until she found them. *"GO ON! TAKE THE FUCKING THING OFF! TAKE IT OFF! TAKE IT OFF!"*

The next moment, the clips would snap open. The helmet would be lifted. Then...

She was back where she was. In the church. The priest was still up there delivering his final words, and all was silent. She felt discombobulated; it must've shown in her dreary eyes as the woman sitting next to her, a friend, leaned in close.

"Are you okay?" she asked.

What a question!

Elena turned to her, blinking, and whispered back, "Yeah, fine."

The pair looked back up at the priest, but this friend couldn't resist one last worrying glance towards Elena. There was no emotion, a blank canvas, and she didn't know what Elena was thinking. She didn't want to. This friend was 43-year-old Imani Keens, a fellow colleague – well, now, Elena supposed, *former* colleague – at the Desmond School for Creative Arts. She looked especially young for her age. Those health care treatments worked brilliantly. Her short black hair, her hazel eyes, and illuminating white teeth made her one of the most approachable teachers in the facility – and generally one of the most approachable people all-round. Her delicate skin looked like it could melt as a chocolate bar would in the sun.

There was never a point where Imani felt indebted to Elena, but being there at her husband's funeral was something Imani felt like she owed her good friend. Elena, Imani thought, was a woman with nothing anymore, and nobody. She needed a friend, and after everything Elena had done for her, Imani wanted to be that friend; she needed to be that friend.

Imani was just about to look from Elena back to the priest, but something caught the corner of her eye; she turned her head, so lightly that it didn't look obvious, and already felt vomit itching to rise up in her throat as two officers pierced the altar, the coffin, and Elena with predatorial glares. *What's the Valeland Citizen Protection Agency doing here!?* Imani asked herself. She couldn't even believe how close she was to blurting that question out loud. Two officers stood, almost hidden, at the back of the church. The one with the hat must've been a higher rank. *No fucking decency*, she thought. *It's this poor woman's husband's funeral. They're not going to ruin today of all days.*

The priest instructed, "Now, if you would all please rise as Elena and I will lead you all out onto the courtyard."

The priest stepped down and walked across to the open exit. An assistant on each door held them open as Imani and Elena slowly rose and walked across. The coffin remained on the platform, and she wanted to take one last look before those red curtains closed; something, though, told her to just keep walking out onto the courtyard. *Just get it over and done with, Elena. Say your thank you's and then you can just go home.*

Elena forgot how clear it was outside. Imani's arm was around her shoulder, and she felt her friend leading her towards the elevated patch of grass in front of them. Laid neatly on this patch of grass were flowers arranged into the name of Elena's husband, all in capitals. Mrs. Sullivan had never approved this gesture, but it was still nonetheless respectable and it was – she had to admit – beautifully done. She had just not wanted to make a massive fuss, that was all.

Turning around, Elena was quite taken aback by the crowd of people that followed them out onto the courtyard. She thought there weren't that many people there at first. Or was it just because they were all spread out like a scattered herd of animals? All their eyes darted towards Elena. She gulped. What was this feeling? Why was she feeling it? It was just the gathering of guests who wanted to pay respect… Pins and needles shot through her suddenly as they stepped forward. A line was being formed, and as the queue grew Elena tried to hide that she was wiggling her fingers to ease the surge of numbness that had spread across her body.

Then she felt a sudden wave of minty breath on her ear.

Imani whispered, "I'm just going to thank the priest."

That comforting touch on Elena's shoulder slid off as Imani made her way back up towards the church where the priest stood, his hands clasped in front of him. The guests moved forward towards Mrs. Sullivan. The numbness, the pain, wasn't easing. *Go away!* she told herself. But it wouldn't. Would it ever?

"I'm sorry for your loss," the first guest in line said, extending their soft hand out to Elena.

Elena accepted it and, with a slight nod, she said, "Thanks for coming."

She said it so quietly the guest thought she had ignored them.

The guest walked off to the side, and this repetitive sequence continued. And continued, and continued, and continued. Anywhere else, that's where she wanted to be. The number of sincere apologies as the line shrunk down to its last few guests had Mrs. Sullivan thinking: *Are you? Are you really sorry? Or do you feel legally obliged to say that just because death is a horrible, yet inevitable, thing that happens to all of us at some point? Are you just being polite?* Why should people be sorry for something that can't be stopped? Like Emmett's death...

"Mrs. Sullivan?"

Her eyes were open, but it felt like she had been asleep for the past five minutes. Shaking hands with everyone was just instinct, but locking onto those uniforms, stern looks and straight postures, Elena had quickly landed back into reality.

*What a horrible thing to think. They meant those apologies.*

*"No, they didn't,"* a voice echoed. *"You know they didn't mean it. Deep down. NOW TAKE THE FUCKING HELMET OFF AND SEE WHAT HAPPENS!"*

"Mrs. Sullivan?"

"Huh?" Elena locked eyes with one of the men standing in front of her. "Can I help you?" she asked drearily.

The man on the right wore what she guessed very quickly was a chief's police hat. The officer's navy-blue uniform all matched, apart from that hat. The hat made him look like he had his full head of hair, but he took it off, revealing a bald spot as shiny as a mirror.

He held his hat close to his chest as he said calmly, "Allow us to introduce ourselves: We're from the Valeland Citizen Protection Agency. I'm Chief Hughes and this is Deputy Cole." The officer who the chief introduced as Deputy Cole wasn't much smaller than the chief – skinnier, yes; less experienced, most definitely. But not really all that much smaller. That wasn't fair. Mrs. Sullivan was probably taking the deputy for granted only because she judged him on his looks; his clean-shaven face, with his hair styled to the side and secured by five tubs of gel, really helped with her assumptions. "We were hoping you could answer a few questions regarding your husband's death."

Elena's shoulders sank. She released a disregarding huff, which was fully intentional.

She breathed, "Whatever."

The officers shot quick unsure glances at one another. She actually cooperated! For a moment, Chief Hughes didn't know what to do next.

"Okay…" Chief Hughes cleared his throat, coughing up his sudden jitters. "So…" Another glance at the deputy. "Are you sure you're okay with…?"

Elena barked, "Yes! I'm fine!"

From the church, Imani turned her head.

"All right, Mrs. Sullivan," the chief said, "what can you recall from the night of your husband's death?"

Elena answered, "It all happened all so quickly. It kind of comes back to me in spurts."

"Okay. What can you remember from that night? Anything before the accident?"

Rubbing her temple with her thumb and forefinger, Mrs. Sullivan said, "We spent the entire day getting ready for dinner. Special occasion."

"Was your husband acting *weird?*" the chief asked quickly.

"Not really." Images flashed back into her mind, of them on that night in their home. She remembered him spending a curiously long time in the bathroom. With the bathroom door shut. The door stayed shut until she opened it fifteen minutes before they were meant to leave for their reservation. "He had been *very quiet* for a huge chunk of the day. If you consider that weird then, yeah, I guess he was acting differently."

Talking, she kept remarkably calm. She couldn't let them break through that thick wall in front of her. If they managed that, then they may've been able to dissect her and manipulate her into saying things that were the furthest things from the truth.

"Okay, thank you. There's something else, Mrs. Sullivan, we would like to ask. We went to the hospital that Emmett attended for appointments, saw his doctor, and she said that an autopsy didn't take place after his death. She said that *you* didn't want one."

"That's right," she mumbled cautiously.

Elena's eyebrows rose.

"Why is that?" asked the chief.

"I was in shock. It felt like I was in a nightmare. I knew he was already dead when I saw him, and I guess I just didn't want to feel worse by hearing the injuries he sustained."

"Mrs. Sullivan, you do realise—"

"What's going on?" Imani rushed over and stood by Mrs. Sullivan. The V.C.P.A chief and deputy fell silent, trying to give her that assertive stare that would say that they were in charge. "Can I help you?"

"Madam, this conversation doesn't concern you," said Deputy Cole.

"Excuse me?" said Imani firmly, her eyes wide. "I don't think it's okay for you to be bombarding this poor woman with questions on a day when she's in mourning. Doesn't exactly put a good name on the V.C.P.A, now, does it?"

"We just need to find out more about Emmett's death," clarified the chief patiently. "Our conclusion so far is that it wasn't a peaceful death in a hospital bed."

The chief closed his mouth, his teeth grinding together as he thought, *Okay, you should've worded that better.*

Imani said, "How insensitive of you!"

Deputy Cole lifted a finger, and started, "Now, Madam, you have no right talking to—"

Hughes raised a hand, silencing Cole instantly as if his hand were an off button, and said as calmly as ever, "No, no, this woman is right, Cole. This wasn't the right time. I apologise, Mrs. Sullivan." Elena said nothing. She offered nothing but a blank stare. The officers started to back away as Hughes added, "But we will be in touch soon."

They walked away. A handful of guests must've seen that as a cue to begin to make their way to the wake's location as they followed the officers out. Imani and Elena remained still.

Imani turned to her friend, placing a hand gently on Elena's shoulder, and said, "Are you all right?"

"Yeah, fine. Thank you."

*Happy as bloody Larry.*

The chief sat there, recalling that talk with Elena from two weeks prior. He sat back in his chair in his private office in the Valeland Citizen Protection Agency building. The only sign of life in the whole building, looking at it from the outside, was that of the light in Chief Hughes's office. The night shift was the norm. He wouldn't dare check his watch, or the clock on the wall, because he knew it would just make the shift drag on. The first glimpse of daylight – that pale shade of blue – shining over the horizon was always the first glimmer of hope for Hughes that he would be going home… for a few hours, at least.

His team were out on patrol across town, from the town centre to the beach and all the way to the outskirts. Many other officers offered to take the night shift, but Chief Hughes always rejected the offer. Although, it was greatly appreciated.

He would say, "I would feel better if I just did it myself."

That had been the motivator behind he and Deputy Cole visiting Elena at Emmett's funeral. It had been an error of judgement, that he would openly admit to his team when they returned, but what he had said was true. Elena knew it, Cole knew it, even Imani knew it: Emmett didn't die peacefully in the hospital surrounded by his family. *Maybe I would do the same if my partner of many years tragically passed,* reflected the chief. *I wouldn't want to make a major fuss either, but I sure as hell would want to know the truth. They didn't get the chance to perform an autopsy, and that was Elena's choice…*

*She knows something we don't.*

There was a knock.

"Chief, it's me," called the deputy behind the door.

"Come in, Cole," ordered the chief.

Deputy Cole poked his head through, the door creaking open, then he opened the door fully and stood in the doorway. The chief noticed his deputy was breathing inconsistently, like he was out of breath. Like he was worried.

"You better come with me."

The chief leaned forward in his chair.

"Yeah?" said Hughes. "What's happened?"

"Our team found something, not far from that old restaurant just outside of town. We fear it might have something to do with Ele—"

The chief shot upright and headed out of the office. He knew something was up with Elena. It was common for the deputy to explain the situation on the way to the scene, but both officers kept silent during the entire drive there. The whole 25 minutes. Signs of night still filled the sky, even as the east felt the first warmth of the fiery glow of the sun.

Most of the town would've still been asleep, but the chief was now wide awake, as if he had taken his fill of coffee.

# CHAPTER THREE

## All A Blur

*She wakes, but she's not in bed. Mrs. Sullivan's conscience tells her that she shouldn't be there; she should be at home in bed, ready to commute to the Desmond School for Creative Arts. Wait! Now, she can have a lie in, can't she? She can stay in this state for a bit longer.*

*The bare trees surrounding her like army men, the crunch of the leaves under her feet, all of it reminds Elena of the many autumn walks she and Emmett used to go on. The adventures. She continues through the wilderness; birds are tweeting in the sweet morning air, music to her ears, and the crunching underneath her remains pleasurable — until she freezes.*

*A light glows in the distance, through the dozens of trees in front of her. It's entrancing, calling to her like a hypnotic ticking clock. She steps closer. The closer Mrs. Sullivan gets the clearer the light is. It's the golden light of the restaurant she and Emmett had reservations for the night he—*

*Elena snaps her head the other way, for something else calls to her.*

*"Go to it, Elena," a voice echoes around her. "You know you want to."*

*She turns away from the restaurant sign and makes her way towards the other sound. Like the sign before, it becomes clearer as she walks closer. A whooshing. Through the trees, a light speeds past her. A vehicle? She begins to speculate where she might be.*

*"The road…" she tells herself.*

*"Now walk to the edge of the road," the voice demands, "and look to your right."*

*Elena does as she's told. The sky above is beginning to become a blend of the previous night's dim blue and the upcoming morning's fiery orange.*

*She feels, she knows, that she's getting closer to the edge of the road. Fewer and fewer trees are surrounding her with every step and the odd whooshing and passing light increases in volume and brightness.*

*There she is. She's at the edge of the road now.*

*"Now, look to your right," she recites.*

*It's the tree. THE tree. And kissing the foot of the tree trunk is the shattered hood of a car. The car's rear seems to still be in good shape, but as she walks to the front, Elena sees the true damage caused. The windshield is shattered, mainly on the passenger side; the airbag has been activated; and wine-red stains are splashed across the hood, even reaching as far as the tree itself.*

*"It must've launched him," she mutters.*

*"Killed him in an instant," the subtle voice says. "That's why you didn't approve of the autopsy. You knew the damage done…" Elena looks around; she thinks she's hearing a ringing in her ears, like sirens. "But, hey," the voice adds cheerfully. "That was the plan all along, wasn't it? He died and you survived."*

*Elena, as if being controlled like a puppet with strings, draws herself away to the back of the car. It's becoming clear that it's their white Rolls Royce. At first glance, it could be mistaken for any old white car. But nope, it's definitely theirs. The licence plate confirms it:* 3ULL1VAN.

*She slowly bends down, grabs the corners of the plate and tears it off with one yank.*

*"It was the plan all along," the voice repeats.*

*"Shut up," she growls.*

*"It was the plan all along. It was the plan all along."*

*"Shut up! Shut up!"*

*"IT WAS THE PLAN ALL ALONG!"*

*"NO IT WASN'T! I LOVED HIM! SHUT UP!"*

*The sirens grow louder, like someone had amped the volume on a set of headphones all the way up, and…*

She had to wake up. And that's exactly what happened.

# CHAPTER FOUR

## Being There For A Friend In Need

Mrs. Sullivan awoke and sat bolt upright in her bed. It wasn't the blinding glare of the sun shining through her bedroom window, nor was it the alarm clock that had been going off for three hours straight by that point. *That voice*, she thought. *The car... They'll find it and they'll think I did it.* The voice needed to go away.

She turned to her nightstand, sat up, and was surprised to see that the time was well past midday, coming close to 1:30pm. The time sunk in, and Elena remembered that there was no need to hurry. Really, there was nothing – and no one – she had to get up for. It wasn't like the Desmond School were going to phone up and ask where she was; that ship had sailed and *firing* her just proved that, no matter how long or how hard you worked for a company, no matter if you poured your heart into the workplace, you could always be replaced.

Blanking the ajar door to her right as she walked across the landing, Elena had her heart set on the bathroom. Letting the water drizzle from the showerhead, like a gentle patter of raindrops on a bus shelter, relaxed her as well as woke her up. She still couldn't believe it: 1:30pm! Never had she woken up that late before. Then she reconsidered the fact she *just didn't have to*. Not for a job, not for her husband. Not for anything or anyone.

Could there be a silver lining here? This could be the chance to become her own woman. She was sure she was eligible for retirement, if not now then soon enough, and the pension she had been waiting for ever since joining the Desmond School after returning from Oxford was waiting for her. *How about a well-deserved holiday? Not the moon, though.* She lifted her head, allowing the water to spray pleasurably over her. It was a relieving feeling that had not been felt in so long. She smiled at the prospect of a holiday. *Ooooo, where to go?*

*But…*

*What about everything else?* The smile quickly vanished as she stepped out of the shower. Looking into the mirror, she saw eyes that she almost did not recognise, and she thought about Emmett. *What would he say? Sure, he would want me to enjoy life and not crumble. But the car… I know they're just going to get the wrong idea.* And she didn't just mean the V.C.P.A; *everyone. How about you do the holiday after all this blows over? But the car—*

*Oh, shut up! It was just a nightmare. An allusion. That wasn't you, Elena. It's NOT you. Tell yourself that, now!*

"It's not you," she said to her reflection. "Stop thinking about it."

*"What? You want to forget about me?"* she heard Emmett say. *"Why!?"*

"What? No! Th-that's not…" She let out a nervous chuckle. "You know that's not what I meant. Come on, you know I will never forget about you."

*"But you could."* The voice lowered close to a whisper. *This* wasn't Emmett. *"And you will. Come on, Elena, don't kid yourself. To forget is what you really want out of all this. Isn't it?"*

"Stop it," demanded Mrs. Sullivan.

*"Isn't it?"*

"I said to stop it!"

*"ISN'T IT!?"*

She cried, "STOP IT!"

Elena felt herself pull her arm back, her fist clenched. Like a bullet, she swung and with that single punch the mirror shattered into many sharp pieces, landing in the sink. Her heart was trying to escape from her chest; the pounding hurt. But it wasn't until she realised what she had just done – *she*, Elena Sullivan, a woman Emmett called the sweetest in the world – when the gash across her knuckles started to sting.

She looked down at her hand. Streaks of blood raced down her fingers; a few drops leapt from her fingertips and landed on the bathroom floor. The pain was there… It had been for over a month. Her feet were planted on the floor, like she was being held down by a magnet. She kept still; the more blood that flowed down her hand, the more that warm wave made her tingle. Like the pleasurable spray of the shower. Like the sea of a Spanish beach.

The grand doorbell rang like a belltower.

Elena looked up and around, as if remembering she was wrapped in a damp towel in her bathroom. Oh yeah, and she had just smashed a mirror with her bare fist.

The doorbell rang again.

"Just a second!" Elena called.

The self-destruct button on panic mode had been pressed. Blood flowed endlessly out of her hand as she kept a grip on the towel around her waist. She ran across the landing, leaving the bathroom door open, and went back into her bedroom.

Changing with only one hand was easier said than done, but Elena managed it. She wrapped her grass green fleece around her as she went downstairs to the front door. There was one last ring as she reached the bottom step.

"Coming, I'm coming," she called again.

Elena reached out and opened the door, hiding her bloody hand behind her back.

"Hi, Elena."

"Imani?"

Imani put on a smile, but there was a concerned look in her eyes. In one hand, she held a bunch of flowers – a nice variety, Elena thought – and the jean jacket and slim-fit trousers was also a good look. She still didn't get why she was at her house, though.

"Are you okay?" Imani asked.

"Why wouldn't I be?" Elena answered.

The fake smile and the constant shifting of the eyes told Imani that something was wrong. Either that, or she was in the middle of something and the last thing she needed was for someone to interrupt.

"Okay…" said Imani slowly. "I… I just wanted to check in to see how you were doing, that's all. Thought these might cheer you up."

She presented Elena with the flowers.

"Um… Thanks," said Elena.

Elena held them in her good hand, her other hand still behind her back. Imani noticed this and darted her eyes down. Elena tried to hide it even more, but it must've made her look incredibly stupid because the more she tried, the more Imani looked sceptical.

"What's wrong?" she asked. Before Elena could even answer, Imani reached for her arm and lifted it close. She looked at the bleeding knuckles, then back at Elena. What she did to injure herself, Imani didn't know, but it wasn't something that could be ignored. "Oh. my God, Elena. What happened? Come on, let's get this cleaned."

Elena stepped to one side and was forced to let Imani in. Imani kept a tight grip around Elena's wrist as she led her like a dog on a leash up the stairs, dropping the flowers halfway up.

"Imani!" a stunned Elena cried.

Elena was sure she felt a crack in her shoulder. But she felt Imani's grip loosen as she scanned the landing; none of the rooms looked like a bathroom. She turned her head and there it was, the bathroom… and the—

"Christ, Elena! What happened?"

Imani was like a worried parent, letting go of Mrs. Sullivan and entering the bathroom. She bent down on one knee and picked up the shards of glass, literally and figuratively putting the pieces together as she looked from the shards and up to the shattered mirror. All while Mrs. Sullivan fiddled with her fingers in the doorway.

"I… um… I *fell*," Elena lied.

Imani glared at Mrs. Sullivan and at her bleeding hand. It was the furthest thing from the truth, Imani thought. *You fell and everything else is fine but your knuckles?* she wanted to ask. *Just go with it, Imani,* she told herself.

"Right," she said, cupping the glass gingerly in her hands, scanning the room for a bin.

"There's a bin in my room," Elena murmured. "The last door," she added a bit more clearly when Imani passed.

The bin was by Elena's bedroom door and Imani brushed her hands clean of the glass. Elena watched as she walked back up to her. Together they walked back into the bathroom and Imani turned on the cold faucet. She grabbed Elena's wrist and made her reach out under the water.

Elena hissed and winced when the water made contact with the cuts. It was like dipping a toe into a swimming pool for the first time – icy upon the first contact, but then she became used to it after a few moments.

The bloody water swirled down the drain and specks of blood started to stain the sink. As the water continued to pour, Imani washed away the stains with her hand. Elena pulled back from the water; the blood was more-or-less gone, and all was left was the slits on each knuckle the blood raced from. She heard the faucet creak off, and Imani turned back to her. The smile she presented when Elena opened the door was no longer there. This was purely a look of concern.

The air filled with the plinking of water droplets from the faucet as the pair stared at each other for a moment longer.

"Elena…" Imani started. Elena felt a lecture coming. That was the last thing she needed right there; she obviously didn't want to snap at Imani, a good friend who felt like the only person that had been there for her since the incident. "Fancy a coffee?"

*Um…* Elena was now the one who looked perplexed. *How do we go from something that looks like a literal crime scene to you asking me to go for a coffee?*

But still, the idea was promising.

Mrs. Sullivan nodded slightly, and then she huffed out a quiet, "Yeah."

The exhaustion began to hit her like the recurrent waves of a tsunami. She had just woken up, so how could she be tired? Elena's mouth was gaping wide as she let out a yawn. Imani had to let out a chuckle before she took Elena's good hand and led her back downstairs.

"Okay, but let's get your hand wrapped up first. Last thing we need is for you to start bleeding out again." They were halfway down the stairs, and Mrs. Sullivan bent over and picked up the bunch of flowers. They weren't ruined, thank God – otherwise she would've felt terrible – but they weren't as neat as they had been when she had first seen them. They continued down the stairs as Imani advised, "Perhaps get yourself to the doctors in the morning, or this evening. Just to make sure nothing's broken."

Elena nodded at this advice. They reached the bottom step and turned into the kitchen for what Elena guessed whatever they were going to wrap her knuckle in. There was only some wet kitchen roll. It would do – it had to. Imani assisted Elena in tightening the roll around her wrist; she tried as gently as possible, but there had been a couple of times out of the silence when Elena couldn't help but let out a wince.

"Thank you for the flowers, by the way," said Mrs. Sullivan, smiling.

Imani didn't reply. She just looked up and gave her a smile of her own. Imani wasn't usually this quiet. What was going on? *First, the flowers, then helping me with the mess, now she's offering to take me for a coffee?* The coffee mate date was starting to become quite the routine, but these other kind gestures stumped Elena. *What are you sugar-coating, Imani?*

The coffee shop they were accustomed to stood on the corner of Weather Lane and Knox Street. These main roads were home to a lot of Valeland's more local businesses, but many considered that to be the heart of the town; the people, those who commuted 24 hours a day, 5-to-7 days a week just so they could put food on the table. Yeah, like all towns across the nation, Valeland had its Tesco's, McDonald's, and Boots Pharmacies, but nothing else gave the Valeland folk a giddy feeling inside like when they would support a business that grew from the mind of a local like a seed in the spring.

Elena kept her wrapped-up hand out of sight and in her leaf green jacket pocket as Imani continued to lead the way. Elena knew the way to the coffee shop, too, but although neither of them had said a single word for the entire walk, there was still that sense of authority that radiated off Imani. The cafe logo (a coffee mug topped with a twirl as if drawn on with a thin-tipped pen which was meant to be whipped cream) above the entrance became clear as they turned onto the street corner. Even before they pressed the handlebar of the entrance door inward, both Imani and Elena inhaled that strong, soothing smell of coffee beans.

*Entrancing.*

Imani pushed the door open, setting off a gentle jingle in the cafe. They walked in, and the smell was stronger than ever. It made Elena want to allow the scent to float up her nose, forcing her eyes to roll behind her eyes and elevate off her feet, gliding towards the counter like a cartoon character. *That's ridiculous*, Elena thought as Imani continued forward. She even allowed herself to chuckle. *Impossible.*

*"Oh, Elena, how wrong you are. Nothing is impossible when you think about it. Just like how everyone around you thought it was impossible for Elena Sullivan to commit such a heinous act. Despicable, that's what you are. What was once impossible... became inevitable."*

Elena gulped, darting her eyes around the cafe. Imani was already by the counter. Tables were scattered around. Some were occupied by couples and families, others by people hard at work on their laptop. Most likely this place was where they found peace. *I need a place like that*, Elena thought.

"Elena!" called Imani, waving her over. "Come on, what d'you want?"

Mrs. Sullivan exhaled deeply and walked towards the counter. It was when she reached it that she saw that the counter had been formed by a glass case displaying baked goods: carrot, chocolate cakes and red velvet; biscuits and cookies; and behind the counter and the young blonde waitress that served them was a shelf holding a selection of sandwiches, above them a chalkboard menu with the writing practically erased.

She leaned on the counter, squinting at the menu. After a beat, she huffed and stood back, looking at the waitress.

"What is there?" asked Elena.

The waitress turned, her ponytail whipping the air as she glanced back at the menu, and looked back at Mrs. Sullivan and Imani as she answered, "We have lattes, americano—"

"Yes, a latte will do," answered Elena quickly, unbothered by the entire selection.

Imani gave her a look before the waitress asked her what she wanted.

"Just the same, please," she said.

"Okay… two lattes…" the waitress recounted. Elena had already turned around and found a table for two by the entrance. "I'll send them over when they're ready."

"Okay, thank you."

The waitress got to work, and Imani headed over to where Elena sat. The round table looked like it couldn't house more than one cup of coffee, never mind two. They sat opposite each other, the eye-contact being kept to a minimum during the silence. *Say something now*, Imani told herself, *before she starts to think something weird is going on.* Elena's back was straight against the chair, looking towards the counter with a distant expression.

Imani planted her forearms on the table and leaned forward slightly. She opened her mouth to say—

"Here you go. Two lattes."

They both looked up and it was the waitress who served them at the counter. The cups and saucers rattled as she placed them slowly on the table. Imani clasped the cup with two hands, sliding her middle finger through the small handle as she lifted it towards her lips; her eyes were now constantly on Elena, who stared down at the coffee as if it was from a different planet – eyebrows sharp, and her face scrunched up.

*"Since when did Elena Sullivan start drinking coffee?"*

*Since she needed you out of my fucking head*, Elena thought, *that's when.*

39

"Elena?" said Imani. Elena looked up, darting her eyes around the cafe once again. She wasn't entirely there, but Imani was relieved she had got her attention. "I was..." *Take it slow*, Imani told herself. "I apologise if I'm getting completely the wrong idea, but is something troubling you?" she asked cautiously.

Her gaze sharpened again, and Imani took a quick sip of her latte, shifting her eyes past Elena to the wall behind her. Elena lifted her cup close to her lips and felt the froth coating over her throat as she took a gulp.

Placing the cup back on the saucer, Elena said deeply, "What'd you mean?"

"W-well..." Imani stammered. She gave herself a moment to take a breath before continuing. "Elena, it's okay to *not* be okay. You know that, right?"

"I'm f—"

Imani snapped, "Honestly, I don't think you are." Mrs. Sullivan wrapped her hands around the mug and stared down at the coffee inside. "People are here for you, remember that. We're here for you. I... I'm here, Elena. And personally, I think you might need to take a break, get away from all this. I can tell you haven't been yourself since Mr. Sullivan's passing, but perhaps a holiday of sorts might just be what you need."

"Why are you being so nice to me?" mumbled Elena.

"You were there for me when I started out as an assistant at the Desmond School. And I just want to be there for you. Isn't that what friends do?"

Elena shrugged and said, "I guess... I guess it's just been harder than I thought. I've been sleeping, but it's felt like I've constantly stayed awake since that night. I'm sure I don't dream; nothing, that's what fills my mind when I'm sleeping. But I can still hear Emmett in my mind, or someone. I think it's him, though. Sometimes I can just tell. How weird is that?

My imagination doesn't play tricks on me, yet I can hear my dead husband's voice when I'm awake…"

"It could be a coping mechanism. You know, a lot of people picture the one's they've lost and have conversations with them."

"Whatever it is, I still feel nothing. Every day is the same… like life isn't even worth living. He made my life worth living."

"Elena, there's always more than just one person or thing that makes a life worth living. That's why I think a trip might be good for you."

There was a curious look on Elena's face; Imani could see her friend was contemplating the idea. *Please, God*, thought Imani, *she needs this break. Make her say yes.*

"You really think a trip away might be good?"

"I'm sure of it," cheered Imani. "I can even help you look for places if you want."

Mrs. Sullivan smiled, and that was all Imani needed to know that Elena had accepted the idea.

*Praise the Lord above*!

# CHAPTER FIVE

## Blessed

### FOUR WEEKS EARLIER – THE NIGHT

Mrs. Sullivan had told Emmett to go on without her, and she'd catch up; this night was going to be perfect.

Over the years there had been many celebratory nights like this one. A few that came to mind as she applied lipstick in front of the bathroom mirror were the nights they graduated from Oxbridge, when they received the jobs at the Desmond School for Creative Arts, and every wedding anniversary. There was just something about this upcoming anniversary; that exciting but uneasy gut feeling had tormented Elena for an entire week already.

It could've had something to do with the fact that she didn't know what Emmett had bought her. She had her suspicions, but one thing about Emmett was that he always bought gifts she never expected but always turned out to be absolutely indispensable. No doubt that that was going to happen this time round too, but there was still that sneaky suspicion.

She pulled a couple of loose strands of hair back behind her ears – the finishing touches – and now she was ready to have the best night with the best person. Her dark blue dress was tight enough, but not so tight as to be classed as slutty. Emmett wasn't into all that, but she gathered from very early on in their relationship that he appreciated how well-kept she was. He said it was one of the best parts about her. Elena chuckled suddenly, and thinking back, he always said that about everything. He still did up until that night.

She smiled at herself in the mirror. *Well-kept indeed, Elena Sullivan. Bloody-well-kept.* The then soon-to-be Mrs. Elena Sullivan tormented herself leading up to their wedding all those years ago, constantly saying she had to be more than well-kept; she had to be beautiful. This was meant to be her day, the day her decision to spend the rest of her life with Emmett became legally binding. The *I do* came before the marriage officiant even said his lines, and there was an uproar of emotion when both sides of the family watched Elena jump into Emmett's arms for that kiss, joining them together forever.

The day of their wedding was always clear and detailed in her mind, especially on their anniversary. But it was also what she thought of whenever the pair had a tiff. A simple reminder she still loved him. Some of the things she said in arguments made her sound like she didn't love him at all, and it was the same for Emmett. Yet, an argument was only a rare occurrence, so when one was brewing, both husband and wife instantly felt sick inside.

*Things are said in the heat of the moment, and we don't mean them; though we all have taken back things we've said, really nothing said is ever taken back.*

"Tonight will be perfect," she mumbled, still smiling.

But she continued to play with her hair – it had to be perfect. *Everything* had to be perfect. Everything thus far had been ticked off the checklist: the dress, the hair, nails, lipstick, Emmett's present from her, and making him leave early so she could triple check everything. She walked into their bedroom, and on the bed was the small Gucci handbag she needed;

unzipping the bag and pouring its contents all over the bed, she huffed in relief when the little square box she required fell out. Scooping it gently in one hand, Elena held it to her chest as she kept reminding herself that she had the gift in there and it was safe.

Just a glimpse of what was inside the box, Elena had to divert her eyes. The encrusted crystals on the ring twinkled like faraway stars in the night. The box gave a slight clap when she shut the lid, and then she stuffed it back in her bag, along with the rest of her belongings, including her make-up pouch in case she got self-conscious about her appearance in public and had to freshen up.

The heels that matched her dress stood perfectly in line with one another on the bottom step. Mrs. Sullivan ignored them at first, for when she entered the kitchen and placed the bag on the bench she scurried for her mobile. Of course, it was at the very bottom of the bag, like digging something out of a bottomless pit.

"Were handbags created by Mary Poppins?" she recalled one student asking her in a seminar one time. "Is that why you can find anything in them?"

The student's question made her chuckle when she picked up her mobile. Elena started to dial and the phone began to ring.

*"D and P's Taxis. Can I help?"*

Elena tilted her head away from the phone for a second; they'd never answered so quickly.

"Hiya, can I have a taxi straight away, please?"

*"Who's it for?"*

She answered proudly, "Mrs. Elena Sullivan."

*"And... Where would you like to be picked up from?"*

"3 Consat Road."

*"Okay, a taxi should be with you in ten minutes or so."*

"Thank you very much."

Then Mrs. Sullivan hung up and waited.

Ten minutes on the dot. Mrs. Sullivan waited on the street, her handbag hanging from her shoulder and her leather jacket on, as the taxi pulled up to the curb. She hopped in the backseat and caught the driver watching her in the rearview mirror.

"Off anywhere nice today, ma'am?" asked the driver.

"Devine, the nice restaurant in the hills, by the motorway."

"Oh, yes. I know the place." The driver started to pull away, turned back around, and cruised along beside the curb. Elena's handbag sat on her lap, and she stared out the window. Most of the lights in the passing houses were on – *They're leading the way*, she thought – and the bright lamp posts glowed a tranquil orange light, like a fire on a winter's night. "Special occasion?" the driver asked.

Elena felt a grin grow on her face as she said, "Oh, yes. Very special."

The drive was nice. Quiet. The way she liked it. She had nothing against taxi drivers personally, but the idea of them being obliged to start random conversations while on your way to a destination, although the idea might have been kind and polite, came across as nosy. Elena got why they did it, but why ask about someone's life story if you're never going to see them again?

Still, the drive was nice.

They pulled up in front of the restaurant after the 20-minute drive. From the curb, a red carpet led them towards the glass doors under that glowing yellow sign, *Devine*, in neat, cursive writing. After paying the driver and thanking him, Elena stepped out onto the red carpet; a movie premier wasn't what she was attending, but she knew if there were any paparazzi around, she'd be the centre of attention. On these bitter-sweet days, she *was* always the centre of attention because she could. It wasn't often she felt like this, but when she did she wanted people to bask in her efforts.

A doorman in what she thought was a cute little bowtie stood by the door, awaiting her and the guests that followed. His slight nod was the normal greeting Mrs. Sullivan received when going to Devine. The doorman opened the door without a single creak and Elena walked in, being met by a stand and a smartly dressed waitress with a bright smile on her face.

"Welcome to Devine," she said, all of her teeth showing, "do you have a reservation?"

"Ah, yes," answered Elena politely. "My husband is already here. Sullivan, the name is." She looked past the waitress and, in the far corner, under an abstract painting she found impressive, Emmett was sitting at a cloth-covered, candle-lit table that had been decorated with a small vase of flowers. "There he is," she called, pointing and waving over to him.

The waitress looked behind her and saw him, and said, "Ah, okay. Well, let me take you to him."

Elena followed the waitress, passing the circular tables reserved for larger groups of people and zig-zagging her way through the square tables for the couples. Emmett stood up as they arrived, with the waitress pulling Elena's seat out for her. Elena couldn't take her eyes off her husband – the smooth suit, the clean-shaven face, the smile… She smiled back as she and Emmett sat down together.

"Hi," Emmett said. "You look… radiant."

Elena tried not to blush.

The waitress said, "I'll get someone to take your order."

Emmett looked up and said, "Thank you."

As the waitress left, Emmett and Elena just kept staring at each other and giggling like a pair of children. Neither of them could believe they were there, at this stage in their lives. It hadn't really crept in yet that this day marked another year of them being together as husband and wife.

"Can you believe it?" Elena said. "It's been this long."

"I know," whispered Emmett, still partly stunned by this reality. "Have I already said how amazing you look?"

Elena chuckled and said, "You can make an effort when you want to, too, can't you?"

"Well, I do try."

They both laughed.

A waiter came across and stood at their table, cradling a silver bucket with a guaranteed fresh bottle of Devine's finest champagne. Elena couldn't recall the restaurant serving champagne like this before... They weren't doing it with the other tables.

The waiter placed the bucket on the table and said, "Compliments of all of us here at Devine. For the happy couple."

Elena caught her husband grinning at her. Then the waiter spun around, launching his arm forward as if to present them with something; Elena looked past the waiter and her jaw dropped – with Emmett smiling proudly – as another waiter came walking forward with possibly the biggest bouquet of flowers she had ever seen. Behind this waiter, another waiter quickly tuned a violin then started to play a slow, peaceful song. Elena covered her mouth, about to come to tears. She felt that all eyes were on them, seeing in the corner of her eye all the guests smiling and applauding.

Emmett then slid a small, purple fabric box towards his wife. Elena let out a chuckle as she cupped the box in one hand, opening it with the other. A diamond ring, just like their wedding ring. The violin stopped playing and there was silence. Everyone's full attention was on the couple.

Emmett leaned forward and said softly, "I love you more than the day I first set eyes on you. And I always will. Happy anniversary, my darling."

"Happy anniversary, love. I love you, too." She matched his tone and she leaned forward into a passionate kiss. The guests applauded. The first waiter popped open the bottle of champagne like a firework above them, and a chorus of whoops followed the bottle opening. From then, she *knew* it was going to be a perfect night. It already was.

The night went on as both of them had hoped.

Price didn't matter that night, nor did the amount of champagne Emmett had consumed. The bottle was gone when the night concluded, but Elena knew it hadn't hit him as much as it would've if he hadn't had any food. After paying, they linked arms and strolled out of the restaurant like the happy couple everyone saw them to be. A perfect night, that's what it was. Simply perfect; nothing more, nothing less.

Their Rolls Royce pulled up as they exited Devine, and Mrs. Sullivan tipped the vale before entering the driver's side.

"You can't fault Devine," said Emmett as they came out onto the main road.

"Yeah," said Mrs. Sullivan, her eyes fixed on the road ahead, "my steak was perfect."

They wound round the hill and came up to a set of traffic lights and a roundabout; the exit they needed was what led them off the hill and onto the motorway.

The lights flashed amber then turned green, and the Rolls Royce turned smoothly around the roundabout to the second exit. Both of them enjoyed these quiet night drives, with only a few cars passing by, their headlights like stars. Because of the woodlands that heavily populated this area of Valeland and the hills, the motorway wasn't as straight as driver's would've hoped the road to be. Still, at least the drive was peaceful.

No traffic, no accidents, no problems… *Nothing.*

*Nothing.* Suddenly, *nothing. Darkness was closing in around her like walls… Her mind went blank. Mind blank, blank mind. Gone. Nothing. Her vision was gone. Hearing was still there but only just; Emmett's voice, a car horn, then BANG!*

*A whiplash? Screeching tires? Glass smashing?*

Mrs. Sullivan woke up in the emergency room, with her husband, Emmett Sullivan, dead.

She remembered being discharged only after a few hours as her injuries were said to be not as fatal as the doctors originally suspected. Despite this, Elena wasn't leaving her husband's side. They would've had to drag her out if she wasn't allowed to see him one more time. Still, even a month on, Elena didn't know the true cause of death. The last thing she recalled was that she was the one driving. *She* was the one driving. *She* was the one.

*I was driving,* she thought. *It was me… But it wasn't. It was. It wasn't. Yeah, it wasn't me. It had to be someone else. A reckless driver drove us off the road. Yep. Because it wasn't me.*

"Yeah, Elena," she told her reflection in the bathroom, "keep telling yourself that."

She knew it to be true.

# CHAPTER SIX

## Surveying The Scene

The Valeland Citizen Protection Agency closed the motorway off for closer examination on the Rolls Royce that crashed into a tree, one night four weeks ago, ultimately killing Emmett Sullivan. Not Elena.

Chief Hughes surveyed the crash like a painting in a museum. He stroked his chin. The tree hadn't flinched. His team had already set about and finished cutting the highway off with a set of cones and police tape. Hughes studied where the Rolls Royce connected with the tree, Deputy Cole slowly coming up behind him.

"Anything?" the deputy asked.

"Nope." The chief shook his head, folding his arms. "Clearly the reason Elena survived was because of the airbag. Mr. Sullivan went straight through the windshield, landing on the car's hood. A part of him could've connected with the tree. Do you see the blood patches here?"

Hughes rubbed his fingers down the tree's rough bark, showing the stains of blood. Deputy Cole nodded, noting the information. But then an idea popped into mind, a possible argument against the chief's theory.

"But," he started politely, "surely Mr. Sullivan wasn't stupid enough to not have worn a seatbelt?"

"Cole, even with a seatbelt, considering the speed the car was driving at plus the force as it connected with the tree, I'm surprised it didn't send Mrs. Sullivan flying, either."

"So, we've established that Mrs. Sullivan was the one driving?" guessed Cole.

"She had to have been. The reports from the hospital state Emmett was dead in the ambulance. Mrs. Sullivan, on the other hand, was just unconscious."

"We're going to treat it as a homicide, then?"

Hughes tutted and said, "Despite the possibility, Cole, we can't just jump to conclusions."

"Chief!" a voice called.

Hughes and Cole looked behind them, and a fellow officer waved them over to the back of the car.

"What is it?" said the chief.

The officer kept their eyes down; Cole and Hughes looked down also and saw something that sprouted a whole bunch of new possibilities. There was the brief idea that it could've flown off upon impact, but the V.C.P.A chief and deputy would've been kidding themselves. The licence plate had been torn off.

"Chief?" said Cole, catching Hughes' blank stare. The cogs in his brain were turning, and the realisation may have been setting in: Mrs. Sullivan might not be as innocent as she appeared. "What shall we do?"

The chief answered slowly, "Get someone to pick up the Rolls Royce." His eyes were still on the patch where the plate would've been. He didn't want the theory to be true. "We have to see Mrs. Sullivan."

"Are we going to take her in, Chief?" asked Deputy Cole.

"No... *Not yet.*"

As part of the V.C.P.A, they had to keep an open mind; Chief Hughes was right, they couldn't jump straight to conclusions. As much as they may have had to. It was now up to Mrs. Sullivan to tell them the truth. To tell herself the truth.

# CHAPTER SEVEN

## Wondering

*A whiplash? Screeching tires? Glass smashing?*

Mrs. Sullivan sat in the lounge, trying to keep the vomit down. She wondered if anyone else got that sickly feeling where you think something bad was going to happen. She tried to push those feelings to one side and wanted to brainstorm places to go for her trip.

*London? That's a great place for sightseeing. Living in the big city is the dream for many, isn't it? Not for you, Elena, it's not. You want somewhere peaceful, like Cornwall or Scarborough. A little seaside town. That's more like it—*

*Darkness.* Suddenly, *darkness—*

*Or how about Edinburgh? A place full of history—*

*Blank mind, mind blank—*

*Where else is there? Norfolk? Norwich? COME ON, ELENA! There's got to be somewhere—*

*Gone. Nothing.*

*It's no use.* And it wasn't. Her mind was elsewhere, and she was frustrated with herself because of it. *It.* She leaned her head back, staring up at the ceiling. A long sigh escaped her, and at that moment there was a knock on the door.

Elena didn't budge. Another knock.

She hissed, "Fuck off."

Another knock. She obviously hadn't said it loud enough; Elena groaned as she stood from the couch and made her way to the door. *Any other day would've been better… Any other day when I'm not here.* She opened the door and there stood Chief Hughes and Deputy Cole of the V.C.P.A.

"Hello, Mrs. Sullivan," greeted the chief. "How are you?"

Like she was lost in her own world, Elena said nothing. A worrying blank stare. The chief and deputy glanced at one another and continued to wait for a response. They tried to make themselves look like their minds hadn't been made up already.

*"They know, Elena,"* that familiar voice – not Emmett's – said, ringing through her ears.

Still with that blank stare, Elena muttered, "You know…"

Hughes and Cole glanced at each other again then back at Elena. *Curious. Suspicious.* They still couldn't leap to conclusions so soon. Even if she was trying to admit to them what she had done. The chief kept in mind the slight possibility that Elena didn't commit vehicular homicide.

"Excuse me?" said Cole.

"You know…" started Mrs. Sullivan. Then a smile spread across her face as she added, "You know, I'm actually doing fine." The sudden jolliness in her voice made both Chief Hughes and Deputy Cole step back. "In fact, I'm grand. Why don't you come in and I'll put the kettle on?" she said wryly.

They stepped in as Elena made her way towards the kitchen.

Hughes reached out to stop Elena as she went for the kettle and said, "Oh, that won't be necessary, Mrs. Sullivan." She turned around. "We just wanted to ask you a few questions."

"About…?" *Don't sound stupid,* Elena thought. *You know this is about Emmett.* "My husband?" she added.

*"You know what they're going to ask,"* the voice said, *"just like how they know what you did."*

"Yes," answered the chief.

Cole added swiftly, "If that's okay with you, of course."

"Yeah," said Elena. Her smile faded away then reappeared. "Okay. Take a seat."

The chief and deputy sat themselves down on the couch as Mrs. Sullivan took her place on the other end. From his pocket, Cole revealed a small notepad and a pen. Elena had it figured out: *If they've been to the crash, their minds have been made up. They're going to see the licence plate and see that it's registered to me... But I know I didn't do it.*

That didn't matter. She was the prime suspect; she survived and Emmett didn't. That was the reality. And the truth – Elena's truth – was that she didn't intentionally murder her own husband. However, convincing the V.C.P.A. would be easier said than done.

"First of all," started the chief, "we wanted to apologise for turning up at your husband's funeral. It was inappropriate of us to do that and to think you'd be in the right state of mind to answer questions regarding his death at the time."

"It's fine," Elena said, waving her hand to add to the reassurance. "Don't worry about it."

*"You know they know..."*

"Great," said the chief, leaning forward. "So, to begin, what can you tell us about the night your husband...?"

Elena thought, *At least he has the human decency to not say my Emmett was murdered.*

She replied, "It was our anniversary the night Emmett passed away. Neither of us could wait, because we had reservations for Devine – you know, that lovely restaurant. We had it planned for weeks. Anyway, that night Emmett headed off in the Rolls Royce before me because I wanted to finish getting ready. I never liked him waiting for me. So, I got a taxi up to the restaurant and... it was *perfect*. Just perfect. Emmett surprised me with a violinist and champagne when I arrived."

Cole started jotting down notes. "The night went on, we had our food, enjoyed each other's company as we always did, then we set off home in the Rolls Royce."

The blank stare returned.

"Then?"

Mrs. Sullivan gulped repeatedly, trying to hype herself to finish the sentence.

"Then… I don't know what happened. I must've blacked out or something, because the next moment I woke up in the hospital."

"Blacked out?" repeated Hughes, raising an eyebrow.

"Yep," Elena clarified. "One minute we're driving along the motorway, the next I'm in the hospital."

"That doesn't make any sense," said the chief.

"Tell me about it," scoffed Elena.

"So, you don't remember the exact time you crashed?"

Elena shook her head and said, "That's all I remember."

"Hang on," said Cole, looking up from the notepad. "Mrs. Sullivan, you said Emmett surprised you with a bottle of champagne."

"Well, it was for both of us," Elena clarified again.

"Okay," continued the deputy, "you've also said that you drove home in the Rolls. You do understand that under UK law it's illegal to drink and drive?"

"Yes, I'm aware of the law, but I only had one glass. I was under my own control when I was driving."

Chief Hughes asked, "*Were* you, though, if you say you blacked out? Do you happen to be a drinker, Mrs. Sullivan?"

Elena shook her head rapidly like the accusation was ludicrous and said, "Not at all."

"So perhaps one glass was enough," suggested the chief.

"Mrs. Sullivan," the deputy intervened, "we should really place you under arrest for having a drink—"

The chief cut Cole off with, "But we're not going to do that, because that's not why we're here. I know you to be a reasonable person, Mrs. Sullivan. I'm asking you to really think about that night, what led up to that devastating incident. Maybe the drink provoked you, and you're just telling yourself nothing happened."

Elena's eyes grew wide with shock. The chief had struck a nerve there, but he had to bring it up. Mrs. Sullivan started to turn a beetroot red, like she was holding her breath.

"How *dare* you," she hissed. "Are you really insinuating that I killed my own husband?"

Deputy Cole put his hands in front of him as he said calmly, "We're just trying to get to the bottom of why this happened. If you are telling the truth and this was just an unfortunate accident, then we need to find an alley that can take us to that conclusive result."

"But Mrs. Sullivan," the chief carried on, "if you're lying to us then it's going to be a lot harder for us to help you. The last thing the V.C.P.A wants is to say they've arrested one of the most respected teachers at the Desmond School for Creative Arts. Please... Elena, help us help you."

Mrs. Sullivan looked down at her hands. She was seeing double as she started to shake her head lightly. There was their answer; she would've just been going over old ground if she said anything else. *Blank mind, mind blank. Darkness. Gone. Nothing.* She couldn't remember if she wanted to.

Cole looked down at his notepad and informed her, "We investigated the crash earlier today. You're probably aware that the passenger's side of the windshield took the most damage. That's how we've come to the cause of death. But there was one other thing..." Elena looked up as the chief and the deputy glanced at one another. The all-clear look from the chief led the deputy to finish his statement. "The Rolls Royce has been tampered with."

"Wh-what'd you mean?" mumbled Elena.

"Mrs. Sullivan, the back licence plate had been taken. Now, we're considering all possibilities here but if the crash wasn't intentional then perhaps someone tried to kill you both? At any point driving, did someone try to cut you off?"

"I... I honestly... No."

*"They never believed this idea, Elena. Their minds are made up. You did it. You fucking did it!"*

Mrs. Sullivan cleared her throat and said, "I don't know why someone would steal the licence plate, either. Probably a bunch of delinquents thought it was funny. I-I-I... If you want anything else from me, then I'm sorry. I can't help you because everything I've told you is all I know."

Both Hughes and Cole sighed. The deputy put the notepad back into his pocket as he and the chief rose from the couch.

"Okay..." he said.

They started to walk around the couch and back towards the front door. Mrs. Sullivan followed a few steps behind. But before they walked out, they both turned to Elena.

"Before we go, Mrs. Sullivan," said the deputy, "can I just ask one more question?"

"If you must," she said.

"Did you love your husband?" he asked.

Mrs. Sullivan smiled and replied, "More than anyone will ever know."

Cole nodded and followed the chief out. As they walked down to their police cruiser, Mrs. Sullivan heard a faint "thanks" but she had already slammed the door shut. She turned around and allowed herself to lean against the closed door. She looked around at the house, which she and Emmett had built together over decades of love. Of course she loved him. What a thing to ask a grieving widow!

*"They're not going to stop. The investigation will continue until they find you guilty… Don't bother trying to tell yourself otherwise; it's true. You should start looking at places for your trip."*

But she couldn't think about a trip; Elena slowly slid down the door like the tears upon her cheek. She dropped until she sat upon the floor, and she wailed into her hands until she had no more strength to feel as bad as she did.

*"Come on, darling. There's always hope. Don't wallow in your grief. I'm never truly gone. I'm always here, and I'll be with you whatever you decide."*

This was the voice she wanted to hear. *Emmett.* It was just a shame she couldn't hear it more often.

# CHAPTER EIGHT

## Refreshing, Indeed

Over the course of the next few days, Elena kept herself to herself; she remained in her house as if it were hibernation season, and she had received no human contact since the chief and deputy asked her about Emmett. It was a good thing, really, to have this time to herself. Time to herself meant time to process what had happened since the accident… and what was about to happen. People grieve in their own way, but one's own way isn't exactly the *right* way…

Chief Hughes sat in his office in the Valeland Citizen Protection Agency building, head in his hand, just trying to put the pieces together; he had done the night shift again, but he was wide awake. It was coming up to 5:30am but, from a single glance outside, one would've assumed it was coming up to midnight.

Deputy Cole had called in ten minutes prior, barely raising a conversation, then left to go out on his morning patrol. He assigned himself to scout around the seafront, and it wasn't the first time. Hughes knew how peaceful it was down there, but always let the man be. There wasn't much hassle at this time in any part of Valeland, anyway, so there was nothing wrong having a few minutes of peace before daybreak.

One end of the beach was marked with a holiday park, with many of the caravans and bungalows that stood on the grounds being privately owned. Cole struggled to find a suitable spot for himself and the police cruiser. The other option – the option Cole eventually went with – was on the other end of the beach, which was marked with an empty car park and a rusty cafe that looked like it had survived many harsh winds brought in by the tide.

After parking by the cafe's entrance, Cole walked into the sound of a jingling bell above the door. The counter in front displayed homemade cakes and sandwiches that smelled mouth-wateringly sweet. A lot of the cafe had been occupied by sets of tables and chairs, but no customers. But that wasn't really surprising at this time of morning, Cole considered, and it meant quicker service.

The woman behind the counter had a red apron wrapped around her, and she presented the V.C.P.A deputy with a charming smile. She looked young and well-kept, like someone who cared, not someone who was in it just for the money.

"Good morning," she said pleasantly, "what can I get you?"

Reaching the counter, Cole answered, "Just a tea, please, thanks."

"One tea... Milk and sugar?"

"If you don't mind."

The woman kneeled down under her side of the counter and placed a teapot and a mug on a tray. This wasn't the first time Cole had visited this neat little cafe; it was, however, the first time he had seen this new girl at work... He watched as she prepared his tea, then looked to the far window. Still dark. That was okay.

"£2.50, please," the waitress said.

Deputy Cole reached into his pocket and pulled out all the loose change he had. He handed it to her in exchange for the tray of tea.

As he took it and stepped back from the counter, he noticed her look and said, "Keep the change."

They smiled at each other, with the waitress keeping her eyes on the deputy as he made his way to a table by the far window. Surely, he would get the best view from this spot. The first sip instantly warmed Cole up inside. The waitress pottered around the counter, straightening the plates of display cakes and sandwiches, but doing so with one eye watching the V.C.P.A deputy.

"Let me know if you need anything," she said shakily.

Cole looked over and smiled back at her. This girl's standout features were that bright smile, those rosy cheekbones and her tied-up strawberry blonde hair. She turned away, as did the deputy. The tide was in and the deputy didn't ever want it to go out again.

*Mrs Sullivan can't stop herself from shaking, no matter how much she tries. SHE JUST WON'T STOP! It's like pins and needles all over her body but worse; it's more like knives and forks. And she can't do anything about it.*

*The pillow on which her head had rested is no longer there. She can't fathom how that is, because it feels like she's still lying down; everything around her is spinning, as if she is on a fairground ride set to maximum power. She has that sickly feeling in her stomach now as well as the constant pinch of the knives and forks. But where has the pillow gone?*

*Mrs. Sullivan hears thumping, so that means she's walking. Right? She has to be, and her question is answered when she is met with a tsunami of wind. That clears her bearings. If anything, surely stepping out of the house and walking down to the main street wouldn't have been as agonising if she had been wearing shoes, which was also the case with her nightgown. Not appropriate at all, yet she still continued down the street.*

*"I don't care anymore,"* she whispers to herself.

*"You don't care,"* that voice repeats. And the voice is right. Elena suddenly feels some sort of satisfaction – a form of comfort – finally agreeing with the voice that she's been trying to ignore for so long. *"You know,"* the voice adds, *"the V.C.P.A don't believe your bullshit."*

*"They don't believe my bullshit,"* Elena echoes.

Stones are digging into her feet. They could easily be bleeding by this point, and she has no idea because all she feels is the dry pavement scraping against her soles. The wind is getting stronger, and she starts to sense a change in the air – the fresh, cool, salty air.

*"Do it, Elena, you know you want to."*

Her soles are now warm, grainy, and she hears the tide crashing onto the beach. The sand is more comforting than the pavement, and the sound of the waves is even more relaxing. She does want to do it, because why else would she be here at the crack of dawn; the sun is beginning to rise in the east, and it sends something down her body which washes all the pins and needles – everything – away. She's never seen the sunrise, but that paint palette of a sky – the navy blue, the pale yellow, and fiery orange – is still stunning to see.

*Now, there really is nothing left…*

*"Do what?"* she finds herself asking quietly.

*"You know exactly what. Go on, do it. You know the truth; they know the truth… Everyone knows the truth."*

*"Everyone knows the truth,"* she says.

*Nothing…*

Deputy Cole sipped his tea, the sky showing hints of the sunrise. *Wow*, he thought. *Beautiful as always.* Then he turned towards the counter where the young woman stood. *Beautiful as ever.* They smiled again at each other, and the bell above the entrance jingled. They both watched as a short, tubby lady waddled in, wearing the exact same red apron as the waitress.

"Good morning, Granny," greeted the waitress.

"Morning, hon," the woman replied, her voice scratching against her throat every time she tried to talk. "Is everything done?"

"Yep," the waitress said proudly. "Everything's been unloaded in the back. We should be good for the next few weeks."

"That's good." The lady nodded as she walked behind the counter. Cole sipped his tea; one eye was still on the horizon, while the other was on the grandmother and granddaughter. They embraced tightly as the woman whispered, "This cafe is everything. It's a part of our family, hon. I'd rather die than see it go under."

The waitress hushed her grandmother and placed her hands on her shoulders.

"Now, stop talking like that," the waitress said lightly. "Nothing's going to happen to us or to the cafe. We'll be okay." Her grandmother nodded and smiled as they embraced again. "I'm going to see if him over there wants a refill."

She slyly pointed over to the deputy. Granny glanced over at him and back at her granddaughter; a look as if to ask her granddaughter if she thought she was daft. The waitress immediately caught on and scoffed. Young love, she remembered that feeling well enough.

"Okay," said Granny, winking, "go and give him a *refill*."

Cole glanced over to the counter and saw the older lady hand the waitress another teapot from under the counter. He quickly shifted his eyes back to the blueing sky as the waitress came over.

"Would you like another?" asked the waitress to Cole, reaching the table and presenting the teapot.

"Oh, please," said Cole, trying to act as if he didn't realise she was there at first.

She slowly poured, and asked, "You scouting the area for someone?"

She saw that his eyes were back on the beach.

Cole chuckled and answered, "What makes you think I'm a police officer?"

"Well, for starters you came here in a V.C.P.A cruiser… and the badge and uniform were a massive giveaway." Cole peered down at his uniform and chuckled, as did the waitress. "I'm Ally, by the way."

"Deputy Simon Cole." The waitress looked over to her granny, who instantly gave an approving nod. Ally sat down at the table with Cole and they couldn't stop smiling at each other. "So, you've been here long?"

"My family's run this place for years," said Ally. "That's Granny P over there…" Cole waved over at Ally's grandmother. "She and my grandad bought this place when they were just 18."

"Wow. I've seen your grandmother in here, but never you."

"I normally work in the back, but with Grandad falling ill, Granny needed more help manning the cafe. I'm hoping to take it over some day."

"Oh, nice. That'll be great," said Cole. "So what—"

Something passed Ally's shoulder, catching the deputy's eye. And it wasn't the sky or the beach, but a figure staring out at the sea.

Ally asked hesitantly, "Is something wrong?" She turned in her chair and caught sight of the figure, too. "Who's that?"

"I-I don't know…" the deputy answered.

She looked back at Cole and asked, "Are you not going to have a look, Simon?"

"Let's see what she… *they* do first, Ally."

They were on a first name basis; Cole felt like she was taking a shine to him, and vice versa. And above all that, even before he had the chance to ask her out, he had already lied to her; he would've bet his yearly salary on who the figure was.

*Mrs. Sullivan steps forward and now she can feel the water at her ankles. She stands for another moment and takes the deepest breath she's ever taken and exhales. That was the last of it, surely. Now there really is nothing.*

*"Go on, take another step," that voice orders.*

*She does. She can feel the water swallowing her whole — just one bite — and the water is now at waist height; she stops, her eyes closing, letting the sea breeze smack her across the face. Spreading her arms out as if for an embrace, Elena knows that she's going... She's going to do it; she's going to go and nobody will know. Nobody will care. It's the easy way out, and the easy way is the right way. It is. The right way. The right way to go. Go, go away, end it all, she has to... do it... She has to do it or everything will catch up.*

*"Can I do it?" she mumbles.*

*"Of course," the voice clarifies soothingly.*

*"I can..." says Elena again, this time with confidence. "I can... And it's the right thing to do. Goodbye."*

*Goodbye; goodbye forever, and when we say goodbye for good, it ends. It's all over. There's nothing left, and we're gone.*

*Mrs. Elena Sullivan begins to lower herself, really being swallowed up; the water is now above her breasts. As she lowers even more, she feels more like she is being drawn in. Something's pulling her, but it isn't the light people say they see just before death. Darkness, that's what. Because when we're gone, we're gone. No way of coming back...*

*"Elena!" a distant voice calls. "Please don't do this. This isn't you." She feels a presence, a presence that might almost be familiar, but she's not completely certain if it's the person she hopes it is. She rises just as the water reaches her neck and the voice calls out again, "Don't! This isn't the end."*

*That did it; somehow that tells her that Emmett is there with her. She can live on, can't she? Imani reminded her of that, telling her to take a break and start fresh. To start anew. And with Emmett telling her the same thing, perhaps, she presumes, this is in fact the right way forward.*

*The idea of happiness is coming back to her and is sounding less ridiculous. But she won't know until she gives it a try...*

*She hears Emmett's distant voice once more: "Live your life well, my love. It might have been the end for me, but you've still got time left before you."*

Deputy Cole and Ally turned their attention back to each other, mirroring each other's expressions, eyes wide and jaw on the table.

"What the hell was that about?" Ally asked, leaning in.

Cole gulped and said, "I honestly have no idea, but I need to... something's clearly not right."

Neither of them talked during a prolonged silence; Ally started to feel a tad uneasy. The image of what she and the V.C.P.A deputy had just witnessed together was quite powerful, and Cole himself had been fighting the temptation to once again jump to conclusions. His mind bluntly came to the assumption that that figure had tried to kill themselves, and nobody wants to witness such an act. Something drew them back, though, he recalled, and it was something to take into consideration.

It wasn't something Deputy Cole could keep to himself for long, he knew that, and Hughes had to hear about it. He didn't get a good look at the figure, their face looking out towards the horizon, but one thing he did note down was that they weren't wearing appropriate clothing.

"Look," Cole said, rising from the table, "it was lovely to meet you, Ally, but I have to report this back to the chief."

He tucked his chair in, not expecting a response, but Ally said, "Don't worry, I understand. I hope to see you in here again."

They smiled at each other, and nothing else was said. The bell jingled above the door as Cole left for his cruiser, and he knew what had to be done; he would have to save asking her out for later, and instead he would direct his attention wholly on Mrs. Sullivan and this new piece of… he wanted to call it *evidence*.

The drive back to the office was a silent one. There was not much morning rush-hour traffic – thank God – and the traffic lights were on the deputy's side. But that was all external; within, his mind was racing, forming equations, hypothesising what these recent events meant, and where these events would lead.

He parked up and headed straight for Hughes's office. It was no surprise that he was still there, wide awake and keeping himself busy by completing some forms that probably had nothing to do with actual police work. Cole called that part of the job the *boring stuff*; when he brought Cole on the force, the chief quickly grasped that he was more of a field guy rather than being stuck in an office answering calls all day.

Deputy Cole didn't think to knock, and Chief Hughes was startled by him running in and skidding to a halt in front of his desk.

"Cole? What is it?" said the chief, pushing the papers to one side.

"It's… It's Mrs. Sullivan, Chief…"

"What about her?"

"I-I might have something on her that could help us determine what really happened."

"Well tell me!" the chief said eagerly, leaning forward and resting his elbows on the desk.

"I was at the cafe, you know, the one I normally go to, and I looked down at the beach and saw a figure."

"A figure?"

"Yes, a figure," continued Cole, "and they started to walk into the sea."

The chief thought it before the deputy had said it.

"They tried to drown themselves?" guessed the chief.

The deputy said, "Yes, but then they stopped, second-guessed their decision I think, and left."

"Did you get a good look at this figure?"

"Unfortunately, no, sir. All I remember is that they looked like they were in some sort of nightgown."

"Right… So how does this link with Mrs. Sullivan? You don't think it was her, do you?"

"Well, it could've been…"

"Come on, Cole. What have I told you about jumping to conclusions…?"

"Yes, I know," argued Cole, though he meant no offence, "but just hear me out: Do you not think it's curious how, when we questioned her, she basically kicked us out of her house when we brought up Mr. Sullivan? Do you not think there's remotely a chance that the crash was fixed for just the driver's airbag to go off and not the passengers? And say if the figure was her, she's probably realised she can't get away with what she's done so she tried to kill herself. She's hiding something, Chief. I don't know what it is, but I just have that feeling."

"Okay." The chief considered Cole's reasoning. "But that doesn't explain why she decided at the last second to *not* commit suicide."

Deputy Cole shrugged and agreed, "That's what I can't figure out either, Chief." Both of them sighed, and the chief rubbed his face. Then Cole added optimistically, "Who knows, maybe she's realised doing the right thing and turning herself in will be better for her. Better for us all, actually."

They both chuckled and knew how highly doubtful that that was even a possibility.

Chief Hughes always lived by the idea that you couldn't make a decision until you got every side to the story; he also knew on the odd occasion that there was only one side to a story, and this was one of those times. He liked Mrs. Sullivan, he had respect for her – and other than Deputy Cole, there weren't many others he respected – and listening to his deputy's reasoning opened his eyes that he was probably just postponing turning her in because of said respect. The *evidence* was all there – the car, not wanting to talk, the weird way she had been acting since the funeral – and perhaps now was the time to act.

With another sigh, the chief said quietly and regretfully, "All right, Cole, we'll go to see her again."

The chief's walkie-talkie suddenly crackled. This wasn't the time.

*"Chief,"* a female officer's pronounced voice came through, *"there seems to be an incident at Valeland Station. Assistance is required."*

Hughes unhooked the walkie-talkie from his belt and held it up to his mouth as he replied with a groan, "Okay, we'll be right there." It crackled again as the chief hooked it back on his belt. He rose and said to the deputy, "Come on, Mrs. Sullivan'll have to wait."

The V.C.P.A chief and deputy left the offices to attend the scene at Valeland Station; they had to wait until they could get to Mrs. Sullivan, but if one thing was for sure it was that Mrs. Sullivan wasn't going to wait for them.

# CHAPTER NINE

## A New Chapter

Mrs. Sullivan jolted up, gasping as her eyes opened wide. She looked around, gathering her bearings, and it quickly set in that she was home. She was safe in bed, but she wasn't safe from the night's sleep she had; she got out of bed and looked down at the mattress. Her eyebrows narrowed at the sight of the massive wet patch that soaked through.

*Okay, Elena, fair enough that everybody has nightmares once in a while, but pissing the bed is a disgrace. You're not bloody seven.* She patted her backside and that too was damp, like she had fallen asleep during a thunderstorm – one that was located entirely on her bed. She tore the sheet off the mattress, rolled it up in her arms, and went down to the kitchen to throw it in the wash – along with her nightgown.

As she did so, Elena tried to ignore the throbbing headache that came with waking up that morn—

She gasped again as she took in the time on the kitchen clock: two in the afternoon. *Are you serious? A day wasted!*

Mrs. Sullivan shrugged it off after putting the wash on and taking a seat in the lounge. Thoughts crept in and out of her mind, like pedestrians arriving and leaving a bustling station, and she was pretty much helpless in trying to stop them.

*Why did I have an accident last night? That's never happened before! What to do with the last remaining hours of the day? Will I go to see*

70

*Emmett? How's Imani? The Valeland Citizen Protection Agency really believes I have something to do with MY Emmett's mur... death? Ha! Please, don't be absurd. Still... what should I do for the rest of the day?*

She looked around, nibbling on her thumbnail like a mouse enjoying a slice of cheese, and then Imani came back to mind. She remembered the conversation they had in the cafe... Then what Imani had specifically suggested... And then she recalled agreeing to the solution. *With nothing else to do, Elena, you need to act on it.*

But first, it was best to at least freshen up.

After a quick shower and changing into a new nightgown, Elena proceeded to head back into the lounge and go for the bookshelf nearest the right wall. She crouched down and under the bottom row of books – the Shakespearian row – Mrs. Sullivan easily pulled out a small drawer which from a distance, or upon first sight, would easily be missed.

Hibernating in the drawer was a Dell Studio 15 laptop – an Emmett-bought possession – and she took it with her back to the couch. The dust the screen had collected told Elena how long it had been hidden away there, and she'd be scared to admit to Emmett that she hadn't used it since they purchased it.

Blowing on the screen as she flipped the laptop open made the dust spread off into particles, *like confetti*, she thought, and she logged in. The laptop immediately took her to the Google homepage. *Now... Where to go?*

Going abroad was off the table, not because she couldn't afford it but simply because she didn't want to. Abroad was too far, like the moon; millions of miles up into the sky was just too far, no matter how tranquil it would be. Nobody there to disturb her. She could be alone; she could get away. *Earth to Elena, you can't get away with going to the moon. Come back down and be realistic about this: Where can you go?*

She typed in the enquiry *U.K destinations to go for peace*, pressed the search button, and a series of websites popped onto the screen in a matter of milliseconds. Minutes passed and no articles or lists appealed to Mrs. Sullivan's taste and desires; all the top ten lists she skimmed through consisted of the same places – mainly featuring Brighton, Cornwall, and Scarborough. An article on the best coastal towns in the UK caught her attention, offering a moment of hope, and a couple of places seemed to pique her interest. Her eyebrows raised at two specific locations – St. Bees and Newbiggen. She scanned through pictures of St. Bees, and it seemed nice enough, peaceful and spacious, but too close to Valeland. Newbiggen was on the other side of the country, a twenty-to-thirty-minute drive from Newcastle. Again, it seemed nice enough, but it was just too small.

Mrs. Sullivan knew she was being as picky as a child with food when looking at places to go. After half an hour of looking at places, she let out a sigh, about to slam the laptop shut. A place not too large, but not too small, that was what she wanted; a place where things happened, but she could have her moments of peace; a place where nobody would know her, but she could meet some lovely people. *The perfect place. Paradise.*

As was the case with Google searches, the most popular articles and sites were at the top of the page and the lesser-known ones were at the bottom. She started to think, *The lesser-known the article, the lesser-known the town.* So, Elena scrolled all the way down to the bottom and the last headline at the bottom read in bold: **Crazy Lady Appoints Herself Mayor of Fictional Town**.

Scepticism and intrigue – beauty and the beast – they just go together, and Mrs. Sullivan clicked on the article. It wasn't a recent article, that was for sure, with the year being 1977. Something that had tugged at Mrs. Sullivan's interest was that there were no photos that came with the article. It must've just been an issue that got lost in the pyramid of newspaper articles, because surely if somebody had made the accusation that they were the mayor of a town nobody had heard of people would look into it; either that, or the person was mentally challenged and just seeking attention.

The latter was the most probable, Elena thought, but as the article went on, she saw a quote supposedly given by the "mayor" themselves.

"Now, I know what you're all thinking: *Somebody randomly proclaiming to be a mayor, they're just mad.* But I assure you that that isn't the case. We as a town are proud to be independent and given its short, controversial history, we understand why you won't want to help. I just want peace, and to do that requires taking small steps. I didn't grow up here, but, when I came across a bunch of settlers and saw how they made a home for themselves, it made me think that there is a chance for everybody to be happy. A short drive from Newcastle, between Berwick and Alnwick, we are Castlehead – proud and determined."

It moved Mrs. Sullivan as she read along; this mayor had a vision, an aspiration to make the town a better place and nobody believed her – or believed *in* her – and that was probably what led to the town vanishing off the map… if it ever was on it.

"Castlehead…" she considered. "Sounds nice."

*That's the place, the place to get away, Elena. Don't think about it too much because you'll just second-guess your decision and won't go. And you know what'll happen if you don't go: you'll get caught. Everything will catch up with you and then you won't be able to get away. Get away, for your own sake. No time to waste.*

And this wasn't that echoey voice, that voice she knows shouldn't control her mind. It sounded like it, sure, but Elena just knew this was all her.

*No time to waste. Act on it.*

First thing Monday morning, Elena pulled up outside the Desmond School for Creative Arts. She looked through the gate and saw the grounds in front of her. *It's the last time you'll be here, Elena*, she told herself, *make it count.* A smile grew on her face as she looked on, students between the ages of 11 and 16 going about their day; study groups sat in circles, scattered around the grounds and under trees to avoid the glare of the sun, while other kids came in and out of the buildings, leaving or attending lessons.

Mrs. Sullivan remembered the feeling well, and nobody could take away those memories. It was her experience at the Desmond School for Creative Arts – along with spending every moment with Emmett – that made her want to work at the establishment – to teach what she had been taught, to be able to show the future generations that no matter the setbacks they could always move forward. Not anymore, she couldn't, and knowing that, her smile faded.

"Mrs. Sullivan!?" someone called from up the path. "You're back?" As they came towards Elena and the gates, she saw that it was the security guard from the day she was let go. In his hand he held a Costa takeaway cup and sipped it as he expected an answer from Elena. "Are you coming back to work?"

"Well, unfortunately not as the last time I was here I was fired. I was told I needed time to myself."

"Wait, what?" The guard tilted his head forward just to make sure he had heard her properly. "From what I've heard, you didn't—"

"Anyways," added Elena spontaneously, "that doesn't matter anymore."

She didn't have time for excuses. If they thought it was the right decision to let one of the best teachers they had go, then that was their choice. She knew she was moving onto new things, now, and even if she didn't have the chance to tell Desmond during this visit, she had no animosity against her former employer for it.

"Would it be a problem if you could allow me to see Desmond? I need to let him know I'm leaving."

"Oh… um… okay, yeah, sure."

With his free hand the guard pulled the gate open. Elena gave him a thankful smile as she entered the grounds. She followed the path up to the main buildings, honouring the statue of Lord Alfred Vale with a pat to its base as she walked past. She knew what a visionary that man was, Lord Alfred Vale, and she knew how many lives he had impacted; it was those kinds of people, she thought, that everyone should try to live up to.

"Make a difference; petit or grand, it's still a difference," was one of the many influential things he said.

Walking into the main building, Elena headed straight past the reception desk and towards the stairs.

"Hey!" the receptionist called, lifting herself from her chair. "Hey, you, Mrs. Sullivan!" the receptionist called again. Elena continued up the stairs, blocking out the receptionist's voice. She didn't see it as ignoring, she just wanted to talk to Desmond, that was all. It wasn't as if she meant harm to anyone. The receptionist walked around the desk and started to follow her up the stairs, continuing to call out her name. Elena imagined the voice being a seagull constantly squawking. Finally catching up to the former teacher at the top of the staircase, the receptionist added, "I really need to know what you're doing here, Elena. Desmond told you to take a—"

"Yeah, I know he fired me. I was there." Mrs. Sullivan kept staring straight ahead as the pair paced down the hall. "I just need to speak to Desmond for a moment," she added.

"Okay," said the receptionist, "but you know you have to book an appointment."

"I don't mean to be rude, but I'm aware of the rules here. I worked here a lot longer than you have, and all I need is five minutes with him. I've got a lot on my plate and, believe me, after this you won't see me again."

Elena and the receptionist froze at the headmaster's closed office door.

Beyond the door, they heard Desmond say, "Everything's here, Cole: the contract, the boy's personal details, everything."

"Thank you, Desmond."

Elena's instant thought was, *Why was Deputy Cole speaking with Desmond?* And with that thought came an ounce of sick rise in her throat. "At this rate, he should be able to start this time next week." Okay, the conversation wasn't about her. *But it's the end of the conversation,* Mrs. Sullivan thought. *I could've been brought up at least once, and then I'll have to face the Valeland Citizen Protection Agency again.*

They heard footsteps and the door opened. It was Deputy Cole, who openly grimaced at Elena. "Mrs. Sullivan," he acknowledged, sounding like a dog growling, "what're you doing here?"

"My business here has nothing to do with you, Deputy, so if you're going to make assumptions about me then you'll probably be wrong, as usual."

Deputy Cole kept the pile of papers he held close to his chest and said nothing more. He walked off, feeling Elena's eyes still on him. She wasn't scared to stick up for herself when needed. She was just *scared.*

"What was that about?" the receptionist whispered once the deputy turned a corner.

"Nothing," said Elena.

Just then, Desmond Edwards called Elena in. He had heard her, and both Elena and the receptionist entered. He was seated and looked very relaxed.

ST. JUDE'S — A CASTLEHEAD NOVEL

"Headmaster," the receptionist said politely, standing in the doorway, "I told her she had to book an appointment but—"

Desmond lifted a finger and said, "It's okay. Get back to work."

"Yes, sir," the receptionist said and closed the door behind her.

Elena looked at Desmond in his chair – very relaxed and smiling at her – and the smile felt like a way for him to tell her he was expecting her arrival.

"Take a seat, Elena."

And she did. The headmaster's fingers tangled together as he planted both of his hands on his chest, sitting back even further in his chair. *At this rate, how has the chair not given way?* Elena thought. But that wasn't why Elena was there, so she had to get the chair and Desmond's weight out of her head.

"Sir…" she started. "I-I do apologise, honestly, I really do, for just barging in like this but it's just that—"

Desmond raised a finger again, instantly hushing Elena, and said in a reassuring tone, "Mrs. Sullivan, it's absolutely fine. I've been meaning to talk to you, anyway, about possibly—"

"Look, sir, please let me speak first. I know the decision you made, you thought, was for the best. And now *I'm* doing what's best for me. I've decided to move."

That may've been what Elena wanted to speak to Desmond about, but that certainly wasn't why Desmond wanted to speak to her; he leaned forward, the chair creaking as he did so, and rubbed his beard as he tried to process what he had just heard. Giving her that break a couple of weeks after her husband's death was for the best, Desmond was still 100% sure about that, but he wasn't so sure about Mrs. Sullivan wanting to actually leave. If anything, Desmond would've at least assumed Mrs. Sullivan was 100% *against* the idea of moving. An image of that day flashed in his head, and he saw Mrs. Sullivan coming into school and expecting to work; from how adamant she was about working and saying she was fine to wanting to move in such a short space of time didn't add up. With a raised eyebrow, he came to the conclusion that something wasn't right.

"Okay..." he muttered slowly, still stroking his beard. "Do you really think that's what you should do?"

"Yes," announced Elena. "After thinking about it, sir, I have to say this might be good: a new place, a new environment, new people, all that. I feel it – I *need* this."

Desmond Edwards couldn't argue with her. Although his original idea was to bring her back to work, starting from the next week, he thought back to how she was when Emmett first passed; that had been the reason behind his decision to let her have an extended period of leave. So, if this was something that she felt she needed, then Desmond would be happy for her.

Desmond said with a slight shrug, "Well, good for you, Elena. Where is it that you're going?"

Elena didn't expect her former employer to engage for a second. She appreciated it, actually, although it made her want to move even more.

She leaned forward, too, and said brightly, "Northeast."

Desmond's eyebrows rose and he guessed, "Oh, nice. Newcastle?"

"Nope. A place called Castlehead."

Desmond's face dropped and his heart began to pound.

*Something's up with her*, thought Deputy Cole as he turned into the next hallway before the stairs. *Chief always says to not jump to conclusions, so I won't*. With the papers still close to his chest, Cole turned back around and made his way back up to the headmaster's office. *I'll just investigate and prove it*.

Of course, as he expected, the office door had been shut. Cole couldn't come up with a good enough excuse to walk back in; even if he did, it would only disrupt their conversation, so he wouldn't have been able to gather any new possible information about what Mrs. Sullivan was up to. He inched forward until he could see his own reflection in the smooth wooden door, then he turned his head to press his ear against it.

"But why Castlehead?" he heard Desmond ask.

"It's just someplace different, isn't it?" answered Elena.

*Castlehead?* Cole repeated in his head. *As in the Castlehead Criminal Investigation Department?*

Back inside the office, Desmond shrugged again and repeated, "Well, yes, I guess so, but *why* Castlehead? There are many other small towns in the U.K."

Elena tilted her head and narrowed her eyebrows. Desmond's tone had shifted very quickly after she had told him where she was moving to. It sounded like he was against the move now.

"Sir, I don't get it. What's wrong with Castlehead?"

Desmond rubbed his temple, thinking of the kindest way to describe the town to her. He wasn't going to force her not to move there, as he didn't have the right to do that, but he did think it would be good to give her a bit of background.

"Elena, where exactly did you find out about Castlehead?" he asked.

"It was some article I found online. It was well-hidden, and one of the few things there was about the town."

"What article exactly?"

Elena explained, "It was about some woman proclaiming to be the mayor of the town, but nobody would listen to her. At first, I thought she was crazy or just wanted attention but, when I did a bit more digging, I found that the town does exist."

"It exists, all right. Madam Mayor and I are in close contact with one another."

"You've been there?" asked Elena.

Desmond clarified, "I've visited a few times. Nice enough when you're just a tourist, but you soon realise those cracks that are in every town are more like black holes in Castlehead."

Elena sat back and asked, "How'd you mean?"

"A lot of things have happened in that town. When the town was beginning to expand, many local governments tried to seize Castlehead's ownership but after one look at its history they turned away. Valeland is the only town that has regular communication with Castlehead. Other things led to the town being erased, from maps and from history, such as people being... well, people and simply causing conflict." He saw Elena's disheartened face; he sensed how excited she had been at first. As one of the school's best teachers, Desmond felt like he couldn't let her down. "Look, Elena, I'm not going to scare you out of moving there, but if you do go, please just be careful. Most people there want to leave."

Elena smiled at Desmond, who under that beard smiled back. In that moment, Mrs. Sullivan started to believe that if Desmond hadn't fired her then, she wouldn't have found the confidence to start a new chapter.

"Thank you, sir," she said.

"Do you have anywhere to stay?" Desmond asked.

"No." Elena shook her head lightly. It was the only thing she hadn't sorted out. "Not yet."

"Okay. If you are going to move to Castlehead, I'm going to help you. I'll contact a friend of mine who lives there, tell her you're coming, and she'll set you up until you get on your feet. Mind you, she's a bit rough around the edges, as is the place itself, but you'll get used to her."

"I'll keep that in mind," Elena chuckled. "I appreciate the help, sir."

"Any time."

"Shit," mumbled the deputy, stepping back from the door.

He started to hear footsteps and that was his cue to dart down the hall and back outside into the courtyard. It was bad enough Elena wasn't admitting to what she had done, even after the chief had given her chance after chance, but with Elena Sullivan moving to Castlehead it had put the Valeland Citizen Protection Agency on a timer.

Chief Hughes had to know.

Mrs. Sullivan accepted the piece of paper Desmond handed to her; he had written down the address of his friend. She glanced at the location – *Carson Estate* – and then headed for the door. She was about to turn the door handle, but Desmond called her back.

Still seated, he said, "You'll be missed, Mrs. Sullivan."

"Thank you."

"All the best to you, Elena."

She opened the door and walked out of the headmaster's office for the last time. *All the best*. This was the right choice. It was; it had to be; it *needed* to be.

# CHAPTER TEN

## I Spy

For a Monday afternoon, Deputy Cole thought the Valeland roads were quieter than normal. He kept one hand on the wheel as he took out and flipped open his phone with the other. Yeah, okay, it was against the law but did the rules really apply to him if he was working *for* the law? Besides, the call was urgent.

Driving along, Cole planted his phone in between his shoulder and ear as it rang. Ten seconds later, the call was answered.

*"Hughes here,"* said the chief.

"Chief," started Cole, trying to sound less panicked than he actually was. It didn't work; his pitch was high and he talked fast like a chipmunk on coffee. "I've just been to the Desmond School for Creative Arts to finish the deal with Desmond about signing that lad to the junior detective team, and I saw Mrs. Sullivan there."

*"Wait... She was there? Did you speak to her?"*

"No, we only passed in the hall when I left the headmaster's office. But I overheard them talking."

*"And?"*

"Mrs. Sullivan is planning on moving—"

*"Whoa, hang on a second... Moving? What'd you mean? Moving where?"*

"Castlehead, Chief. What should we do? We can't just let her get away."

*"I know, I know. Give me a second…"* Cole did give his chief a second, and it was all Hughes needed. *"Okay, here's what we're going to do…"*

"Yes?"

*"Nothing."*

Was the chief pulling Cole's leg? Do nothing?

"Chief, I'm not following."

*"Let me make a call. I have a contact in Castlehead who can keep an eye on her."*

Then the chief hung up. Cole chucked his phone on the back seat and continued driving, doing the only thing he could; he had to trust that the chief knew what he was doing.

In the V.C.P.A building, sitting at his office desk, Chief Hughes hung up on his deputy and switched from his mobile to the landline on the desk. He held the handset to his ear as he dialled the number for his Castlehead contact. All done with a grin smeared across his face. He knew what he was doing. Soon, Mrs. Elena Sullivan wasn't going to be Valeland's problem, but if there was anyone who could solve a problem like Mrs. Sullivan then it would be his contact.

When Hughes heard the contact pick up, he greeted them in a low tone, "Hey, it's me. I need a favour."

*"Hi, me, I'm sorry but we're not a charity."*

"Oh, come on."

They both laughed.

*"Hi, Hughes, how's everything in the west?"*

"That's kind of why I'm calling. We're investigating a possible murder, and the suspect is, well, leaving for Castlehead. I don't know when."

*"What's the name?"*

"Elena Sullivan. I can send you all of the information we have on her as soon as I put down the phone."

*"Okay, but if she's a suspected murderer and she hasn't left town yet, why doesn't the V.C.P.A just put her in her place? You are the chief after all."*

"You know I don't work like that. We've interrogated her more than once already and if we confront her a third time, she'll not engage with us. Plus, there's been an incident at Valeland Station that's taken up a lot of our time, so just in case she, you know, gets away—"

*"You want us to keep an eye on her, should she actually come—"*

"So, you can make sure she doesn't become more of a danger to civilians."

*"She's that bad, huh?"*

"It's mainly just my suspicions, as of now, and a couple of events that have occurred in the past couple of weeks."

*"From the sound of it, I know exactly where she belongs."*

"Where? A psychiatric ward or something?"

*"I was thinking more like the morgue, but a looney bin works, too."*

"So, you'll do it?"

After a beat, his contact said, *"Yes, of course. You know all I want is to keep this town safe. Send me the information you've got on her."*

"I will do. Thanks, man. I owe you big time."

*"Nah,"* his contact scoffed, *"it's absolutely fine. We're all in this together, aren't we?"*

"Always. Thanks, again."

That was the perfect time to end the call.

Roughly 150 miles east, the Castlehead Criminal Investigation Department's chief, Derek Pattison, hung up the call with his fellow chief of police, Chief Hughes. Pattison and Hughes did things a little differently, but they both wanted the same thing;

that was all that mattered. Unlike many police departments around the country who never fully comprehended Pattison's values, Hughes understood. How they couldn't was mind-boggling to Pattison.

They were simple: make the world a better place…

*Better* – that's why he was the chief of police. To make the world better. To make people better. It was his job, it was his life, and he knew how the world should be – in his eyes. Brief, yes, but the call with Hughes had Pattison thinking; through his years as chief of the C.C.I.D, Pattison had dealt with people like this Elena Sullivan before, but the fact that she was moving to *his* town at this time wasn't ideal. It never was ideal when those kinds of people were involved, Pattison believed, but this time meant more to him than usual.

He sat up straight, scooched his office chair forward and logged onto his computer on the desk in front of him. He shifted the icon to the bottom left of the screen and clicked on the symbol of a half-open envelope. A list of emails popped up and at the top was the latest one from Chief Hughes, flashing blue as if begging to be clicked on. The email had been attached with a file labelled **Mrs. Elena Sullivan** in bold writing. Pattison hunched over even more, his eyebrows sharpening as he read the file…

It was only then that he truly gathered what Chief Hughes meant; she had been denying all accusations that the Valeland Citizen Protection Agency had offered, as most suspected murders and lunatics did, but the evidence was all there, too – her spouse dying in a car crash, which she survived, being seen down by the beach, becoming defensive once confronted… *A lost cause*, Pattison thought.

The chief clicked off the email, shut down the computer and slouched back in his chair, turning to the window to his left. It was a nice view of the town he called home, a place that was precious to him, and it was about to be infested by more vermin. He rubbed his prickly jaw as thoughts and ideas came to him.

These types were different to your average criminal; evidence may point towards them but who can say it was actually them? That's why constant surveillance has always been essential, so you could catch them out like spotting a ghost with a flashlight. They're haunted by themselves. However, Elena was haunted by something more, and after reading the file Hughes had sent him, Pattison had it in his mind that something needed to be done.

At that moment, being lost in the Castlehead view and in his own world, Pattison turned around at the sound of a knock at his door. His trusted Deputy Ton walked in.

"Chief?" he said.

"Yes?"

"It's Madam Mayor," Ton informed his chief. "She wants to know about the development of the hotel."

With a sigh, the chief said, "Tell her they might be stumped."

Ton nodded and left the office.

Pattison looked back out the window and wondered once again, back in his own world. *Madam Mayor... Ha! I've known since the beginning that this is a bad idea.* Despite his own opinions, he had offered to oversee the project. A luxury hotel for all, he recalled Madam Mayor describing it as, and he remembered laughing at the idea afterwards. The final decision, as always, was down to the mayor, and part of that decision was because of Pattison's input. That place couldn't stand there any longer. Pattison didn't care if the mayor's naivety got the better of her for practically her entire career, it had to go. Refurbishing it as a hotel, though, wasn't a suggestion offered by Pattison.

And what a glorious coincidence this Elena Sullivan was coming, hopefully to ruin everything. *Bad for society*, thought Pattison, *but amazing for... me.*

*Do better. It's what has to be done.*

# CHAPTER ELEVEN

## The Drive

Coming to the end of the first week of March meant that spring was on its way; when Imani woke up on the morning that Elena was leaving Valeland, she was stumped for a moment, thinking she had slept through until the afternoon. But her eyes weren't deceiving her – the sun had risen before 8am that morning, and her alarm was beeping.

It was a day Imani knew she had to get through, even though she was dreading it; Elena was actually leaving, and Imani deep down wasn't ready for it. What a statement: Mrs. Sullivan was leaving Valeland. Okay, okay, Imani was the one who had suggested to her that she should take a break, but she never thought she would actually go through with it. It was her home. Elena had been there when Imani had moved to Valeland; she was there when Imani had been hired at the Desmond School for Creative Arts; Elena had been there; Elena *was* always there for her.

Saying that Imani felt indebted to Elena for all the things she did for her was being a tad overdramatic, but that was how Imani felt. The thought came to mind every so often. Elena was there for her, and so she was going to be there for Elena; that's what friends did for each other. Elena didn't ask either, but Imani was going to help her pack the last of her things. Apparently, Elena wasn't taking much. Imani didn't know why as she saw most things in that house of hers as priceless, but Imani understood. *New town, new life, right? If you're moving to an entirely new town to get away from the norm, why would you want to take everything you own? It'll just be a reminder of what made you want to move in the first place. You might as well stay home.*

She got out of bed and immediately changed into some bottoms and a shirt she didn't mind getting dirty. Elena hadn't told her specifically what they'd be moving. *Be prepared, just in case*, she thought as she changed.

Single? Yes. Lonely? No. That's how Imani liked it. Her semi-detached home on the corner of Grove Road – a part of a warm, homely (obviously) suburban area – was everything she could have wanted from a house. Two bedrooms, one turned into a storage room, a kitchen with an island counter, a washroom with a walk-in shower, and a lounge which was a little small. But like the house itself, it was big enough for her.

Downstairs, in the kitchen, Imani poured herself a coffee and a bowl of Kellogg's Corn Flakes, before making her way into the lounge. The remote control was already sinking into the couch as Imani sat down, the cereal on her lap and the coffee down by her feet, and she caught the stick just before it was lost down the back of the sofa.

The television on the stand by the wall facing Imani flickered on. She got a signal eventually and the screen presented Imani with the local news channel. A woman sat, wearing a black suit jacket and shirt, in front of a screen presenting less important news stories. Chomping on her Corn Flakes, Imani had to turn the volume up just a touch to hear the woman's polished voice.

"We wish the family the best," the reporter said. *Probably a death*, Imani guessed as she continued, shovelling spoonfuls of cereal in her mouth. "Now, back to Valeland," the reporter on screen continued. "We have a special guest in the studio to give us an update on the events at Valeland Station. Please welcome the chief of the Valeland Citizen Protection Agency, Chief Hughes." The camera zoomed out, and both the reporter and Chief Hughes were in view. "Welcome," she greeted him.

"Thank you for having me," he said with a nod.

The reporter leaned forward, all ears, and asked the obvious question: "What can you tell us about the events that occurred at the station?"

Imani had heard about what had happened, but she didn't want to start leaping to conclusions. A news story that makes it onto the front page of every local paper surely means it's a big deal. That's what the town, and the V.C.P.A (apparently), were treating it as. She, probably like most morning viewers, wanted to unearth all she could about it.

The chief answered, "The events in question put many civilians in danger, and the damage caused by the train has led to immediate repairs on parts of the station. Luckily, as far as we know, nobody has been killed. However, more than two dozen people, six of them children, are still in a serious condition and are the main priorities of the hospital. We have reprimanded some key suspects, and we are led to believe that they were all in kahoots with one another. This was, in fact, a planned attack. But as I've just said, there were no fatal deaths, and I can now confirm that the station has been reopened. A couple of platforms are still out of commission, which may cause delays on some services."

"Well, there you have it, ladies and gentlemen," the reporter said with a smile, "you've heard it right here on the Channel X Morning News at Eight that—"

Imania clicked the TV off. The weather forecast was next on the news lineup and she didn't care for it. She necked her coffee while still holding the empty cereal bowl in her other hand, then she took the bowl and mug into the kitchen. She left them on the kitchen counter by the sink as she went back upstairs to grab her coat and bag.

She still couldn't believe Elena was actually leaving.

"And we're clear!" the lead cameraman called out.

The reporter and Chief Hughes both rose from the desk as the studio bell rang, signalling a break. They shook hands.

"Thank you once again for coming on, Chief," said the reporter, still shaking Hughes's hand.

"My pleasure. I'm just happy that all of this Valeland Station debacle is sorted," the chief replied.

They left the set on opposite sides. Deputy Cole was waiting in the wings, his arms folded, with a determined look on his face. The chief and deputy stood close, looking above and around them for any possible hidden mics or cameras; it was a news station after all.

"Now we can focus back on Elena, right, Chief?" said Cole.

Chief Hughes answered calmly, "Don't worry about it, Cole. I made the call to my contact in case Elena does in fact decide to leg it out of here."

Cole leaned in even closer and growled, "But Chief, can't we just catch her as she's leaving? It'll make things a whole lot easier, then we can put this whole mess behind us."

"Ah, Cole," breathed the chief, following it up with a tut. "Patience is key. It'll all work out in the end."

Deputy Cole stepped back, unsure of what his chief meant by that. He said nothing more as they made their way out of the studio. For weeks, he had been suggesting to Hughes to just bring Elena in, because they all knew deep down that she was guilty – the evidence was all there – but having Hughes reject the suggestion every time didn't add up. And yet, perhaps it finally did. Not jumping to conclusions… Holding off on Elena's arrest… This *contact*…

Now Deputy Cole had finally come to a conclusion: Chief Hughes knew exactly what he was doing.

Mrs. Sullivan needed to take it all in. It was hers and Emmett's dream house. It *was*. Even with this move to Castlehead being a 100% definite, Mrs. Sullivan couldn't bear to see the house go to anyone else. It still felt like home, even with her most important items packed. She looked in the mirror in the bathroom – one of the things she wasn't taking – and stared at herself for a full minute. She was already in her boots and an overcoat.

"No, Elena," she said, "don't be doubting yourself at the last second." All the paperwork had been fast-tracked to be signed in a matter of days – Elena had the money to do so – and with that signature now on paper, there really was no turning back. She cleared her throat and told herself, "You want to do this. You need this. Do it."

She stepped out of the bathroom and made her way across the landing into her bedroom. It was empty, apart from a wooden bedframe and a wardrobe with no clothes in; she took the room in, and she closed the door behind her as she made her way back onto the landing. As she stepped onto the stairs, she felt her pocket.

*Still there*, she thought.

She couldn't lose the papers. She walked down the stairs; by the door were a set of boxes labelled in black marker **More Clothes**, **Knickknacks**, **Books**. The kitchen had been left the same way Elena had always tried to leave it – spotless. The lounge was very much the same (the couch, the bookshelves, the coffee table, the piano), most of the furniture remained there. The bookshelves looked hungry to be filled.

Imani pulled up outside Mrs. Sullivan's house, making sure she didn't block the driveway. She switched the engine off and, before opening the door, she looked out the window and saw that the boot of Mrs. Sullivan's substitute car (a dark red Volkswagen Polo) was open, and also that there was no 'for sale' sign standing at the front of the property.

*Has she already sold it?* Imani asked herself.

She headed up the drive as she pressed the button on her car keys to lock her car, before stopping at Elena's front door. Taking a quick glance at the open boot of the Volkswagen, she realised that this departure was becoming more real with every second. A case was haphazardly planted in the boot, sitting on an angle. The case looked too big for the car. Imani breathed in for five seconds, then out again for five, before she knocked.

The knock at the door startled Mrs. Sullivan. She turned from the lounge and walked up to the front door.

"Elena?" called Imani from the other side. "It's me."

She opened the door and both women smiled at each other.

"Hello, Imani," Elena greeted, stepping aside to allow her friend in.

Stepping in, Imani looked up and around the house. *Wow*, was all she could think. It's said that all houses seem bigger when there's nothing in it, whether it be furniture or life, and this was exactly the case for Elena's house. She took in the lounge, noticing the abandoned sofa.

"You couldn't get anyone to take the couch?" she asked.

"Oh, no, no," said Elena, leaving the front door open as she stood by Imani, "don't you worry about that."

Turning to Elena, Imani asked, "Well, what'd you need?"

Elena stepped aside again, presenting the boxes by the door, and said, "Just these…"

*That's it?* Imani didn't understand. She was there to move a few boxes that would've been extremely light? However, she did realise that her friend was older so perhaps she couldn't do the back-and-forth trip from boot to house more than twice. There was no need to argue against Elena's needs, though.

"Okay," she said. "Also—"

"The case, I know," Elena butted in, chuckling. "I need help with that, too."

"That's fine, Elena."

"Thank you, Imani. You take those two boxes…" Elena pointed at the boxes labelled **Knickknacks** and **Books**. "And I'll get this one…" She had already started to lift the box labelled **Clothes**. Imani smiled. That definitely was the lightest of them.

"No problem," said Imani, going for the two boxes.

Having only taken the one box, Mrs. Sullivan was the first to go out the door and place the box down by the car. Imani stacked one box on top of the other; her head tilted to the side to see where she was going. She made it to the car in one piece, also placing the boxes down by the car.

They directed themselves to the boot and the case. The case was too big for the boot. It would've been more of a struggle to put it in the backseat. The stalemate with the suitcase was similar to the kind a person found themselves faced with when their case reached the weight limit for a plane. They could feel the impact of the disruption they were causing to the people behind them, knowing all of them were eager to get on the plane so they could get their holiday started. Part of her felt like that; when she glanced back at the house, she felt like she didn't want to go (*No, Elena, you need this. Do it*) but when she looked back at the case, she felt all the more desperate to get out there and onto the road.

*You need this…*

"So, how are we going to do this?" asked Elena, her hands on her hips, examining the case.

Imani leaned forward, her head nearly in the boot.

"Hang on," she said. There was a pull-lever on the back of the backseat. "Let's get the case out." Elena grabbed the bottom as Imani took the top handle and pulled the case out. They placed it on its wheels and Imani leaned forward, back into the boot. Elena watched on; Imani reached for the lever and the seats jolted downwards, creating more room in the back.

Backing out of the car, Imani said proudly, "There you go."

Elena kept quiet, veiling her impressed look with a smile. *You have a teaching degree and you didn't know what that lever was for? Elena Sullivan, come on now.* If Emmett were there, she probably would've laughed it off, but here with Imani she had to feel embarrassed. *This technology...* She held that thought. If Imani knew what Elena was thinking, she would've thought, *Technology? It's a Volkswagen Polo, not a high-tech laptop. Elena, it's done now. Don't worry about it.*

"Let's get it back in then," Elena said.

Imani nodded and grabbed the top of the case again, with Elena taking the bottom.

They lifted it together, tilting their heads forward so they didn't hit the door, and Imani suggested, "Put the case on the seats, then the boxes can just go here."

That was what they did; after piling the boxes on top of each other in the boot, they were able to close it easily as if nothing was in it. The boot slammed shut, and Imani and Elena looked at each other. This was it.

Elena said with a smile, "Thanks for everything, Imani. It means a lot."

"No, Elena, thank you," Imani responded. "Keep in touch, yeah?"

"Of course." Elena stepped back and walked to the driver's side of the car, opening the door. Imani followed, expecting Elena to already be buckled up and ready to go. But Elena held the door ajar and turned around. "Before I go, I almost forgot to give you something."

"Elena," said Imani, waving her hands in front of her, "you really don't have to get me anything—"

"No, no, hang on."

Elena reached into her pocket, pulling out a folded piece of paper. She unfolded it and presented it to Imani. Imani leaned forward and read the sheet closely; at first glance, she already saw it was a document of sorts – an important one, too, like a contract – and even after skimming through it, she couldn't really understand what exactly it meant.

"What's this for?" she asked, taking the document with both hands.

"It's for you." Elena smiled, starting to feel the sting of tears in the corner of her eyes. "I feel like I had to do it. I *wanted* to do it."

Imani let out a shocked chuckle.

"I… I…Wha… I mean… Why? I-I don't get—"

"*Shh.*" Elena stepped closer, spreading her arms out. "You don't need to say anything."

They hugged tightly; Elena could feel the document scrunching up against her back as Imani wrapped her arms around her. They separated and Elena saw Imani had allowed a tear to flow down her cheek.

"Thank you so much," Imani croaked. She cleared her throat, wiped her eyes with her free hand, and added, "But how did you manage it? I thought it was a pain to get one of these."

Elena grinned and answered, "Nothing's a pain when you have money."

Imani nodded knowingly, and they hugged one more time.

When they had split again, Elena reached into her other pocket. She pulled out a set of jingling keys, which included the keys for the Volkswagen, and she tore the only golden one from the set. Handing it to Imani was like handing down a family heirloom to the next generation; Elena, although half-excited for starting her new chapter and half-regretful of the decision, felt only pride in her choice. She knew Imani would take the utmost care when it came to what she handed to her. That was the level of trust she had for her friend.

Mrs. Sullivan tucked the keys back into her pocket and got in the car. Imani stepped forward and held the door ajar.

Peering down with a broad smile for her friend, Mrs. Sullivan, Imani asked, "So, do you know where you're going?"

"Yeah," said Elena as she twisted the car key into the ignition. "But I have to make a pitstop first."

"Goodbye, Mrs. Sullivan."

Elena looked up, and said, "All the best, Imani."

Imani shut the car door and stepped back as Elena drove out of the driveway. Elena honked the horn. Imani waved. And that was it — a new chapter. Imani glanced back down at the document, then looked at the house Elena and her husband had treasured for so many years. One last look at the document, Imani felt tears arriving. She couldn't believe Mrs. Sullivan would do such a thing…

## DEED OF GIFT

This Deed of Gift is made on 6$^{th}$, March, 2009, between Mrs. Elena Sullivan of the following address: 3 Consat Road, Valeland, United Kingdom (hereinafter referred to as the 'Donor'). And Ms. Imani Keens of the following address: 1 Grove Road, Valeland, United Kingdom (hereinafter referred to as the 'Donee').

For further reference, when jointly discussing the Donor and Donee, they shall be referred to as the 'Parties'.

- The Donor is the beneficial owner of the Gift in question, and desires to present the property to the Donee as such.
- The Donee has accepted the Gift from the Donor.
- Both Parties agree that this is a legally binding contract and any discussions regarding ownership details shall take place in a court of law.
- Both Parties also agree, should either the Donor or Donee want out of this Deed of Gift, such discussions should also take place in a court of law.
- The Donee is being gifted:
  - The Transfer of Ownership
  - Tax Map References of Property 3 Consat Road
  - The Property Itself

The Property consists of the land addressed at 3 Consat Road, Valeland, United Kingdom.

**Donor Name: Elena Sullivan**
**Donee Name: Imani Keens**

Mrs. Sullivan knew it to be the right thing. She couldn't have given the house to anyone more deserving or more trusting than Imani. The thought of selling it made Elena's stomach churn; but that wasn't happening, so there was no need to worry. It was as she pulled up on the curb by the Lily Park entrance that the thought started to fade.

There was one more person she had to say goodbye to.

Some semblances of life started to sprout from the tree that shadowed Emmett's resting place; the leaves brought with them the vibrant feeling of spring. Elena liked the idea that one's spirit was forever held in something else after they passed on, like an heirloom, or a picture, or a house, or even a tree. She liked to think Emmett listened and watched over her, like a guardian – a protector, as all good husbands and wives would for each other. She liked to think there was something *more*. Reality, though, showed her just that – reality – and the reality was: Emmett was gone and Elena lived on.

"Hello, my love," said Elena at the foot of the gravestone. The leaves and branches shaded her from the sun breaking through the clouds above. "I... I just wanted to... I'm sorry for not visiting, I've just been..." She gulped and took a breath. "Actually, to tell you the truth I don't know why I haven't come to see you." She chuckled and added, "I shouldn't be scared, should I? You wouldn't be mad if I told you I was moving, would you? No, of course not. You would encourage it. I just know it."

*"It's your time now, darling,"* she envisioned him saying, as if he were standing there before her. *"Make the most of it."*

"Yeah, you're probably right," said Elena. She looked around; nobody was around. It was just her and Emmett. *Her* Emmett. The two of them together... "This *new chapter* should be good," she added. "You would say that, too. I know I've been torn on the idea of starting fresh, but now is the time."

*"The time to escape,"* said the voice that she swore wasn't Emmett's. *"The more time you spend here, the easier it is for them to catch you. Because you did it!"*

"For fuck's sake! SHUT UP!" cried Elena.

She heard footsteps behind her, and turning around she noticed a mother and daughter had been frozen, their eyes glaring at her. It was then that she realised she was in a public space. It wasn't just her and *her* Emmett.

Elena tried to look apologetic, but the mother had already started to drag her daughter away. *Crazy lady, that's what they'll call me*, Elena thought. Then she turned back to Emmett's gravestone.

*"Honey…"*

Emmett was back.

"Yes?" Elena whispered.

She knew it, but she needed to hear it:

*"It's time to go."*

"Yeah… You're right." She walked up to the gravestone and placed her hand on top of it. Cold, still, lifeless… *Like Emmett.* Because he wasn't really there, only living on in her imagination. This was her decision, and it was for the best. "Goodbye, Emmett. This wasn't supposed to happen."

Mrs. Sullivan turned and walked away, coming out of the shadows of the tree and making her way down the gravel pathway to the entrance where her car was parked. As she got back into the car and started the engine, though physically he wasn't, she knew Emmett was there. Or she had believed he was.

*"Goodbye, my love."*

The drive was like how she thought about her walks – relaxing and necessary. Turning onto the highway, heading east, Mrs. Sullivan thought, *Wow, I'm actually doing it. It's actually happening… I'm getting away with… No! I'm moving on, and I'm very happy about it.* She kept telling herself that as her hometown of Valeland, England, slowly faded in the rearview mirror.

There was something about driving in the middle lane all the way that made Elena feel safe – as her walks did. She knew she wouldn't have such a tight grip on the wheel, and she could sit back, comfortable but alert, and drive without any worries. She remembered what the article said: *A short drive from Newcastle, between Berwick and Alnwick, we are Castlehead – proud and determined.*

"Proud and determined," Elena muttered. "I… am proud," she continued, unknowingly putting pressure on the accelerator, "and determined to remain that way always. I am proud to be your wife... I was always proud to be your wife, and I was always proud of you." Flashes of Emmett and his smile came to her. "I was always proud—"

The car swerved sharply...

A series of car horns roared behind her, and like her morning alarm, they immediately woke Mrs. Sullivan up; she steadied the car, and she was back in the middle lane. Her heart still beat steadily, but after a deep breath, Elena focused on the road in front of her again. It was the road to a new life, and she couldn't wait. Happy as Larry to be starting a new chapter.

But then, from the lane to her left, Mrs. Sullivan felt the vibrations under her Volkswagen of a car speeding up beside her. She turned her head as the car honked, and although her sight over the last year or two hadn't been the greatest, she saw crystal clear that the bloke driving in the blue Ford was giving her the middle finger.

Then the car gained speed once again and drove off in front of her. The further the car sped away, the smaller the car got, almost like a speck on a screen. But there was a sudden urge...

*"Go on,"* a voice was telling her. *"You know you want to. Emmett would've said that it's your life, so do what makes you happy. Going after him will make you happy."*

Elena's lips curved slyly, and she rammed her foot down on the accelerator, determined to find the middle finger man in the blue Ford.

With an eye on the speed at all times, Elena drove as fast as she could. The middle lane didn't matter now; she swerved in between lanes, the indicator clicking once every couple of minutes. She came to the conclusion very quickly that the left lane was best for observation, so she didn't miss any cars passing her peripheral vision.

Driving on but slowing her pace, she scanned over the two lanes now to her right. She passed an exit, knowing it wasn't for Castlehead as she had only been on the road a little under an hour. Her eyes, just then, locked onto a vehicle in the far lane. The grin returned, and she flipped on the indicator once more.

She had returned to the middle lane.

She sang, "I spy... with my little eye... a blue Ford..."

The Volkswagen sped up just a touch as she came up behind the Ford; she wasn't daft enough to openly show the driver that she was next to him again, so she kept a car's length behind the Ford.

*"Go on,"* that voice hissed. *"Do it. Spin him off the road..."* Elena tilted her head down and looked at the tyre she was closest to – the bottom left – and she pressed on the accelerator a tad more. *"Go on, you're getting closer. Closer... Closer. Almost there, and he'll get what he deserves."*

The front bumper of her Volkswagen was almost kissing the Ford's rear left tyre. One nudge to the right, and she'll teach him a lesson on who to flip off.

*Wait!* Mrs. Sullivan thought.

The grin vanished. She steered away from the Ford and aligned herself back in the centre of the middle lane. *What was I about to do? What was going to happen? You idiot, Elena, you could've bloomin' killed someone. Focus! Focus and get back to thinking about your new life.*

She had passed an hour on the road already, and she knew then she was over halfway through her journey. Closer to Castlehead then home; a short drive from Newcastle, by Berwick and Alnwick. They were places she had only heard of.

"That's funny," she said to herself. The sudden thought, *Funny how you're moving to the place only a few have heard of, rather than the places charted on maps,* made her chuckle. "That's funny," she repeated.

Driving became relaxing again; no rude men flipping her off, no mad drivers, just people getting from point A to point B. A campervan crawled on in front of her, and that somehow made the drive even more relaxing. People would've just overtaken the rundown vehicle, but not Elena. She liked it; a vehicle on its last wheels; most probably a family taking her out for one last ride – an end of a chapter for them.

*But the start of a new one too*, she thought.

In the distance, it looked like a landscape painting. Elena saw hills, undoubtedly full of uneasy, winding roads that felt as unpredictable and precarious as a rollercoaster. The hilltops looked like they reached the clouds, and the hills themselves appeared to be the first line of defence – unbreakable and intimidating. Guards protecting something sacred, like Buckingham Palace, don't budge; neither did these hills. Down by the feet of these barricaded hills was a blanket of trees, their leaves beginning to shine, anticipating the arrival of spring later that month. Above, the sky was trying to break through the light clouds, with the sun already doing so, now beaming through a set of clouds to Elena's right, causing a glare on the windshield.

She lowered the shade above her head, and that made everything clear once more. A green sign was coming up, with an exit. Driving closer, she raised her foot from the accelerator so she could read what it said. Continuing on the highway would take her to Newcastle, but this next exit would lead her to—

The name had been almost completely scratched off; the only visible letter remaining was just enough to tell Mrs. Sullivan where she was heading.

*C.*

C for Castlehead.

# CHAPTER TWELVE

## Welcome To Castlehead

Mrs. Sullivan took the exit. The road led her down to a set of traffic lights – with the amber light out of use – and a roundabout. *Look at the hills*, she thought, *and you'll go the right way*.

The traffic lights turned green and she took the second exit towards the hills. It was an isolated, perfectly straight road with grazing fields on either side. No cars in front, and no cars behind; the sign back up on the highway probably made it seem like the road was closed. That was Elena's guess as she continued on.

Ascending the hill, making sharp zig-zagging turns at unpredictable moments, the road wasn't exactly flat or smooth. Cracks and bumps made the car jump and gave Mrs. Sullivan that feeling where everything in your body rises into your throat then suddenly slams back down like a broken lift. The road levelled out for a few moments as she ascended further up the hill, but—

BOOM!

That feeling returned suddenly. Mrs. Sullivan took a deep breath and steadied herself. *Anticipate it, Elena. Breathe in, breathe out, and you'll anticipate it*. The road flattened again as the road curved around. A set of trees shaded Elena and the car from the sky above; she drove on cautiously, as the road was narrowing.

She crossed her arms, turning the wheel; the curve was tight and she feared brushing up against branches or tree trunks. The curve ended with the treeline. Elena could see the light of the sun now breaking through the clouds, shining down like a spotlight on the town that stood at the foot of the hill Elena was now on – and the many others that surrounded it.

This was Castlehead.

Mrs. Sullivan began to descend the hill. With quick glances, she saw the town below her; heads of buildings looked like floating specks, the people commuting in the town weren't visible to the human eye at the height Elena was still at, and from her point of view, it resembled nothing but a normal town.

Descending further, Elena drove into a field of trees; this time, the trees made it seem like an eclipse had occurred. Everything around her as she continued was trees, pointed branches, and an ocean of dirt. The road was uneven, but not so much to make her feel sick. It just needed repairing. She swung around another curve, and it was on her left, on this curve, where Mrs. Sullivan had seen the first man-made structure in over two hours, since she was back home in Valeland:

A gravel walkway, decorated by flowers sprouting an array of colours (red, blues, yellows, and whites) like imploring lights on an airport runway, led the way up to a grand brownstone mansion. Old, but still standing. Whoever had lived within that stunning piece of architecture, Elena thought, must've been very important. Like the mayor, or someone of that stature. If she found the time, Mrs. Sullivan considered visiting it properly, if it were actually open to the public. Now wasn't the time, so Elena drove on.

She sensed that she wasn't far from civilization; the further she descended the more forms of life she encountered.

A rabbit ran out, narrowly missing the Volkswagen. Elena didn't budge. A car passed on the other side of the road. She definitely wasn't far from town now, but she wasn't out of the blanket of woodlands on this hill yet. She hunched forward and saw a billboard by the side of the road, greeting civilians not to Castlehead but to a place Elena suddenly assumed was a holiday resort of some kind.

The board stood on two large wooden pillars; behind the bold writing was a cartoonish sun, its golden rays contrasting with the neon green painting of the grass. In black writing, the board greeted Mrs. Sullivan to Sunvalley Park.

Behind the billboard, she saw another gravel driveway, guarded by trees as it led down to a circle of caravans. She didn't see much, but in the centre of the circle was a pile of wood, as if for a campfire. *Oh, it's a campsite.*

Again, though, now wasn't the time to visit, so she continued driving down the hill. She pressed on the radio, and it crackled while trying to gain a signal.

*"And that was Kelly Clarkson's hit song, My Life Would Suck Without You."* The radio presenter sounded young and excited to be hosting a radio show. As Elena had reached the bottom of the hill, stopping at a set of traffic lights, the presenter added, *"Coming up next is Right Round by Flo Rida, featuring Ke$ha."*

The light turned green, and Elena found herself on a street aligned with a set of local shops. Cafes, hairdressers, off-licences – just like any other normal town. Mrs. Sullivan felt like she had to explore more, rather than head straight to her new home. It was a whole new experience, so she supposed she should make the most of it.

*"This just in!"* A powerful voice shot out of the radio. Elena jumped. *"Early this morning, the body – which has now been identified as Sharron Rose – was found dead in the living room of her home,*

*Wardle Gardens. The C.C.I.D's chief, Derek Pattison, has issued a brief statement regarding the matter, claiming he is disinclined to reveal any more information. There have been no reports on Sharron's husband, Anthony Eccleby, and her daughter, Isabella, and their reaction to this terrible event; the only thing that can be confirmed is that neither Anthony or Isabella were at the scene—"*

Elena turned off the radio when she reached another set of lights. Driving deeper into the town allowed her to take in the hills surrounding this place. She thought it was a neat place – apart from the fact that the first news report she heard was about a death. *The family must be devastated*, she thought as the lights turned green. She kept her eyes on the road, the shops aligned on each side not grabbing her attention.

Round a roundabout, and a left and a right later Mrs. Sullivan looked up from the road; thankfully, the lights at the end had caused a queue of cars, so she could take it in. A grand church stood tall, looking over a cemetery. A sturdy brick wall with front and side metal gates protected this sacred place, and to her very little knowledge of this new town, Elena assumed that this was the only church in Castlehead. Another place to visit should she get the chance.

Then as the queue crawled nearer to the end of the road, she was now third in line –

Mrs. Sullivan thought, *Maybe it's time to see my new home. You're here for a while so you'll have time to see everything in time. But still… There's so much I need to see. The home isn't going anywhere – Yet, neither is the rest of the town. Oh, bloomin' hell! Just continue giving yourself a tour!* She was now at the front of the queue, the light turning amber, and Elena indicated left.

*You've still got the rest of the day to kill*, was her reasoning behind deciding to keep on driving around town.

The minutes went on, and Mrs. Sullivan went down busy roads and narrow suburban streets that she'd eventually have to get used to. This area seemed nice; all the houses had reasonably sized front yards and drives, most likely three-to-four bedrooms, and there wasn't a single scrap of litter on the streets. The place in which Elena was going to be staying was offered by Desmond – how could she reject her former boss's generous offer? – but after settling in, these clean suburban streets she drove on currently sat at the top of the list for future places to live.

Roughly every other house had a plaque by the front door – Mrs. Sullivan didn't count how many specifically had a plaque – and it clicked that the plaques featured the name of that specific house. An odd thing to do on a surface level, but when a house has its own name, then whoever lives there has made it their own. Elena liked that idea.

*Luna*, Elena thought, *That's a nice name.*

At the end of the road, she caught the street name: Chess Street.

*Chess Street – top of the list.*

And where there was a suburban area, Elena knew a community school wasn't far away. Two blocks down, she turned right onto one straight road. The road had two points – a top and a bottom, or a beginning and an end – and when driving along Elena quickly saw on her right the main entrance (great, black metal gates) to a secondary school.

Through the gates, steps led down to the main reception. On either side of the school were two main fields, the one on the left side of the school was accompanied by two rusted, warehouse buildings. *Sports halls*, Mrs. Sullivan guessed correctly. Passing the school and coming up to the end of the road, Elena saw a lamp post with a bus stop sign attached to the top of it. Around eye-level, also attached to the pole, was the bus schedule and at the top of this schedule was the name of the bus stop and the school. Thomas Hill High.

The day had started to enter its latter quarter and Mrs. Sullivan was still driving around. She wasn't lost, she started to tell herself. Basically, not having a map or any sense of direction in this new place, she was really very lost; but she told herself she wasn't, and that was all that mattered.

"How can someone be lost when they want to find everything out for themselves," mumbled Elena, unknowingly turning onto a scene of a crime.

Police tape and a road closed sign cut the street off halfway. A police car was parked on the curb by the house at the end of the street, and police tape and a road closed sign had also been placed at the other end of the street. But Elena tried to get as close to the tape and sign as possible without being noticed; that wasn't hard, she thought, given that there was only the one police car and officers were nowhere to be seen.

At that moment, a figure left the house. Elena parked up, intrigued. The figure was in a police uniform. *What is he doing?* Elena thought, not taking her eyes off the officer as they locked the front door. They walked up to their cruiser, and just as they put their hand on the car door, they turned their head and noticed the Volkswagen. The officer was male, quite tall — even from a distance — and his hair was greying, a moustache coming in. As he crouched under the police tape, still waving his hands, Mrs. Sullivan gathered that he was trying to tell her not to be there.

At the hood of the car, the officer motioned to Mrs. Sullivan to unwind her window. She did so, and he bent over, resting a hand on the car roof.

"Can I ask what you're doing here?" the officer asked.

"Apologies, officer, I didn't realise there was a crime scene," she answered honestly. A quick glance at the house then back at the officer, Elena put two and two together. *The home of the Sharron Rose woman...* But she thought to ask. "Is that...?"

"Yes, it is," snapped the officer. He double-taked from the house, then back to Mrs. Sullivan. He remembered receiving the email from Chief Hughes. "You shouldn't be here," he added.

And she *really* shouldn't have.

"I understand, officer. I'm... Well, I'm new here and I'm just trying to find my way around town."

"Oh..." He acted surprised. "Where is it exactly you're trying to get to?"

"Um..." Mrs. Sullivan pictured herself back in Desmond's office at the school, when he graciously offered her a place to stay. He had said something about contacting a friend, and it was just as she rose from the chair he had passed her a torn piece of paper with the friend's name and the address. It was a part of an estate, wasn't it? By a park, she remembered vaguely reading. The place was rough around the edges. "Car-Clarkson- No! Carson Estate, is it?"

"Ah, yes," the officer breathed, nodding. "It's not too far from here, actually. Just head back down where you came, make a left, keep straight and after a couple minutes, you'll find yourself by Carson Park. From there, you won't get lost."

"Okay, thank you." She started to reverse and the officer stepped back. Elena looked at the house again, Wardle Gardens, and stopped reversing. She called back to the officer, "Can I just ask why you're the only officer here?"

She couldn't fully understand herself why the question came out. The officer was taken aback also, looking at the house. Of course, he wouldn't tell a crazy suspected murderer the real reason.

He came back up to the car and said, "I wanted to have a look for myself, after forensics and everything had been done."

"Would your boss allow you to do that?"

The officer shrugged, parted his lips into a grin, and said, "It's good that I am the boss, then."

"You're the police chief?"

"Chief Pattison," the officer replied, introducing himself.

Mrs. Sullivan regretted asking the question. She must've sounded so rude; when it comes to the police chief, you should just obey their orders. But not Elena Sullivan, no, she goes ahead and allows curiosity to get the better of her and asks more questions. *Well done*, Elena thought, kicking herself inside.

"Oh, right," she said. "I'm Elena. Mrs. Elena Sullivan."

"It was nice to meet you, Elena," said the chief, extending a hand through the open car window. She accepted it, but Pattison added firmly, "But I think it's best you get home, now. I don't want people passing by thinking the wrong idea."

"No, certainly not. Good luck with everything, officer. I hope everything gets sorted."

Mrs. Sullivan reached down for the lever and rolled the window up. Pattison waved the reversing car off, that grin reappearing.

*It will get sorted*, he thought. *At any cost.*

*"Chief?"* a voice crackled from his police radio attached to his belt buckle. *"Chief?"*

He heard the call more clearly that time.

"Yes, Ton, what is it?" asked Pattison, holding the radio close to his mouth.

He ducked back under the police tape and officially re-entered the crime scene. As his deputy spoke, Pattison unblinkingly kept his eyes on the Wardle Gardens house.

*"Taylor wants to know when you're coming in,"* Ton said.

Pattison rolled his eyes as he replied, "I'll come in when I come in." *Honestly that woman thinks she's the bloody chief. Not as long as I'm here.* "I just have a few things to do," he added more calmly.

*"Okay, it's only because you haven't got a team out there with you, and we need to know when you're bringing Anthony Eccleby in for questioning."*

The chief entered the Wardle Gardens front yard and looked around; the carnage the cars crashing into the garage caused, being the first to see that corpse on the sitting room floor, Anthony and Isabella nowhere to be seen – it all left the course of action clear.

"Ton, tell the team I'll handle Anthony. And they need to get a forensics team out here," the chief ordered. "We might have to fear the worst."

In Pattison's mind, the worst was the C.C.I.D not understanding why Anthony did what he did; no questioning was needed. It was protocol, though, so he had to just go ahead and get it done. He couldn't make people suspicious; suspicions meant delays.


Mrs. Sullivan followed the chief's directions, and he was right. It wasn't like she doubted him, she was relieved to have finally known where she'd be living. *You're here now, Elena, just get yourself settled.* Maybe her conscience was right. She had been driving for hours; anymore time spent driving and she would probably forget how to walk.

The chief was right about the area known as Carson Estate. Passing the park, Elena caught three young lads (maybe eleven or twelve) lighting up fags. The police probably didn't bother with this part of the town due to the community's overall stubbornness to do what they wanted. Bins had toppled over, a stray dog walked along the path with its tail tucked between its legs and its head down – *Probably just finding someplace warm*, she thought – and there wasn't a single wall or bench clean and free of graffiti.

Elena's eyes were fixed on her surroundings; she shifted her eyes quickly back to the road and slammed on the breaks, the wheels screeching against the asphalt.

A hooded man, whose face was covered in filth, his figure reminding Elena of what could only be described as a zombie, had stumbled out in front of the car. He turned his head, his eyes hooded and casting shadows down his cheeks, but Elena knew he was looking at her.

"Watch what ye doin'!" the zombie man howled, thrusting his arm forward, almost tumbling over his own feet as he did so. "Ye fackin' cun'! Wha' street corna ye live on, eh?"

Elena kept her cool as the man somehow managed his way to the other end of the street. She took the next left, completely missing him falling face first like a plank at the bottom of a set of stairs. The street she had turned onto had brought her to a crumbling apartment complex. She found a space in between a white van and a motorcycle, assuming this was the place.

From the glove compartment, Elena shuffled for that small piece of paper Desmond had given her. She looked at the name – Carol Holmes – then the address – Carson Estate, Castlehead, England, CH10 9TT. The road sign by the main entrance of the apartment complex clearly read Carson Estate. And above the door was that very postal code.

*Just unpack later*, Elena told herself. She hopped out of the car and walked into the complex. Caution tape in the shape of an X blocked the way to the lift on her left. Out of bounds. In the far corner of the room was a door that stood by the sign of the stick figure rushing up some stairs. The door to the stairwell... By that door, against the opposite wall to the entrance, was a high desk where a grey-haired woman sat jotting something down, unbothered by Elena's arrival. The blood red carpet, Elena noted, also needed a good wash;

actually, on a closer glance it looked like it was actually supposed to be a lighter shade of red.

Elena got the shivers out and walked up to the desk. *Be nice, Elena. Desmond said she was a bit rough around the edges, so if you're on her good side, she might not kill you.*

*Kill? Kill-kill, kill you? She won't kill. Why kill… Kill. Don't kill. Kill you, kill you, she'll kill you. Kill you, you kill. You kill, kill you. Kill. Kill. Kill! Kill! You'll kill, you'll kill. You're ill, ill-kill. Ill. Kill. You ill? You ill? You ill? Hey! You ill?*

Wait…

"Hey!"

Elena looked down at the woman. She was glaring back at her.

"Huh?" blurted Elena.

The woman asked for the fifth time, "Are you ill? Please don't make me call a doctor. Can't be arsed with that shite."

"What? No. I was just… I was just…" Elena was just… She couldn't remember. "Anyways, I'm—"

"Elena Sullivan," finished the woman bluntly, her eyes now off the new arrival and back down to the paper she was writing on. She muttered quickly, "I'm Carol Holmes. You dare make a Sherlock joke! Desmond told me you were coming at some point. Let me show you to your apartment."

"Oh…" Elena stepped back. "Okay… Thank you very much."

"Yeah, yeah. Come on, I'm going to close up in a bit."

Elena watched Carol step from the seat and walk around the desk; Elena got a good look at her – *What was left of her* – and was even more surprised by the diminutive stature of this woman. *Short* with *grey hair that ran all the way down to her back* and *wrinkles appearing every second?* Elena put them all together and thought, *She's like one of those goblins in those fairy tales Mother used to read.* Carol was in grey jogger bottoms and an oversized jacket. *Definitely making yourself welcoming towards the people who live here*, Elena thought sarcastically. And Elena wasn't good with sarcasm.

But she said instead, "Closing up?"

Carol waddled past Elena, leading her through a rusted door that brought them into a narrow stairwell. They started climbing the stairs as if on a hike, each metal step clanging.

Carol's voice echoed as she answered, "Had to enforce a curfew six months back." Elena tilted her head to try and get a glimpse of Carol's face as she spoke, for the owner of the building had her eyes entirely on the steps in front of them. "Some little shits tried to break in. C.C.I.D did fuck all, as suspected, but nothing's happened since neither."

Elena gulped and managed out, "My stuff's still in the car, so could I at least get them before you do?"

Carol huffed and explained, "Is all your stuff really that important?"

For the first time climbing the stairway, Carol looked back at Elena fully; she caught on that Elena didn't appreciate that remark. So, she reassured her with a roll of the eyes, "There's a key to the front entrance on the set I'm giving you. But don't try to disturb the others. They can get arsy, and the walls and everything are very thin."

*Yeah*, Elena thought, *I gathered that.*

They had reached the top where they were met with a door. Carol opened it and Elena followed. They were in a hallway full of doors with apartment numbers on them; some numbers were missing, falling off, or dangling upside down. Carol suddenly stopped in front of door number 3.

"Is this it?" Elena asked.

"No," growled Carol, "I've just decided to stop here to introduce you to your *precious* neighbours. Yes, it's your apartment!"

This was needing some getting used to.

"Oh, well... um... Thanks, again, Miss Holmes," stammered Elena.

"No, no," denied Carol, shaking her head. "None of this *Miss* crap. It's Carol."

"Oh, well... um... Thanks, Carol."

*Bloody hell*, Carol thought. She stuffed her hand in her jogger bottoms pocket and pulled out a keyring with two silver keys and a label of the door number attached to it. Carol passed it to Elena, who took it gently.

"It's normally easy to get mixed up with which key is which," explained Carol, "so I recommend people who live or stay here to put a mark on their door key with a pen or something. And don't lose them! There's only one key for each apartment."

Elena nodded; she didn't need to be told twice.

"No problem," she said. Elena saw the label on the keyring. *33*? "Wait, why does the door say...?"

"We lost the other three."

Elena went with it and said, "Oh, I see."

"Right, I'll be downstairs for a little bit longer if you need to ask about anything else," said Carol. It was the politest thing she had said to her, Elena thought. "But, honestly, please don't," she added swiftly.

Carol walked off back down the hall, and Mrs. Sullivan jammed one of the keys into the door – with luck, it was the right one – and... it opened.

Elena's mouth opened, and her eyes started to water – and not because she was crying. She felt like somebody had shot all the smells of a dumpster through her nostrils. She stepped in. The door shut on its own accord. By the door was the only light switch in the room that seemed to be the entirety of her new home; a low, twin bed laid against the back wall, against the left side wall was a chest of drawers that sat on a slant, and on the right was a chair and a desk, and on that was a microwave.

*Where's the toilet? Actually… on second thought, just leave the toilet. I'll ask in the morning.*

Adjusting to her room took a good half hour to forty-five minutes. The word Elena used to describe the room to herself was musty. She sat on the bed and took it all in, sinking through the mattress to the metal bed frame. After that time, Elena picked out the essentials from her car – clothes and washing utensils (her books could be left until the next day) – and sure enough as Elena made the round trips down to the car and up to her room, Carol Holmes was nowhere to be found. Still, she got what she wanted sorted done before it got too late, and she was in bed at the reasonable time of 10:52pm.

*BANG! CRASH! BOOM!*

Mrs. Sullivan woke up the next morning with a shooting pain rushing down her spine, all the way down to the back of her knees. She turned to her side, seeing what her new home looked like on the side. Weird, but it was still the same – small and concrete, like a prison cell.

She sprouted up suddenly, noticing the door was sitting ajar by about three inches. That wasn't right; she was sure she locked the door the previous night.

Elena climbed out of bed and went over to the box she had left full of clothes to change from her nightgown to a blouse and chinos underneath. Afterwards, she shot straight out the room – double-taking to make sure the door was actually closed – and rushed down to the reception.

"Carol!" she called, her voice shaking as she made her way down the final set of stairs…

In the reception, Carol was at the desk, her arms waving about as she talked to the Castlehead Criminal Investigation Department officer. The officer stood there, arms folded, nodding at everything Carol was telling him.

"Listen, Deputy," said Carol, "I know Carson Estate is a shithole but, Jesus wept, we haven't had this kind of ruckus in years."

"Has anyone identified who might've broken in?" asked Deputy Ton.

"No. All their stories are the same. They heard a lot of banging and crashing through the night, and the person was talking to themselves."

Just then, Mrs. Sullivan ran in and skidded to a stop next to the C.C.I.D deputy.

"Carol, somebody's tried to break in!"

"Yes, I know, Elena. Why d'you think Deputy Ton's here?"

Elena looked up at the deputy, both of them nodding in acknowledgment of each other's presence.

The deputy asked Elena, "Did you hear anything, ma'am?"

She reflected on the previous night; carrying the boxes to her room was a pain, Carol mentioned something about a curfew, and she went to bed just before eleven that night. The sleep wasn't good, but she had obviously slept all the way through until morning as she hadn't heard any signs of a burglar.

"No," she said. "I woke up this morning, and my door was open. I don't think anything was taken, thankfully. But how do you expect me to feel safe here knowing that somebody tried to break in?"

"Ma'am," said Ton politely, "I've got what I need, so I'll head back to the station and we'll look into getting more security for the building. And we'll get a few officers down to scout the area for anyone who looks suspicious."

"Are you serious!?" roared Carol. "You'll look for somebody suspicious? Mate, the whole of this estate is fucking suspicious in the eyes of the C.C.I.D!"

Ton stepped back as he repeated, just as calmly, "Like I said, I'll get this info down to the station and we'll get it sorted."

He started to walk back to the entrance.

Carol grimaced and muttered, "Yeah, you fucking better."

In the doorway, Ton looked back at Carol and Elena. Elena was as quiet as a mouse, but still vulnerable; she looked like a wandering patient, scared and dishevelled.

"Carol, before I forget," said the deputy, "did anyone tell you what the burglar was saying as they broke in?"

"They swore a lot," answered Carol bluntly.

"Right…"

"Oh, and something about needing to kill," she added.

A theory came to Ton.

"Do you think the burglar was looking for someone who might live here? A target?"

"How the bloody hell should I know?" Carol said in an impatient, high tone. "You're the officer. Now, go down to the office and sort this shit out," she mocked.

Ton left without another word.

As he did, Elena snapped her head back to the desk and Carol.

"And what about me?" she asked.

"What about you?" replied Carol, her eyes off Mrs. Sullivan and down on a piece of paper.

"Someone breaks in, everyone's lives are at risk, and I can't sleep without getting paranoid," Elena explained.

With an exhausted sigh, Carol said, "*Fine*. I'll take a look at the door, and I'll see about getting a new lock."

"Thank you." That was all Elena wanted to hear. "I need to get out for the day, to clear my head. Any places you recommend?"

"Not really."

"Well, do you not have a map I can take a look at?"

With another exhausted sigh, Carol bent down and chucked a crumpled sheet onto the desktop. *God, this woman's difficult*, she thought as she sat up.

"There you go," she muttered.

Elena took the map and unfolded it. This was what she needed the previous day. Examining it was like looking at any old map; it had all the street names, main regions, key locations, and all that. At the far right of the map, she noticed a motorway leading to a stretch of yellow that looked out to what was labelled as the North Sea.

"There's a beach?" Elena asked, realising she might just have a place to let her mind rest after all.

"What gave it away? The yellow bit on the map that says Jaxson Bay, or the fact we're a coastal town in the northeast of England?"

*This woman's going to take some getting used to*, Elena thought.

But she let the sarcasm pass by and asked nicely, "Can I take this with me?"

"No," Carol instantly replied.

"Why not?"

"Because it's the only map we have."

"I'll bring it back," Elena argued, keeping a steady tone.

"Ugh… Fine. You better, or you're replacing it."

"No problem. Thank you."

Elena heard Carol groan as she folded the map up neatly and walked out to her car. In that moment, the beach really did seem like a great idea.

How different was it to the beach in Valeland? Probably not so much… Jaxson Bay – sounds very welcoming, doesn't it? What if it didn't have the same effect on her? What if it *wasn't* like the beach in Valeland? Then that meant she couldn't allow the sound of the waves crashing onto shore to wash over her, to clear her head; she would still be in reality and that wasn't what she wanted when she looked for a few moments to herself.

On the map, it seemed like it was going to take a good twenty minutes to half-an-hour to get there; even so, the town was so much easier to navigate with a map rather than just letting the car take her anywhere. *Oh, yeah!* she realised. *That's the school I passed...* Then a few minutes later: *And there's the church.* After ten minutes, she was out of the town and back into a more suburban area where she came upon a roundabout. The sun caused a glare and Elena struggled to read the signs, but the map told her the exit dead ahead would lead her onto the motorway towards Jaxson Bay.

Gladly, the motorway wasn't packed, maybe because it was still before noon. She kept driving, the Volkswagen bouncing along steadily. With not so many drivers, Elena was allowed to take it easy and think about what she might see at this new beach.

*An ice cream van driving along, perhaps*, she guessed. *Kids rushing into the sea with their buckets and spades... Parents finally getting a break... Is the North Sea compatible with surfers? I don't know. Oh! Amusements! There's got to be amusements! But wait! You might be a bit old... Rubbish, there shouldn't be an age barrier. Emmett loved theme parks. I's always be so nervous, but he'd still drag me onto that huge rollercoaster. His hand... hands... held mine... held mine to calm me, and it did. He held someone else's, though. You told yourself that, and you stuck with your gut and...*

She glanced to her left. *What the...?* On the map, that she'd laid out flat on the passenger seat, it didn't look anything like what she was now seeing. A decrepit building on its last life, would have been a more accurate description. She saw an upcoming dirt track turn off up towards the building. *The beach could wait, couldn't it?* Elena indicated and exited the motorway, passing onto a dirt track that led her through a set of trees, up the hill to a locked gate and wall surrounding the building. Parked by the wall were a line of three vans advertising construction.

Elena parked up and got out of the car. She stepped towards the padlocked gate. She glared through the bars to the building; a fresh front door contrasted with the rotting bricks of the building itself. The crucified Christ above the door, though wooden and asleep, stared right through her. *Catholic made*, she assumed. *An old schoolhouse?* It was the right size. Two floors, possibly a lower ground floor. She wondered what was going on.

"What are you doing here?" a voice said from behind her.

Elena jumped around.

It was a man.

# CHAPTER THIRTEEN
## Clarke Smith

The man was in stained overalls, as if he had been working on the building that very morning. He must've come from the van. He folded his arms and had a serious glare on his face; his full head of hair, greying on the sides, told Elena that he could've been somewhere in the late thirties region. He wasn't slim but not big – *stocky* was probably the right word – and he continued to stare at her sternly as he awaited an answer – or an excuse – as to why this woman was just loitering there.

"I said what are you doing here?" he asked.

"Sorry, sorry," Elena said shakily. "I'm new here and was passing through—"

"You're new?" This man seemed surprised by that. He explained, "Well, this facility isn't open to the general public yet."

"What is this place?" asked Elena.

"It's called St. Jude's. It used to be a medical institute, but Madam Mayor decided to have it refurbished into a hotel."

"Oh, I see," Elena said.

"Yeah. We managed to keep it mostly open before the millennium. People were divided by the facility's purpose. Some thought it was what the town needed, while others thought it was too extreme. Some are still even torn over whether or not it should be a hotel."

"But it's a medical institute. Surely, it was for a good cause?"

"It was no normal hospital," the man corrected her.

Elena grasped what he meant by that and said, "For someone in construction you seem to know a lot about this place."

"Oh," the man chuckled. "I'm not a construction worker. I volunteered to help out because I used to work here. Most of the team in fact consists of former doctors."

"Sorry."

"No, don't be. I can see why you thought that I worked in construction."

He glanced down at his overalls, then back up at Elena.

"Was this your permanent job before it shut down?" Elena asked.

She was fully invested now, and she thought it to be polite that this man was taking the time to give her a bit of a history lesson. The man cocked his head towards the building Elena now knew to be St. Jude's, and he chuckled, somewhat nervously, Elena thought.

"Oh, God no. I own a pharmacy in town. This was a job on the side. I couldn't do what the other doctors did full-time. Sorry, where are my manners? I'm Clarke. Clarke Smith."

Clarke Smith extended a hand.

Elena accepted it graciously and said, "I'm Elena. Elena Sullivan."

"Well, it's very nice to meet you, Elena. How long have you been in Castlehead for?"

"Just a day," she answered. Clarke said nothing, and silence quickly filled the air. Elena began to contemplate an idea. She had settled in – kind of – and now she needed something to do... She had already told herself there was no way she was spending every single day in that dumpster of an apartment complex. "You wouldn't, by any chance, need an extra pair of hands?"

"Have you had any experience in manual labour?"

"Not much. I was a teacher for a time at the Desmond School for Creative Arts."

*"Where?"*

"A very exclusive school in Valeland," Elena clarified.

"I think Thomas Hill High might be a better fit for you then, Elena," Clarke suggested thoughtfully.

"No, I don't think so." Elena looked at the building, then back at Clarke. The intrigue was still there, and after what Clarke had told her about the brief history of St. Jude's, it only further piqued her interest. There was just *something* about it. "I moved here for a change in my life after… anyways, yeah."

She had her goals. Clarke respected that. He didn't want to offend her, of course, for he knew she was a proud, respected woman. He just thought perhaps a woman *of her age* shouldn't be doing manual labour. *Surely her husband does all the work*, he thought.

But he said instead, "Okay, then." He shrugged, accepting how keen she seemed. "Why don't you come over for dinner and we can discuss the job more?"

"Oh…" Elena placed her hand on her heart, her face going pink. "I'm flattered, Clarke, but I think I'm a bit too old for you."

Clarke laughed.

"No, I didn't mean it like that. I'm married and I have a son. My wife can cook us a delicious meal, and I could tell you more about the town and St. Jude's. So, you're not coming in blind."

"Oh I apologise…but I don't know." She instinctively tried to sound more flustered than she actually was. She added nervously, "You see, I'm still trying to come to terms with this move. I only offered to help for something to do."

"Okay, then," Clarke replied. "That's disappointing, but it's your choice, I guess." Elena thought that that sounded rather passive-aggressive. "Why don't you start next week? There's a couple of things the team needs to discuss with the mayor and the chief, and I wouldn't want you getting involved in all that malarkey."

"What does the chief of police have to do with refurbishing this place?"

They both turned to St. Jude's.

Clarke explained, "It's well-known Madam Mayor and Chief Pattison work together extremely closely. Rumours suggest Pattison influences some of the decision making, including changing this place into a hotel. I think he was one of the people against St. Jude's. But that's just my opinion, so don't take my word for it."

"Okay." *What kind of place is this?* she thought. And she didn't just mean St. Jude's. "Well," she started awkwardly, "it's been a pleasure talking to you, Clarke." She started to walk back to her car. Taking a hold of the handle, she called out, "I'll see you next week."

Clarke stood by the gate and waved Elena off as she reversed and headed back down the bank to the motorway. Clarke grunted as he couldn't wrap his head around why she would reject his generous offer like that. Nonetheless, he knew he had to get on with tearing off the old wallpaper in the building.

As she found herself back on a noticeably busier motorway, all Elena thought – as if she just had a brain fart – was: *Where was I even meant to be going?*

# CHAPTER FOURTEEN

## Amongst The Trees

She still needed to find a way to stay away from the apartment building. The map sat laid out flat again on the front passenger seat as Elena drove back into town, seeing if there was anything worthwhile. As she drove, she did suppose, however, that at least she had a job. She really did appreciate the offer to go over for dinner at Clarke's... So why didn't she go?

*You told him*, Elena reassured herself, *that you just needed time to adjust to Castlehead. That was all. Sometimes that's all people need — time. He understood my situation... Yeah, yeah, he did...*

*"No, he didn't!"*

*The* voice...

Elena peered up at her rearview mirror above the dashboard, like someone was there sitting in the back.

She reached an impasse; on the road, she told herself, not the voice. The traffic lights quickly flashed green and she continued on. Though the feeling that someone was on her tail was still there, shaking it off was no simple task. *You're just trying to find something else to do.* That was it—

*"No, you're not! Keep running, go on. I fucking dare you. Run from what you know, the truth, and keep telling yourself that the fictional, perfect world you live in is real. Accept the offer and see what happens."*

"I said no," cried Elena.

*"There's always light at the end of the tunnel. Isn't that what they say? You know it's true. Even if something seems wrong, and it is, get through it and reach the light. Go towards the light; embrace it and your new chapter can truly be written."*

"Can it?" Elena muttered.

*"Of course…"* Somehow the whisper of this voice felt loud. Elena had no choice but to listen. *"You're not so different from everyone else. Everyone drowns out a bit of themselves so they can try to focus on what they think matters. No one can move on alone. And that's what you are – alone."*

"I am."

*"Yes. Say it again. Say it again. You know you want to."*

"I am alone," Elena said more clearly. *But I want to say it again…*

*"Then go on! Say it a-fucking-gain!"*

Elena cried, "I AM ALONE!"

Like a bolt of lightning, a surge of adrenaline rushed through Elena. She took the next turn sharply and slammed on the accelerator. The engine growled as the car sped down the main road; Elena's eyes were locked on the end of the road. A three-way junction. She only had the choice of left or right. If she continued ahead, she would end up in a florist's.

*Stop!* The sudden thought popped in. *Stop while you can!*

Elena leaned back as far as she could, hammering her foot on the brake. The car screeched to the end of the road just in time. She caught her breath as she took the left and kept to the 20mph speed limit.

She needed somewhere, anywhere to stop to just take a break. Driving onward, the map was no longer a factor or a great deal of help, Elena looked out all of the car windows for a half-decent place to stop.

The next turn took her onto a road with parking spaces on both sides for people who needed to explore the rows of shops. Elena was one of those people. Lucky for her there was a perfect space in between a red Range Rover and a grey Mini Cooper. Taking her time, concentrating, parking up was a piece of cake.

Shutting the door, Elena peered over the roof of her car and her eyes locked onto a glorious image; a treasure trove for people like her. She fell in love instantly, and for a second all feeling in her body had gone away. Drunk on relief, Elena let out a bright smile; that was definitely where she was going to go. As she crossed the road, the green logo of the shop became clearer. Though, for people like Elena, all she needed to do was to notice the books on display in the windows, the green block letters of the store and then she was transported to heaven: *Waterstones*.

*Peace at last.*

For people like her, Waterstones was a safe haven. Like most stores within the Waterstones chain, the one Elena rushed into included a small cafe by the front left window; it wasn't anything much, but at least it was a place to take a moment to gather one's thoughts and relax. The store itself stretched all the way back, which was a lot further than it looked, to a set of fire exit doors. Along the walls to both sides of her were the heavenly bookshelves; hundreds and thousands of books to choose from. You want non-fiction? You would head down to the bottom to the non-fiction section. You want horror? That genre was stationed next to the cafe, the shelves mostly taken up by Stephen King novels. You want crime? That was more around the middle of the store; from Agatha Christie to James Patterson, this Waterstones had it.

Also, like other stores she had been in, Mrs. Sullivan saw that the latest releases were on display on a series of small tables by the front right window. Instead, Elena went for the cafe and found a two-seater table by the counter. She sat down and her head fell into her hands; her ears pricked up every time she heard a snippet of a conversation from other customers at the cafe or people intrigued by a book they had seen on a shelf and arguing with themselves whether to get it or not because they knew they had so many other books to finish off.

"Excuse me," a soft voice said.

Elena looked up and saw a baby-faced girl young enough to be her granddaughter (*Working just to get the money in*, Elena thought upon noticing her); the girl wore a Waterstones shirt underneath a tight apron. She held a small notepad and pencil, constantly presenting Elena with a pleasant smile her boss probably forced her to keep up.

"Yes?" said Elena.

The girl hunched over and asked, "Would you like anything?"

"Oh, no thank you," said Elena, shaking her head.

The girl played with the pencil in her hand, suddenly nervous, and she told Elena quietly, "I'm sorry, ma'am, but if you're not going to order anything then you can't sit here." The girl gulped at the brief agitation shown on Elena's face. "I am sorry," she said again.

Elena shrugged and said, "Fine, just a black coffee." She looked away and rubbed her forehead, the pencil scribbling on the notepad sounding more like nails on a chalkboard. "Four sugars," she added quickly.

"I'll get that for you as soon as possible."

The girl walked off behind the counter to start working on the order. Elena was alone again, and she let her head fall back into her palms. If she knew one thing, it was that she wasn't tired, but other than that she didn't know what was going on. It could've been the guilt of rejecting Clarke's dinner offer. *He seemed like a nice bloke, as well*, she thought. *Nerves*. It could've been that, yes. It could've been nerves due to starting a new job she had no past experience in.

The whole point of this move, she remembered again, was to begin a new chapter, to try new things. So, in hindsight, Elena couldn't hate herself for accepting the position. *Actually, you offered! Ugh. Why did you do that, you stupid woman?* She took a deep breath. *It's okay, it's okay. Everyone has second thoughts.*

"Everyone does," Elena murmured.

A quick glance up from her palms, Elena saw the young waitress come over with a cup and saucer. She placed it on the table, still with that pleasant smile glued to her face.

"Black coffee, four sugars," she announced.

"Thank you, sweetie," whispered Elena with a slight nod, a signal to walk off and attend to other customers. Elena brought the coffee closer to the edge of the table, getting a good look at the black liquid. At first, its smell was putrid, but her nose adjusted to it quickly enough. "Coffee and a good book..." she muttered.

Elena looked around. Nobody heard.

*Coffee and a good book*, she recited in her head. A good old coffee and a good book – to readers, there was no better way to escape. No distractions, just you entranced by every word on the page, drawing you in deeper with every page you turn. That was what Elena appreciated about literature – all forms of it, in fact – and it was crazy to her how something as simple as a coffee served in a Waterstones could bring back such fond memories...

## 1969

By the wall securing the perimeter of the Desmond School for Creative Arts, in the far corner behind the school where nobody could distract her, Elena sat against the stump of a strong tree. The leaves and branches shaded her from the sun above; she tried to block out the singing birds in the cloudless sky, wanting to be even more immersed in the book she had resting on her lap. The sixteen-year-old even had her hair tied back so strands of it wouldn't get in her eyes as she read.

She was almost halfway through the novel, when she paused to take in the passage she was on reading:

*The twinkling stars seemed to be even more beautiful through the telescope. Though the log Walter and Nieve sat on was rough, it didn't bother them. A clear night meant a perfect night to wonder what was beyond the world they lived in; Walter's telescope was a way to reach even closer to the far ends of the universe, and he wanted to share it with Nieve. He wanted to share everything with her.*

*He positioned the telescope at a forty-five-degree angle. Nieve sat patiently.*

*"Go on," said Walter, jerking his head towards the telescope.*

*Nieve looked nervous at first, unsure about the offer. The last thing she wanted was to harm their friendship by breaking the telescope; it was a device she hadn't really interacted with before this point.*

*"Are you sure?" Nieve mumbled, her head still down.*

*"Of course," Walter reassured. He reached forward as if going towards a nervous puppy for the first time and grabbed Nieve's hand. Pulling her forward, Walter positioned her eye at the lens. "Just look through there," he told her.*

*Roughly 240,000 miles from Earth, the moon shone. But to Nieve as she stared in awe through the telescope, she felt like she could touch it. She felt like she was there. She sat back from the scope and looked at Walter with possibly the biggest grin she ever had on her face.*

*"That's incredible," she breathed, both her eyes and Walter's locking.*

*"It is, isn't it?" said Walter, smiling pleasantly back at her.*

*They both tilted their heads back, looking at the stars staring down at them. Tonight was a night Walter hoped the stars would align. After a brief silence of admiring what was before them, Nieve exhaled, ready to spark another conversation.*

*"Walt?" she started. Walter turned to her. "Do you think there'll ever be a time where we travel beyond the moon? The moon landing was spectacular but there's got to be more out there."*

*"I'm sure there is," replied Walter. "You never know, there might be a time where we figure out how to even live on the moon."*

*"How amazing!" Nieve whispered, still awe-inspired by Walter and the stars.*

*"We could even go beyond the moon," added Walter. "Hugh Everett theorised that there are an endless number of possibilities, other universes that exist with ours."*

*"Like a multiverse?" suggested Nieve, scooching a touch closer to Walter.*

*"Exactly. But it's just a theory."*

*"Okay…" Nieve inched closer, their fingertips touching. "And theoretically in how many universes are we sitting here?"*

*"I'm hoping… in every universe."*

*They leaned in, the stars aligning like Walter had hoped, and their lips—*

"Afternoon, Elena!"

Elena knew that voice, and yes, he distracted her from reading the best part, but he could never anger her. Emmett Sullivan – a lean figure, slick black hair, and bright eyes – stood over her.

"Hello, Emmett," Elena responded politely, folding the corner of her page so she didn't lose her space.

"What are you reading?" asked Emmett, kneeling down to get a look at the cover. He read out, *"Space: A Wondrous Place by Sara Kelly.* Didn't she write *The Winds of Change?"*

"Yes," squeaked Elena. "She's magnificent, isn't she? Her messages are so moving."

"Yeah, she is," Emmett agreed. "So, how's this book?"

Elena closed *Space: A Wondrous Place* and passed it to Emmett so he could get a good feel of it.

She said, "It's really good, as expected. It's about a forbidden love, but it has a much deeper meaning."

"Ah, I see…"

Emmett took a quick glance at Elena and then flicked through the book. You couldn't beat the smell of a new book. So, the book was about a forbidden love? Emmett thought there was nothing forbidden about the relationship between him and Elena. They had both been raised to succeed; that was why they were attending the Desmond School for Creative Arts, because they were worthy of it. Emmett knew he would one day be worthy of marrying this stunning ray of sunshine, on top of being successful, but on the odd occasion they still enjoyed a little bit of *fun*.

"Can I have it back?" asked Elena. "Please?"

"Yes, of course."

Emmett had an idea.

Elena reached for it but, just as she was about to take it, Emmett tugged it back. A proud grin spread across his face, knowing he had got her with that simple joke. She tried again, but it was the same result: Elena was too slow.

"Emmett," huffed Elena, reaching out once more, "come on now."

But she still couldn't get the book back. Emmett jumped up. He really was acting childishly, Elena thought, in the grounds of one of the most exclusive institutes in the United Kingdom. If any students or teachers saw what he was doing, they would've thought he needed to go back to nursery.

"You're going to have to catch me if you want it," laughed Emmett, jiving backwards before scampering off.

Elena rolled her eyes but let out a little chuckle. She rose and entered a light jog; good space was made between Emmett and

Elena, and Elena noticed he was heading for the wall. Those who used their creativity and mind were never meant for physical exercise (a ridiculous myth in the creative arts, sure, but in this case it was true), so Elena hadn't been able to catch up.

*What's he doing?* she thought as she jogged. Emmett had reached the other end of the wall and chucked the book over to outside the perimeter before scaling the wall himself. He couldn't be serious!

Elena called out to him – he had one leg over the wall – and she added, "This isn't funny!"

She was saying the opposite of how she was feeling. This was what she liked about him. Serious and passionate about what he wanted in life, but he also knew how to have a good time. She hoped this side of him would never go away. He was out of the school grounds by the time Elena reached the wall; she jumped up, her hands anchoring over the top. Elena wheezed as she pulled herself up.

"Hey!" a distant voice from within the grounds called out. Elena looked back and saw a staff member rushing towards her. She looked out to the herd of trees that Emmett must've ran into. "What do you think you're doing?" the staff member exclaimed.

*Go,* Elena's instinct told her. *Go for Emmett, get him!*

And the book of course.

Elena laughed and lowered herself out of the school grounds, rushing into the herd of trees. Grass flattened and twigs snapped underneath her feet as she ran deeper into the woodland. Rays of sunlight broke through the leaves and branches overhead, guiding her even further in. Emmett was nowhere in sight. He had to be found.

"Emmett!" she called out. "Ready or not, here I come!"

No reply. He didn't want to give himself away.

A rustling bush stopped her dead in her tracks. *He's close.* She did a full 360 turn but there was still no sign of him. She snapped her head around to the sound of another rustling bush. Then, glancing up, the sun had failed to continue to send its rays down. *Dark. Alone. This isn't funny anymore.* Emmett had gone, and he wasn't coming back.

*"Yeah, admit it,"* a voice told her. *"You know he's not coming back."*

With every word, it seemed to get even darker. Elena spun around frantically, unsure of where to go.

"No, he's just playing around," Elena argued.

*"Wrong! Emmett always plays around… You just don't want to think it. You can't help it, though, can you? Happy wife, happy life! What a load of shit. He doesn't love you like you think he does. Manipulation can be an invisible act of torture to the victim."*

"No! Get out! Emmett, where are you?" Elena cried.

*"But you're never going to leave him—"*

"Emmett!"

*"Because secretly—"*

"Emmett!"

*"—you like what he's doing. Don't you? Don't you? You know he's wronged you already, but you're stopping yourself from telling him because—"*

"Because I love him. Emmett, please!" Elena cried.

She drew herself away, her hands like a pair of claws on her hair. Her eyes were wide as tears streamed down her face.

*"Because you love him? No, no, no, try again, Elena. You're not telling him so he can dig a bigger hole for himself! You evil bitch! Wrong! How wrong!"*

"Fuck off!"

*"But it'll feel so right."*

"AHHHHHHHHHHHHHHHHHHHH!"

Elena wailed. Above, a flock of birds soared away. She collapsed to her knees and uncontrollably sobbed until she wheezed. Breathless.

She was too distracted – too hurt by what she knew – to hear the crunching of twigs in the distance.

A guardian angel on her shoulder, she imagined, that was how soft the hand that grabbed her felt. Elena sniffled and tilted her head onto the hand, using it like a pillow. There was no need to open her eyes; she knew it was Emmett. He placed the book on Elena's lap and brought her in close for a hug.

She sobbed gently. Emmett shushed her.

"It's okay, it's okay," he whispered, his mouth pressed up against Elena's ear as they stayed in the hug. "*Shh*, I'm sorry, Elena. I didn't mean anything by it. I was just playing around."

Then Elena opened her eyes, putting together what he had just said. But after a moment, she allowed it to slide. Time stopped when being comforted by her Emmett. He *was* there; he *had* come back; he *wasn't* leaving; he *hadn't* wronged her, and he *wasn't* going to. That little voice in your head, the voice that spits out all your doubts like phlegm when you're unwell, isn't always right. The voice was never going to leave, it was something Elena, like everyone, had to live with. Containing it could work, so that was what she was going to do. How long she could last, she didn't know, but one thing that she hadn't had any doubts over was her Emmett Sullivan.

## 2009

Emmett always liked the Waterstones store, ever since the branch opened back in the 80s. The Sullivans were fixated on all forms of literature, and Waterstones had all they could ask for. Sitting there, her coffee untouched, Mrs. Sullivan remembered the countless hours they would spend in a store, picking out a collection of books and then ending their regular visit by having a coffee in the cafe.

Emmett wasn't there anymore, but even so, it was nice thinking about him without getting upset. That day north of forty years ago was the first proper time Emmett showed that he wasn't going anywhere.

Their love for books led to the belief that there was nothing literature couldn't teach them. Not having a television wasn't because they had entered their later years; it was a choice from the beginning. Just like sitting there in Waterstones was a choice. Elena looked around, making a choice, and thought about purchasing a book to add to her collection that she hadn't even unpacked. There was no harm in seeing if there was anything new or interesting. *Treat yourself, there's no harm in that either.*

She rose from her table, the coffee still untouched, and walked off down the store. Shelves after shelves overwhelmed the aisle leading down to the back, and Elena looked at all of them as she walked. At the top of each shelf a sign labelling the book's genre drew customers in to search for something that best fit their taste.

*Fiction... Hmm... Probably not. Young adult... definitely not. Wait! What about horror or thriller? Oh, that's an option.* She continued down the store. Where was the horror and thrill...? *Hang on! What did that say up there?* She reversed a couple of steps and looked up. *History.* That was the one.

Elena nudged past a couple of young-looking customers to get a better look at the selection. The section varied from worldwide history to U.K history, to—

That was odd. No local history?

Mrs. Sullivan bent down to the bottom shelf and scrolled her finger across the books' spines to catch even the name of the town. To no avail. She stood upright again and found a book exploring the United Kingdom through the centuries; a hefty book indeed, whose weight took Elena by surprise when she pulled it out of its space. On the cover there was an intricately drawn outline of the U.K, Northern Ireland included. Skimming through it, Elena caught on quite quickly that at the start of every century section there was a somewhat updated photo of the nation.

Then it clicked. *Go towards the back*, which she did, *and there'll be the U.K from 1900 to 2000*. On the picture was marked all the major towns, cities, and historical landmarks across the nation; Elena dragged her finger down from the top of Scotland, through Edinburgh and the border, to Berwick-Upon-Tweed, and then she passed an unmarked Castlehead and straight into Newcastle.

It was safe to say that a functioning town like Castlehead wasn't founded after the millennium. *No history books on Castlehead, as if it doesn't exist*, thought Elena. *Just like how St. Jude's wasn't marked on the map I borrowed.* Once the book was back in place, Elena turned around and realised the two young customers were still there. Looking at them properly, Elena saw they were both girls of around fifteen or sixteen, with pale skin and straight black hair. Similar features made Elena quickly assume they were related.

"Excuse me, girls," said Elena.

The girls turned to the random woman that had approached them, and the one on Elena's left said, "Yes?"

"Who are you?" the other asked.

Elena said sincerely, "I'm sorry to bother you, and this might sound like a very weird question, but are you both students by any chance?"

The girl's glanced at each other and took a quick step back.

The girl on the left said hesitantly, "*Yeah…* Why?"

"Thomas Hill High?" asked Elena.

"Miss," the right one said firmly, "what is this exactly about?"

"I'm just curious… about the history you get taught." Elena thought quickly. "You see, I'm starting at Thomas Hill High as a new teacher, and I just want to get a heads up on the specific topics the school teaches."

That was a bit of a relief for the girls, and things felt a little less uncomfortable. It was still odd to have this random woman approach them to ask about their school lives, though.

The right girl explained, less tensely now, "Well, neither of us do GCSE History, but during, like, Year 7, 8, and 9, we learned basically just the usual stuff. The World Wars, Medicine, the Victorian period—"

"Any local history?"

The left girl butted in, "Not really. Most Castlehead history is just, well, events, honestly. The Mayoral Election assassination that happened in 1977 is the main one, I think."

"What about the settlers that founded the town?" suggested the other.

"Settlers?" said Elena.

"They came sometime before World War I."

"What about St. Jude's?"

"I think," the left girl said, "St. Jude's was a topic at some point, but a lot of things we learned about it was just when it opened, what it was used for, and when it shut."

"Oh! And that it was meant to be demolished," the right girl added.

*So maybe that's why it's not on the map*, thought Elena, *because it was going to be demolished and so there was no need for it to be on the map.*

"Thank you so much," said Elena, scooching past the girls without a single farewell.

The girls watched her go towards the cafe counter and hand a waitress some money before she left. The woman seemed like she was in a rush. The girls turned back to each other once again.

"That was weird, right?" the left one said.

"Oh, yeah," agreed the other. "Definitely."

Mrs. Sullivan speed-walked back to her car across the road. She loved how she had gotten the same thrill from learning now that she did way back when she was a student. As she drove, the excitement of knowing there was so much to uncover about this town was infectious; Emmett would've been the same, too – eager to learn more. Her initial action of volunteering at St. Jude's was – she couldn't lie to herself – just for something to do, but she now knew as she entered Carson Estate that it could also be a brand-new learning experience and may actually make this move worthwhile.

Pulling up to her apartment building, the rumbling of the engine had been overpowered by a series of roaring cries that sounded like it was coming from the park. Or possibly even from beyond that, once the door was open. Elena knew not to make anything of it – frankly, it wasn't any of her business – but the constant high-pitched yelling made her think a catfight had broken out. Above all, though, she made sure she hadn't forgotten the map.

Elena walked in, the lights were on and Carol was still at her desk.

"Evening, Carol," greeted Elena. All she got in return was a grunt. Placing the map on the desk, Elena added, "Is there any news?"

Carol glanced up; to Elena, Carol's eyes seemed like they were starting to roll to the back of her head. It was a menacing look that made Elena feel queasy, along with hearing the worst possible kind of update about what happened that morning.

*"On?"* asked Carol.

"What'd you mean, *on?*" Carol sensed the impatience in Elena's voice. "I'm talking about the break-in last night."

Carol fully tilted her head up this time before answering. A quick thought came to mind: *I didn't think she had that kind of tone in her.*

"Oh, that," she said. "Look, Elena, something about the C.C.I.D that you need to know is that they don't give a shit about this part of Castlehead. Expect an update from them in about... never."

"Why wouldn't they do anything about it, or anything that happens around here? Coming in just then, I heard screaming over the park. It sounded like, pardon my profanity, someone was being murdered."

"I couldn't tell you, Elena," answered Carol honestly.

Carol didn't have the kind of a social life that would allow her to know, really; that, and the fact she didn't give a shit ensured her ignorance. That was how Elena saw it, and that was probably how most people living in the building felt. The Castlehead Criminal Investigation Department supposedly not doing anything about the serious crime that had taken place that very morning just made Elena feel more nauseous. She told herself, *If this happened in Valeland, the V.C.P.A wouldn't have slept until they figured out who had broken in.*

Elena shook her head and mumbled, "Goodnight, Carol."

She headed towards the stairs, not seeing Carol's slight wave as a response. One step, two steps—

"Oh, Elena!" called Carol. Elena reversed down the steps and Carol came back into view, still seated at the desk, her feet dangling from the chair. "We might be able to get a new lock for you before the start of next week."

Shrugging, Elena argued calmly, "So what am I supposed to do until then? I'm just not going to have a door?"

"Christ, I'm not that cruel," spat Carol. "No, the door still works, you just can't lock it."

That wasn't exactly the best substitute to Elena's predicament, but she supposed it would have had to do for the time being.

"Goodnight, Carol," she said, starting up the stairs again.

She didn't hear Carol's response, for she had surpassed the first floor: "Goodnight, Elena."

# CHAPTER FIFTEEN

## First Day

The days leading up to Elena's first day volunteering at St. Jude's were fairly quiet – if you classed hearing the constant cries coming from across the park as quiet. Elena had very much kept herself to herself, not leaving her apartment any more than once a day for essentials such as food and drink. The reason being, as it may have been obvious to anyone who knew who Elena was – which was no one in Castlehead (not properly anyway) – that she was thinking a lot about St. Jude's and the town as a whole; she couldn't let go of what the girls in the Waterstones had said, what Clarke had briefly told her, and just about everything else too.

Monday morning – the majority of people dread this day of the week because it was back to the grind. For Elena it was the beginning of the grind, you could say; she woke up, feeling fresh in the rundown apartment building she called home and put on what she deemed suitable for a job like the one she had at St. Jude's – a flimsy white top she barely wore, a worn-out pair of tracksuit bottoms that had so many mud stains on them that their original grey had faded, and a set of old trainers she and Emmett used to wear.

She shut the door behind her before heading down to reception where, unsurprisingly, Carol was sitting at her desk. But this time she was flicking through a set of documents instead of writing on them. That was new.

"Good morning, Carol," said Mrs. Sullivan cheerfully.

"Mornin', Elena," responded Carol in a much less enthusiastic pitch – fumbled and uninterested. Elena stood in front of the desk, leaning forward as if to rest when really she was trying to get a cheeky glimpse at the documents. Carol glanced up. "The council," she spat.

"I'm sorry?" said Elena, acting confused.

"These documents," Carol clarified. "They're from the Mayor's Office. They think I shit money."

"Okay, well…" Elena was stumped, trying to consider ways to divert the conversation onto something more appropriate. "Is there any news on the lock and the intruder from last week?"

Carol's eyes were set on the documents, not Elena, as she replied bluntly, "Lock should be fixed today, and there's nothing on the break-in."

"Still nothing!?"

"You seem shocked," Carol answered bluntly.

"They're the police of this town!" Elena growled. Carol looked up. "I understand having other things to take care of but, for heaven's sake, surely they have enough officers to work on more crimes than just one!"

"It's all that Sharron Rose malarkey; that's they're main priority," Carol established, seeming to also be offended by the idea that the Castlehead Criminal Investigation Department didn't frankly give a rat's arse. Then she looked Elena up and down. "And where're you off to? You look like a chimney sweep from the Victorian times."

"Oh, this?"

Elena looked herself up and down. She didn't like wearing this kind of stuff. *Icky Elena Sullivan! Dirty!* But a thought flashed in her mind…

*"You're in Castlehead, Elena!"* That voice… *"Nobody will care."*

"This," Elena continued, listening to her head, "is what I'm wearing today. I'm helping out with the St. Jude's refurbishment."

Carol's eyebrows rose, and she exclaimed, "Bloody hell, I wouldn't go anywhere near that place. Some mental stories have come out of there."

This was Elena's chance to get some intel. Reliable or not, it was still intel at least.

"Yeah? What kind of stories?" she wondered.

"Depends on who you ask, really," said Carol, shrugging. "People say it was meant to help the unfortunate and unwell. Others say it was practically a torture chamber."

"How come?"

"Once you walked in," Carol said slowly, "nobody would come out the same. That's what they say, anyways."

"Who's *they*?"

"The papers, news channels, anyone who would make money from a false headline."

"Ah, right. The man I spoke to about the job said they're refurbishing it into a hotel. Very exclusive, apparently."

Carol scoffed and said, "Only someone with one brain cell would want to stay there."

"So do you believe the stories?" asked Elena.

"God, you don't stop, do you? I like to say that if you haven't witnessed something, you're in no place to have an opinion about it."

It made a lot of sense to Elena that someone like Carol would say such a thing. That must've been why she seemed so dormant from everyone else, distancing herself from the outside world.

"Hmm," said Elena. Perhaps it was best to leave the conversation at that. "Okay, well, I'm going to go."

She began to turn, but Carol stopped her by saying, "I don't know if you'll find out much about that place, but one thing's better than nothing."

Elena left the building and went off to the St. Jude's Medical Institute with that last sentence looming in the back of her mind. She knew how true it was.

St. Jude's stood, as dormant as a volcano. It dominated the top of the hill, although it was as frail as someone in their nineties. It was truly a sight to behold, especially for someone who was a student of many academics, as was Elena. She parked up by the line of vans that were still fixed in the same place they were over the previous week, and there was Clarke Smith to meet her at the gate. His arms were racks for the folded clothes he held.

"Good morning, Mrs. Sullivan," he greeted her as she got out of the car and closed the door. "You're actually the first one here."

Now standing in front of Clarke, Elena asked, "Really? Where is everyone?"

She looked around. The row of vans told her that she was most likely the last one there.

"Everyone will come as the day goes on," Clarke explained, thrusting the folded clothes in front of her. They were overalls, matching Clarke's. She took them as he added, "I actually wanted to talk to you before everyone came, too, to be completely honest with you, Mrs. Sullivan. Put those on and I'll show you around and tell you what the plan is going forward."

Clarke walked off and Elena did as she was told. Though she put the overalls over the clothes she chose to wear that day, it wasn't exactly appropriate to be changing outdoors. She did it anyway; there was no need to cause a fuss.

Once the overalls were on, and they had started crawling up her backside irritably, Elena met Clarke at the main door to the institute. The door outshone the rest of the building, being a fresh white with golden hinges and a handle. They must've just put it in place.

"So, what is it exactly that you want me to do, Mr. Smith?" asked Elena.

Clarke jerked his head towards the door, and said, "Follow me." He opened the door and the pair walked into an area with a countertop covered in a plastic sheet; the floor was blanketed in a thick cloth. The entire interior had that thick intoxicating smell of paint. Directly in front of them was a narrow hallway, brightened by flickering lights, and they took the hallway down in what Elena suspected to be the main area of the institute back when it had been a hospital. Clarke added, trying not to trip over the cloth, "We've already had the new flooring fitted. So, before anything else, we're just painting the walls. Once we get those done, we can start on the rooms."

"Are these them?" asked Elena, directing her attention to the steel doors in the four walls around them.

They looked like doors meant for a jail...

"Yeah, and there's going to be more rooms downstairs." Clarke pointed to the far end of the room where a wooden door stood. "Along with a restaurant and bar. Where we're standing now, we're going to fit in a staff room."

"Is there anything down there at the moment?" asked Elena, motioning towards the door carefully, but not without some growing excitement.

She peaked through the single glass pane that was built in the door; there was an endless staircase heading into a pit of darkness. An abyss. Why they didn't construct the building to have multiple floors instead of building downwards was an odd choice (Mrs. Sullivan had never been in a place like this before) and yet Elena got the jitters when she wondered what was down there. She waited by the door like a child ready to go to the playpark.

Clarke Smith stepped forward and said gingerly, "Before the refurbishment began, we cleared out pretty much everything. Records and archives have been shifted elsewhere."

Elena felt like Clarke didn't want to reveal too much to her, with this being her first day. That was exactly what he was trying not to do. But she couldn't help it, she admired the history held within fascinating places such as this one.

She went on to ask, matching Clarke's gingerness, "Anywhere in particular?"

Hopefully she had come across as curious and not desperate, like an officer interrogating a witness or suspect.

"I couldn't tell you, Mrs. Sullivan. I wasn't the one to arrange for the records to be moved." He clasped his hands, and with a leap in his pitch, he added, "Anyway, that's none of your concern. Now, let's get started."

*None of my concern?* Elena wondered.

With that, she knew she wasn't going to see downstairs anytime soon.

Soon after, Clarke had assigned Elena the task of helping to paint the walls – to add multiple layers, to make sure the white would set and look fresh – and she got to work. In some cases, like getting those intricate details in the corners and edges, Elena had to use the range of brushes Clarke took from one of the vans, setting them down by the hallway leading to the reception. Mostly she would use the roller. That was easier; she didn't have to bend down as much using it.

Clarke was in and out throughout the day; there would be spurts where he would help with the walls, or start on another section of St. Jude's – not downstairs – and there would be other times where he wasn't seen for anything up to an hour.

"Sorry, just the missus," his excuse was. "Very needy," he would add under his breath. Or his excuse would go along the lines of: "It was Madam Mayor just asking how we're getting on."

The more this went on leading into the afternoon, Elena quickly accepted that it didn't matter what his excuses were. This was what most days were probably like, and all she wanted to do was get as much work done as possible. Clarke was correct in telling her that morning that more and more workers would arrive as the day went on, because by 1:00pm the main area of St. Jude's was packed with a range of workers. From fellow painters, to carpenters, to construction workers, there were so many tradespeople that Elena started to feel out of place. It was secondary school all over again; she had no idea what the plan was going forward, or whether she was going to be asked to help with construction (there was no way she was doing that), or anything else that required even an ounce of strength. It was true that Emmett wasn't the greatest at jobs like this either, but his impeccable intellect made him somewhat more capable than his spouse.

"Here," a fellow painter said, his face having more paint on it than Elena's overalls. "Did you hear what happened at the pub the other night?"

For a second, Elena thought the bloke was talking to her.

"Oh, aye!" someone else answered. The sound of this woman's scratchy northern accent forced Elena to tuck her neck into her shoulders and for her fingers to lock. Nails on a chalkboard. "Wasn't there, like, a massive scrap or something?"

"Yeah. Gill and Susan were foaming. All because a lad didn't win a fucking karaoke contest."

The lass surmised, "Bet he was mortal."

"Apparently he blacked out after the scrap."

The pair howled with laughter. How someone could've found that funny, Elena thought, was incredibly rude. Everyone else who was there probably had their night ruined because of that fight. It reminded Mrs. Sullivan of how Carol acted when she asked about the break-in and if the C.C.I.D had found out anything. Looking back, Carol was so nonchalant about it. Elena wasn't brought up to look down on anyone, but in this case these people needed to care more. If this was just a couple of instances Elena had thought, she dreaded what else was going on in this town.

She loved it.

"How're you getting on, Mrs. Sullivan?"

Elena placed the roller down on the cloth under her feet and turned. Mr. Smith stood there smiling, admiring the paint on the wall and looking at Elena approvingly for her great efforts.

"Yeah, I think I'm doing okay for my first day," said Elena.

They both stood back and looked around. Everyone was getting on with what they needed to do. Elena noticed planks of wood had been placed in the middle of the area. They would be for the new staff room Clarke had told her about that morning.

"There's still loads to do, but keep it up. Thanks again for the help, Mrs. Sullivan. It was very kind of you to offer."

"To be completely honest, I just needed something to do."

They both chuckled, but it was the truth.

"Yeah, I understand what you mean," said Clarke, stuffing his hands in his pockets and huffing out a gust of air. "Don't get me wrong, I love owning the pharmacy but it's sometimes good to do something different."

Elena nodded and said, "Yeah, you're right."

Clarke added, "But always remember what's important. People lose themselves when they forget."

What exactly was important to Elena? That was the question at that moment. Emmett, for one; that was the most important thing in her life. *But he's gone.* What else was there, then? To be happy. That was a good one. A priority even. That was why she had moved... wasn't it? Valeland had been a reminder of Emmett, and the life they had. She was happy then, that was important. Was she happy now? Perhaps *that* was the question.

She was quickly growing to like this guy, Clarke Smith. It seemed like he was a man who stood by his morals. That could be either a good or bad trait in people, depending on how they presented themselves and those morals. Mrs. Sullivan began to reconsider a certain offer.

"Mr. Smith?" she started.

"Yes?"

"Is the offer to come for dinner still on the table? I was rude the other day not accepting, and I would love to meet your family."

"Of course, Mrs. Sullivan! I'd love for you to come over. How does the end of the week sound? The twentieth?"

With a nod and a genuine smile, Elena said, "This Friday? That sounds great."

Amidst this conversation, and the others that happened around them, there was the faint sound of approaching sirens. A few minutes later, there was a knock on the front door. Clarke raised a finger, excusing himself to attend to the door. From the sirens, everyone had a good idea who it was. They were right.

Clarke returned, leading Chief Derek Pattison of the C.C.I.D through the hallway. It wasn't just those two, Elena noticed thanks to the shadows gliding towards them on the walls. A woman was with them too.

"Good afternoon, everyone," she said, taking the lead.

Everyone stopped what they were doing, and a sudden rumble of whispers grew.

"What the fuck?" one man said.

A woman leaned towards the woman next to her and said, "What's Madam Mayor doing here?"

Mrs. Sullivan heard the comment. That's who that slim woman was, her dress darker than her skin, complimenting her figure.

Madam Mayor stood in the centre where the planks were and said, "I thought I'd come to see how everything was going. It's looking good, but remember we are on a schedule. We've almost completed planning for the grand opening ceremony."

Clarke stepped forward, entering the mayor's peripheral vision.

"Madam Mayor," he said, sounding panicked suddenly, "with the utmost respect I must tell you we aren't as far into the project as you may think." Past the mayor's shoulder, Clarke caught Pattison shooting him a glare. "We need more time," he pleaded.

Madam Mayor looked around at all the workers, what they had done thus far, then back at the chief. Pattison also looked around, and to his left noticed a very familiar woman. She was watching on like everyone else. An immediate bad judgement call on Clarke's part for hiring a crazed bitch like Mrs. Elena Sullivan. Chief Pattison had to think on his feet.

"Okay, fine," the mayor obliged, caving into the begging look Clarke gave.

Mrs. Sullivan locked eyes with Pattison for a split second. She gave a slight wave, remembering him from Wardle Gardens.

The chief leaned forward. Madam Mayor shivered at the breath she sensed by her ear. She glanced up at Pattison; he seemed worried suddenly.

He kept an eye on Mrs. Sullivan as he whispered to his mayor, "Madam Mayor, can I have a word with Clarke for a moment?"

Clarke remained still. He hadn't heard what the chief had asked.

"Okay, but make it quick, Derek," said the mayor. "I need to get back to the office."

Pattison retained his straight stature as he said firmly, "Clarke, I need to have a word."

The C.C.I.D chief led the pharmacist through to the reception area, and they stopped by the front entrance. There was a sudden fear in the chief's eyes that Clarke hadn't seen before. Pattison's eyebrows sharpened. He clenched his fists by his side. Clarke had no clue what this sudden change in mood was about.

"What's the matter?" whispered Clarke.

"What is *she* doing here?" hissed the chief.

"I'm sorry, I don't—"

"Elena Sullivan!" the chief clarified. He hoped she hadn't heard. After a beat, and after having received no response, Pattison was clear to continue. "Why is she working here?"

"She... volunteered."

"And you just gave the job to her?"

Clarke explained, "We need as much help as we can get, Chief." Off the chief folding his arms and grunting, Clarke added, "What exactly is the problem, anyway?"

Pattison glanced back down the hall. No one was there. They were in the clear, still, and the chief could tell Clarke.

"We're looking into her. We received a tip from the V.C.P.A that she was moving here."

"And that's a problem *because*..."

The chief rubbed his face – Clarke didn't grasp the seriousness of this situation – and after a couple of deep breaths to contain his frustrations, he said, "We think she might have something to do with her husband's death."

"Woah! Hang on a second... You think she murdered her husband?"

ST. JUDE'S — A CASTLEHEAD NOVEL

"We don't know for sure, that's why we need to be careful. And it's not just that." *There's more?* thought Clarke as the chief went on. "We think she might not be all..."

"All what?"

"All... *there.*"

Now it was Clarke who rubbed his face down. He couldn't believe what he was hearing. He stroked his chin as he processed what he had just been told.

"Christ," he exclaimed. "She's coming over on Friday to meet Caroline and Aaron."

The chief stood back, biting his lip. His nails dug into the palms of his hands as everything circled in his mind, like a race gone horribly wrong ending in a disastrous crash. Many injured and some dead. That might be the outcome if they didn't do something quick. The conversation he had with Chief Hughes flashed in his mind. It aggravated him more now than it did back then; they didn't take her in because there was no solid proof that she did anything, and now here she was in Castlehead leaving Chief Pattison to deal with the problem, endangering the lives of many.

"Okay..." said the chief finally. There may have been a way they could catch her out. "I need you to do me a favour, Clarke."

"Yeah?"

"I want you to find out as much about her as possible on Friday. Look for cues, *signs* that show us she needs to be fixed." The chief saw the uncertainty in Clarke's eyes, so he added quickly, "I'm sure the last thing you want is for her to be poisoning the mind of your little boy."

"Of course not," cried Clarke.

"Exactly. She's out of line. I know she won't say anything to the likes of me or Ton, but she *will* talk to someone who she at least mildly trusts. And if you can get what we need out of her, we can give her the help she needs and everything will be fine. She won't be a burden. The last thing we need is another disaster on our hands, not like Sharron Rose."

"I understand, Chief."

"Good. Just treat her normally and she won't suspect a thing. Now, I've got to go drop the mayor off and talk to Anthony. Plus, if I spend another minute in here, I'll be sick. Between you and me, it's a fucking waste of time trying to reopen this place. What good did it do? It definitely didn't help people." Chief Pattison didn't allow Clarke to answer. He turned to the hallway and called out, "Madam Mayor!"

Madam Mayor was heard saying her goodbyes to the workers – Clarke quivered at the fact he now knew he had hired a possible murderer – and she came through smiling. Nothing else was said. Pattison held the front door open for Madam Mayor. Pattison entered his C.C.I.D cruiser, with the mayor leaving in her private black SUV. It was common knowledge that the mayor was escorted to most places. They left and Clarke shut the door, releasing the air from his lungs like a balloon.

From what he expected to be a normal day turned out to be the complete opposite. If Elena hadn't accepted the invitation, she wasn't going to meet Caroline and Aaron, Clarke wouldn't have agreed to do what Pattison asked of him. Nothing was more important than his wife and little boy. He couldn't allow Elena to do anything; he had to keep a constant eye on her when Friday came. Caroline and Aaron couldn't know, though; Clarke wouldn't know what to do with himself if they ended up roped into all of this. *It'll just be like a normal dinner party*, he told himself as he made his way back down the hall. *They'll play their roles perfectly, and they won't know that…* The realisation had started to set in. *Oh, God! There's going to be a murderer in my house.* He had to make sure it didn't go south.

All the workers – Elena included – stared at Clarke as he entered the area. His voice was gone. Even in the dim light, his suddenly colourless complexion was noticeable.

"Mr. Smith, are you all right?" asked Mrs. Sullivan.

He looked over to Elena. Air entered and left his body naturally.

"Treat her normally," Pattison had told him.

"Yes, Mrs. Sullivan," said Clarke. "Everything's fine. Get back to work everyone."

By the end of it, somehow, it turned out to be a very productive day.

# CHAPTER SIXTEEN

## Dinner With The Smiths

"Is everything ready, sweetheart?" called Clarke from his bedroom, buttoning up the ironed white shirt that went with his suit trousers and polished shoes.

"Yes, darling," answered Caroline from the kitchen downstairs.

It was short notice but Caroline thought it was very polite of her husband to bring his friend over. All he had told her was that her name was Elena Sullivan and that she was new to town. Over the few days leading up to the eventual Friday night dinner, however, Clarke seemed to be shook by the idea. When Caroline would ask him about it, he would say he was fine.

Aaron was in his bedroom getting in the last couple of minutes of playtime before Elena arrived.

Looking at himself through the mirror, Clarke called, "Come on, son!"

"Okay, Daddy," said a faint voice from the next room.

Clarke's reflection in the body-length mirror stared back at him as he shakily managed to do up the top button. What on earth was he doing? This night had to go smoothly; all he had to do was keep an eye on Elena and get some information out of her – casually, though, not like she was being questioned by the police. That was all. Nothing more and nothing less. It was that simple. Right? It wasn't like Mrs. Sullivan was a suspected murderer... Oh, wait! What on earth was he doing? Being stupid, that was what.

*Do it for the family*, he thought. *For their safety.*

After a deep breath, Clarke allowed himself to relax and make his way downstairs. He passed the front door and continued down the hall and into the kitchen. Behind the kitchen door was the cooker, stove, and his beautiful wife Caroline Smith attending to the meal that was almost ready. Her usually curled hair was tied back to stop it from getting caught by the smoke and flames that sprouted from the frying pan. The vegetables sizzled as she tossed them. The apron she wore protected her blood-red dress if the pan spat at her.

"Smells lovely, sweetheart," said Clarke, coming from behind and pecking Caroline on the cheek.

"Dinner's almost ready. Everything's set up in the lounge," said Caroline, taking a quick glance at her husband before focusing back on the cooker.

At that moment, a timer on top of the microwave next to the cooker tinged. That was Clarke's cue to leave and let Caroline complete the finishing touches. As he left, Caroline pulled down the oven door. Clarke made his way back down the hall and stopped at the bottom of the stairs.

"Aaron, son! Come on." His voice raced up the stairs and into the bedroom of his son, the four-year-old Aaron Smith.

He had been dressed in a matching outfit to his father. He raced down the stairs, froze at the second step from the bottom and made the leap of faith to the floor where Clarke met him, catching his son in his arms. Both father and son chuckled. Caroline loved hearing that sound.

Clarke held Aaron close.

Aaron leaned forward, as if to reveal a secret, and whispered, "I want an ice cream."

Clarke chuckled again but shook his head lightly.

"Maybe after dinner, if you're good."

Clarke wouldn't get any backchat from his son. As he believed most parents should, Clarke tried to model his son after himself. A parent's job was to lead their child in the right direction. Aaron was a good boy because of it. At a young age he quickly learned the difference between right and wrong.

They went into the lounge; the television on the stand affixed to the opposite wall was off – as it should be when the Smith's hosted dinner parties like this – and a folded table was placed in the centre of the room. Clarke put Aaron down and admired the set-up: a white cloth covered the table, a chair had been placed on each side of it – one for each person – and in front of the chairs were plates and cutlery. Three wine glasses and a plastic cup with a straw stood by the plates. It wasn't what you'd get in a Michelin Star restaurant, but it would have to do.

Aaron looked up at his dad and said softly, "What am I having, Daddy?"

Clarke called, "What's the kid having, sweetheart?"

The father and son heard a light voice come from the kitchen, "It's a surprise."

"Oh, a surprise," whispered Clarke eagerly, bending down to Aaron.

Aaron smiled, beginning to shake his hands. Clarke loved it when Aaron got all giddy over *surprises*. It made him smile, too; Aaron was so innocent, funny, and good-natured. He was a good boy. As he should be. He was going to go places, make so many friends, and make a life for himself. Clarke could feel it.

There was a knock.

"Is that her?" squealed Aaron, now bouncing like Tigger. Hearing his dinner was going to be a surprise, that they were having a guest over, and all of that with the added bonus of getting an ice cream later, Aaron's happiness was uncontainable. He rushed over to the door. "Come on, Daddy," he squealed again.

"Okay, okay," chuckled Clarke. He stood by Aaron in front of the door, wrapping his arm around his shoulder. Turning his head, he called again, "Sweetheart, she's here."

Caroline called back, "Just a second."

"Caroline!" Clarke barked suddenly. Aaron shuddered. "I said she's here!"

Caroline dashed through the hall to the door, wiping her hands on her apron as she did so. She stood on the other side of Aaron, avoiding Clarke's glare.

"Sorry, honey," she said softly.

"And take the apron off," Clarke added in low tone.

"But I still—"

"Now, please." Caroline untied the apron and tossed it to the side, falling on the skirting board below. Clarke nodded approvingly and ordered gently, "Open the door, honey."

Caroline reached forward and pulled the door open. The Smith family presented Mrs. Sullivan with bright smiles.

"Hello," said Elena shyly.

"Hello," greeted Clarke, motioning Elena into the proud Smith household. "Make yourself comfortable." Elena scooched past the family and removed her black jacket, placing it on the banister, revealing a mossy green dress which would likely not be the most appealing choice to a modern eye. It suited Elena, though. It was one of her favourites. Clarke saw the dress and said in a soft, kind tone, "You look lovely."

"At least I know now I haven't overdressed," Mrs. Sullivan joked, eyeing the dress Clarke's wife was wearing and the shirts the men had on.

They all chuckled politely before Clarke introduced Elena to the family.

"This is my smouldering wife, Caroline," he said.

Caroline waved at Mrs. Sullivan.

"Nice to meet you, Mrs. Sullivan," she said, nodding.

"Likewise," answered Elena. "Oh, and please call me Elena."

"Okay. If you'll excuse me, dinner's almost ready."

Caroline returned to the kitchen.

"And this," Clarke went on, nudging a smiling Aaron forward, "is our son, Aaron."

Elena bent down, one hand on her kneecap and the other extended for a handshake. Aaron stepped forward with his father still nudging him and shook the guest's hand.

"Hello, Aaron," said Elena. "I'm Elena. You seem like such a lovely boy."

Clarke nudged Aaron once more and said, "Say hello, son."

"Hi," said Aaron, stepping back.

Nerves suddenly kicked in. This person was weird. He had never seen her before. Why was she in his house? This wasn't right. Aaron looked at the stairs that took him to his room; he just wanted to play, never mind the ice cream, this guest, and surprise dinner.

"Let's go through," said Clarke. He ushered both Mrs. Sullivan and his son into the lounge. "Take a seat, Mrs. Sullivan. I'll get Caroline to bring the drinks in."

"Okay," said Elena.

As Clarke left the room, he said, "Aaron, you sit down where the cup is."

Aaron shimmied over to the seat where the plastic cup was. Elena watched him lift himself up onto the seat, and how he tried not to look at her. He was blinking fast and fiddling with the cutlery. Elena never had experience working with children under the age of twelve, but younger people being nervous when meeting new people was a habit she commonly saw, even when working at the Desmond School for Creative Arts. It was those first day jitters, just in a home environment. The first thing she needed to do was make the subject feel comfortable, making him feel like he could engage.

"So, Aaron, how old are you?" she asked.

Aaron kept his head down as he muttered, "Four-and-a-half."

"Wow," Elena exclaimed, her mouth wide. "Four-and-a-half! You're a big boy, aren't you? What do you like to do?"

This time, Aaron looked up and said, "I like to play with my cars."

"Oh, cool!" Elena caught Aaron's lips curving, just a little. *There we go*, she thought. "They can go so fast, can't they?"

"Yes," agreed Aaron cheerfully. "But not as fast as Lightning McQueen."

"He must be super-fast, then." *Just act like you know what he's on about*, Elena thought. *Look at him*. Her strategy had worked. "Does that make him the best?"

"Yeah, he is."

Clarke walked back in, clamping the neck of a bottle of red wine in one hand and cradling a carton of fresh orange juice in his free arm.

"Sounds like a fun conversation," said Clarke, walking past Elena to where his son sat. He opened the carton of orange juice and started to pour. Aaron reached for the cup, but Clarke snapped, "No, no, son. Leave it."

"Sorry, Daddy," said Aaron, sitting back.

After pouring, Clarke said, "It's okay." He went over to Elena, presenting the wine. "A drink, Mrs. Sullivan?" She accepted the offer, and Clarke twisted the cork out the bottle with a pop. Caroline whooped from the kitchen, and the grown-ups laughed. As Clarke poured, he asked Elena, "How are you finding working at St. Jude's?"

He put the bottle down on the table, sat in the closest seat to where he stood. Now, he could relax. Now, he could try to get something out of this woman.

"Yeah," said Elena, nodding, "I'm liking it. It's something I've never done before, so I will admit I was nervous when I started but I settled really quickly."

"It certainly looked like you did," Clarke agreed. They both took a sip of the wine. "So, what was it like working as a teacher in Valeland?"

*Strike a nerve*, he thought.

"I've always been fascinated with the idea of learning new things. Me and my husband went on to Oxbridge, and we got jobs at the Desmond School when we returned home."

"Your husband?" That could be something... "You were high school sweethearts, as they say."

"Uh..." Elena took a gulp of the wine. "Yeah, if that's how you want to put it."

Aaron said suddenly, "Where is he?"

Elena and Clarke turned their heads to the boy.

"I'm sorry?" said Elena.

"Where is he?" Aaron repeated, oblivious to the subject he had brought up.

"Aaron!" snapped Clarke again, this time more harshly. But he thought, *That's my boy*! "I'm sorry, Mrs. Sullivan. That's not approp—"

Elena shook her head, then necked the rest of the glass.

"No, don't worry," she said to Clarke. "It's just a question." She looked at Aaron. "He's... not *here*."

Elena knew she couldn't use such phrases as *dead* or *passed away* in front of a young child who most likely didn't understand the concept of death yet. If it were anyone else who asked such a rude question, Elena wouldn't have taken it as well. She knew that for a fact. However, she still needed to change the subject quickly.

Thankfully, Aaron didn't really comprehend what she meant by saying her Emmett wasn't there with them.

Clarke grabbed the wine bottle, shaking it as if to ask Mrs. Sullivan if she wanted more. She tilted the glass in Clarke's direction for him to pour. Drinking was a great way to ease the tension; for Clarke, it was a great way to ease the flow of information too.

Clarke said thoughtfully, "I'm sorry, Mrs. Sullivan. It must've been very hard on you."

Like he wouldn't have believed.

But she said, "Thank you." Now it was time to *really* change the subject. "You said you owned a pharmacy in town?"

"Yes, I do," said Clarke.

He didn't want to talk about himself. That wasn't what Chief Pattison needed! But he remembered what the chief said to him at St. Jude's. He had to make her feel comfortable. *Act normally and she won't suspect a thing. Wasn't that it? Act normal.* With that in mind, Clarke had to just go with it.

"How did that come about?" Elena asked.

"I don't really know, honestly. I guess I thought it was the best way to help people."

"That's why you worked part-time at St. Jude's," concluded Elena.

"Yeah, but like I said to you the other day, I couldn't do what the *actual* doctors did in that place. They're the real heroes."

*Doctors are heroes, very true*, Elena thought agreeably. *You also said St. Jude's was no normal hospital.* The girls in Waterstones… What was it that they had said? *Something about the institute only being a brief topic… When it opened… and… oh, yeah! And what it was used for.*

They both kept their voices low, even though Aaron was in a world of his own, sipping his orange juice.

"Were you allowed to do any kinds of procedures on the patients?" she asked.

"No," replied Clarke bluntly. He thought of adding something more. He couldn't make himself sound too out-of-sorts. "I didn't have the qualifications to do such things…" He told her that he acted like more of an assistant than a doctor. The memories made his toes curl inside his pointed polished shoes. *Stretchers… Rooms… Closed curtains… Hiding… Hiding downstairs… Wincing… The sights and sounds, at points unbearable… The instruments they used – Oh, God! The drilling sound, those high-pitched drilling sounds! The screams – who could forget those screams? Rumours can be true. The doctors did what they did to help those people. They're heroes… because they fucking survived.* He had to say something else to break the silence. "But what they went through…"

Clarke couldn't even finish the sentence; those doctors were Godsends. How they managed to get through a single day with those unwell folks, he didn't know. Clarke shivered, and so did Elena at the thought. *Those poor patients*, she thought. Someone walked over her grave and somehow she loved it. There had to be a library somewhere in Castlehead.

Elena replied simply, "Oh, right."

The adults sipped their glasses of wine; Elena was almost done with her second glass while Clarke was one gulp away from finishing his first. It was then that they heard footsteps from the kitchen.

Clarke topped up his glass as Caroline walked in with a small plate, putting it in front of Aaron. The surprise dinner was fish fingers, chips, and salad. Aaron's face lit up as he dug into his food. Caroline went back out of the room to fetch Elena and Clarke's dishes. As Caroline walked in, a plate in each hand like a professional chef, Elena also topped herself with a third glass of red. It was going down nicely, and it would be even more pleasant with what Caroline had prepared. Caroline placed the dishes down and Elena's jaw felt like it had dropped on the plate itself.

A beautifully done beef wellington with cooked veg in a sauce sat in front of Clarke and Elena. For the third and final time, Caroline left the room and brought one more plate back in for herself. Her dish. She sat down in the last remaining chair and reached out for the bottle of wine.

Elena passed it over.

"Thank you, Elena," said Caroline, pouring her own glass.

They were ready to eat.


Like Mrs. Sullivan had hoped, the dinner and wine went down nicely. It did the trick. You know a meal is good when talking is kept to a minimum. As the meal went on, Caroline kept glancing at her son to see if he was okay – he was, which was good – but shifting her gaze across to Elena, Caroline saw nothing in those eyes as Mrs. Sullivan ate. It could've been because she was enjoying the meal, but there was something... *something* about the way Elena constantly kept her eyes on young Aaron Smith. It was like she had been spelled.

She still ate the food, though, so at least a part of Mrs. Sullivan was still with them.

Caroline finished the last of the veg on her plate, cleared her throat after swallowing and said, "Is everyone finished?"

She rose quickly before anyone could respond. All the plates were cleared so, yes, everyone was finished. Caroline snatched all the plates and carried them out the lounge. The wine was also gone, so she grabbed the empty bottle, too.

On her way out, Caroline heard her husband compliment her: "That was lovely, sweetheart. Thank you."

Clarke looked at a smiling Aaron.

The youngster saw his father's authoritative look and shouted, "Thank you, Mammy!"

Clarke then looked at Elena.

"Yes, thank you, Mrs. Smith!" she said. She was completely back with them. "That was lovely." She lowered her voice, directing her focus onto Clarke as she added, "Your wife is a great cook."

"Ah, well, thank you, Mrs. Sullivan," said Clarke. Aaron sat back, his head down. It looked like he was waiting, but his bowed head made him look like he was in a sulk. Clarke whispered to him, "You're excused."

Aaron got down from his seat and darted out the room before going back upstairs. It was playtime again. Elena chuckled at how energised he had suddenly become.

Elena said, "He's very sweet."

"I am blessed to have him as a son," said Clarke. He needed to get the conversation back on track. "Do you have children?"

Elena reached for her wine glass but remembered it was empty.

"No, me and my Emmett weren't fortunate enough to be blessed with children. In saying that, however, I think me and my Emmett focused more on ourselves and our professions."

"Focusing on what's important to you," said Clarke, nodding. "I respect that," he said honestly. "Did you not consider adoption?" he asked.

A sober Mrs. Sullivan at this point would've thought that question was stepping over a boundary. But three glasses of wine in – she wanted it to be more, truthfully – she thought to just see how the conversation would play out.

"Adoption was never on the table," she answered. "If I were to have children, which now for obvious reasons I can't, I would want it to be my own. I know families can be born through adoption, and it makes me happy knowing that people feel fulfilled when adopting a child, but personally the child has to be mine. And Emmett thought the same. I know he did."

Clarke and Elena looked at their wine glasses and knew what the other was thinking.

"Caroline, babe!" Clarke called.

From the kitchen, he and Elena heard, "Yeah?"

"Can you bring in another bottle of wine, please?"

"Yeah, I'll bring it through in a minute."

Clarke knew Caroline was clearing up the kitchen, most probably doing the dishes. He knew to just let Caroline finish them before coming in with more wine, rather than appear rude by demanding to give them the wine that second. He turned his attention back to their guest before he allowed it to get to him that his wife couldn't do a simple task and give them the wine like he had asked. If he had wanted it *in a minute*, he would've asked *in a minute*...

"Was Castlehead a place you and your husband always wanted to come to?" he asked Elena.

"Not exactly," said Elena shakily. "I hadn't even heard of this town until I found an article about the mayor. Like St. Jude's, I just needed a change and the next thing I know I'm passing the ownership of my house to a good friend and I'm saying goodbye to the town I grew up in."

"It must've been hard, moving away from everything and everyone you've loved."

"Very. Especially with my Emmett's passing still fresh in my mind at the time." Emmett's passing was always in her mind. "And it just came to a point where... I couldn't deal with everything all at once."

"I understand," said Clarke.

*No*, thought Elena, *I don't think you do. Nobody will ever understand...*

"I know my Emmett would've wanted me to be happy," she added, "and I am. I made sure I left Valeland with everything in order, and I... it was when I was driving that it hit me."

"What?"

"That I can now live my life knowing everything's all right."

Caroline walked in with a fresh bottle of red in hand. She placed it on the table, in between Elena and Clarke.

Clarke looked up at his wife, his lips curling upwards nervously, and breathed, "Thank you."

That weak, shivering gaze reminded Caroline of how her husband had been acting all week. She didn't know why, but there was something more to this dinner than her husband was letting on.

Clarke took in every word Elena had said, wondering what it all meant. Nothing had been said that could've been used as solid evidence against Mrs. Elena Sullivan, and that wasn't what Chief Pattison asked. He kept that in his head all evening. He continued to analyse what Elena had said before Caroline came walking in with the wine; she could live her life knowing everything was all right... That could've meant anything – general affairs, such as handing in one's resignation letter, or saying your goodbye's – but this was a bloody suspected murderer. It didn't just mean *anything*. From what Elena had said about her recently deceased husband, it sounded like they loved each other as a married couple should. There were no grey areas when it came to discussing their life together; upon a quick reflection as Clarke poured the freshly opened bottle of red, it had looked like Aaron had struck a nerve when he asked where Emmett Sullivan was...

Death is natural, and it's a sad reality that it will happen to everyone eventually. Even so, being a part of life, it's always been taboo and a sensitive topic to talk about... Clarke thought it was okay to discuss these things. He had buried both his parents by the time he was twenty-seven, and as hard as it was, he had a family to attend to and push through. Which he did. So, to him, why was it so hard for Elena? She said it herself that she was happy, and that was what Emmett would've wanted.

*Unless she IS hiding something,* he assumed, watching her drink her… *How many glasses has she had?* Her haphazard posture as she sat, the droopy eyes – yep, she was well on her way towards having a hangover the next day. That was beside the point. Clarke was going off track. Ultimately, he had come to the conclusion that Mrs. Elena Sullivan was masking over the grief and guilt; Mrs. Elena Sullivan was masking over the harsh reality that she was responsible for her husband's death.

Caroline walked in and finally sat with the grown-ups. She poured herself a glass, and now it was time to relax.

She leaned forward and asked Elena, "Do you have any plans for the coming days?"

Elena exhaled, blinking rapidly as if to stay awake as she answered, "Yes. No, not really. B-but I do wan' oo see if… if there's a library here."

"Yes, there is," said Caroline. "You're a fan of reading, then?"

"Oh, yes!" cheered Elena. "Very much so. I-I-I wan' oo read up on St. Jude's."

Clarke's eyebrows narrowed.

"What can a book tell you that I haven't told you already?" he pointed out.

Elena scoffed, and said, "Pish-posh!" She angled her wine glass towards Clarke. "You ha-haven't been living as long as St. Jude's has. I wan' oo know the h-history. You said i-it's no normal hospital."

"Well, what I meant—" Clarke started.

"*And* you said you didn't witness *everything*," snarled Elena. "What the fuck have I got to lose?"

For someone who upon first impression seemed like a well-educated, sophisticated woman, Elena was showing a whole different side of herself towards Clarke and Caroline.

"So, you won't be attending the funeral, I suppose?" asked Clarke.

Just hearing the word *funeral* made Elena's spine tingle.

"What? What funeral?" she said, double taking between Clarke and Caroline.

"The funeral for Sharron Rose," Clarke clarified.

That name rang a bell… *Sharron? Sharron Rose? I don't know a Sharron, but that name…* Oh, yeah! Elena had first heard the name on the drive. Her body was found dead in her home. She thought wrongly, *Imagine waking up to that in the morning.*

But she said, "When is it?"

"This Sunday, actually," answered Caroline.

"Oh… I-I don-don't know," said Elena. "I-well, are you going to be there?"

The couple looked at each other. Their minds were made up, and the excuse was fool proof.

"I don't think we will," said Clarke. Caroline nodded agreeably but remained silent. "We don't want to be subjecting Aaron to that kind of atmosphere just yet."

Silence fell suddenly in the room. They all took awkward sips – Elena's was more a gulp, necking the dregs of the glass – until something else was said.

Caroline said gently, "What'd you mean before?"

"Huh?" Elena's mouth was wide, drool visible even from Caroline's seat at the far end of the table.

"You said about St. Jude's that you have nothing to lose looking into it?" clarified Caroline.

"Well, I fucking don't," wheezed Elena. "I live in a fucking shithole! I have no job! I ki… My husband fucking left me!"

Caroline's eyes were wide with freight and concern. She looked at Clarke, tilting her head towards Elena, trying to give him a signal to do something, to at least calm her down or change the subject.

Clarke whispered, "Mrs. Sullivan, you might want to keep your voice down. We don't really want Aaron hearing—"

"Oh, I'm *sorry*, Your Majesty," she blurted out.

"Clarke," said Caroline, "can I have a word with you for a minute?"

The couple rose and left for the kitchen. Caroline slammed the kitchen door shut behind her.

"What is *wrong* with her?" she hissed. "Actually, better yet, what is wrong with *you?*"

"What'd you mean? I'm fine," said Clarke, his voice breaking and his eyes darting around the room. "I didn't know she couldn't handle her drink."

"This isn't about the drink, Clarke. All week, every time I asked about tonight, you've been acting strange about it. Like you didn't even want her to come. If you wanted to cancel, you should've just told her."

He couldn't tell her what this night had really been about, even if he wanted to.

Clarke said, "I was just… *nervous* about tonight. She's been through a lot, clearly, and maybe she just needs a friend."

"Okay." Caroline shrugged. "But do you not think she's been weird all night?"

"Of course I do," said Clarke through gritted teeth, "I'm not stupid, woman! Don't worry about her, all right?" He lifted a finger, and added in a raspy tone, "I'll sort it out. She's just had one too many. I'll call her a taxi and everything will be fine."

They held hands. Clarke took a deep breath, peering into his wife's reassuring eyes. Caroline copied the deep breath, and after a moment, she believed what Clarke had said; he would sort it out, whatever *it* was.

They walked down the hall, turning past the stairs and stopped by the doorway into the lounge. Clarke raised a hand, with both he and Caroline keeping silent. Elena was mumbling to herself. Clarke poked his head in, and Elena had her head bowed, swaying back and forth. From the doorway, neither Clarke nor Caroline made out what she was saying; after an all-clear nod from Caroline, they both stepped in and sat back down.

Elena was still mumbling with her head down. Clarke and Caroline were invisible to her.

"The car... the fucking car. Fuck off. That's what you can do." Mrs. Sullivan wasn't directing her voice to anyone but herself. "Fuck off. You... you're telling me stuff I already know. Sh-shut up. Go on, s-s-say another word. I dare you. Say another... another word about Emmett. It was... was... wasn't my fault, okay!? It wasn't my fault."

*"It wasn't? Was it not?"*

"S-shut up!"

*"Do you see what happens when alcohol enters your system? People get hurt. That's why drinking wasn't a casual desire, unlike opening a book. But you're weak. Yes, you are! When there's no way out, when you need to find an excuse, you give in to the poison! You weren't the wife Emmett wanted, Elena. You just didn't want to face the truth. That's why you did it."*

Clarke leaned forward, placing a hand on her knee, and asked, "Elena? Are... are you okay?"

Elena looked up and around. Her eyes were full of bewilderment. She was a child lost in the shops, or the woods, and her hands were rapidly shaking. She finally looked at Clarke, and her gaze softened.

"Wha-?" managed Elena. "Wh-where am...? Huh? Oh, oh, yeah. I'm okay." She rose nervously. "I think... I think I'm going to go home."

Before the Smiths knew it, Elena was in the hall by the front door wrapping her coat around her.

"Wait, Mrs. Sullivan," said Caroline, rushing to her. "Do you not think getting a taxi home would be safer?"

Caroline turned to a blank-faced, unimpressed Clarke, hoping he would agree.

Elena shook her head and said, "No, I-I'll be fine. The air might sober me up. The wine's gone straight to my head."

She laughed, but her attempted humorous remark didn't even get a chuckle out of her hosts. Either way, Mrs. Sullivan preferred the walk.

"Are you sure?" asked Caroline, unconvinced.

"Yes, I'll be fine," repeated Elena.

Clarke stepped forward, putting an arm around his wife's shoulders.

"Sweetheart, if she says she's okay then I believe her. Get back safe, Mrs. Sullivan. Thank you for coming."

"Thanks f-for having—" She burped, sharing the smell of the wine she had consumed so readily. "Thanks for having me."

She opened the door to the refreshing evening air, not looking back at her hosts as she stepped out onto the top step.

"See you on Monday," said Clarke.

As Mrs. Sullivan descended the steps to the gate, she heard the door slam shut behind her. She liked the walks. She liked seeing what the walks brought her – the sights, the people, and everything else in between – and she did hope it would help her clear her head.

*"Go on, Elena..."*

Back in the hallway of the Smith's two-bedroom house, Clarke and Caroline stared at each other. Clarke knew that look on his wife's face – the glare of disappointment, confirming she wouldn't be giving him pleasure anytime soon – but he had a reason for just letting Mrs. Sullivan leave in the state she was in. He had got what he wanted. The mumbling wasn't rock-hard evidence, but it was better than nothing, and it was something to pass onto the chief.

Caroline didn't need to know that. What it looked like to her was nothing more or nothing less than a rude gesture from her husband that Clarke undoubtedly knew she'd forgive him for the next morning.

"I'll check on the boy," she said, brushing Clarke's arm off her shoulder. She was halfway up the stairs before turning back around to her husband who watched her. "That woman needs help," she added.

Clarke chuckled, and said, "She needs more than fucking help, babe. I'll be up in a bit. We can just put the table away in the morning."

*A rough surface, uncomfortable on the palm… SMASH! Shattered to pieces, like a heart after a dark truth…*

# CHAPTER SEVENTEEN

# Remembering Sharron Rose

This was the second time in under two months that death had entered Mrs. Sullivan's life, so only God could've known by this point why a little bit of her wanted to attend the funeral of Sharron Rose. Elena sat on the edge of her bed, bending down to tie the thread-thin lace of her black heels and matching black dress. The 8th of March, 2009, edition of *The Castlehead Chronicle* that Elena must've found in an old corner shop sat rolled up next to her. Or it probably came from a bin, considering how crumpled it was when she unrolled the paper. But she couldn't remember.

She read the front page once again:

### THE CASTLEHEAD CHRONICLE
### Date: 8/3/2009

**The residents of Castlehead are saddened to hear of the sudden news that the body of beloved citizen, Sharron Rose, was found dead early yesterday morning in the lounge of her home, Wardle Gardens, with a bullet to the head.**

**Authorities aren't certain why the unfortunate event has occurred so suddenly, but they initially suspect that it had been suicide.**

We were unable to talk to her devoted husband, Anthony Eccleby, or her daughter, Isabella, but on behalf of Castlehead, we are sorry for your loss, and we are all thinking of you at this sorrowful time.

Castlehead residents, family, and friends are all formally invited to attend Sharron Rose's funeral at Central Cemetery in two weeks' time, 22/3/2019, to pay their respects to one of Castlehead's most beloved citizens.

If there was one thing Elena took from being a teacher for as long as she had been, it was that she could easily point out mistakes. Whoever wrote this article – she couldn't find the author's name at the bottom of the page – clearly didn't get it proofread before publication, for 22/3/2019 didn't sound right. Common sense engaged, and Elena knew it was meant to say: 22/3/2009.

Nevertheless, there was no use in heading to the papers and complaining; the funeral itself was more important. Mrs. Sullivan had no idea who this Sharron Rose was, but apparently she was beloved by many. Now Elena was a Castlehead resident, so she did have the option to pay her respects; she may've not known her personally, but this day was important to her loved ones, like Anthony and Isabella, and that's what made her decide to go. People who she barely knew, or didn't even know at all, paid respect to Emmett; there was that moral obligation for her to do the same.

*Emmett would've done the same.*

There was a knock at the door, shocking Elena momentarily. She went up towards it and called out, "Yes?"

In the hallway, Carol the receptionist said, "There's a taxi here for you."

"I'll be down in a minute."

She grabbed her coat, wrapped it around her shoulders, and made her way out onto the hallway. Carol was already back down in reception. Elena was met with a taxi driver of Indian descent by the front entrance, and out front was a grey Ford with the taxi service logo plastered across both rear doors. Mrs. Sullivan hopped in the back as the driver started the engine; as she buckled up, she put her coat completely on.

"So, where are we off to?" asked the taxi driver, watching Elena through the rearview mirror.

"Central Cemetery," Mrs. Sullivan replied, looking out of the car window.

They drove off until they reached the first set of traffic lights, which were red. That meant five minutes of waiting, which would feel like five hours.

"Ah, you must be heading to the funeral," the driver guessed.

"That's right," Mrs. Sullivan mumbled.

Red, amber, green. Ready, set, go. The car turned left then there was an immediate sharp right onto a road leading to a roundabout.

Mrs. Sullivan kept looking out of the window; she knew by the shops that spawned along the road they were driving on that they were out of Carson Estate. Like a child in the backseat, staring out of the window made Elena tilt her head back into the seat. She felt herself dozing off. *No, Elena, you can't get drowsy now.*

"Very sad."

That woke her back up.

"Huh? What?" she let out.

They had only just gotten around the roundabout as the driver repeated, "Very sad, the death of Sharron Rose."

"Oh… right… yes, very."

*Bloody hell*, thought Elena carelessly, *for someone whose first language isn't English, he really likes to talk, doesn't he?* Now that she was completely awake, and now that she wasn't going to get any peace because of this yammering taxi driver, Elena sat up straight and tried to look engaged in the conversation.

"Relative of yours?"

"No," Elena said instantly, turning her head to hide her raised eyebrows. If she was a relative, surely she would've been travelling with the family. The fact was that she wasn't a part of the family. Not a part of it whatsoever. "Just..." she started to add with a whisper. "Just... paying my respects."

From afar, as they turned once again, the church's belltower looked like it reached beyond the clouds. *Like all the way into space*, Elena thought as they pulled up to the front gates of Central Cemetery.

She paid the driver, and as she stepped out of the car, she heard the driver say, "Sorry for your loss..."

Her eyes were on the gates but her mind was on the taxi that was now halfway down the road; she was sure she had just said that Sharron Rose wasn't a relative... and yet the driver still apologised for the loss. *Unless... unless... no! The apology couldn't have been for anyone else.* The driver wasn't sorry for Emmett's death. The driver must have meant this Sharron Rose woman; he could've just forgotten she told him there was no relation there, and the idea of a funeral led to him just saying it. Yeah, that's all it was.

*It was too late for apologies.*

Taking a deep breath, Elena slid the front gates open; the wind must've shut them, she assumed. The gravel pathway crackled like a campfire as she walked up to the church, leaving the gates open behind her. Drawing nearer to the church, she saw that there was a side entrance, too. By the gate was a pile of earth and a newly dug grave – Sharron's grave.

Elena froze as Central Church's grand brown doors opened wide before her; she took a step back awkwardly, shivering at the prospect of the two rows of people slowly walking out of the church believing she was just some stalker. The people were all in black — suits for the men and dresses with veils for the women — and both rows were led by a father and a daughter. *That must be Anthony and Isabella.* From where Elena stood, though, she couldn't get a good look at them, but she did watch on from a distance as they made their way to the newly dug grave.

The guests were followed by a set of pallbearers hauling Sharron's coffin. Everyone waited patiently as they came to the grave and manoeuvred the coffin onto the lowering device. Elena took a step back and allowed herself to get transfixed by the church's remarkable structure. Quite a sight, really. Its ageing architecture was charming, and it made her smile and think how great it was for a structure to remain up and healthy for as long as Central Church had. Her instinct told her these grounds had seen its fair share of weddings, funerals, and traditional Sunday services. If anyone asked, Elena would openly admit she wasn't an avid believer, but it was still something she appreciated; it made her feel happy knowing such beliefs brought so much comfort and peace to people.

It had appeared that all the guests were by Sharron's resting place as they all formed a semi-circle around the foot of the grave. Isabella stood in between Anthony and a much older looking man. Possibly one of Isabella's grandfathers. The doors to the church remained open, however, and one more single figure made their way out to the church's entrance, looking up at the sky.

From neck to feet, the man that stood at the doors spectating the burial was draped in a navy-blue robe. Elena stepped towards him, and she saw he had had his hands clasped together. Noticing the woman that stepped towards him, the man bowed his head.

"Bless you, my child," he said.

He was almost too quiet to hear. Elena smiled back, accepting the blessing. With his quiet voice, and the sheet of white hair upon his head, he seemed quite a mild man; he had an average build and wrinkles around his mouth that he just accepted were there. Certain things came with years of blessing those around him.

*Go on*, Elena told herself. *Ask him, he might have an idea of who Sharron is…*

*Was…*

"Excuse me," she said. To sound more respectful, she added, "Father."

A welcoming smile was on the priest's face as he said, "Yes?"

"Hi, I'm new here and I was wondering if that service over there is for Sharron Rose?"

"Ah, I see," said the priest with a chuckle, "I thought I hadn't seen you here before. Yes, it is. You aren't the first person to ask today." They both looked at the burial taking place, and Elena saw a line of black cabs parked outside the side entrance. They were most probably there to take them to the wake. "As you can see, she was liked by so many."

"Yes, thank you," said Elena. She glanced back at the priest and asked, "Aren't you supposed to be over there?"

"No. Sharron's father, Harold, asked to say a few words instead. They asked me to do the service."

"Ah, I see," said Elena. "I'm sorry, where are my manners? I'm Elena Sullivan."

"Avner. Father Avner."

"So, Father, was Sharron…" She didn't know how to put her question into words. "Was she… you know, faithful?"

"The Rose-Eccleby family aren't of faith, no."

"Then…"

Elena raised a curious eyebrow.

Father Avner finished her query: "Then why did they choose a church?"

"Yes," admitted Elena nervously. "I didn't know that was allowed."

"It's not a matter of if it's allowed, Mrs. Sullivan. It's a matter of why can't it be? Some aren't too pleased with some of the decisions I make regarding services such as this one, and regarding the church itself. But you can't live vicariously through anyone else. Otherwise, why else would God give us our own minds? It's better to determine if a decision is good or bad through time, not when you make it. Take now, for instance, are you, Mrs. Sullivan, going to actually do what you've come here to do and pay your respects to a beloved member of our community or are you just going to try to make up another excuse to keep this conversation going so you don't have to face that fear?"

That got Mrs. Sullivan thinking.


It was an emotional day for everyone, especially those who knew Sharron Rose personally − that being her father, Harold Rose, her six-year-old, Isabella, and her husband, Anthony Eccleby. As it felt for most people when they'd first heard Sharron had died in a *serious accident*, it still didn't feel real.

But only one man knew what really happened. And it would remain a mystery to those around him for ten long years.

Nobody had evidence that the incident involved Anthony in any capacity, and nobody suspected he was either. *Thank God for that*, he thought every time the incident replayed in his head. People had quickly come to accept that it was just an unfortunate event that could happen at the most unexpected of times and even to the happiest of people.

And yet, perhaps Anthony *was* expecting it. He knew that she wasn't well and hadn't been herself for some time. He told himself that some people can recover very well after reaching their breaking point, but Sharron wasn't one of them; she knew *it* – the pain – had to end. She knew she had to end it all.

Maybe Anthony could've done more…

By how many people there were around Sharron Rose's grave, Elena imagined that not everyone managed to get a seat in Central Church. Or some additional seating had been put in place. Those who knew Sharron knew of her popularity across Castlehead, while those who didn't know her all too well got a glimpse of it during the service. Mentions of charity work, volunteering, and her selfless acts had put a smile on all the guests' faces. Isabella, Anthony, and Harold were blessed with the good-natured soul that was Sharron, always seeing the bright side, never trying to let anything get to her… Toxic positivity, some may've called it, but her family couldn't deny that her smile – the smile Isabella inherited from her – lit any room she was in.

Unbeknownst to Mrs. Sullivan, Anthony requested Harold to lead the way to the altar as the entrance song played. He had asked on a day when the sun didn't shine and Sharron's death slowly became reality, with Harold accepting graciously. Because it was his daughter. He wasn't leading the way or making a speech at his daughter's grave for his son-in-law. They both knew, despite their differences, that they had to keep smiling for Isabella – who didn't know what to think leading up to the funeral, because there was no way a six-year-old, even a bright girl like Isabella, was able to fathom the loss of their mother. They had to stick together for her. They had to keep her safe, and they had to do things they thought were the best for her and that was why Anthony didn't allow his daughter to read the article.

"Too horrible," he would tell her whenever she asked.

Another frequent question she would ask: "How did Mammy die, Daddy?"

It stumped Anthony the first time Isabella asked it, but he couldn't say nothing to her so he said, "Mammy wasn't well, darling."

He wasn't lying... just *stretching the truth*.

By the time it reached 1:00pm, Mrs. Sullivan shuffled away from the church and started to make her way towards the burial. Father Avner smiled at first as he watched, but that smile faded into disappointment when Elena drew no attention to herself, sneaking past the crowd and heading for the side gate.

She hoped no one had noticed. She was about to exit the grounds, but an invisible force stopped her. *Come on, what is it that you're really afraid of?* Elena turned around. She had buried both parents and a husband in her lifetime, but nothing could match the pain, she realised, of losing a child.

*"They're hurting, Elena,"* she heard Emmett say. *"No death is more important than another. It doesn't matter if you know them or not."*

"You're right," she mumbled, bowing her head.

She turned back around and leaned against the wall by the side gate to watch the end of the burial. The coffin descended six feet under. Isabella clutched her father's hand, Anthony held back tears – if there were any left – while Harold remained stoic in his posture.

Nothing but guilt. Nothing but relief.

Anthony shivered suddenly. Was it pain? Or, as they say, had someone walked – trampled – over his own grave?

He sighed, "Why didn't you take me instead?"

That was that. The earth had started to cover the coffin, and people had started to make their way to the taxis which would take them to the wake. The guests went down in numbers as did the taxis that waited for them. And for the fifteen minutes this happened, Mrs. Sullivan watched every moment.

The remaining three at the grave were Harold, Isabella, and Anthony. The two men seemed to be talking, but in hushed tones; they had to protect Isabella.

"Our taxi'll be here in a minute, Anthony," whispered Harold.

All six eyes were on Sharron's tombstone.

"Bella," said Anthony, his voice low yet gentle, "go and wait for the taxi with Grandad."

"Okay, Daddy," said Isabella.

Elena saw the little girl take her grandfather's hand and they started to walk her way. They passed her with mirroring smiles and left the grounds, waiting up the main road. Elena stayed put. Anthony looked around and saw by the church doors Father Avner and then the funeral director they had hired to make the arrangements. With everyone gone, Anthony thought this to be the right time to thank him.

He walked up and heard the funeral director say, "Thank you once again, Father, for letting us have this service on your grounds. It means so much."

The two shook hands.

"It's my pleasure, Mr. Montague," said Avner. "Many people believe grounds like these should be exclusive only to those of faith. The higher-ups opted for me to even be laicized, but I pleaded my case and I'm still here. Praise the Lord."

Anthony reached into his trouser pocket and said, "If we're saying our thank you's here, here's a little something." He gave Avner and Montague a £50 note each. They started to shake their heads in protest, but Anthony didn't let them get a word in. "You've done so much for us, please just take it."

"Well," said Montague, "that's much appreciated, Anthony."

"Bless you, my son," said Father Avner, sticking the money inside his robe. "My heart goes out to each and every single member of your beautiful family."

"Thank you," said Anthony with a smile.

With a light wave goodbye, Montague started to head down towards the front gates. Anthony and Father Avner stood silent, letting the light breeze wash over them. But under the smile Anthony presented the priest, there was an unsure gleam in his eye. As if he didn't know what to do next.

"What's bothering you, Anthony?" the priest asked.

*Other than the fact I've just buried my wife...* thought Anthony instantly.

"Father..." started Anthony, shaking as if getting a feeling back into his fingers. "Father, do you think God will forgive us? You know, for not doing more? For not seeing the signs?"

"I think he will," said the priest with a reassuring nod. "Anthony, I believe that one mistake doesn't defy who you are. You can't blame yourself for Sharron's passing, and I'm not going to tell you that the pain or guilt you might be feeling will go away tomorrow. But tomorrow is another day, and it's another day closer to the time you will come to terms with what's happened."

"And are you sure you were okay with us having a service here? Even though we're not of faith?"

"Everyone is welcome here, Anthony. Remember that."

"Okay... Thank you, Father."

Anthony stepped away from the priest and church. *Everyone is welcome.* He walked towards the side gate, with one last glance at his wife's resting place. But it wasn't just the grave that made him stop. A woman in a black dress, with long straight silver hair was watching him by the gate. She looked nowhere near intimidating; she had more of a nervous innocence about her. He didn't notice her during the service, nor during the burial either.

He decided to call out to her: "You know if you wanted to join us, you could've just done so? Everyone was welcome."

"I-I was going to," Mrs. Sullivan answered as she approached the man and the grave. "But… *something* didn't feel right about it."

They stood face-to-face. His charm and kindness radiated off of him, and Mrs. Sullivan sensed by how articulate his voice was that he never meant any harm to anyone. He looked like someone who just wanted the best for everyone. *Quite a handsome chap, too*, she thought. White teeth like cleaned mirrors, neat brown hair, tall and lean – he would've been her type, if she was younger.

"What do you mean?" he asked.

"Nerves, I guess," admitted Mrs. Sullivan, folding her arms and shrugging. "I think I'm still trying to adjust to this place."

"Ah, you're new. How are you finding Castlehead?"

Mrs. Sullivan chuckled and said, *"Different."* Anthony chuckled, too, and Mrs. Sullivan added, "My husband would've tried to make the most of this place, but I'm not him."

"Yeah…" The mention of this woman having a significant other tugged at Anthony just a touch. He had a feeling that this husband was no longer here, like Sharron, and that was why she didn't want to attend. "My Sharron was the light in the family," he added as he looked at the grave.

Mrs. Sullivan followed his gaze and looked at the tombstone:

IN LOVING MEMORY OF SHARRON ROSE
DATE OF BIRTH – 5th MARCH, 1979
DATE OF DEATH – 6th MARCH, 2009

"Emmett made me a much better person," said Elena. "I never loved anyone the way I loved my Emmett." *Until...*

She shook her head and quickly reminded herself that this was a day to remember Sharron Rose. Anthony looked at this woman, knowing how she felt. He knew by the way she talked about her husband she would've done anything for him, and that's how Anthony felt about Sharron.

Anthony recalled Sharron's last words being: *"If you really loved me, you would end my misery."*

And he did. He did it for her.

Anthony cleared his throat and said, "Yeah, the love was — and still is — there."

"Daddy!" called Isabella from outside the grounds.

A smile appeared on Anthony and Elena's faces when they heard that sweet voice.

"Well, I must be going," said Anthony. "Are you coming to the wake?"

Mrs. Sullivan shook her head and said, "I better get back, sorry."

"Okay, no worries."

The pair started to walk towards the side gate. But they made sure it was a slow one.

Elena said, "How's your daughter coping?"

"Honestly," said Anthony with a shrug, "I don't know. I don't think she really knows what's going on. She's amazing, though. She gets that from her mother."

"Yeah, I bet."

Just a few steps away, now.

"Have you got kids?" asked Anthony.

"Emmett and I," said Mrs. Sullivan, "we focused on ourselves. We had each other... That's all we needed."

As Anthony and Elena left the Central Church grounds, they looked to their right and saw a waving Isabella, Harold, and a taxi.

"Mr. Eccleby!"

Anthony and Elena looked to their left. Chief Pattison was walking towards them, and Anthony immediately rolled his eyes. He raised a finger towards his father-in-law and daughter to tell them to wait a minute. He and Elena took a step towards the chief.

The three met, forming a triangle. Mrs. Sullivan quickly noticed Pattison was here for Anthony, and Anthony alone.

"How are you doing, Anthony?" the chief asked.

"How'd you think, Chief?" replied Anthony.

"Look, I'm going to go," said Mrs. Sullivan. "It was nice talking to you." She walked past the chief and said in a low tone, "Nice to see you, Chief."

The chief narrowed his eyebrows and said unpleasantly, "Mrs. Sullivan, it's a pleasure as always."

Anthony didn't make anything of the exchange between the two. Elena walked down the road as Anthony looked back at the chief, his eyebrows also narrowing sharply.

"What do you want, Chief?"

"I just need to talk to you, Anthony," said the chief smugly.

Shaking his head, Anthony said, "No, no, nope. Not today. Not on any day, Chief. I'm sorry, I already gave my statement to the C.C.I.D and the paper. So, if you don't mind, I have my wife's wake to attend."

Up the road, Harold and Isabella still watched from the taxi – Harold more intently than Isabella.

"What's taking Daddy so long?" Isabella groaned.

"I don't know, honey," said her grandfather.

Back by the side entrance, the chief said to Anthony, "Yes, you gave a statement to my team, but you didn't give a statement to me."

Anthony huffed, the chief getting a good whiff of his breath, and he muttered, "Look, can we just do this on a different day? I really got to—"

The chief butted in then: "Anthony, I'm going to make you an offer you can't refuse, so if you don't want to hear me out then go but, in my *professional* opinion, I think it'll be better for you and your family if you stay and listen."

"What'd you mean? What offer?" Anthony barked.

"The Castlehead Criminal Investigation Department believes your statement. I, on the other hand, have my own theory."

"Oh!" snarled Anthony. "This will be good. Let's hear it."

"The C.C.I.D believes your theory, but I went to Wardle Gardens the day after *it* happened—"

"Well done," said Anthony sarcastically.

"No, Anthony. Well done to you. I know it must have been extremely hard for you to do what you did."

"Chief, I really don't—"

"Come on, Anthony. Don't bullshit me. I know you did it."

"She killed herself, Chief," said Anthony.

"Anthony, we both know she didn't have the capacity to kill herself. Maybe something happened and she told you to end it for her. To put her out of her misery, and you obliged." The guilt across Anthony's face started to become more visible to the eye. "It may not feel like it, but you've done the right thing."

Anthony wiped a tear away from the corner of his eye as he said, "So now what? You're going to take me in for questioning, or just straight up throw me in jail and throw away the key?"

"Oh, on the contrary! There's no place for *people like that*. I'm sorry to say it, I know she was your wife, but you knew something had to be done. Why'd you think I'm the chief of police? To make this city a better place. People like you and me know what has to be done to keep people safe. Can you imagine what would happen if your poor, little daughter found out the truth that her own father killed her mother? She's not, though, because as a *loving* father you're going to do whatever it takes to keep her safe. So, my proposition is that if you don't say a word, I'll do my part and keep the C.C.I.D away from the investigation. For as long as it stays between us."

Anthony heard a slight click come from Pattison's trouser pocket, and he glanced down; a pistol, loaded and aiming for his gut with nobody around to see it…

He sighed and whispered, "Deal."

"Good boy," said the chief with a smile. He put the pistol back in his pocket and started to turn away. With one last glance over his shoulder, Chief Pattison said, "Some people aren't made for this world, Anthony. Remember that. Not a lot of people will see that now. But you *have* done a good deed, for yourself, your family, and for Castlehead. This town needs cleansing, this town needs help, and the only problem is that people aren't opening their eyes to see it. I'll make sure they do, just as I have done with you." Anthony said nothing; he couldn't. "Now, haven't you got a wake to get to?"

The chief strode off down the road. Anthony turned around, and Harold and Isabella were hopping in the taxi. Harold was in the front with the driver and Isabella sat in the back. Anthony joined his daughter.

Isabella looked up at her father as he strapped himself in, and asked, "Who were you talking to, Daddy? You were so long."

"Oh," Anthony forced a happier tone out as he spoke. "That was just the chief of police, darling. He wanted to send his best wishes to us, and hopes we're okay… which we are, right?"

"Yeah," Isabella replied.

The taxi drove away from the church grounds, and not a word was said during the entire ride. All Anthony could feel was Harold's eyes piercing him a doubtful glare through the rearview mirror.

## 2019

Anthony felt himself lean over Isabella, spotting the remote sinking into the bottomless pit that was the back of the sofa. The sixteen-year-old's eyes were glued to the morning news, chomping away on her bowl of cereal. Anthony had that *feeling* that something was coming…

"In other news," started Steven, the news reporter, sitting next to his female co-host in the studio, clearly reading from a script as he spoke, "local police have still yet to confirm what really happened that night in 2009, when Castlehead lost its favourite daughter, Sharron Rose." Anthony slowly reached towards the remote, like he was trying not to scare off a deer, as Isabella seemed to have lost all interest in what was happening around her. "However, Chief Pattison has personally allowed us to announce that the force suspects that Sharron's death wasn't an accident, and that she may have been—"

Anthony swooped the remote up and turned the TV off with a single click. Isabella popped up instantly with that Sharron-like look on her face, cradling the bowl in one hand whilst her free hand was placed on her hip.

"What'd you do that for!?" she cried. "We might have actually found out the answer to what happened—"

"Isabella," Anthony interjected calmly, "they're probably wrong. You know what the C.C.I.D are like; they just want recognition for something they're not even a part of."

He flung the remote back onto the couch and added, "If they had found something – *anything* – they would've found it ages ago. Now, go on, get dressed... Now!"

His daughter stomped into the kitchen and placed the bowl in the sink with a clang and charged upstairs. Anthony's gaze followed her up the stairs until she entered her bedroom. The bedroom door slammed shut, feeling like it rattled the entire house.

Anthony paced around the bottom of the stairs between the kitchen and the lounge, rubbing his face down to calm himself. He was mad at himself for doing what he did; Isabella did deserve to know the truth, but the argument that always fought against Anthony telling her was that she'd never forgive him. He couldn't lose his daughter, too... Then he'd have nothing.

As he looked up at the chandelier, an idea sparked up; Anthony leapt into the kitchen and went to the cupboard under the sink. His back cracked as he reached down and pulled out a bouquet of roses. (He had no other place to put them, otherwise Isabella would've found them). They had been Sharron's favourites.

*This should clear the air*, he thought as he walked back to the bottom of the stairs.

After a few minutes that felt like half an hour, Anthony called up the stairs, "Come on, Isabella!" His formal voice echoed through the house. "You're going to be late, and you *do* remember how impatient your mother got."

Anthony checked his Apple Watch on his wrist. 9:45... In fact, *he* wasn't even ready himself.

He heard from Isabella's room: "Two seconds, Anthony! I know! I'm just finishing off my makeup!" In her room, putting on the finishing touches, she rolled her eyes at the sound of her dad's voice and murmured without him hearing,

"I know what she was like. She *was* my mother. I... was... there."

These final touches made her red lips even more red and made her cheeks pop a rosy pink. Not too much to make her look skanky, but just enough to make her look a little healthier than she already was. That amount pleased her mother, and that was all that mattered. It hadn't just been her looks Isabella had inherited from her mother, but it was also her attitude; if she was in a mood, it wasn't the voice of an angel you'd hear, but rather the voice of an old woman's screeching through a megaphone. Before everything that happened, Anthony wouldn't see much of this side of his daughter – and even for a good while after the incident, too – however, it was as she'd gotten older and entered her tween years that the heated screaming matches mainly started.

Anthony looked up once more as Isabella emerged at the top of the stairs. She took a slow walk down the steps.

"What have I told you about calling me *Anthony*? I'm your dad. D-A-D. Dad!" he reminded her.

Hearing this, Isabella grinned and her walk started to become a strut. Like a model, she showed off her knee-length skirt over her skin-tight leggings, her white polo, a smart jacket that went down to just under her waist, and she had the flattest of shoes on too. As smart as a student attending school, her father couldn't help thinking.

"Sorry, *Dad*," said Isabella, now staring into her dad's eyes and him into hers. The tension in Chessington Close was still there, but it had died down after a moment of silence. Isabella looked down, noticing the bouquet – and that he wasn't dressed – and said calmly, "Why are you not ready? I thought you were coming, too."

Isabella kept that evil glare on him, and she sensed that Anthony didn't have the courage. Within, though, Anthony had to appear very apologetic, diverting his gaze away from his daughter. He had no intention of going, not after what was said on the news.

"I'm so, so sorry," he finally burst out, hunching his shoulders to seem more vulnerable.

The rage boiled up inside like a kettle, but the heartbreak was the clearest thing on Isabella's face. Anthony tightened his grip around the bottom of the bouquet as Bella's eyes started to well up with tears. She felt betrayed – again – by her father. It was as if she was being stabbed in the back by a thousand knives, although this wasn't the first time he had chickened out of doing something involving his dead wife, so deep down Isabella didn't know why she was as surprised as she was.

"But it's her birthday," she clarified. "And you lied."

"I didn't lie. No," Anthony argued.

Isabella pointed her finger ruthlessly at him and cried, "You did. You did, you did, you did. YOU DID! YOU DID! YOU DID!"

"ENOUGH!" Anthony shocked himself by how that had come out. The velocity was unstoppable. Isabella quietened, and there was another moment of silence. He thought he had shattered the windows, just as Isabella had felt he had shattered her heart by not wanting to visit his wife's grave. He didn't care if it was a complete stranger or his daughter, Anthony wasn't going to allow anyone to stand there and call him a liar and rub it in. "I... just... can't... make... it."

Isabella started to whimper like a puppy. Normally, this would've been the time to comfort his daughter, but Anthony couldn't stop thinking about the news and what the Castlehead Criminal Investigation Department let them *insinuate*. Not *reveal*. He presented the roses to Isabella, and she accepted them peacefully; not another word was said between them as Isabella brushed past her father and left without a fuss.

When Isabella walked out of the doors, she was in too much of a state to make sure they were shut behind her. Anthony had to shut them properly, yet he did it so softly, in fact, that he barely heard them click together. All he could do now was sit in the lounge, on his side of the couch, basking in his relief that the episode was finally over. Still he couldn't help but sigh, such was the guilt that meant that the image of all three of them together as a family was becoming unbearable.

Sharron Rose had been dead for ten years, but Anthony still hadn't put all the pieces back together again. As would anyone having to live with the guilt… as would anyone who had done what he had.

He rubbed his eyes desperately, leaning his head back and hoping to snooze, but the sweet sound of Sharron's voice drifting forever through his mind stopped him. Anthony felt her telling him that he could've gone for his daughter, no matter how hard it was. He could've gone for Isabella, yes, but he didn't. Sharron always said, back when she was alive and well, that if Anthony wasn't going to join in on a family activity, he could've at least gone for Isabella. He would tell anyone that he listened to his wife, and at points he did, but something else was nibbling away at his patience as well as the thought of his family.

*The lying scumbag*, he thought as he started up the stairs to his room to fetch his phone. He scrolled through his contacts as he walked back downstairs and found the man he wanted to give a piece of his mind to.

The phone rang and there was an immediate answer.

*"I was hoping you'd call, Eccleby,"* Chief Pattison said on the other end.

Anthony pictured the chief slouching at his desk, unbothered, in his office on the top floor of the C.C.I.D building.

"What was that?" Anthony growled.

*"What was what?"*

"You know damn well what! The morning news…? Sharron Rose…? The C.C.I.D suspecting she was murdered…?"

*"Hmm… Are you saying she wasn't?"*

Anthony pictured a smug grin plastered across Chief Pattison's face as he spoke.

"You bastard, we had a deal."

*"Yes, Anthony, we did. But I'm not the one who broke our deal…"*

Anthony gulped, but he tried to keep his composure. If he stuttered or struggled to get any words out, the chief would have him on the ropes.

"What are you talking about?" asked Anthony, shaking his head vigorously.

*"Our deal was that if you kept your mouth shut, I'd do my part in keeping the C.C.I.D away from the case."*

"Yes," Anthony spat, "exactly. So why so suddenly are the police *suspecting* a murder?"

*"Anthony,"* started the chief, *"for ten years I've managed to keep my team away from what really happened that night. Your secret isn't the only one I keep, so much so it's become a running joke that the C.C.I.D are notoriously bad at what they do. I told you ten years ago what I do as police chief is for this town. For a better future. Nothing more, nothing less. I do what's right, and for a moment there, I had faith that you would do the right thing, too. However, like this town, you've disappointed me."*

"Chief, I swear I—"

*"Who did you tell?"*

"Nobody…"

*"Stop setting yourself up for a worse outcome, Anthony… Just tell me. Tell me, and I'll make it all go away."*

Anthony thought for a moment, and answered once more, "Nobody."

*"Really?"* the chief asked. *"Really?"* He was as calm as he had been this entire conversation. It was scary. *"Well, let me cast your mind back to the Christmas holidays... December, 2018... Thomas... Hill... High..."*

Anthony felt like throwing up his entire insides.

He muttered, "H-how...? W-wha-? How did you...?"

*"Ah, so you did tell someone?"* clarified the chief with a content sigh.

"How did you know?"

*"This is my town, Anthony. I know a lot of different people in a lot of different places, who'll be willing to do anything for me. That is because they can see what I'm trying to do. I thought you knew that."* The chief almost sounded disheartened. *"Clearly I was wrong. With Sharron, you helped me."*

"What?" managed Anthony.

*"She would've died either way, Anthony,"* clarified Pattison with a chuckle. *"Whether in the hospital, your sitting room... or even St. Jude's along with that nutter who came here from Valeland. You really thought putting Sharron in that freak house would've helped her? Everyone thought that place was built to cure people..."* Another chuckle. *"Look at how that turned out. At least you took my advice and didn't send her there. Shame it's the only time you've listened."*

Anthony dug his fingers into the side of his phone, unintentionally pressing the volume button. He bit his lips so much he tasted blood.

"You're a dead man, Pattison. A fucking dead man!"

*"No... I'm not. And I beg you, please do not try anything stupid. A lot of people are going to get what they deserve, and I don't plan on making you one of them. You will soon realise I'm the good guy. One way or another..."*

Then the chief hung up.

Anthony looked around. He wanted to make himself believe he considered what the chief had told him when he revealed what had happened to the man in Thomas Hill High in December, 2018. However, the more he thought about it, the more he hated himself. To protect Isabella, he would've taken the secret to the grave with him, but he knew it was just a spur of the moment thing... *I just spat it out*, he wanted to believe.

He slammed the phone down to the shiny floor with such ferocity that pieces flew everywhere and landed all around him.

"AAAAHHHHHH!!!!"

*What to do now...?*

# CHAPTER EIGHTEEN

## Day Off

### 2009

Mrs. Sullivan realised that was getting used to the new routine as she pulled up to St. Jude's the following Monday. She hadn't been working there long, and she had no past experience in this line of work, but she had started enjoying it; walking into the institute with everyone already manning their post, she worked hard to get things done – and it was going well. Parking up and seeing St. Jude's somehow still stable, Elena thought of it like a body. The workers were the muscles and organs, St. Jude's' structure were the 206 bones, and the atmosphere the hotel would eventually bring would be, well, the heart.

The muscles and organs weren't functioning properly on this overcast Monday. However, for Mrs. Sullivan as she stepped out of the car into a flock of workers talking over each other by the entrance, it had never been like this before. The commotion, the discombobulation. Everyone panicked, and the truth of it quickly became clear when she walked up to the crowd, asking the reason why they were acting like a bunch of children arguing over the rules of a game; it was because of the absence of one Clarke Smith.

Around the edge of the crowd a short redhead woman turned and noticed Mrs. Sullivan.

"What's going on?" Mrs. Sullivan asked her.

The woman shrugged and said over the continued noise, "Clarke hasn't shown up. Everyone's been appointing themselves in charge!"

"Okay," said Mrs. Sullivan, "thank you…"

She couldn't even recall this girl's name.

"Grace," the redhead said.

"Thank you, Grace."

The teacher inside Elena had started to boil. This was the kind of anarchy she expected from the Desmond first years, not a crew of workers halfway through their life. Mrs. Sullivan understood the situation now, and she made her way through the crowd to the centre. All eyes needed to be on her. A common technique used to shut the students up in class was for the teacher to raise their hand until they noticed, and they'd gather that the teacher was waiting for them to pay attention. That wouldn't have worked in this situation; these weren't kids.

"Quiet!" she roared, her voice cracking. Everyone turned to Elena in the centre of the crowd. She cleared her throat and added, "Right, let's do this like adults. As Clarke would be expecting us to work. It's come to my understanding he hasn't shown up today. I'll find out what's happened. I know he's the leader of this operation under the mayor and chief, but reacting like this is unnecessary! Now, let's work like mature adults!" Her tone settled as she asked, "Now, can anyone tell me if we have any deliveries coming today?"

"Yes," a man a couple rows back called out, "carpets for the rooms, and the bed frames."

"Okay, great," said Elena. "A small group of you shall focus on bringing those in today, and please make sure they have the right order. Everyone else, we're moving onto the rooms and downstairs today. If any of the walls need an extra

layer of paint or two, you know what to do. Any questions?"
*Silence…* "No? Let's get started."

She had been working there a little over a week, but it
already felt natural. Every day Mrs. Sullivan had been there,
Clarke Smith was there, too; as she painted, or helped to bring
stuff in and out of the institute, Clarke was always there, either
overseeing everything that went on or getting himself involved.
The day went on and it didn't feel right without him there.
Elena didn't have his number to check up on him, nobody
knew why he wasn't in, and he hadn't even found the time to
give them a heads-up about this concerning absence. Was it a
sudden fever? Probably not in mid-March, no. Had something
happened to Aaron or Caroline? Oh, no! Elena hoped to God
nothing like that had happened!

More so after the dinner she had with the Smiths, Elena
appreciated Clarke taking her in and making her one of the
townsfolk. She had to do something. Clarke not being in
wasn't right. *Something* wasn't right. Not knowing what that
*something* was niggled at her until the end of the shift.

# CHAPTER NINETEEN

## Actions Have Consequences

Chief Pattison knew by the faraway look in his eye, the dishevelled hair and the unkempt beard that was settling in for the long haul, that Clarke Smith hadn't slept ever since the reports came in about what happened to his pharmacy – back on Sunday morning. Sunday and Monday night were everlasting to Clarke; the chief hadn't got any officers to examine the scene until Monday, not even Taylor (whom everyone knew Pattison didn't want on the force), and not knowing how serious the situation was kept him up all night.

Clarke stood next to the chief, and they both examined the front of the pharmacy. No other officers were at the scene, but the chief had informed Mr. Smith the previous day that officers had taped up the entrance and the front window that had been smashed had been boarded up.

"Could it have been kids messing about?" suggested Clarke naively.

"I don't think so, Clarke," said the chief. He shook his head and added as he took a step closer to the taped entrance, "Deputy Ton stated that somebody tried to stop whoever this person is, but a further accident was caused. Paramedics were called that night, too."

"Bloody hell," exclaimed Clarke. "I don't get it. Something like this has never happened before."

"Are you insured?" asked the chief.

"You have to be when you're in business, Chief. But I'm going to have to take some time to sort out the affairs."

"Of course, Clarke. I'm sorry about this," the chief said solemnly.

"Don't be. It's not your fault." Clarke wiped his face down with his palm. He knew the window would be fixed, and soon enough his pharmacy would reopen too, but that didn't mean what had happened killed him inside. "This is my livelihood, Chief. I don't care if someone breaks a window, or breaks in, nobody's going to take that away from me."

"Definitely not," mumbled the chief, his eyes still on the shop.

He had a theory.

"So, do you have an idea who might've done it?" asked Clarke.

"Yes, I do."

Off the sly grin the chief presented, Clarke knew exactly what he was insinuating.

"No, I'm sorry, Chief, I don't think it's her. Remember, she was at mine for dinner the night it happened."

"That is true, but you have to remember we received a call around midnight. The time adds up, and she's not—"

"Yes, I know she's not right in the head! But how do you suppose we catch her when there's no evidence against her? I've already told you she didn't reveal much at the dinner."

"Uh-uh-uh," said the chief, shaking his finger, clearly implying he disagreed with Clarke. "From an outside perspective, you'd think she's just grieving. Grieving badly, at that. She's also riddled by guilt. You told me nothing much was brought up about Emmett's death..."

"Yes, that's common with most people who grieve a loss. They don't like to talk about it."

"But the reason she doesn't want to talk about it *isn't* because she's grieving. It's because she's scared she'll let something slip... *The car.*"

"It's not evidence, though, Chief. All that night proved was that she's a sad, lonely, challenged woman." Clarke motioned to the shop and added passionately, "But *this*, this is evidence that someone is out to hurt me. Or even worse, my family. And I'm not losing the most important things in my life over a rock being put through my window."

"Okay, okay," said the chief soothingly, "I understand. Are there any cameras in your shop that might've captured anything?"

Clarke said, deflated after his (what the chief saw it as) rant, "No, I've already checked."

The chief bit his lip.

"Right, okay. I'll have to get someone to look into the security footage around here."

Behind them, they heard a powerful engine coming to a stop. Chief Pattison and Clarke turned around to see a chauffeur of a black SUV open the rear door closest to the curb. In black heels, tight jeans and a jacket (very casual for someone of her stature) Madam Mayor stepped out. She glared sharply at the chief and Clarke, then looked past them at the pharmacy. She wasn't impressed.

"Madam Mayor," said both the chief and Clarke.

"Chief. Mr. Smith," said the mayor.

"What are you doing here?" asked Clarke.

Madam Mayor explained, "I found some time out of my day to come down to see how everything at St. Jude's was going, but then I heard about this and presumed you'd be here."

"Clarke," said Pattison quickly, "I'll look into the footage to see if I can find anything else."

Then, the chief walked off around the corner to where he had parked his police cruiser. Madam Mayor and Clarke stood staring at each other. Clarke's knees began to wobble. He couldn't figure out why he felt nervous all of a sudden; it could've had something to do with the fact he wasn't at St. Jude's and he thought the mayor expected him to be there. There she was, but not disappointed. She stood authoritatively but had an empathetic glimmer in her eye.

"I'm sorry this happened," said Madam Mayor softly, turning to look at the store.

Clarke let out a forced chuckle and said, "Yeah, a lot of people are apparently."

He thought straight after saying that the mayor would be offended. But off her look, still an empathetic one, she wasn't.

"I understand needing to take time off, Clarke," she said. "I don't want you to feel like you *need* to work at St. Jude's."

Clarke Smith knew how important reopening St. Jude's was to Madam Mayor. It was actually how important it was to her that made him sign on for the job. She had a vision; the St. Jude's Medical Institute had also been a vision — to help people. Chief Pattison, on the other hand, had a *different* vision. Clarke sensed that. The whole plan of trying to find out information about Mrs. Sullivan's life, the whole idea that she was the one behind vandalising Clarke's life's work, and the whole theory of Mrs. Sullivan being a murderer thing, it made Clarke wonder why they hadn't just recommended a specialist to help her. If she had lived in Castlehead when the institute was open, there was no doubt in Clarke's mind that she would've been a patient with these rumours against her.

Inside, he felt sorry for her in some ways. That didn't make sense, he knew that, but there was also that little bit of him that hoped these theories weren't true. Putting everything to one side, Mrs. Sullivan seemed like a genuine person; some would've probably called her *proper British*. He didn't know anyone personally who called her that, but he thought that was how people saw her on a surface level.

*Ah! Conflicting thoughts:* they're what make us human.

"Thank you, Madam Mayor," said Clarke sincerely.

"Hopefully everything will be sorted before the ceremony," said the mayor brightly.

Clarke said, not so brightly, his mind still racing, "Yeah? I hope so, too."

St. Jude's was the least of his concerns.

"The ceremony has been booked. A few weeks until it takes place," announced the mayor. Clarke snapped his head towards her. She went on. "This *incident* shouldn't derail the schedule?"

"No," said Clarke blithely. "I'll just let the team know I won't be there until further notice." Then an idea sparked… "I'll get Mrs. Sullivan to give me regular updates so I can pass them onto you or Pattison."

"Okay, that sounds great. Thank you, Clarke."

Madam Mayor reversed and jumped back into her car. Not a wave goodbye or anything; she had driven off, leaving Clarke to concede with the closure of his business until everything was back in order.

*Everything will be okay,* he thought. *Don't lose your head over it. The chief will come back soon enough with the footage and you'll see, Clarke. It'll all be just a huge misunderstanding. Just some kids goofing about. That's all. In that case, there's no need to take further action…*

*Mrs. Sullivan, you still have to consider her. Don't forget! Don't forget that she got herself pissed at the dinner. Don't forget she's a murd… No, she's not! There's no proof. Pattison just wants it to be true so this mess can be put to bed. Yes… But…*

He couldn't stop himself from thinking: *What if the chief's right?*

What if Chief Derek Pattison was right all along? About everything?

*Then everything will be okay.*

# CHAPTER TWENTY

## Faint, Paint, And Pain

A couple of days had passed and Mrs. Sullivan took up the role of leader when she was at St. Jude's. Everyone was working accordingly, even Elena – she still had to contribute – and slowly but surely everything was beginning to come together. The bed frames had been delivered on time, as did the carpets. There were still rooms to go over with paint, but that was the least of the crew's worries.

As was the case with the students she had taught once upon a time, there seemed to be more enthusiasm radiating off the workers when the middle of the week came. And as she guaranteed, it was because the week's end was within arm's reach. The building rumbled with conversation and hard work – a comfortable atmosphere, Elena thought – and there was no sign of anyone slipping.

The reception had started to resemble Madam Mayor's vision of a hotel reception rather than the dull entrance to a medical institute. The protective cloth had been removed from the floor, showing off the glistening marble floor that led through the main hallway into the main hotel area. Construction had begun on the new staff room that was planned to be in the centre of this main area, surrounded by the newly painted white walls and the strong doors of the rooms. Work still needed to be done on the rooms at this stage, that was the workers' main priority.

Update on downstairs: Barely been touched.

"It looks great," said Elena, admiring the practically finished reception area alongside the redhead girl Mrs. Sullivan quickly remembered this time her name was Grace.

"Yeah, it really does," agreed Grace.

Update on Clarke's presence on this day: Absent-

Clarke walked in, his jaw falling at the sight of the reception. Elena and Grace hadn't yet noticed him, until thirty seconds later.

"Wow. Brilliant job!" he said gaily, forming a wide smile.

Elena and Grace turned around.

"Emmett- Clarke!" Elena hoped neither Grace or Clarke caught that slip-up. "Where have you been? We haven't heard from you in days!"

"How have you been?" asked Grace.

"Yes, yes, I'm fine," said Clarke, motioning with his hands for them to settle down. "It's actually why I'm here. Mrs. Sullivan, can I have a word outside?"

"Of course," said Elena. Before leaving, she murmured to Grace, "Keep an eye on everything."

It was spitting outside. Mrs. Sullivan had to fold her arms for warmth, for all she had on was a stained top and bottoms she had worn for three consecutive days. She had started to taste the scent, never mind smell it. They stood by the row of vans.

They were close enough for Elena to also get a gust of coffee breath as Clarke said, "I'm sorry I haven't said anything about not being in recently. Everything's just *a lot*, at the moment. I was meant to come in yesterday to talk to you, but I got caught up in *stuff*."

"What's happened? You *can* tell me."

"The night you came over for dinner, somebody vandalised my pharmacy."

"Oh, my God!" cried Elena. It felt like the air had been taken out of her. She didn't know what to say to comfort or support him. Looking past Clarke, all that came out was: "That's awful."

"Yeah. A rock went straight through the front window," Clarke added.

*A rough surface, uncomfortable on the palm… SMASH! Shattered to pieces, like a heart after a dark truth.*

"Wow…" mumbled Elena, now with her head down. She still didn't know exactly what to say. "What happens now?"

Elena's stomach started to swirl around, like a whirlpool of uneasiness and sorrow.

Clarke explained, "It's a waiting game, now, Mrs. Sullivan. I've closed the shop until repairs begin. Thankfully, nobody was hurt. Chief Pattison said he's looking at the security camera footage from that night to see if they can spot who did it." Mrs. Sullivan nodded every couple of words, keeping her anxiety at ease. Why did she feel like this suddenly? Clarke added, "So, yeah, with everything going on I'm not going to be able to make time for St. Jude's. Not until at least all this is cleared up."

"Yeah, yeah, I get it." She nodded. She kept looking around, as if distracted. "I'm… If there's anything you need me to do, you know I'm here."

"That means a lot, Mrs. Sullivan." He had set the rumours and everything to one side. It really did mean a lot for someone to say that they were there for him. "Thank you." Elena still seemed distracted; she hadn't taken in the gratification. "Are you feeling okay?"

"What!? Oh, yes! Most definitely!" she blurted out too enthusiastically. Clarke raised an eyebrow and stepped back. Elena had to quickly think of an excuse. "There's a lot to get on with, that's all."

Clarke nodded, and said, "You can say that again. I have to talk to the insurance company about getting the window replaced." He started to walk off, and Elena followed. "Can you let everyone know I've come over, and tell them they're doing a great job?"

"Yeah, yeah, of course," said Mrs. Sullivan.

Mrs. Sullivan stepped towards St. Jude's while Clarke stepped towards the gate. He had parked outside the grounds.

"Thank you, Mrs. Sullivan," said Clarke, getting one last look at St. Jude's and Elena. They were quite a distance from each other, but Clarke managed to see the little smile Elena revealed. "Take care of yourself."

"I... I will."

She turned back to St. Jude's and walked through to the reception. Grace was still there. She didn't have to wait for Mrs. Sullivan.

"Is Clarke gone?" she asked.

Something had changed. The sickly feeling vanished. Mrs. Sullivan took one more thorough look at the reception, relieved, then looked at Grace.

"Yeah," she said, swallowing deeply.

"Is everything okay?"

"Everything's fine."

Elena and Grace walked through to the main area, their footsteps silent on the new floor, and as expected, it was empty with the half-done staff room standing sturdily. Elena shut her eyes and took a deep breath, leaving Grace to wonder why she had frozen.

"Mrs. Sullivan?"

Elena opened her eyes at the sound of her name. Back to reality, the sickly feeling was gone and forgotten, and the goal was clear: Finish St. Jude's without any more setbacks.

"Everyone!" Elena called out, her voice echoing off the walls.

Automatically, groups of workers had exited from all the rooms around her and Grace. Most of them were in their matching overalls and held paintbrushes and rollers in their hands. They assembled a circle around Elena. She was the teacher once again, on stage in the main hall of the Desmond School for Creative Arts, giving the weekly announcements. Nerves were non-existent when it came to speaking in front of crowds.

"Yes, Mrs. Sullivan? Is something wrong?" the man right in front of her asked.

"No. I just needed to let you all know that Clarke showed up just before-" That caused an uproar of *what*'s and *really*'s. Elena shut it down instantly. "All right, all right! He couldn't say hello because he had somewhere else to be. What he wanted to let you know, though, is that he won't be working here until further notice. He's fine, so don't worry. There was an incident at his pharmacy recently, and he needs to focus on that. So, to help him, we need to get on with what we've been doing, and make sure everything is perfect for the reopening of this place. Is that clear?"

She received a chorus of yesses before everyone resumed their positions in their respective rooms. They continued on with their jobs, and after a couple of minutes to herself, Mrs. Sullivan decided to join in and do her bit rather than be the unofficial leader.

The room closest to the door that led downstairs was where Elena had been working for the day. She had skipped lunch and kept painting. One wall had been completed, and by 3:00pm she was ready to move on to the wall opposite. The original wall hadn't even been painted; it was just crumbling concrete.

She hopped over to the wall with a roller in hand and the pallet of white paint in the other. *Use the same technique – up and down.* Elena bent down, placing the pallet on the floor and covering the roller in the thick white mixture of resin, additives, and solvent. Standing back up straight, Elena thrusted the roller forward-

She froze. An inch closer and the roller would've connected with the wall. Something caught her eye. Elena placed the roller back down and took one step closer to her discovery. Steadying herself by placing her hands on the gritty concrete wall, Elena squinted and saw markings. They were faint markings; it had become clear as she squinted the best she could that these markings were a series of vertical lines of about two centimetres tall. She stroked her finger along and counted the lines.

*Six.* She didn't think she missed any. The rumbling conversation happening outside the room faded as Elena allowed her full attention to upon these markings. She had no clue what they meant, but she had remembered reading books about prisoners keeping tallies of how long they were trapped for. The markings could've been that. Or something else. Maybe it was just a sign of how long the building had stood and hadn't been looked after properly, leaving the concrete to wear away. If that was the case, then the whole wall would've done the same and there would've been a lot more mess to clean up. Elena concluded they were markings of a patient.

That hunger, that teacher's instinct, to educate herself in the history of this place returned. *Now's not the time*, she told herself. She shook the fascinations out of her head and picked up the roller once more. The markings were the first things she painted over. The squelching sound of paint being rolled onto a surface was becoming satisfying to hear.

Very satisfying. The motion of moving one's arm up and down felt normal by this point. But she still couldn't forget the freshly covered markings—

*Just get this wall finished and you'll be finished for the day, Elena. You know there's more to those markings than meets the eye, but the wall needs to be done. However, those markings tell a story... Okay, stop arguing with yourself. What you really want is for everything to be okay with-*

"Don't even think about finishing that sentence, Elena Sullivan!"

"What?" Elena whispered.

That fucking voice was back...

*"You know exactly what! Stop lying to yourself. About everything."*

Elena chuckled, "I'm not lying."

*"You actually feel sorry for Clarke after what he did to you?"*

"He did nothing to me."

*"The dinner... None of them wanted you there. They didn't even try to stop you from walking home. How could they do that to you? How could he do that?"*

"How could *he* what?"

*"Leave you in that state. Even though he knew all too bloody well you were hurting. You had your doubts."*

Mrs. Sullivan dropped the roller. Paint splattered by her feet. She stared at the partly painted wall. Nothing else was around her.

"He *did* leave me," she muttered.

*"Yes."* The voice was soothing. *"And you did something about it. A good thing. I think you know what to do next..."*

"I know what to do next," she repeated robotically.

She jolted forward...


Grace was the first one to find Elena in that state on the ground. The paint was all over the floor, and a splodge of red was plastered on the wall over the white. Trickles of the red dribbled slowly to the bottom like raindrops on a window.

It was Grace's cry for help two minutes after coming out of her state of shock that brought a group of workers into the room to help Elena off the floor. She was out, and they didn't know how long she'd been out for, or how long it would take for the ambulance to arrive.

Mrs. Sullivan jumped awake. It was that feeling one got when waking up from a nightmare, or more accurately, a night out. She wasn't fully awake when she sat up; the first thing she felt was the tightness of her back from lying on the firm mattress. Opening her eyes, her vision was still blurred. Disorientation was an understatement. Her initial thought was that, from the strain in her back, she was in her Carson Estate apartment.

"Woah! Woah! Woah! Calm down, Mrs. Sullivan."

"Huh?" Mrs. Sullivan turned her head. Grace was there by the bed. They were in a windowless room, like a prison cell; other than the filthy mattress and the bed Elena sat on and the first-aid kit Grace had, the room was desolate. "Grace? Wh-where am I?"

Coming back around, Elena's head was pounding. As well as her back being as tight as a triple-knotted shoe, Elena's head felt restrained by something. A soft fabric of sorts. She touched her forehead, and felt a bandage wrapped around it.

Closing the kit, but with her eyes on Elena, Grace said, "You're in St. Jude's. Downstairs. You've had a bit of an accident. We tried to call an ambulance but Oak Castle Hospital is manic at the moment."

"How-how come?" mumbled Mrs. Sullivan, still adjusting to the bleak surroundings.

"I work as a doctor at the hospital, that's how I know," Grace explained. She rose to her feet. Mrs. Sullivan remained on the bed. "We had to act quickly. You were losing blood. So, we found this room and a storage unit, that's how we found this mattress. Blood pressure seems to be fine. You might have a mild concussion given what we *think* happened. Can you remember anything?"

"Um…" Elena hadn't settled her focus on Grace yet. She was foggy and had this bewildered look on her face. "I… I remember starting to paint the wall. Then… Then everything went blank. Did anyone see what happened?"

"No, but we think you may have had a fall and, on the way down, you've cracked your head off the wall."

Elena started to stir, shifting her legs off the bed.

"I… I need to…" she started.

"No, not yet." Grace knew Mrs. Sullivan wanted to get home. She had dealt with patients at Oak Castle Hospital who wanted to be in the comfort of their own property. And like the patients, Elena didn't argue against Grace's professional opinion. "I'm going to stay with you for a little while, and depending on how I think you are, I'll take you home."

Elena knew the other option was that if she wasn't good she'd be taken into hospital for further examination.

"Okay," she whispered.

Grace lifted the first-aid kit by the handle and said, "I'll be back in a minute."

She left the room. Mrs. Sullivan continued to look around. A few moments had passed and her vision had started to become clearer. All the rooms in the building were the same – windowless and without character. She sighed and took a good look at the walls around her. Fully adjusted and confident that she was fine, Elena saw that this room – like most of the rooms downstairs in St. Jude's – hadn't even been touched.

The walls on either side of her, and the wall in front of her too, closed in – that's what it felt like – when she noticed there was also an engraving on each of the walls in sight. These weren't faded markings, however, but rather an actual word. Capitalised. Bold. Badly written.

*Kill.* That was the word.

*Kill. Kill. Kill.* Left. Right. Straight in front.

The patient who originally commandeered this room had a thirst to kill. *Well done, Elena. What gave it away? Possibly the three walls that read 'Kill'? Well bloody done.*

Grace was more than a minute. It was more like twenty. Elena paced around the room, getting the feeling back into her legs, as if she was waiting for someone to be finished in a cubicle. Eventually Grace did return. Without the first-aid kit. She didn't seem surprised that Elena was up and walking, but she didn't seem concerned either. Worryingly, that tickled Elena.

"How are you feeling?" asked Grace, standing in the doorway.

"Not too bad," said Elena.

She didn't know how she was feeling, really.

Grace stammered for a beat, then asked, "Do you think you can go home?"

"Yeah, I think so," said Elena instantly. She answered when she heard the word *home*. "I think that'll be best," she added.

"Okay, then."

Grace guided Elena out of the room, down a long stretch of hallway. They passed a set of locked double-doors with a piece of paper stuck to it reading *The VIP Experience.* That was the restaurant-bar the crew also hadn't begun work on. A little bit further down were more empty unfinished rooms and to their left was the set of stairs that took them back up to the main area. Looking up made Elena feel dizzy; she didn't tell Grace, simply because getting home was what she wanted.

They continued out onto the grounds, and behind the row of vans was a rusted orange Kia – Grace's car. Elena's

Volkswagen was still parked outside the gate, but Grace shook her head, protesting that she was in no condition to drive on her own. Grace offered to drop the car off the next day.

"Jesus!" cried Elena. "What time is it?"

It was pitch black outside.

"You were out for six hours."

"What?" said Elena, getting in the front passenger seat.

"Where'd you live?" asked Grace, starting the engine.

"Vale- I mean, Carson Estate. That apartment building opposite the park."

"Yeah, I know the place."

The drive certainly didn't feel like fifteen minutes. Because once Elena's backside hit the passenger seat, she fell back asleep. Grace nudged her awake. Elena adjusted to her surroundings faster this time. On her left was the park, and on her right was her apartment building. She took a deep breath.

"Thank you for everything, Grace. You're a good person," she said.

"Don't worry about it." Grace shrugged. Elena pulled the door handle, and she was about to step out onto the road but Grace stopped her by saying her name. Elena turned as Grace continued: "Please don't feel like you have to come into St. Jude's for a while. You need rest."

"I understand," said Elena softly.

Then she stepped out of the car, walked around the front with a wave to Grace, and entered the building. She heard Grace's car drive off in the reception area. Elena couldn't figure it out, but there was an overwhelming sense of relief and joy seeing that miserable cow Carol sitting at the desk.

Carol looked up and said, "Fuck me! What happened to you?"

She was referring to the bandage around Elena's head. *Duh*, thought Elena. *What else would it be?*

As Elena walked, she said, "I had an *accident* at work. But I'm fine now."

Carol scoffed, and said deeply, "You don't bloody look it."

"I assure you I am."

"Well…" Elena was ready for the next sarcastic remark. Carol said, "That's the important thing."

Why wasn't this Carol around more often? Elena smiled and started up the stairs to her apartment. Carol thought not to go into detail about why Elena had the bandage around her head, but if she hadn't seen her return that night then she knew something would have probably been wrong.

Elena didn't even change. She stomped over to her bed, and once her bandaged head hit that brick-like pillow, she was gone. Ultimately, it was going to be the best sleep she had had since moving to Castlehead.

# CHAPTER TWENTY-ONE

## Patrol

Thursday night was the odd night out when it came to patrolling the Castlehead streets. Pattison and Officer Laura Taylor were guided by the streetlamps as they drove along in the chief's cruiser. They both preferred the action to office work, and it was off that similarity alone that both of them would be at each other's throats most shifts.

Officer Laura Taylor fought for justice. She was straight-laced, slim but not the tallest, and she always put in the work when it came to looking professional and solving crimes. Her mousey hair was pulled back into a ponytail, so much so Pattison couldn't help but glance at the single strands of grey that showed. She rarely had her hair down anymore, but she didn't care. She was out to be the best, and the best meant making sure everyone else's lives were safe, even if it meant risking her own. Pattison couldn't deny she was one of the best. He would hold his hand up and say he was impressed with her calibre of work if he had to, but his counter argument to that would've been something along the lines of: "But she's trying to fit into shoes that are just too big to fill. She very often forgets her place."

Long story short, from the chief's perspective, jealousy ran through Taylor's veins.

They trotted along Liberty Street, a narrow road cutting behind the big Castlehead Tesco and a rival store next door. The chief and the officer kept their eyes peeled; it was these kinds of streets where trouble was caused. The cruiser wasn't even hitting 20mph when it passed the back of the Tesco.

In between the two stores, an alleyway led to the conjoined car park. At this time of night, the car park was an empty field. Nothing but asphalt and painted-on parking spaces, some of which happened to be declaring itself to be for disabled customers or for families. Those spaces were nearest the stores' entrances. Another factor that played into the car park being completely isolated until the early hours of the morning was that this Tesco wasn't a twenty-four-hour establishment. Weird, right? But, hey, things were done differently for some reason. In fact, things were often done differently in this town.

"Wait!" Taylor shouted.

Pattison slammed on the breaks and asked, "What? What is it?"

The chief followed Taylor's gaze towards the alleyway.

"Something's going on," said Taylor.

The tall buildings on either side of the alleyway blocked the moon from shining down a spotlight onto the scene. It wasn't until both the chief and Taylor hopped out of the car and got closer that they noticed the commotion that was happening before them.

"Hey!" barked the chief. "C.C.I.D!"

Now in the alleyway, the officers heard grunting and the sounds of fists and feet flying. A group of *hooligans* were beating up a defenceless soul. The lack of light meant neither the chief nor Taylor could get a good look at the group.

"Hey!" cried Taylor. "Stop what you're doing!"

The group spread out, pausing the beatdown on their target. The target was barely stirring on the ground. *Oh*, thought the chief, *so they take notice of Taylor! I'm the fucking chief, I give the orders. I control the situation*. Pattison rushed forward and the group scurried off down the alley and into the car park.

Pattison rushed to catch up with them while Taylor knelt down beside the victim. From the back of her belt, she unhooked her small torch – an essential when scouting out at night – so she could get a proper look at the damage done. She glanced up quickly once more, and her boss and the group were out of sight.

In the moonlight and out of the alley, it was clear now that there were three of them. Pattison chased them across the car park past the Tesco towards the exit where a lever and ticket machine stood. Of course, at this time the lever was down.

"Hurry! Hurry!" one member of the group cried, out of breath.

"Go on, just crawl under!" another one said.

They were directing their orders to the third member who reached the lever first, who attempted to leap over it as if he were a parkour expert. He wasn't, so he failed miserably. Pattison had to keep a straight face, but it was rather amusing watching these amateur criminals – probably kids off their heads on drugs and booze – using all their strength to lift the lever up so they could crawl under it.

Pattison reached them and stopped to embrace what was happening before him for one more moment.

"You know you need a ticket for it to work," he remarked, removing his pistol from his pocket.

The group gave up. They turned around and Pattison held his gun on them. All three of them must've seen better days in their youth; they all had messy hair under the black hoods they wore, their trousers – two of them were in ripped jeans (as if that was cool) and the other was in tracksuit bottoms – were covered in blood and dirt stains, as were their overcoats. They had surrendered, ready to be taken in.

"It's not what it looks like," the one in the tracksuit bottoms said.

All three of them straightened up and formed a line in front of Chief Pattison. His gun was still on them, in his right hand. With his free hand, from his belt buckle, he unhooked something none of the criminals could make out and attached it to the front of the gun.

"I'm sure it's not," said the chief, sounding unbothered.

That *something* the chief clicked onto the front of the pistol was made from a high-quality metal alloy that diluted the sound of the gun when shot. It was a suppressor or silencer.

"No, honestly," said one of the guys with ripped jeans.

"Believe us," said the other.

Chief Pattison rolled his eyes, letting out an exaggerated scoff. The number of times he had heard these kinds of excuses – the fact that people like this even existed made him feel sick. They had no right to do what they did to that defenceless victim back there. If there was a valid reason behind the beatdown, then fair enough, he thought, but from the looks of it and from their lame excuses, these lowlifes were trying to weasel their way out of this predicament.

And for that...

Three whispered hisses followed.

Three men, each of them shot in the head. That would be three fewer doses of poison for this town. The chief stuffed the suppressed gun into his pocket and walked back to the alley. It was going to be a long road ahead for the chief to get where he *needed* to be, but nothing was going to stop him from making this town a better place. He had done Castlehead a great service. He had saved a life. Taylor flashed the torch on the victim – male, around the six foot range, copper-skinned. He needed to be taken to Oak Castle Hospital after getting a close look at his bloodied face, contorted left arm and right leg, shaggy, torn clothes, and as he struggled to catch his breath Pattison saw four teeth were missing like ten pence pieces missing from a purse.

"Let's get him in the car," whispered the chief.

Taylor and the chief pushed the man up from his back – they didn't want to cause any more damage to his arms by pulling him up – and they dragged him across to the cruiser, his arms draped over both officers' shoulders, his legs dragging behind him like the bottom of a battered dress. Pattison let Taylor lay the man on the backseats while he himself hopped in the driver's seat, switching on the engine and sirens. Taylor took the front passenger seat, and Pattison put his foot down.

"What happened, Chief?" asked Taylor.

Pattison kept his eyes on the road, his face emotionless, as he said deeply, "They resisted. Had to take action, Taylor. I did what had to be done." Before Taylor could voice her uncertainty – surely there was something else he could've done? – the chief ordered: "Get a team to handle the bodies, tell them to get in touch with Doctor Medica so he can give us an analysis on the corpses as soon as possible. I want them back by morning."

Taylor said, "Yes, sir."

The chief didn't care for the tone, but he kept on driving, staying silent while Taylor made the call.

Chief Pattison and Officer Taylor spent the night in the waiting room at Oak Castle Hospital while the staff there examined and worked on the man. By sunrise, a doctor informed them that he was stable, adding that he wouldn't wake up for at least a few hours. That was fine. All Pattison needed was for him to be alive.

By 10:30am, both the chief and Taylor were fully awake, thanks in part to the Costa Coffee refill station by the front entrance of the West Wing.

"I'm going to get another one," said Taylor, showing the chief the empty plastic cup. "Do you want one?"

A row of attached blue chairs were against the perimeter of the waiting room. Taylor rose from her chair at the end of the row. Pattison remained seated in the chair next to her, looking down at his feet.

"No, I'm fine," he said, shaking his head.

Taylor walked out of the waiting room, leaving Pattison alone. Visiting hours didn't apply to the Castlehead Criminal Investigation Department, whether it was an emergency or not. Pattison imagined the hospital would begin to fill with family and friends of patients around midday. At least it gave him time to think.

*This is a place people can be helped*, he told himself. *Not St. Jude's.*

Five minutes later, the door swung open and in came Deputy Ton holding a file. The chief suddenly rose, meeting his deputy in the middle of the room.

"The DNA sample we took last night came back," said the deputy, handing the chief the file.

"Any good news?"

"Yes. All his records are in there. I passed a doctor and she said he's stirring and awake."

"Thanks, Ton."

"But you have to be slow with him, Chief."

"Don't worry. He'll talk to *me*."

The chief, the file tight in his hand by his side, walked to the room at the very end of the hall where the man had been placed. The door was open three inches, and it screeched as Pattison pushed it open slightly more so he could enter.

Lying on the hospital bed – from the door he looked like he was lifeless – the man was on a drip, his left arm and right leg in casts. Next to the bed was a beeping heart monitor. He was definitely stable; his heart was consistent according to the monitor. As the chief walked up to the foot of the bed, he noticed the doctors had stitched up his face, just above his eyebrows. The black eyes, along with the scars on his cheeks and chin, would've had people guessing that the man was in a serious car accident rather than a beatdown in an alleyway.

Under the injuries, however, was a middle-aged, copper-skinned guy who, though alive thanks to the miracle workers of Oak Castle Hospital, had very little to contribute to this world. The purple shadows around his eyes made it hard for him to recognise who was standing at the foot of the bed; to the chief, the man's eyes were slits. The man struggled to turn his head both ways, but he managed it under the tight pain that came with it.

"Where…?" he mumbled. "What…?"

Pattison didn't move from the foot of the bed, and opening the file he said, "Sean…" There was no way he was going to try and pronounce that surname. "You're in Oak Castle Hospital. You were the victim of a severe beatdown last night in an alleyway by Tesco's." Sean's lack of response indicated he had no recollection of the night. "Me and one of my officers found you and brought you here to safety."

"What… happened…? What happened to the—?"

"They've been taken care of. Now, as the chief of the C.C.I.D, I am a very busy man, so tell me why those scumbags did this to you."

"I-I don't—"

"No excuses, Sean," said the chief like a parent you couldn't hide anything from.

"A-all I remember…" The air catching the back of Sean's throat made him hack. "I remember walking. I had been—"

"You had been drinking. The doctors found alcohol in your system when they examined you. Doctor Medica told me he had also found alcohol in the systems of the men who beat you. Given your age, and the reports back from Doctor Medica, I'm going to assume this wasn't a planned attack, and that the guys who beat you senselessly were just three kids trying to make a point to themselves. I'm going to assume you had no previous contact with them."

"No… I didn't."

"But…" Pattison tutted, getting one last glimpse at the information provided on Sean's file before shutting it and taking a step up towards the heart monitor. "That isn't a valid reason for me not to pull the plug."

Sean gulped. There was nothing he could do. There's nothing you can do when your life is literally in someone else's hands.

The full cup of coffee in hand, Officer Taylor stopped in the doorway of the waiting room. Her boss wasn't there. She grasped quickly that he must've been checking on the man they found.

She turned back around into the hall and headed down towards the victim's room. On her way, she took that dreaded first sip of a hot beverage she guessed most people hated. The patient's door was ajar, and Taylor could hear muttering from Chief Pattison. Perhaps this was meant to be a private conversation; she stayed in the hallway but kept just close enough to the door so she could hear what was being said. It wasn't eavesdropping, she thought, if it was viable information that could help the poor victim, the C.C.I.D, and the town.

She had her rights as an officer of the law. She had her rights as a human being.

"I'm going to give you a chance I don't give many people," she heard the chief say.

In the room, Sean cleared his throat and murmured, "What do you mean?"

"That file was filled with your records, Sean. And boy do you deserve to rot in prison for life or to have that life artificially shortened. In the state you're in now, either would work. You're going to give me a reason why I shouldn't kill you. Because if I do, it'll be one less of *you* in this town."

The chief bent down towards the plug socket into which the heart monitor was connected. He clamped his hand around the head of the plug, ready to pull…

"Because," coughed Sean, "I'm trying to do better."

The chief released his grip around the plug and rose. His expression was serious, no hint of emotion. *Because I'm trying to do better.* Trying to do better was all Pattison wanted. He kept his eyes locked on Sean.

"Good boy," he said. "But you're going to have to prove it."

"How?" asked Sean.

"Doing better is what I believe in, Sean. I believe this town can do better. To do that there needs to be order. The last thing I want is for people in this town to believe they can do what they want. You're going to work for me and help make this town a better place. The place it used to be. The place it *needs* to be."

Taylor took a step back from the door. The chief had said the three boys had resisted. Did he just kill them? If that was the case, then those boys lost the right to give their take on it. She didn't want to justify their actions unless Sean wasn't telling the complete truth, but killing for the sake of it... It wasn't like they had weapons after all.

What was going on? Taylor couldn't even remember the initial reason she wanted to find the chief, so she walked back up the hall to the waiting room where she sat back down. Did that mean all those times the chief said past criminals had been taken care of they weren't sent to the Big House but instead secretly killed? No interrogations? No further investigations? Bullets to the head and that's that? For what reason? Because it was what they deserved? If all of this was true, then had she been working for the wrong person all along?

Or on the other hand, all these theories could've been that – theories, that was all. Pattison had always been passionate about what he did, and he had a tendency to take business into his own hands when something needed to be done. One of the first things Taylor learned when getting into this career in her early twenties, straight out of graduating from university, was that you couldn't base anything on theories and ideas. Evidence was crucial. All she could work off was Pattison's word about those three boys; he said they resisted.

# CHAPTER TWENTY-TWO

## Library Visit

If you had asked Mrs. Elena Sullivan three months ago that she'd be in a new home in a new town, using her free time to look into a mental hospital, then she would've laughed in your face. Even a few days later, she still felt like she had an obligation to be working at St. Jude's, but she understood why she couldn't. Taking some time off due to the injury she sustained was, looking back, the best option. Elena removed the bandage around her head, and the scar above her eyebrow was a glowing red. It was going to take time to fade, she wasn't stupid, but the pounding pain had gone. That was a plus.

She was going to use her time wisely today and finally take the chance to go to the library. The library in the Desmond School for Creative Arts had everything one needed for studies and casual reading. Walking into it felt like escaping to Wonderland. She couldn't resist the desire to do a full 360 spin to look at the mountains of shelves, keeping all the books neat and in their place. It was like that scene in *Beauty and the Beast* when the Beast shows Belle the library in the castle. A masterful piece of storytelling, that film was, despite the uncomfortable Stockholm Syndrome undertone it carried. Kids may not have been able to see it, but for someone whose specialty was literature and storytelling it was much more evident.

There was very little chance the Castlehead library was as magical as the one in Valeland. Either way, she saw libraries as the prototype internet. Most libraries had a section dedicated to town history. That was what Elena had to look for. She wasn't going to roam about and bring home a collection of books to read. She kept that in her head as she changed into a smart white shirt, jacket, blue jeans, and shoes. Good enough for this breezy but sunny weather.

What a surprise! Carol was at the reception desk when Elena went downstairs.

Elena walked past the desk towards the entrance and said, "Good morning, Carol."

"Mornin', Elena," mumbled Carol. Then she quickly looked up and called out, "Oh! Elena, wait!" She stepped away from the desk and rushed over to Elena, who turned and faced her. She had an envelope in her hand. "Someone came by this morning and dropped this off for you."

Carol handed Elena the envelope and went back to her desk.

"Thank you."

The envelope was addressed to her in neat block writing. In it was a piece of A4 folded three times over. Unfolding it, she saw the same block writing and it read:

**Dear Mrs. Sullivan,**

**Grace told me about what happened the other day. I've been rather busy and since I'm not able to find time to visit you personally, I thought a letter would be best. All I wanted to do was ask if you were okay. I was horrified when I first heard what happened. But I'm happy to hear nothing was severe and that you're taking time off.**

I understand things haven't been easy for you the past couple of months. With the move and all. But I'm here for you, and so are Caroline and Aaron. We care about you deeply and want the best for you. I hope, once you're 100% and everything gets sorted with my pharmacy, we could meet for a coffee.

Until then, I wish you well, Mrs. Sullivan.

Thank you for all the help with St. Jude's.

Yours sincerely,
Clarke.

Mrs. Sullivan held the letter close to her chest and smiled. That was a lovely gesture. She folded it back up and put it in her jean pocket. She couldn't lose it. She didn't want to. It was a reminder that maybe she wasn't entirely alone.

When she walked out of the apartment building, her mind was set on going to the library. That was what got her out of bed that morning. Mrs. Sullivan automatically got in the car and started to drive. Her hands were on ten and two, as they should be. There was no map this time, there wasn't any need for one, and not having it meant she could grow some independence when it came to knowing the roads of Castlehead.

She was out of Carson Estate and remained under the speed limit. It wasn't a target, and driving at a steady speed meant she was able to take in everything around her. It was easier to keep a look out for the library. Nearing ten minutes in the car, Elena found that she was on a narrow road passing Thomas Hill High. The gates were shut, but over the fence Elena saw a group of students playing football on the field. At the end of the road, she had the choice of turning right or continuing on straight ahead; she kept to the same path and, a couple of minutes later, on the corner of a junction,

Mrs. Sullivan saw a red sign in front of a single floor building resembling a bungalow that said: **Castlehead Library – For All**.

*All* included Mrs. Sullivan.

She passed the library and found an alleyway behind the building: parking spaces. She parked up in front of a locked storage unit, and the sudden chill she received when getting out of the car made everything tingle. She shook it off, put on a smile, excited to learn once again, and headed up the alleyway to the main road. Standing by the sign, Elena examined the building like an inspector judging whether or not it should remain up or demolished. This was nothing in comparison to the library in Valeland. It wasn't fair to compare; it wasn't like Castlehead was home to the most prestigious creative arts school in the United Kingdom.

The doors slid open as Mrs. Sullivan stepped forward and she walked up to the reception desk. A young-looking girl – twenties, perhaps (why did girls always look older than they were?) – with curled brown hair and a bright smile manned the desk. Elena looked past the desk for a second and saw the shelves of books, and no readers. The few comfy chairs that had been scattered around for people to get some reading done in peace were barren, the books on the shelves – it didn't matter which section, whether it was fiction or nonfiction – were neatly stacked, as if they hadn't been touched. The internet was a valuable asset to the world, sure, Elena thought, but she knew there was no better sensation than carefully taking a book from a shelf, getting a glance at the blurb, and deciding to have a read. And the internet didn't have that fresh book smell.

Still, Elena didn't need books. *You need information*, she reminded herself.

The receptionist welcomed Elena with great posture and a bright smile. Elena smiled back, glancing down at the receptionist's striped buttoned shirt and the nametag clipped on her left side. *Emilia Michael.*

"How can I help you?" asked Emilia giddily.

*Okay,* Elena thought, *this girl is definitely younger than she looks.*

"Good morning, darling," said Elena, "by any chance do you have a history section?"

"We do indeed," said Emilia. "It's by the nonfiction section. Are you looking for anything in particular?"

"Local history," specified Elena. Emilia looked understanding, but Elena muttered nervously, "About St. Jude's."

Emilia's face dropped. Her face went from welcoming and bright to as if she had just experienced a nightmare. *Is that sweat?* Elena asked herself. Nobody wanted to talk about St. Jude's in this town, did they? Why?

After a moment, Emilia tutted and said, "I'm sorry, ma'am, but there's no books about that place. There never has been."

Mrs. Sullivan wasn't going to give up that easily. She kept her cool, taking a deep breath; there was no need to cause a scene. Elena knew that there were a lot of people who worked in customer services who would just be as blunt as a poorly kept pencil. They didn't want to be bothered.

*But...* in fairness to this Emilia girl, Elena saw her expression and it seemed almost apologetic. Genuine. *But...* she wasn't going to just leave. There *had* to be something on that nuthouse.

Elena shrugged suggestively and said, "How about any records?"

Emilia pressed her lips together and shrugged, shaking her head.

"Sorry," she said quietly. "We don't have that kind of information here. You'll want the Mayor's Office for that. But there's no way you can get in without an appointment."

"Okay…" Elena nodded, contemplating her next move. "So, how do I get an appointment?"

"Oh, it's quite easy," said Emilia, that bright tone returning, "you just call them up-"

"Okay, great!"

"But you probably won't get an appointment until…" She huffed like a horse, and added, "I don't know, maybe 2070."

Despite her age, Elena understood sarcasm – though she didn't quite appreciate it – and this was the definition of it. She thought Emilia was trying to be funny, but the young girl obviously didn't know how serious this situation was. She needed information. Needed it. She *NEEDED* information. Even if she tried, Elena understood clearly that she wasn't getting an appointment at the Mayor's Office. As a teacher, she worked off facts – not opinions; okay, her profession was a tad hypocritical as the whole point of teaching literature meant considering ideas that hadn't been explored before. In this case, however, Elena needed solid proof. Not someone's opinion.

Elena wasn't going to give up. If there was a benefit to working with students, it was that she knew how to make them feel guilty. She turned around and slowly headed for the door.

"Okay," she mumbled, a step closer to the door than the desk. She exaggerated a sigh and added, "Thank you anyway."

Emilia watched this poor woman. She seemed desperate. There was no need to have books on St. Jude's simply because nobody asked about it. Everyone had heard the stories. There was no need for books. She thought about that place, and the history. Her great grandfather was there for the opening, she remembered him telling her. He had worked all over town, bless his soul, just for his daughter and herself to have a good life here. And that included St. Jude's. Bless his soul. It was he who she had heard the stories from. She believed them, and then... *The scrapbook*, she thought. *Oh, my God! The scrapbook could help!*

It had been on display for a short period of time six years ago, but everyone avoided it. *Would he be okay if I brought it out just this one time?* Emilia asked herself. There was something different about this woman; she was the only person who had come in asking specifically about St. Jude's. There must've been a reason why.

*I'm sorry, Grandie!* she thought, glancing upwards.

The doors slid open, and Elena was ready to step out into the breeze.

"Hang on," Emilia called. Elena instantly snapped her head around and leapt back to the reception desk. Emilia went on: "There *might* be something in the back, if you'd like to come through."

"You're a life saver," said Mrs. Sullivan.

Jerking her head to the side, Emilia added quickly, "I'll help you find what you're looking for. There's a lot of crap out back."

To Elena, that almost came across like this Emilia girl was adamant she was going to join her in finding more about St. Jude's. She could've interpreted that wrong, but she'd never met a more impassioned receptionist. Emilia and Carol would *not* get along.

Emilia left the reception desk and led Elena through the library, aisles of books labelled under their specific genre. In a far corner, Elena saw there was a colourful children's section; a spotted carpet, low-level shelves of picture-books and fairytales, and an empty chair waiting to be sat on. Elena suspected it was used for a reading club of sorts. The opposite corner displayed a small selection of DVDs to rent for a week; they were in no particular order, and off a quick glance all the films were from the 80s and 90s.

They continued down the nonfiction aisle of U.K history, and at the end was the back wall and a door that was labelled **Staff Only**. Emilia opened the door, stepping aside for Elena to enter. What they walked into was a forest of stacked boxes, loose files and books, and terrible lighting. It took Elena a minute to adjust to the natural, grey light that shone through the high window above them. How in the heck was she going to find anything in here? It clearly wasn't organised. Looking around, though, Elena noticed a lot of the cardboard boxes were labelled in black marker – **Children**, **Young Adult**, **Books That Need Restocked**, among others.

Elena stepped over a loose file and found a box to lean on. She said, "So, how are we going to do this?"

She accepted that they had to start somewhere, but where?

Emilia looked at her, picking up the loose file, and said, "What we need is in one of these boxes. I haven't been in here in donkeys so…"

"So, we just start wherever?" suggested Elena.

"Yep."

So that the search for anything about St. Jude's could be done as quickly as possible, they eliminated the boxes that they *knew* they wouldn't find anything in. The children's box was definitely out of the question, as was the young adult one, and any box that consisted of any forms of fiction. To Emilia's credit, going through the boxes was easy enough, for even the ones that weren't labelled were homes to either certain genres and specific authors. Most files Emilia and Elena picked up were lists of names – names and addresses of people who lent books or DVDs and needed to return them – while a couple were records of monthly revenue.

Elena didn't need any of this.

After slamming shut a file of records, Elena turned around and saw Emilia putting aside the boxes they had already searched through.

"Anything?" said Elena.

Emilia looked up, shook her head, and said, "Not yet. I'm sure it's around here somewhere." She kept on stacking boxes together as she added with a tinge of shakiness, "Please don't tell anyone about this. My grandie would kill me if he knew I had let a customer back here."

Elena looked up from the new file she had found lying on a shelf.

"Your *grandie*?"

"Great grandfather," clarified Emilia. "He was the original owner of this place."

"Oh! So, it's a family business?" asked Elena curiously.

Maybe Emilia's great grandfather knew if there was anything hiding in here. Or better yet, maybe he knew things about St. Jude's.

"*Well…* Not really," said Emilia shakily.

"What do you mean?"

They had both stopped what they were doing.

Emilia explained, "I assume that was his plan. But after an accident in the late seventies that sent him into a premature retirement…" She gulped hard, her teeth digging into her bottom lip. "*Something* changed about him. He sold this place to a couple, then they sold it off to a teacher, I think, and then when I turned eighteen, I decided to take it over myself. He wasn't exactly chuffed, I don't know why, and all he said was that *things* had changed. As well as him."

Elena stood there. This man must've experienced a lot in his life. She wondered if she should follow up with a question that might've been crossing a boundary.

"Do you know if *he* worked at St. Jude's?"

"Yeah, he did," she answered immediately. "It was the last place he worked before his accident."

Elena thought: *I wonder if I'll be allowed to meet him.* Or was that crossing another boundary? Probably, but in for a penny…

"Is he still here?" she asked instead.

"Oh, yeah. For his age, he's still in great health… As far as we know. We don't see him much." Emilia saw Elena's curious look, her head tilted, and Emilia thought she'd better clarify. "The accident derailed his confidence. So much." She took a deep breath, and added quietly, "He won't talk about it. The only thing he's mentioned to me is that…" Then there it was — a flash, a memory. "Oh, shit," Emilia mumbled. "I know where it is."

"What?"

Emilia spun around, climbing over the boxes behind her and under the window she picked up a box which was labelled **Other**. She climbed over towards Mrs. Sullivan and placed the box on top of a small cabinet. Opening the flaps, there was a pile of old scrapbooks sitting there collecting dust. Emilia flicked through some of them, and they were mostly photo albums. It was at the very bottom where Emilia picked up a scrapbook the size of an encyclopaedia. The picture on the cover was a landscape image of the town, lit under a glowing sky fuelled by the sunset.

She turned to the front page. Elena couldn't see what was in it. Emilia then thrust it into Elena's chest. She wasn't expecting it to be that heavy; it pulled Elena down, making her look like she had a hunchback.

"This is it," said Emilia, tapping the scrapbook's cover. "Over the years, Grandie collected newspaper clippings and articles and kept them in here, until his accident." Elena opened to the first page and it was an article from *The Castlehead Chronicle*. Its date: 21/3/1916. As Elena flicked through, Emilia said, "Then he stopped collecting them altogether. I remember asking him when I was a kid why he collected them, and he would tell me that it was history being written right in front of us. After his accident, I asked him why he stopped and he simply said… that I should not ask him that again. *Emmy, there are cruel people in this world,* he told me, *and they're the ones who lead us.*"

The book was open on a familiar article:

## THE GUARDIAN
### Crazy Lady Appoints Herself Mayor of Fictional Town

The article that Elena found online…

"Okay," said Elena. "What does this have to do with St. Jude's?"

Emilia instinctively snatched the book when she took it from her. A second later, she passed the book back and she had flicked onto a page with a clipping from *The Castlehead Chronicle*.

## THE CASTLEHEAD CHRONICLE
### First Man Cured By St. Jude's Medical Institute

Under the headline was a photograph of a woman in a doctor's uniform to the left, in the middle a stocky, balding man in a suit, and on the right an awfully familiar looking man with a full head of hair and a beard. Where had she seen that face before? The man was staring right at her.

"Grandie kept tabs on nearly everything in this town, including St. Jude's," said Emilia. She took the book from Elena again, and flicked to one of the last pages where there was a series of articles. "Before he retired, all of this happened…"

Elena followed Emilia's finger, brushing down the page of headlines.

### THE TELEGRAPH
**Could the Craziness be Genetic?**

### THE CASTLEHEAD CHRONICLE
**Madam Mayor Re-elected! Assassinated Instantly During Mayoral Election Celebration!**

### THE CASTLEHEAD CHRONICLE
**Patient Escapes St. Jude's. Causes Mass Riot.**

Elena's eyes were glued to the page. Though all the articles she had skimmed through seemed intriguing enough just because of their headlines, the last one regarding the patient escaping St. Jude's grabbed her attention most of all. There were snippets of all three articles that came with the headlines, and Elena brushed her finger along the page as she read the last one:

**Last night, a patient at the St. Jude's Medical Institute broke out and ran amok around town. Witnesses claim to have heard him crying and screaming over the acts of "torture" committed inside the hospital. Soon afterwards, the man by the name of Gerald Nate was taken into custody but was quickly released by Deputy Ton on the condition he'd be under strict supervision at all times.**

There was nothing about the riots…

Elena didn't know if this Gerald Nate was still alive, seeing that the article was from nearly three decades ago. 1981, to be precise; what if there was still a chance, though? A chance to get solid proof from a man who had experienced the so-called horrors from within that madhouse. It seemed like St. Jude's had what Elena would call a hit-and-miss track record of *curing* people; it was surely a milestone to release the institute's first patient back out into the real world, but that patient must've suffered through so much *treatment* if other patients (like Gerald Nate) had gone out of their way to break out like a prisoner whilst claiming to have witnessed – and most likely have fallen victim to – the acts of torture.

That was her next move: Elena needed to get more on Gerald Nate.

Gerald was the key.

She had a good feeling.

Closing the scrapbook, and passing it back to Emilia, Elena said, "Thank you so much, darling, for doing this."

"It's my pleasure," said Emilia, accepting the book and nodding gratefully. "But what is it about St. Jude's that you want to find out?"

"I…" Elena shrugged. "I honestly couldn't tell you. It's not just St. Jude's, either. It's this whole town. I don't get it… But I want to. I don't know why." She chuckled as she added quickly, to ease the tension, "Maybe it's the teacher inside of me."

*Or something else.*

Emilia tucked the scrapbook under her arm and said, "Well, *a lot* has happened in this town, ma'am, over the years. If I could tell you everything, I would. But I'm not the right person for that." She cleared the way for the door, and they both headed back through the library. Emilia was back behind the reception desk, and she placed the scrapbook underneath. With Elena back by the entrance, before leaving, Emilia added, "If you find anything else, I know I won't be the only one grateful."

That made Elena smile. But before she left, there was one last favour...

"Could I," she asked hesitantly, "perhaps lend a notepad and pen?"

Emilia knelt down and, from under her side of the reception desk, pulled out an A6-sized notepad and one of those four-colour pens. Elena remembered seeing some of her students use those pens in her class before she was...

What was she, again? Let go or did she quit? Man, that seemed like such a long time ago now. It didn't matter, now. This mattered way more.

She took the pad and pen, waved goodbye and walked out of the library, back through the shortcut to her car. She hopped in the driver's seat but didn't start the engine. She chucked the pad and pen onto the passenger seat, her eyes fixed on the storage unit she parked in front of, and that exchange replayed in her mind. *I won't be the only one grateful.* What did Emilia mean by that? Emilia's great grandfather had some sort of connection to St. Jude's, which could've been the reason he changed. If only Emilia gave her more insight on Grandie. Still, Elena supposed Gerald Nate was a decent substitute.

Yet, despite the fact that her mind was like a suspect board in a police office, trying to connect so many dots, Elena still had to consider that Gerald Nate might've died some time ago. And, even if he hadn't, that she had no clue where he lived.

A phonebook was required.

# CHAPTER TWENTY-THREE

## A History Lesson

*Telephone booths still exist, right?* thought Elena. If they did, they were endangered due to the new tech that people obsessed over, like those iPhone's and those what-do-you-call-its – the Playboxes and X-stations, those beep-boop video game things Elena and her generation didn't understand.

Lucky enough, and to Elena's surprise, as she turned onto the high street the Waterstones was on, there *was* a red telephone booth on the street corner. She parked askew on the double-yellow lines – yes, she knew she wasn't allowed, but it would only take a second – and ran into the booth. The payphone itself had lost its shine. Under the phone, thankfully, the booth was furnished with a book. The paper was thin and the font was, at highest, an 8. The pages thrashed together as Elena turned and turned, looking for surnames beginning with N.

"Come on, please, please, please, please," she mumbled to herself.

Passing pedestrians must've been thinking she was on drugs. Why else would she be in a telephone booth?

The N section was at the tailend of the phonebook. The next letter A. That meant the name was somewhere by the top. And there it was, the name Gerald Nate. Next to it a phone number. This conversation couldn't be over the phone. Next to that was the address. This had to be dealt with in person. 11 Thea Lane, Castlehead.

*Got it.*

Elena tore the page out of the book. *Pfft, nobody will care,* she thought as she rushed back to the car. She hadn't been caught illegally parking, thank God, and she drove off to see Gerald Nate. Suddenly there was a possibility that she might be able to speak to an actual St. Jude's survivor, *and* not receive a fine? Today was shaping out to be a good day.

*Perhaps a call would be easier,* she thought suddenly. *Isn't it just going to be extremely weird if a random stranger knocks on his door to ask about his experience being a patient in St. Jude's? No! You're not stupid, Elena. You don't know who's listening in on those calls. No doubt the police, or worse the bloody Mayor's Office.*

*That's all I need… shit with the mayor.*

*Just take a deep breath…*

*You're doing the right thing.*

*Like moving to Castlehead in the first place, right?*

She pulled up to 11 Thea Lane, Castlehead, England, and she – admittedly with regret – took a look at the house and it was exactly what she thought a house owned by a mental patient would look like: overgrown grass, litter everywhere, the wooden fence around the property ready to collapse under the slightest bit of force, curtains drawn over the front window, and the gutter along the roof of the bungalow swinging back and forth with the wind.

*Lord, help me,* she thought, gulping and picking up the pad and pen. *In these conditions, he's better off dead…*

*Wait! What did I just say?*

There was an open gap in the fence where a gate must've stood at one point. With the pad and pen tucked under her arm, and the somewhat smart casualwear, it came to Mrs. Sullivan again as she walked up to the brown front door that

she looked like an inspector. Or a reporter… *Yes!* That was it
– a reporter. Investigative journalist Elena Sullivan looking
into the dark history of the St. Jude's Medical Institute.

The door seemed to have been shredded and put back
together like a jigsaw puzzle. Elena clenched her fist, ready to
knock, but hesitated; she was under the impression that
nobody was in and, to a lesser extent, that the door would
crumble with the slightest knock. Glancing around, stalling for
time, Elena thought she should've listened to her head –
Gerald Nate was dead, wasn't he? *Look at this place! It looks
abandoned.*

Then she felt something: an itch. A tingle in the back of
her neck. It was the feeling that someone was watching her.
*Hang on! Did those curtains rustle?* Mrs. Sullivan didn't know what
to think anymore. In this situation and generally speaking too,
of course.

*"JUST KNOCK ON THE FUCKING DOOR!"*

*That* voice…

And she did. Quietly. She heard footsteps from within. It
wasn't abandoned. Then she heard the jingling of a lock and
the rustling of a door handle. It creaked open, and holding it
ajar was a greying man with a somehow young face.

"Yes?" he said.

Even after hearing the footsteps just mere seconds ago,
Elena was stunned that someone actually answered the door.

Holding the notepad and pen, Elena said brightly, "Hello,
my name's Elena Sullivan. I'm a reporter from *The Castlehead
Chronicle*—" *God, this guy better buy that I'm a reporter*, she thought,
"—and, um, I was wondering if I could come in and have
a word?"

The man opened the door a little further, and his face
suddenly became more visible. His eyebrows were low, and his
eyes looked like they were two lines drawn by a pencil. It was a

suspicious look. This guy definitely didn't buy the reporter impersonation.

"About?" he asked.

It was at this moment that Elena saw he was in flip-flops with socks — how dare he? — and a baby blue shirt that made him look like he was in a hospital gown. It was too big for him, and the grey bottoms were too baggy. Gerald Nate didn't take care of himself, that was for sure.

"Um…" Elena unconsciously tapped the pen on the pad. The nerves were kicking in.

"About…" The extended pauses made the man raise his eyebrows. He was waiting. Elena finally blurted out, "About St. Jude's."

Gerald's face turned from suspicious to fear in a nanosecond. He glanced back into the black passageway behind him and then back to Elena.

"Sorry," he said, shrugging, "I can't help you. You have the wrong house."

*But this is 11 Thea Lane, and…*

"Wait!" said Elena a bit too loudly. This stopped the man from shutting the door. "You *are* Gerald Nate."

The man stood up straight, and at the sound of the name folded his arms and an apprehensive look grew on his face.

"How do you know about Gerald?" he barked.

So, maybe this man wasn't Gerald Nate.

"Research," answered Elena quickly. "I'm doing a piece on St. Jude's before its grand reopening in a few weeks."

"Yeah," said the man, nodding, "I heard it was being made into a hotel. That doesn't answer my question, though. How do you know about Gerald?"

There had to be some element of truth to Elena's persona. To make it more believable.

"I found an old article," she explained, "that said he escaped St. Jude's. I just want to know *more*. Why. How."

The man looked down at his feet. He always had a gut feeling that this day was coming. He knew Gerald would talk, even if it did bring back the memories, even if it did remind him of what he had gone through. Only he knew what Gerald really went through, and it was those experiences that morphed Gerald into the person he ended up becoming – it explained *why* he was the way he was.

Elena stood there, still and patient – hopeful and desperate – and the man looked at her. He sighed.

He stepped to one side.

"Come on in," he said tentatively.

Elena stepped through the front passage, its black carpet bouncing darkness off all the walls. The man shut the door, squeezed past Elena and led her through a door that took them into a bare lounge. One of those classic televisions with the aerial poking out of the top was on by the back wall, glitching. There was nothing more than a dead fireplace against the wall nearest to them, and in the centre facing the TV was a brown recliner. It didn't fit well with the clear walls and wooden flooring.

The TV – when it wasn't glitching – showed some football match. On the TV's left there was an open door, and Elena got a glimpse at the kitchen counter covered in tins, cutlery and packets of condiments. She didn't know what to do amidst the mumbling commentators on the TV and the awkward silence between herself and the man in the room. She glanced at the man standing next to her, and he gave a look that told her to stay put. Until it was safe to move.

The man stepped over to the recliner facing the TV and kneeled down in front of it. This was when Elena noticed from where she was standing – by the draped curtains that hung on the opposite wall – that a hairy arm rested on the recliner's. The man took the hand resting on the recliner gently, most likely at eye level with the person sitting down.

"Gerald?" he said softly. Nothing but a grunt as a response. "There's someone here who would like to talk to you."

Another grunt.

The man rose and gave an all-clear nod to Elena.

She walked towards the TV and turned to face the recliner. In the chair was Gerald Nate. His cargo shorts and tank top revealed his tree trunk arms and legs, prickled with hair, and was draped in his dark beard. Elena tilted her head down, getting a better look at the lack of expression on his face. Unmoving. Vacant.

*Dead.*

Elena remembered that feeling, that feeling where you can't move. You don't want to find the strength to move. Because you're so hurt. She felt for Gerald Nate. There were no scars or bruises, not a single sign, that reminded or even hinted at the abuse that Gerald endured. They were scars you couldn't see.

Bending down, Elena whispered, "Gerald?"

Gerald snapped his head upwards, the dead glare now on this woman.

"Who are you?" he said unblinkingly.

Swallowing nervously, Elena said, "My name is Elena Sullivan. I heard that you might be able to help me."

"Help you? With what?"

There was no backing out now.

Elena asked, "I heard that you escaped St. Jude's many years ago?"

Gerald's eyes were back on the glitching television. Elena took that as a no; this man was zombified by what happened there. It lived with him for all those years. Elena started to well up thinking about it. She hid her emotions well, though, quickly wiping away the arriving tears. Maybe she shouldn't have tried to look into St. Jude's. What was the point in opening doors to the past that so many wanted to keep locked? All Elena had done was bring back the trauma by simply mentioning the mental institute. Hadn't she? Stupid. She was stupid. She was a stupid woman for doing everything she had done.

She kept still as she processed these thoughts... with no idea what was going through Gerald Nate's own head:

*GOAL! I like football. This is why I love it. The teams have one goal. I thought we had a goal, too – to help people. St. Jude's was meant to help people who thought they couldn't be helped. People who felt worthless. People who had no idea what was going on. It makes me feel worthless, trying and failing despite believing what we were doing was good. I was trapped. I am trapped. Just like the straps on the beds. Tight... Tighter. They had to be tight, until you couldn't move. It was the only way to help. Wasn't it? Ah! I don't know! Nailed in sometimes. Nailed! Nails... Nails? Clang, clang, clang. Hammered into the skull. They were machines that needed fixing. They needed fixing... and charging. Charging? Yeah, they did. Don't tell yourself they didn't because they did. Remember? Remember the shockwave machine? Patients strapped into chairs, doctors – especially Him – amping up the power to its highest. Did it work? Did it fuck! It only drained the lives out of them. Poor things. Hell – that's where we were. Hell. And He was the Devil. Not incarnate – just the Devil.*

This woman wanted to know what happened, and in spite of the pain he felt, Gerald was going to tell her. If she really wanted to know.

Looking back up at her, Gerald said slowly, "The article is wrong..." Elena glanced from Gerald to the other man.

"I wasn't a patient." With every word, it seemed that he had grown more comfortable. "I was a doctor. Twenty years. The reports were wrong, most of the time. Nobody saw anyone walk in or leave *that place*. We fought to help the sick. Some of us thought it would be best to keep what happened hidden from the press. Of course rumours spread like wildfire, saying that we punished those we looked after. Nah, we helped. Or at least we tried to. That was until Howard came in and took over. Twisted son of a bitch believed the patients needed fixing, believed everything had to be pure. Perfect. And he would make sure he got what he wanted at any cost, even at the expense of lives. Lobotomies. Electroconvulsive therapy." He glanced over to the man by Elena. "Even conversion therapy."

Elena turned to look at the man who greeted her, but he was gone. A moment later he came back in from the kitchen holding a file. He passed it to Elena then looked down at Gerald, his lip suddenly trembling and his eyes full of doubt.

"Are you sure you want to show her?" he whispered to Gerald.

"Yes," said Gerald. "Yes, I do, Don."

Elena tucked the pad and pen back under her arm, which she had forgotten she was holding since Gerald started talking, and opened the file. She wasn't ready for the images within. Purple skin. Deep scars on the wrists. Scans of the brain. Elena wanted to be sick. She turned to Don, and he had his hand over his mouth. She didn't want to speculate, but the only way they acquired these images was if…

"I was a patient," said Don, answering the question Elena hadn't even asked. "Gerald was my doctor. He saw there was nothing wrong with me, but Howard insisted on me staying until I was all better. One night, Gerald broke me out of my room and we made a run for it. The article said riots were caused, when in actuality it just caused an alarm to be raised and some of the patients to try and escape as well."

"Then," started Elena, closing the file and passing it back to Don, "why call it a riot?"

"The C.C.I.D were out all night searching for us. They called them riots to give St. Jude's a bad name. To shut it down. To prove a point. That *we* are wrong."

"But you aren't wrong," said Elena.

Don shrugged and said, "Yeah, well, let's just say some people aren't as accepting of those who are deemed different. Still to this day. It's crazy."

Mrs. Sullivan couldn't believe what she was hearing. This was insanity; good intentions didn't always exactly lead to good outcomes, but for some of the doctors in St. Jude's to think what they were doing, pure torture, was good just showed how many fucked up people there were in this town. Not knowing if any of the people she had met during her time in Castlehead were one of them made Elena even more sick.

Her parents gave her a good life, that was certain, and she couldn't thank them enough for how much they did for her to be successful, but society back when she was a kid – typically where she had grown up – wasn't exactly accepting or on board with equality and rights and all that stuff. She knew a lot of women had been stay-at-home mothers and baby makers, and the men had worked; it was also evident looking back on it how the people around her degraded those unlike them. Race, sexuality, upbringing – all of it played a part.

It wasn't just Castlehead. But being able to get away with acts of torture, it sure wasn't therapy, and the idea that the Mayor's Office and C.C.I.D wouldn't look twice at it was utterly ridiculous. Instead, the C.C.I.D aided the medical institute in trying to lock Gerald and Don – and God knows who else – back up in that place. They then went on to call the breakout a riot? Just so St. Jude's received the bad rep?

*How fucking corrupt!*

A single person, however, especially not Elena, couldn't expose all of this. If anything, all Elena would receive is a participation award – for trying.

She then thought what Emmett would've told her: "Trying something is always better than trying nothing."

That was the point of being a teacher. That was why she became a teacher – not only to learn, but to push people to try and become better people than they already were, to shape them into the people they'd become as adults. She shaped the future generations, along with so many educators across the globe, and all to make sure the students had the best lives possible and to make them understand a better tomorrow was possible if they collectively tried.

Off Don's look, Elena said, "Were there any other doctors who…?"

Stuffing his hands in his trouser pockets, Don huffed, "Yeah, there was, come to think of it."

"Carrie," said Gerald suddenly, his eyes laser focused on the TV again.

"Yeah," said Don. "Carrie. Wasn't there another one, too? Oh…" Don shut his eyes tightly, his nose scrunching up as he clicked his fingers. "God, what was his name?"

"Smith," said Gerald.

*Smith…*

"Yes!" howled Don, the memories flooding back, and for some reason he felt proud that he remembered the name. "Smith, that was it."

"Smith?" repeated Elena.

Then Gerald added, "Clarke Smith."

"*Clarke* Smith?" said Elena, leaning forward slightly, checking she had heard that correctly.

Don asked, "Have you heard of him?"

*Yeah*, she thought of answering. *He's only the man who took me in when I arrived here! Gave me a job, a reason to get out of bed. He's got an amazing family and if it wasn't for him, I wouldn't be standing here.*

"Yeah," she said, "he's my fr…" She stopped herself. "He's an acquaintance."

"Has he told you anything about St. Jude's? What he did as a doctor?" asked Don.

"Hang on," said Elena, raising a finger – trying hard not to come across as rude. "He told me he was an assistant."

"He and Gerald did the daily interviews with the patients."

Gerald then mumbled, "0-9-2… 6… 1-3-6… 6… 1-9-3… 6… 2-4-5."

"What?" said Elena, directed at Gerald.

Don said, "They're four patients he looked after." He glanced back and forth from Gerald and Mrs. Sullivan. "Ugh, I may as well tell you."

"Tell me what?" asked Elena.

"Among the tactics, those patients caused Gerald to be… *like this*." Practically comatose. "Some interviews were unbearable."

Elena listened to every word…

## 1980

It was the worst part of the day – if Gerald didn't count the last eleven hours of his shift. The windowless room consisted of plain icy concrete walls, a table, and two chairs. Gerald sat in one, a clipboard in hand, wearing a doctor's jacket, mask and rubber gloves – Howard said they had to take extra precautions with those kinds of people — and in the chair opposite, there was his patient for the day.

Every Monday was Patient 092; every Wednesday was Patient 136; every Friday was Patient 193; every Sunday was Patient 245. There were four different patients, excluding Don, he took care of. But with those identical blue hospital gowns, revealing their backs, most days they all blurred into one.

Some, like Patient 092, stood out with their more *prominent* features.

Gerald had nothing against immigrants, personally, and even he knew the reason Patient 092 was locked up in St. Jude's wasn't because of his racial heritage. When he sat opposite his Monday patient, all Gerald could look at was those beady eyes.

Folding his arms, Gerald asked slowly, "So, have we been okay over the past week?"

This was how he would start every talk with Patient 092.

092 linked his fingers between each other, forming a ball, and kept them close to his mouth. A wave of fear. He couldn't look at the doctor.

*"He's evil. Remember?"* he heard. Gerald waited. 092 heard, *"Say what you always say and everything will be okay."*

Patient 092 leaned forward and after a deep breath, he said, "They get so loud at night." He stumbled on his words, like something wasn't letting him speak. For himself. He continued to try. "It's never been this bad. It… They're too loud."

*"WHAT ARE YOU DOING!?"*

"They all just left me thinking that I am mad. I'm not talking to myself, Gerald. It's them. They won't shut up, telling me what to do, what to say. What to think."

*"You know what's going to happen now…"*

"Am I going mad?" asked 092. He didn't let Gerald reply, nor did Gerald have any intention of replying. It wasn't for him to answer. "I've stopped talking to my real friends…"

*"Because you don't have any."*

"The voices tell me *they* are my only friends."

*"Because we are. We would never do anything to hurt you. It was your real friends that put you in here. We would never do such a thing."*

"They tell me I should trust them. And there's nobody to put me back into this so-called reality I always hear about. I'm so tired, yet nobody listens. Nobody *understands*."

*"We understand. You're mad for thinking that! We. Are. Here. For. You."*

"Shut up," Patient 092 mumbled.

Gerald leaned forward and asked, "What was that?"

"Shut up," repeated the patient. He pushed the chair back as he rose defensively, leaping towards the wall and putting his hands on the cold concrete, his head down. "Shut up, shut up, shut up! SHUT UP! I'M NOT MAD!" Gerald remained seated, seemingly calm as Patient 092 added, "I'm a good person, I always have been. So why am I being punished?"

*"It's because…"*

"It's because I am mad, isn't it? I am mad. I am just crazy."

*One down*, thought Gerald, *three to go.*

Wednesday came and Patient 136 didn't accept the seat they had been offered. They always ended up sitting in the corner, trying to curl up into a right angle themselves. Always on the verge of tears.

They had thoughts. Many thoughts.

Like Patient 092, Gerald didn't discriminate with this patient, nor with any other. He had to be neutral in this line of work, unlike some others on the team. Among other things, like the thoughts – the many thoughts – Patient 136 had an identity crisis for a while. That was how Howard had put it. That was a topic Gerald didn't feel like he needed to bring up; it was *their* choice wasn't it? Not an immediate red flag, as Howard called it.

Gerald leaned back in his seat, casually, looked over towards Patient 136 and asked, "What have you been thinking about?"

Patient 136 kept their face in their hands. "A lot of things. Am I going mad?"

"What makes you think that?" asked Gerald.

"I must be. Because I feel it. And when I *feel* something, it's not good. I don't know what to do. Am I mad? You're the doctor here, tell me." They were growing impatient. "Am I sick? Of course!" They looked up at Gerald, rising slightly, their back scraping against the concrete. "Of course I am. What normal person has thoughts of murdering their sibling? *Why?* Because they thought putting me here was the best option, that's why. I'm... I'm a horrible person. Aren't I? Aren't I? I need to get away."

They still kept to the corner, their head swirling around the room. They couldn't get away. They couldn't run.

"Why do you need to get away?" asked Gerald calmly.

"I need to run. I'm too much of a danger if I stay here. What if I hurt someone else? I can't do that to them. Maybe I should go to the middle of the woods and stay there. Yeah. Yeah, that sounds lovely. I'll be far enough away that I won't hurt anyone anymore. But..." 136 hopped over to another corner. "But..." They slid down it again, hands on their head, fingers trailing through their short hair. "But what if a tree falls on me? What if a hunter mistakes me for a deer? I... I can't go out there. I don't want to fucking die! What if no one finds my body? What if...? Oh..." Then a chuckle was let out. "What am I thinking? Of course these things won't happen. I'm so sick of these thoughts in my head. I want nothing to do with them. I don't want to think about them, but when I push them away, they just get worse. *They keep coming back*. What did I do to deserve this? Am I a bad person? I *am* a bad person. Am I a burden? I *am* a burden. Am I a monster? Well… I'm certainly not stable. I know that. Any stable person wouldn't have these thoughts…" They stood up properly, and tilted their head to the side, eyes fixed on Gerald. "Right?"

*Two down. Two to go.*

Friday: the beginning of the end. It must've been nice for people with normal nine-to-five jobs, getting themselves amped up for the weekend. Two days off. That sounded divine. That sounded like a fucking dream that wasn't going to come true. Gerald knew it, so he had to get on with it.

Patient 193 didn't know where she wanted to be. Her hair was wild as she constantly paced around the room and at times sat down in the free seat. Gerald allowed this to happen; he thought to allow the patients to express themselves freely, rather than restricting them to a chair with straps on it that wrapped the wrists and ankles to keep them in place.

*Keep them in place… like a single-file line.*

Gerald, however, didn't budge from his seat, his chin resting on his hand. Watching Patient 193 walk about like a clueless elder roaming the halls of a care home at night was entertaining, at times. He knew it wasn't nice to think like that but, for a woman who claimed to have a strict routine, she did struggle with deciding where she wanted to be.

Gerald began to ask, "How are you feel—?"

"I'm so happy!" Patient 193 said, ecstatically, her knees bouncing. "All I ever feel is happiness and peace and joy and-and-and-and it's all because of my set routine: wake-up, eat, brush my teeth, work, come home, eat, brush my teeth, sleep." It fell silent for a beat. "It's all so… so…" She started to look around, lost. "I HATE SET ROUTINES! No, I won't take my meds. No, I won't wake-up, eat, brush my teeth, work, come home, eat, sleep, and repeat. I'm good, right? All good. I'm happy. Happy! See?" She skidded across to the table, her hands slamming down, and leaned in close to Gerald. "Look at me," she said, forcibly smiling. "Happy as Larry." She then shuffled back and started to pace around again. "I can't bear to live like this anymore. Why can't I be normal? Why can't I- Do you seriously think I give a shit what people think? Ha! I'm happy, see? Happy as bloody Larry, Harry, Barry or whatever name you're thinking of." Another beat of silence fell over the room. Patient 193 froze and looked at Gerald shyly. She said subtly, "I'm sorry. I didn't mean to frighten you." But Gerald wasn't frightened, not of her. He was frightened *for* her. And *for* everyone else. "I don't know what came over me," 193 added. "Did you know I have a set routine? I wake up, I eat, I brush my teeth, I go to work, I come home, I eat, I brush my teeth... *and* I sleep."

*One more. Just one more to go. Final—*
*Then it starts all over again. Yipty-fucking-do!*


Sunday arrived. All of Gerald's patients were curious subjects; and all of them, off Howard's final say, would end up having the *madness* shocked out of them. Gerald thought it was hard enough for the patients to live with the conditions they had, and to put them through even more punishment was simply wrong. But it had to be done, didn't it?

Did it? *Does* it?

Gerald wasn't so sure anymore.

He locked those thoughts away when he was presented with Patient 245. There was this faraway look in his eye when he sat opposite Doctor Nate. The patient never took that beanie off – only when it was *the other guy* Gerald was talking to.

The previous week was one of those times. A mad look in 245's eye, that thick London accent. Aggressive when trying to convey his emotions, how he felt, and how he felt about who he was. Now there Patient 245 was, the total opposite of the way he had been the previous week. This was common, and Gerald still couldn't anticipate which Patient 245 he was going to talk to every Sunday.

Neither was any better than the other.

Gerald cleared his throat and said in a low, serious tone, "I spoke to *the other guy* last week." 245 was mute. He just looked at his doctor as he went on. "He told me some interesting things about you. Things that you did."

245 raised a finger, and argued, "Don't always believe what he says." There was a steadiness to his Mancunian accent, collected and yet somehow defensive. This man was nothing like *the other guy*. He added, "He's trying to make it seem like I'm the bad guy."

"How so?" asked Gerald.

"I know about the break-in," said 245. "The break-in I was accused of. It wasn't me. I swear."

Gerald rubbed his temple and said, "You were there at the scene, the descriptions given by witnesses fits—"

"I'm telling you it wasn't me. Don't believe me then. You've already made your mind up. I can see it. You and everyone else here, you all think I'm mad but I'm not. I'm not, I'm not. I know what I'm talking about. You see, what you fail to realise is that underneath every human, like a piece of delectable cake, or a snake, are layers that are revealed in scenarios we either dread or desire." Patient 245 suddenly twitched and snapped his head to the side, before facing Gerald once again. "Wait, did you hear that?" Gerald couldn't say he had heard anything. "How did you not hear the smash? I know I wasn't there, but I heard it. Jingle of glass falling to the ground. It was so loud. I didn't... I didn't... I didn't do it. I swear! It couldn't have been me. I wasn't there.

If it was, I would've confessed. *I* wouldn't have fled the scene like that. People say I do things, but I don't. They're just rumours. But, say, if I did believe that it was me, what exactly did I do? Eh? What did I do that was *so bad* that makes me such a bad person? What did I do that made you think I deserved to be here? Because... I can tell you something. I'm not mad. *That's... not... me.*"

It all came down to perspective. The reason St. Jude's was built was because the former mayor believed people could be helped. To make them understand themselves better. That they weren't monsters. But were they mad? Howard believed so, and so did some of the other doctors. They believed these were the right precautions to take; weekly meetings, daily tests, *therapy*, they all believed in the process. After all, the world would be a much safer place because of their work.

Was Gerald the mad one? Was he mad thinking he could help people? Was he mad for applying for the job at St. Jude's? Was he mad for having faith in the higher-ups to do the right thing? Oh, he was just kidding himself, of course he was mad. Everyone is mad. What is normal? Because it certainly wasn't normal what they were doing. To help them. *Apparently.*

*Everyone is mad. Everyone is crazy. We need to understand that. Mad — it's mad what goes through people's minds. Actions speak louder than words, and one's behaviour speaks way louder than one's intentions.*

*Is Howard right? Do we need structure? Do people need to stop making excuses and look at the facts? The facts being that these people are mad. These people are crazy, and something has to be done. I'm mad. You're mad. EVERYONE IS MAD!*

Understand that.

## 2009

"Wow," gasped Elena. "I'm guessing Gerald wasn't the only one who conducted these meetings?"

Don tilted his head towards Elena and said, "No, Clarke and other doctors did, too."

With a shake of the head, Elena said disapprovingly, "I just don't see why Clarke wouldn't admit he was a doctor."

Gerald looked up at Don and Elena.

"He's probably trying to forget," he said. "A great doctor, he was. Didn't always agree with Howard's tactics, but I had to go along with them. I had no choice."

Seeing that apparently Howard – whoever he was – ran St. Jude's for a period, it made a little sense for his influence to have a significant impact on the institute. But Elena didn't know Clarke was actually a doctor... It made sense now, with him working in pharmaceuticals. There was a good chance, in spite of his bluntness, that Gerald was right when he said perhaps Clarke was trying to forget his time at St. Jude's. But then why had he decided to run the institute's refurbishment? Why did he say he was just an assistant, rather than not mentioning St. Jude's or associating himself with the institute at all?

Was it because he knew deep down what he was trying to do was help people? Was it because he didn't want all the shit on him?

Elena knew she had to take him up on that offer for a coffee. Then she remembered he had to sort out his pharmacy and find out who broke the window. The coffee would have to wait. It could've been an offer Elena *couldn't* take him up on.

Stepping away from Don and Gerald, Elena said, "Well, thank you so much for all of this." Then she froze. "Oh, one last thing."

"Yes?" said Don.

"Who's Howard?"

"You don't know?" Don scoffed. "Some reporter, you are. Howard is… He's called Howard Pattison. The chief's father. I'm surprised the chief's even letting the place reopen at all, never mind as a hotel. His father's probably turning in his grave."

"Hang on!" cried Elena. Was she hearing that correctly? "Did you say Howard was Chief Pattison's father?"

It was *all* beginning to make sense now.

"Yep," said Don. "God help this town for as long as that man's the chief of the C.C.I.D."

Don followed Mrs. Sullivan to the front door, holding it open for her as she walked through the garden. He waved her off as she drove away. Shutting the door, it quickly crossed his mind that Elena hadn't used the notepad and pen at all. He shrugged it off and walked back into the lounge. Gerald hadn't moved.

Don walked through to the kitchen and called out to Gerald that he had put the kettle on.

Gerald's response was a grunt.

# CHAPTER TWENTY-FOUR

## Footage

Pattison and Taylor, led by the streetlamps in the night, pulled up to the C.C.I.D building in a cruiser. The chief told his officer to ignore the blue mohawk, chain-wearing freak in the back. With that order, the drive from Carson Estate to the office was a long one indeed.

Empty-handed, Pattison walked through the automatic doors first. Taylor strolled behind, shoving their passenger forward. Pattison told her to cuff him. Extra precautions, he said it was. Taylor knew what to do, she knew how to do her job; Pattison was her boss, she wouldn't deny that, but she felt like she should be entrusted with her duties once in a while.

Ushering this suspect into the reception area, Taylor peered across to the desk and saw Pattison had been waiting for her. He leaned against the desktop, smug.

"Taylor," he said, pointing to the end of the reception area, where it split into two hallways, "take him down to the cells. I'll join you in a minute."

She did so without any argument. But when did Pattison decide she needed 24/7 supervision? She was the best of the best. A simple explanation would've been that he had been supervising her for an upcoming test, or something along those lines, but this was Chief Derek Pattison who was her boss. Taylor knew her boss to go rogue and take matters into his own hands. He wasn't like anyone else she had worked for. Was he afraid that she was vying for his spot as chief? Was that the reason behind this constant supervision ever since they picked up that man who was beaten in the alley? It was something to look into.

Pattison turned around to the receptionist behind the desk. "Is Ton still here?" he asked.

Seated, the receptionist looked up and he said, "Yeah. He's in the security room."

Pattison started to get that excited/nervous feeling in his stomach. This could've been the breakthrough — the proof — the C.C.I.D needed.

He clasped his hands together and said, "Brilliant. Thank you."

"Who's that lad you and Taylor brought in?" asked the receptionist, jerking his head towards the hall Taylor took the suspect down.

"Some smackhead we brought in from Carson. Was up to no good in the park."

As he spoke, a quick image flashed in the chief's mind of him and Taylor cuffing this apparent smackhead. Walking past them with that mohawk... *that* mohawk — it wasn't right. If a hairstyle could scream, "Arrest me, please, I beg you 'cause I'm on my way to fuck up my life," Pattison would place mohawks at the top of the list.

The chief walked away from the desk and headed down the opposite hallway to Taylor. This hall led to a stairwell that would take you up to the office space, but on the way you'd pass sets of doors on either side of the hall. The last door on Pattison's right was the security room.

*Let this be it*, he thought, opening the door.

The room was lit by the twenty screens covering the back wall, underneath them was a thin desktop where officers sat with headphones on. The screens were maps, all covering regions of Castlehead, and they showed scattered dots that flashed red and blue. It was a tight squeeze, with the rest of the room being taken up by two more rows of computers, desks, and chairs. In the seat closest to the door was Deputy Ton; he spun round in his chair away from the computer screen. The fuzzy black and white image on the screen was exactly what Pattison had hoped for.

"Chief!" said Ton, spinning back around to the screen. The chief stepped across, leaned over the chair and Ton's left shoulder. "You're not going to believe this."

"If this is what I think it is, then I *will* believe it, Ton," said the chief. He had believed it for the past few weeks. He had his suspicions, and now this footage was either going to prove or debunk those suspicions. "Let's see it."

On the screen was a paused, high-angle shot of the street where Clarke Smith's pharmacy was located in town. Ton tapped the spacebar and the footage played. A time and date popped up in the bottom right corner of the screen: 01.24, Sat, 21/03/09. The minutes went on and only a couple of cars sped up the road.

"Hold on," said Ton, sensing the chief's growing impatience.

Then they saw it; a figure in a puffy jacket, the hood over their head, and a bag strapped over their shoulder. They faced the store and started to dig through the handbag. In a second, the figure held a rock in their hand.

This was it.

The sound was muted, but Pattison heard the glass shattering in his head. The figure basked in the destruction they caused. The rock rolled back across to the figure's feet and they picked it up. And with their free hand, they took their hood down. Pattison couldn't focus on who it was, as an innocent bystander came into the shot from the top of the road. She put her hand over her mouth and pointed at the vandaliser. She made a run for it, out of shot, and the figure followed her.

Nothing. Ton thought the screen had paused itself. But another second later the vandaliser reappeared, this time ignoring the shattered window.

"Pause it!" ordered the chief suddenly. Ton shivered in his chair then paused it. "Zoom in," the chief whispered. Ton pressed the up arrow key. In the black and white footage, the hair was still grey and that face was still unmistakable. The chief stood up straight, pride radiating off his smile. He added, "Print this off, Ton. Gather yourself and Taylor by the front desk in two minutes."

Pattison headed for the door, but stopped, holding the door ajar when he heard Ton's voice call back to him.

"Wait, Chief, what's the plan?"

The chief turned his head halfway over his shoulder. His lips curved slightly upwards. Ton knew that look.

"What's the plan?" the chief echoed back. "What the V.C.P.A *should've* done months ago."

# CHAPTER TWENTY-FIVE

## The St. Jude's Hotel

What other secrets hid beneath this town's surface? That was the question Mrs. Sullivan kept asking herself when she got home and changed for bed. Howard was the chief's father, Clarke wasn't just an assistant, St. Jude's patients had been the subjects of tests she had only heard of before in the books she read, and Pattison was up to something too. Elena didn't know what, and maybe it wasn't her place to find out, but what Don had told her had stuck with her. He was surprised the chief was even allowing St. Jude's to reopen; if that meant something specific, Elena's best guess would've been that it meant the chief was plotting some kind of mutiny.

*Against St. Jude's?* she asked herself. *Against Madam Mayor? Or against the people of Castlehead?* Whichever reason it was, Elena had a gut feeling that it was all to get what the chief wanted – peace. If peace meant mental and physical abuse, and literal murder. She definitely wasn't the person to stop him; Pattison's power as chief of the C.C.I.D made him untouchable and that meant he had a huge influence on people and the Mayor's Office.

Nobody would believe her if she spat all of this out. Nonsense, that was how people would've seen it. But Emmett would've believed her, and that was all that mattered. He would've believed her. She believed him; she believed the love and trust they had was real.

*Yes, go to sleep on that note,* Elena thought. *I love you, Emmett Sullivan.*

The love they had was real…

*She wakes, and she's still in bed.*

*She shouldn't be.*

*Why?*

*Because she's going to be late. She's going to be late for the grand opening of the St. Jude's Hotel. She swoops off the bed to the sound of a knock at her door.*

*"Come on, Mrs. Sullivan," says the chirpy voice in the hall, "your chariot awaits!"*

*That can't be who she thinks it is… She's never been so happy.*

*Mrs. Sullivan opens the door and her eyes don't deceive her – it's Carol in a sequined dress and flat shoes. It's that moment that Elena looks down and sees she's in a tight navy dress with a black belt and heels somehow more comfortable than any she had worn before. She's not going to be taking them off halfway through the night. No way.*

*"For what?" asks Mrs. Sullivan.*

*"St. Jude's!" announces Carol, smiling. "Come on!" Carol takes Elena by the wrist and pulls her down the stairs. Somehow she doesn't topple over at the speed they move, especially with the heels she has on. They're in reception and Carol adds, "They're waiting outside."*

*Both Elena and Carol smooth out their dresses and walk side-by-side to the stretched limo waiting for them. Elena is in awe and Carol's smile is even brighter. The chauffeur stands by the back door, nodding welcomingly when they walk towards the car. On cue, he opens the door without a word; Elena hops in first – this is really happening – and Carol follows.*

*The roof of the limo is lined with purple neon lights and in front of them and against the side of the limo is a minibar. The chauffeur can be heard shutting the driver's side car door and the engine rumbles to life. They begin to move steadily. Elena is still in disbelief and Carol has already leaned forward towards the minibar, scooping up two tall wine glasses and picking up a bottle of bubbly by the neck.*

*She hands one glass to Elena and also offers her the bottle.*

*"You want me to do the honours?" says Elena.*

*"Of course, Mrs. Sullivan." Seeing Carol smile isn't normal. But this is really happening. "After all, it is your special night."*

*Elena shrugs and says with a grin, "Well… if that's the case."*

*She takes the bottle and the glass, resting the glass in between her knees as she twists off the top and uses her might to get the cork out.*

*POP!*

*"Way-hey!" the women cheer.*

*Elena pours some bubbly into Carol's glass before her own, and she places the bottle back on the minibar. They cheer it, the glasses clink together, and then they drink. They enjoy themselves. Tonight will be good. Life will be good. Life is good.*

*One glass down already.*

*They can't see where they are through the blacked-out windows, but the limo is still driving at a snail's pace. The chauffeur has definitely done this before; he knows to allow Elena and Carol to savour the moment. If this is what tonight brings, then Elena doesn't want the night to ever end.*

*Three more glasses later they feel themselves turning upwards. It feels like the slow start to a rollercoaster ride at a fairground with how the limo is angled. Sounds of car doors shutting and elated conversation can be heard outside. The limo comes to a stop. They've arrived. And they can't wait.*

*The chauffeur opens the door and the women hop out. They are welcomed with a red carpet leading through the open gates towards the entrance, which is lit by yellow fairy lights that spread snake-like around the edge of the building's roof. The building isn't the wooden shack Elena has been working in for weeks on end, but is a strong, clean structure that implores her and Carol to stroll in. Reaching the front entrance, Elena sees the wooden Christ on the cross has been replaced by the name of the* hotel in elegant cursive writing. Her favourite kind of writing. At the door she and Carol are greeted by a man in a tuxedo who stands to the side and sways his arm inward, ushering the arriving guests into the reception area of the St. Jude's Hotel.

Women glow in their expensive dresses and the men are studs in their suits that vary in all dark shades. Waiters and waitresses are in light grey waistcoats, roaming about the reception area and the rest of the facility holding trays of glasses filled with champagne. Complimentary, of course. There is a handsome chap behind the desk, his hair greying like the waistcoat he is wearing, his jaw chiselled as if out of granite, and he locks eyes with Mrs. Sullivan.

Butterflies... Butterflies; but not the kind of butterflies one gets when they fall in love for the first time, more of the kind one gets when they hope something is going to happen.

Carol notices the man walking through the sea of waiters and guests, heading straight for them both. She looks up at Elena and nods knowingly.

"I'm going to go and mingle," she says.

Carol vanishes before Elena can grasp what she's just said. And now the man is standing in front of her; his rugged hands are together behind his back, he stands upright like the tenured professional Elena already knows he is, and he lets out this little smile that makes Elena suddenly very comfortable. She wants to know what happens.

"Mrs. Sullivan," he says, "welcome to the brand-new St. Jude's Hotel. We've been expecting to be graced by your presence. Can I just say that you look absolutely magical."

Elena feels a sheet of sweat cover her forehead. She can't be blushing, not with all these people around.

"Oh... Goodness," she stammers. "I'm honoured to be here."

"The honour is ours," relays the staff member. "Now, come on."

"Where are we going?" she asks.

"Why, you have a spot waiting for you downstairs in our VIP lounge and bar."

*Downstairs? Downstairs? VIP. Lounge. Escape. Peace. Downstairs in the VIP lounge, a place for her to sit in peace, a place for her to escape.*

The staff member guides Elena through to the already open door that leads them downstairs. Everyone stands to the side, making way for them both like they all know who she is. Royalty. Downstairs, they turn right, and Elena hears nothing. No music, no talking, just the windy silence. Suddenly, it all feels eerie. An A-board informs Elena that the next set of doors on her left is to the VIP lounge and bar. The staff member freezes by the open door and keeps smiling at her.

Stopping in the doorway, Elena asks, "Is this it?"

"Yeah," replies the staff member. "This is it."

He walks off.

*This. Is. It.*

Elena walks in and the silence follows her. Cloth-covered tables and chairs take up much of the red carpeted room; to the right is a stage, where a lonely piano awaits its pianist; against the back wall, opposite the entrance, is a brightly lit bar manned by a weathered man in a red suit matching the carpet. Elena thinks the black shirt and trousers, along with the gold name tag just above his breast pocket, go together really well with the red.

She shuffles herself onto a stool and places her forearms on the glass counter. She looks into the unblinking eyes of the bartender. His smile — it's fake. It's an assured drool; he knows who Elena Sullivan is.

"How are you doing tonight, Mrs. Sullivan?" asks the bartender.

"I'm doing fantastic." She squints at the name tag. Archibald. "I'm doing fantastic, Archibald. Fan-bloody-tastic."

"That's good to hear, Mrs. Sullivan." Archibald turns to the display of drinks behind him. Vodka, rum, whiskey, chardonnay, gin… Oh, so many choices. He adds, facing the selection, "What will it be?"

*It's a special night. This is it. Make the most of it.*

Elena glances upwards, processing her choices, then with a smile says, "How about your finest bottle of red."

274

*Archibald turns with a glass in one hand and the finest bottle of red St. Jude's offers in the other.*

*"Excellent choice, Mrs. Sullivan." He places the glass on the counter and pours for her. Half a glass. A decent amount. "There you go."*

*"You're a gem, Archibald," says Elena. "A fucking gem!" Her voice whisks through the entire lounge. She's very happy. After a sip – the wine is delicious – she says, "There aren't many people like you in this world, Archibald. I think I'm like you."*

*"I like to think so, too."*

*"You know exactly what to say." Elena necks the rest of the glass. "What about you? What's your life beyond this counter?"*

*"My life, Mrs. Sullivan? I'm happy with the life I've had. Content with what I've done and what I've got." As the bartender says this, he pours Mrs. Sullivan another drink. "A wife and two beautiful children are waiting for me to get home when my shift is done."*

*Elena necks the whole glass this time. Her eyes are starting to droop; there's nothing behind that glare.*

*"A wife and kids?" she echoes, nodding dramatically. "Good for you."*

*Archibald glances down then back up at her. She isn't wearing a ring. He was ordered to call her Mrs. Sullivan.*

*"Are you married?" he still decides to ask.*

*She tilts her head, as if she needs to think about it.*

*"Yeah," she mouths. "I was... am!" Everything comes back to her all at once. Overwhelming but maintainable. "I was until that day..."*

*"What day are you referring to, Mrs. Sullivan?" asks the bartender, pouring a third glass.*

*She needs the drink before she can say anything else.*

*"Our anniversary," she says after a sip. Elena swirls the wine gently as she continues to talk. "It was a lovely night. We went to our favourite restaurant in Valeland – that's where I'm from – and I thought it was going to be perfect. It was meant to be perfect. Sorry, but nothing was perfect about that night. Perfect doesn't exist; the perfect person doesn't*

exist. *Silly me, silly little Elena Sullivan for thinking Emmett was the perfect person. Yeah, okay, I'm not perfect either – Christ, no one is – and that's why I'm here and Emmett isn't. He did a bad thing, and I did something worse. I see that now. I just didn't want to admit it. He didn't want to admit anything either."*

Archibald leans forward, slyly motivating her to accept what's happened inside, and says, *"Admit what, Mrs. Sullivan?"*

*"There was another,"* Elena mumbles.

*"Another?"*

She clarifies clearly, *"Another me. She was stunning, exactly what Emmett wanted in a woman. And I felt… I felt worthless when he did what he did. Coming home one night, I just knew; the look in his eyes, he had desecrated the love we promised we had for each other. Till death do us part. I never looked at him the same way, but I couldn't bring myself to leave him. Because I fucking loved him, and love does things to people. I couldn't bring myself to leave him, so…"*

Archibald finished, *"So he had to leave you."* Off her look, he quickly adds, *"It's okay now."* Elena looks up, and now Archibald has his head tilted. *"'Cause like you said, Mrs. Sullivan, you're just like me."*

*"You're just like all of us!"*

Elena spins around and there are four people standing in hospital gowns, with that same unblinking glare as Archibald the bartender. Elena can't scooch any further back on her stool; the counter keeps her from falling. She can't move. Everything is numb.

*"What'd you mean?"* she asks.

She doesn't know who to look at.

*"You're just like us, Elena,"* says the figure furthest right.

The figure furthest left interjects, *"But you're the worst out of all of us."*

From behind, Archibald says over her shoulder into her ear, *"There's no point in running anymore. It's what you've been doing ever since you killed your husband – running. You can't run. No matter how fast or for how long, you can't run from the truth. It will always catch up to you.*

*The truth is that you're not okay. The first step to recovery is accepting it. You have to accept everything that's happened." The words are sinking in. To the depths. "You have to accept that people are going to look down on you for what you've done, for how you are. It doesn't matter how hard you try. Accept it, accept your place, and we promise it will be okay."*

*Elena remains on the stool. She's lost all bodily functions. She's lost. Lost.*

*Blinking once, she notices something about the hospital gowns. The sticky labels on each of the figure's chests. Oh, my God. This isn't real. She feels again, stretching her fingers out. This isn't real. Because the figures are dead.*

*Patient 092. Patient 136. Patient 193. Patient 245.*

*Then...*

*Blinking again, Mrs. Sullivan is back in the windowless room she found herself in after blacking out. She's sitting on the edge of the bed, and the markings on three of the walls are clearer now than they were before.*

*Kill. Kill. Kill.*

*The capitalised K...*

*Three K's.*

*092. 136. 193. 245.*

*Add them up, Mrs. Sullivan. What do you get? Go on! You're not a maths teacher, but you are a teacher, nonetheless. Go on! Fucking add them up!*

*666.*

*The bed creaks. Elena turns and Archibald is there, staring forward. "What does this mean?" she whispers to him.*

*"There are so many like us who need help. There's always a chance for people to understand themselves better, but if you don't take that chance..." Elena knows she hasn't taken that chance. "Then, well, you can't be helped."*

*Can she still take the chance? This isn't real. She knows it's not; she needs to wake up. She needs to wake up.*

*Wake up...*
*There is a bang on the door. An iron fist is knocking.*
*Wake up...*
*Another bang.*
*Wake up!*

Elena woke up. She was in her apartment. Thank goodness it was just a dream.

BANG!

The door flew open and Elena, back in her nightgown, jumped up. She raised her hands in the air; a shadow figure stood in the doorway. There was a click, and the figure had something aimed at her.

"Elena Sullivan," said the figure.

It was a male voice.

Elena took a hesitant step forward.

Chief Derek Pattison stared back at her, pistol in hand.

# CHAPTER TWENTY-SIX

## Just Consequences

"Chief Pattison?" said Elena, her hands still in the air. She needed to wake up. Oh, wait! She was, and the chief of the Castlehead Criminal Investigation Department had a gun pointed at her... "What's going on?"

*Remorseless...*

"Mrs. Elena Sullivan," said the chief, "I'm placing you under arrest for vandalising the property Clarke's Pharmacy... and for the murder of Mr. Emmett Sullivan."

When was this suddenly decided? Then she thought about the dream she had woken up from; if the temptation to no longer run and hide was in her dream, then it was surely on her mind. She still wasn't going to let the chief come in here and falsely accuse her of such crimes she didn't com—

*You did commit one of them, Elena,* she thought.

No more running.

She shouted, "This is outrageous. How dare you accuse me of such a despicable act!"

Elena didn't use the plural term.

The chief rolled his eyes, the gun still aimed at her. *This would be so much easier,* he thought, *if she just came quietly.*

"Mrs. Sullivan, can you tell me your whereabouts on Friday, the 20th of March?"

Yes, she could.

Her chin was up and she said, "I was at the Smith's for dinner."

"Between 9:30pm and 6:00am the next morning?" added the chief, his eyebrows raised. "Did you spend the night?"

The chief knew the truth already. All he wanted was to see if she had any final words.

"I walked home," said Elena.

"You walked home?" Pattison repeated. She was digging her own grave. "So, you didn't make any stops along the way?"

"No!" Elena snapped. "Why on Earth would I do that to one of the only people who made me feel welcome here?"

"I don't know." The chief shrugged. He kept one arm up, the pistol still on Elena, while he pulled something from his back pocket. He chucked it over to Elena; it landed by her feet and she picked it up. The paper was folded four times over, and it was a still image of security footage. "Then explain this picture," added the chief, off Elena's look.

Elena looked closely. It was her, that night after Clarke's dinner. She had had a drink, but the walk sobered her up. She couldn't have done that. She came straight home. It was a good walk, she vaguely recalled.

"That's not me," she muttered, shaking her head at the picture.

"That's not you?" echoed the chief, both hands now on the gun. He betted Elena was going to resist. "The evidence is right there. Don't deny. Don't try to hide it."

Elena looked up suddenly. Her eyes wide, offended; what secrets were hidden beneath this town's surface? He wanted to talk about *hiding* things? Contrary to the evidence provided, Elena was positive the chief had done a lot worse than breaking a window.

She felt herself say sarcastically, "Oh, and you're not hiding anything, Chief?"

*Don't push it, Elena.*

"Excuse me, Elena?" The chief's voice cracked. "What are you talking about?"

Did she stump him just then?

"Not long after I arrived, I began looking into St. Jude's," she said firmly. "I found out a lot. I met Gerald Nate, and I came to the conclusion that you're planning on killing thousands just to *make this town a better place.*"

"Did you say *Gerald Nate?* That's impossible."

"*Why?*"

"Because he's dead."

Elena shrugged and said, "I spoke to him, Chief. And he is alive and well."

*Somebody lied to Father!* Pattison thought. It was difficult not to let the sudden realisation get to him. The chief couldn't let Elena hook onto his emotions; he had to remain calm. *Worry about it later*, he thought.

"Whatever he told you," he said, "whatever you found out, it's all a lie. That's why you don't understand. You will never understand. It's people *like you* that drag this community down. Menaces. Problems. People who come here and think they can just do whatever they please... Reality check: that's not how life works."

Elena retaliated with, "And life doesn't work when you act like different types of people don't exist. By just killing them. You know how messed up that sounds, don't you?"

"That's why you don't understand. I *can* do that. People like me who know what's right. *We* can do that. If people don't know their place, then they need to be told."

Elena's mouth fell open and she said, "You're delusional!"

"No, I'm not. I can see clearly. You can't do what you want, you can't be who you want to be. Not without consequences. If *you* people let us give you the help you need, you'll find the right path. I promise. Everything will be okay. I do what I do for the future of this town, Mrs. Sullivan. Not a lot of people see that. I do it for us, for the children, and for the grandchildren that will make up this community in the years to come. And all people need to do is get in line. Let me help you, Elena. You know what you did was wrong. Accept that. Please… Accept that and come with me."

Elena let go of the photo and started to think about everything that had happened. She had lost her husband – her own wrongdoing – who she still loved endlessly, she had gotten herself tangled in the history of an old mental asylum that had nothing to do with her, and because of that she found out the chief was crazy. Like her. Perhaps that's what he was trying to tell her? Was that the core, the centre of all this? If she accepted that something was wrong – that nothing was right – would everything be okay? What would happen if she did go with Pattison? A cell no bigger than the apartment she already lived in, three meals a day, a bed probably more comfortable than her own. And the help she needed.

*No*!

She was fine.

Elena didn't need help. It was Pattison who needed the help. It wasn't her fault that her husband slept with another woman; it wasn't her fault that all of this happened. In that case, why was *she* – and so many others, she presumed – being treated like they were the worst kinds of people? It didn't make sense. Nothing made sense. What was the point of all this? The point… there wasn't one. No point. No point in going with Pattison. No point in running. No point whatsoever. She may as well have been dead.

That was the point of living. To die.

So, that meant there was no point in conforming to Pattison's ways and doing as he asked.

"No," she muttered. "I won't go with you."

*She's pushing it.*

"Elena…" The chief was disappointed. He didn't want it to go down like this. That wasn't the answer he was looking for. "Come on, now."

"No!" she cried. Her hands cut through her hair as she stumbled back, "Get away!"

Everything was closing in.

"Mrs. Sullivan," said Pattison softly, "come on. Please."

Elena squatted down, so that her shoulder blades rested against the frame of her bed. Her head was in her hands and she was wailing. She felt nothing.

"No!" she screamed. "You're not real! I'm asleep! Get away!"

The chief exhaled through his nose. He lowered his gun and kneeled down in front of Mrs. Sullivan. The gun was still in his left hand, and with his right he clamped onto Elena's shoulder. Empathetically.

He whispered closely, "It's all for a good cause, Elena. Let me help you, like I've helped so many others."

*Like how Father did*, he added in his head. Her response – nothing – was all the chief needed. He sighed, his knees cracking as he stood up straight. Elena's hands were still on her head. He angled the pistol downwards. Nobody could say that he didn't try to give her other options.

At that moment, he heard his father's voice. For a second, Pattison was transported back to that day; they were on their way to Jaxson Bay, but Howard had to run a quick errand at St. Jude's, and all Derek cared about was getting to the beach. He waited in the car. He listened to his father, and when Howard returned, the words he spoke to him after asking what had happened rang through his head. On this day in 2009, those words rang through his head as he stood, pulling back the hammer, ready to help Mrs. Elena Sullivan.

*You'll understand one day.*

BANG!


"What was that?" Ton asked, raising an eyebrow.

Parked outside the apartment building, in Pattison's cruiser, were Deputy Ton – in the front passenger seat – and Officer Taylor who sat in the back middle seat.

Taylor had heard it, too. They both knew what that meant – Elena Sullivan was dead. It meant that she resisted. Taylor and Ton kept quiet as the police radio down by the gearshift crackled.

*"Ton, Taylor…"* Pattison's voice came through, the signal not as good in Carson Estate. *"Shots fired upstairs. Come up. Now."*

Deputy Ton and Officer Taylor glanced at each other knowingly through the chains separating the front from the back. Taylor looked like a prisoner sitting back there, like she wasn't a C.C.I.D officer at all. But Ton let that thought go and they both jumped out of the car and entered the building. They rushed towards the desk; Carol had her head turned to the stairs.

"Excuse me, ma'am," said Taylor, her hands on the desk, "shots have been fired. Remain seated and stay calm."

Carol couldn't speak. *What the fuck's going on?* she thought as Taylor and Ton rushed up the stairs.

Halfway up, they heard Pattison's voice yell, "Stay in your rooms! It's not safe!"

Nobody else had witnessed it. They had only heard the gunshot that killed Elena.

They reached the level the chief was on. Taylor and Ton saw he hadn't budged from the doorway to Elena's apartment.

Noticing them, he took a step inside and Taylor and Ton consciously followed.

There she was, lying crumpled on the floor like she had fallen off the bed. She had her head on her arms, like they were pillows, and the two officers and chief took the image in.

"What happened?" asked Ton.

They all stood over Elena.

"She resisted," said Pattison. Taylor and Ton knew it. "I had to do it."

"Jesus," mumbled Officer Taylor.

"Taylor, go downstairs, tell the receptionist what happened and call an ambulance."

"Yes, Chief."

Taylor rushed back downstairs and saw the receptionist, still seated like she was told. It was her eyes that told Taylor she knew something was wrong.

"What's happened?" asked Carol.

"There's been…" Taylor couldn't word it properly. In situations like this, she had to use her words wisely and informing a friend or a relative that somebody had been shot and killed was never an easy task to pull off. "We came to question one of your guests. She resisted. The chief had to resort to certain *measures*."

Carol knew that meant somebody had died.

"Who was it?" she asked, gulping to contain her worry.

"Elena Sullivan." Taylor couldn't bear to witness a breakdown, so she added quickly, "But what I need you to do is call us an ambulance. Quickly."

Carol cleared her throat, wiped her face down, and said with a nod, "Yes, Officer."

Taylor decided to stay downstairs with the receptionist. She needed someone there with her.

Back upstairs, the deputy and chief kept still. Ton turned slightly towards Pattison and tried to see the look on his face. He had seen this look many times before, too; relieved, but with a sprinkle of doubt and regret. *It must've been a last resort*, he thought.

"Are you all right, Chief?" asked the deputy.

"Yeah," said Pattison. They locked eyes, Elena by their feet, and the chief added softly, "It's something I don't like to do. But sometimes it has to be done."

That sealed it for Ton; shooting Elena Sullivan had been a last resort.

On the ride back to the office, with Pattison and Ton in the front and Taylor in the back, nothing was said. Only thoughts raced through all their minds. In particular, Officer Taylor couldn't get that image of a lifeless Elena Sullivan out of her head.

*Okay*, she thought, *she resisted. But did she resist so much she had to be shot in the head?*

Officer Laura Taylor was granted the rest of the night off.

There was no other option.

# CHAPTER TWENTY-SEVEN

## Getting Started

It was all work and no play for the Castlehead Criminal Investigation Department in the weeks that followed the death of Elena Sullivan. Clarke Smith was heartbroken when the news went out, and more so knowing she was the one that vandalised his property. He would never know why. It was done, now, so he just had to get on with life. Taylor started to take more time off; she had to process a few things before returning full time. And on Good Friday, Chief Pattison and Deputy Ton had their fingers crossed that arrangements could be made to have Elena Sullivan's body finally transported back to Valeland.

They were in the chief's office as they discussed the situation. Pattison was swaying in his desk chair and Ton stood by the window that looked out towards the hills, home of Sunvalley Park and Michael Manor, the rest of the town by the hills' feet.

"So, anything from Hughes and Cole?" asked the chief.

Ton looked out at the view and said, "They're going to take her back after Easter. One of the busiest weekends, Easter, apparently for the V.C.P.A."

"The sooner the better."

Facing the chief, Ton asked, "Do we know if she had any family?"

"Nothing was on her records when Hughes sent them over before she arrived."

"Surely someone's got to know her?" suggested the deputy.

The chief didn't know why Deputy Ton cared so much. Elena Sullivan wasn't Castlehead's problem anymore. There were more important things to take care of, such as finding out who Elena had talked to; Howard told the story of the riots in '81, and how he ordered his team to kill Gerald Nate. There was no way he escaped. Nobody escaped the C.C.I.D. Someone definitely gave his father false intel regarding Nate.

They would pay.

"Her records stated that she worked at the Desmond School for Creative Arts," said the chief, "whatever that is. Some people will sort out a service for her, or something. Don't worry."

Ton looked back out at the view and said, "Yeah, you're right."

Pattison was right, in many people's minds. And at some point, *everyone* would know he was right. About everything.

The chief and deputy were both in their own worlds, so they did not notice that there was a knock on the glass door. They saw, in a long fur coat, showing off her ankles, Madam Mayor standing there. This was the person Chief Pattison had been waiting for.

"Good afternoon, Madam Mayor," he and Ton said together.

"Gentlemen," said the mayor, shutting the door as she entered the office.

She glanced back from the chief to the deputy. Back and forth. Ton was the awkward third wheel here.

"Ton, could you give us a moment?" asked the chief.

"Yes, of course. Not a problem," he said.

Ton left the room and headed for the door to the stairwell.

"You were right," said the mayor. She tightened the coat around her; Pattison wasn't a woman, but even he had thought it looked warm. "About St. Jude's."

"Madam Mayor?" The chief thought to play dumb. "So, you've cancelled…?"

"I've cancelled the project, yes." She paced back and forth from the desk to the window as she spoke. "My mother made that place possible. She wanted to help people, but with everything that's gone on, Clarke's Pharmacy, Elena, I decided it was for the best."

"Yeah, I think it's for the best, too," said the chief. "Even as a hotel, I don't think it would've worked out, Madam Mayor. That place was a hospital; that's its legacy." He stood up and placed a hand softly on the mayor's shoulder. That fur was real. He bowed his head, meeting her eyes. "I know you wanted it to stay open, I know you want to live up to the legacy your mother left you. I know you want to make her proud. But St. Jude's wasn't it. Rather than revelling in the past, we need to anticipate what's to come."

Madam Mayor stepped back and clapped her hands together. *Anticipate what's to come.*

"Yes," said the mayor, "and on that note I need to head back to the Town Hall. I have to finish off the plans for Easter Festival on Sunday."

Chief Pattison sat back down and waved the mayor away.

Alone in his office now, Pattison considered what had happened over the past few months. Anthony was going to keep his part of the deal. St. Jude's was shut – just like he and Howard wanted – and it wasn't going to reopen. What he did as the police chief was for a good cause – the words of his father replayed in his head at times like this (times he felt proud) – and something told him it was all going to pay off.

He was taught by his father to be patient, and that was how Pattison lived his life. The C.C.I.D never escalated the situation with Elena Sullivan; it was up to her to look into St. Jude's, and that decision led to that night in the apartment building. Pattison bided his time and knew what to do in the moment. It had to be done, after all.

From a drawer underneath his side of the desk, Pattison took out a rectangular-framed photo. It was of him pushing away from a hug from his father; one of those imperfect photos that end up being the most treasured. They looked silly and happy as father and son.

Any son – or any child, even – would want to make their dad proud. Looking at the photo of the two of them, Derek knew Howard was proud of him for what he did. It may've been a small step, but a small step can go a long way. Howard lived by many of those philosophical phrases and riddles. *Power is control, not beyond it*, that was another one. He liked to think Howard made that one up, but at times like these it made sense – it made more sense as the chief.

There was one more. Howard first uttered the phrase the night they came back from the beach. They were cosy, the television was on, the fire crackling like they were snowed in, and Derek had asked him when he could become chief of the C.C.I.D.

Thinking back, Derek repeated the words to the photo: "All good things come to those who wait." He smiled at the photo, as if Howard was actually smiling back at him. The chief nodded, suddenly feeling a rush of determination and pride. He added, "It's time."

And time can't be stopped.

# EPILOGUE

## JUNE, 2020

News got around Castlehead quickly, with social media and whatnot, about the events that took place at Thomas Hill High before the May half-term holiday. For a day, the C.C.I.D had thought they had heard enough of it, and the dying-down period had begun; then Aaron Smith was found with his throat slit in his cell in the C.C.I.D offices.

The CCTV footage showed Aaron sleeping, his back to the camera and Pattison, Ton and the mayor walking in. They turned him over, and there he was. Dead. The team had started to consider it as suicide after a couple of weeks. And that was the story they had gone with. Pattison was told *The Castlehead Chronicle* were going to release an update in the coming weeks, but no such article had been released yet.

That meant one thing: There was a bigger story to tell.

Chief Derek Pattison sat in his office in the C.C.I.D building, stroking his jaw, contemplating his next move. Why hadn't they released the article yet? When that happened, that meant the town could put the past year behind them. Clarke Smith was dead; Caroline Smith was dead; Aaron Smith was dead. On top of that, they had to make sure the kids that were involved with the events that occurred over the past year kept their mouths shut – something told the chief they wouldn't – and with one of them (Jason Rayne, Pattison recalled his name being) moving to Valeland during the holiday, it was easier said than done.

Nothing else could mess up the plan, and with that thought, Pattison might've jinxed it.

Before Sean could walk in, Pattison gestured for him to enter the office. What a difference eleven years made; Pattison remembered the day he gave Sean a chance, a chance for redemption, to show he was willing to change for the better. His wounds had healed quicker than expected, though the scars were still there, and now eleven years later Sean stood there in front of Pattison in a suit. As the chief's right-hand man.

It was safe to say he had proved himself.

Sean cradled a rolled-up edition of *The Castlehead Chronicle*. Was this the front-page article Pattison had been waiting for? Off Sean's concerned look, his lips together and eyebrows high on his forehead, Pattison quickly suspected otherwise.

"Chief, you might want to look at this," said Sean.

Pattison snatched the newspaper from him and flattened it out on the desk. Sean had never seen his boss pant so hard or so fast before, his cheeks bursting purple. Sean wondered how Pattison would've reacted, but this was nothing like how he had imagined. Chief Pattison always seemed so collected, even under pressure; that was what shook people.

"FUCK!" the chief wailed.

He rose with such force the desk chair bounced off the wall, denting it. Sean flinched and jumped back as Pattison shoved everything – notepads, files, pens, paper, and his laptop – off the desk with such rage Sean thought for a second he might have had to call for Ton. Pattison panted, his chest inflating and deflating rapidly, his hands firmly on the desk, his fingers spread. Strands of the hair he had left dangled down, shadowing his eyes as he looked at his feet.

"Chief?" mumbled Sean. "What do we do?"

The chief glanced up, a feral drool on his face, his eyes wild and mad. He pounced down upon the papers he had flung across the room and picked up the one Sean had brought in. His nails were going to go through it, such was the force he held it with.

Whipping the paper down onto the desk, flat so Sean could see the front page, Pattison leaned in, eyes darting in all directions. Did he need a doctor?

"This…" Pattison's voice shook, maybe even his entire body, "cannot happen!" He pressed down on the headline and repeated, "This can't happen! Do you understand that? DO YOU UNDERSTAND THAT!?"

"Yes, sir."

Pattison collapsed in his chair.

"Good," he mouthed, nodding.

It was a nod that rattled.

All that adrenaline had drained away. He reached out for the paper again, and tried not to quiver as he held it.

If there was any time to make a move on this operation, it was now.

Time waits for no man. If people started to get ideas, time would run out for Pattison.

"What do you want to do?" asked Sean, his head tucked into his neck like a child afraid to be told off.

The chief arched his head, looking over the paper. There was only one thing he could do.

"What we're meant to do as officers," said the chief. "Take action."

With one last look at the article, Chief Pattison knew it was time.

Time couldn't be stopped…

And it certainly couldn't be wasted…

## THE CASTLEHEAD CHRONICLE
### A New Agency Emerges and Makes a Statement. Former C.C.I.D Officer, Laura Taylor, Leads the Fight for Justice.

THE STORY WILL CONTINUE IN:

*The Way – A Castlehead Novel*